The Wayfarer

BY

ZACHARY M. KEKAC

This is a work of fiction. All characters,
organizations, and events portrayed in this book
are fictional, imagined, or otherwise not real.

SEA OF VIMARAY

CRESCENT COVE

ARETH

WAYPOINT TAVERN

VERDANT FELLS

HIGH FELL

WOADOLOAM FOREST

DRAGONGRAVE

ARISHNA VALLEY

RUINS OF ARYTHOR

THE WEST OF EAVE

WYRMSPINE MOUNTAINS

AEGIS

Dedication

To the creators whose creations have served as the inspiration for my own.

To the adventurers who show that the point is not in the success, but the attempt.

To the delinquent, degenerate, and depraved individuals I name friends.

To those I name family;

Mom. Dad. Keelyn.

To my past self, whose arrogance is the reason this story began.

To my present self, who was the one who did the writing.

To my future self. I look forward to meeting you.

To Alicia. Because of course.

Atlas

Passage I: Midst

"We venture into the unknown hoping to return with something new. Something unlooked for. Something forgotten."

– the Wayfarer

Chapter I: Arkym
• Stirring of Spring •

The Wayfarer stood on the rim of insanity, smirking. His insanity was a thing of forgetting, his smirk a thing of many meanings. It was an arrogant expression, taunting madness to take what mind was left to him; it was grim, a solemn understanding of how little left there was; it was weary, wreathed with the sorrows of a man desperate to remember.

His attention lingered within his mind, the rim on which he stood the threshold of his forgetting. He looked over, down into the descending asylum of hidden self below, where the threads of his memory were hoarded, struggling to peer through the darkness, perceiving nothing.

Above the pit of his forgotten past, in the conscious region of his mind, lingered the few threads of self that remained, each flickering with soft, shifting light, the wistful hue of memory. But they too were fraying, being dragged down into the dark unseen hollows of his unseen self. He was losing himself to himself, knowing that he knew not at all why. That memory was gone too, first of all things forgotten. He knew it was there, at the bottom of the asylum, in the abyss of his mind. He knew too that the only way to retrieve it—the only way to the truth—was the Shadow's.

Drawing his attention from within, the Wayfarer returned it to the world without. Here he stood not on the rim of insanity, but the rim of the sea. It was night, moon limning the dark with silver. He was perched atop the cliff of a crescent-shaped cove. The waters beneath were calm, the sea feeding the cove through a small channel between the crescent's tips was not. It hammered into the half-moon wall of black stone, waves so immense they shook the bones of the land as they struck, making it seem as if the world itself tilted with them.

3

The Wayfarer focused on a black mass at the center of the cove. A small isle of stone.

There on that isle stood an asylum, not of his mind, but of the waking world. Not a place for common folk, afflicted with common ailments of the psyche. There were fairer places for them: kinder, more understanding. No. It was a place for rare folk whose nature it was to unravel the world around them. A place where they could unravel nothing but themselves. It was an asylum not for the sanctuary of those within, but to spare the world without.

Arkym.

The Shadow spoke, naming the asylum. The Wayfarer turned to face it as it stood beside him, a wraith wearing his likeness, a doppelganger wreathed in darkness. He called it the Shadow because to give it any other name, any true name, would be to give it a sense of reality that might well unravel the reality of him. It was a silhouette he alone could see, a voice he alone could hear—his own silhouette, his own voice, lilting and wayworn.

It wears me well.

It turned to him, knowing his mind.

Do not linger.

The Wayfarer knew the Shadow's mind as well. Inasmuch as one can know a thing born from one's own madness. Inasmuch as one knows anything of themselves at all. The wraith was a thread of himself. He knew this, though he knew not how. He imagined it was a part of his inner mind hallucinated into existence. A sickness of the psyche. Rare, but not unheard of. He had no proof, nothing to substantiate his belief but the feeling in his bones. It was a part of him. Perhaps the part seeking self-preservation, guiding him to salvation. Perhaps the part desiring to deceive the

4

self, to devour it, for no reason other than having the ability to do so.

Needless consideration. The Wayfarer would go the Shadow's way no matter what it was or what it wanted. It had led him this far. It would lead him further. To the truth—to the end. Or so it claimed. He did not trust it. He had no choice; no time to wager with, no other option to hedge against. If he hesitated, he would lose the last of himself. He would wander witless in a world which would forget him as effortlessly as he was forgetting it. So, with no other way open to him, the Shadow's way he went.

The way led here, to the cliff overlooking an asylum for madmen unfit for the world. The message was clear: his madness was linked to one once imprisoned on the isle. A man he himself had put there. A man he once named friend, dearest of all. A friend he'd betrayed to preserve everything else: his family, his world.

A thought slid into his awareness. He looked to the sea, the sky, the asylum, realizing he had no memory of arriving. It was unsettling, but unsurprising. That was the way of forgetting. On the wind of the first thought came another. *Did I say farewell?*

His eyes grew distant as his inner eye wandered within his mind, searching for his wife, his son, a parting embrace as he began his journey. That memory wasn't there. In place of it he felt something in him stirring, rising up, rising out. He looked up, wild-eyed, to find the Shadow staring, seeing everything that was surfacing the same as he was.

It was another memory, forgotten, returning. It consumed his awareness. He felt the Shadow step into it, a crooked warden swaggering into the asylum, swinging a skeleton key. A thing of his madness, his madness a thing of forgetting, the Shadow was, paradoxically, a thing of remembering too.

The Wayfarer watched in his mind's eye as a memory returned to him, the Shadow narrating as it unfurled.

Her voice came over the garden hedge, singing in the spring winds,
a song she sang of memory, of love, of you:

> *...Fair few still walk the ways of old,*
> *Those trails tread by foolhardy souls,*
> *Who wandered where none had before,*
> *Through grove, and moor, and silver shore.*
>
> *For in those elder days they say,*
> *To wander was the only way,*
> *In lands untouched, in lands unknown,*
> *In wood, and vale, and hall of stone.*
>
> *Their journey roved and wrought a word,*
> *For leaf, for moon, for bone, for wyrm,*
> *Each name a thread in stories told,*
> *Each tale, each myth, worn ancient old.*
>
> *Of dragons dark and brooding lone,*
> *Of forest eaves 'neath dusken gloam,*
> *Of havens hewn from argent white,*
> *Of realms beyond the seams of light.*
>
> *All memory scrawled upon a page,*
> *All fable passed from Age to Age,*
> *From ash to ash and shade to shade,*
> *A shade of dreamer's distant days,*
>
> *For even ash of Ages gone,*
> *May grow a wood, a world, a home.*
> *Where tale and myth may find yet still,*
> *A youthful and foolhardy will.*

To follow those wayfaring ways,
To know now and forever say;
Far into dusk their trail does go,
Far into dusk their trail does go…

Her song ended. She spoke. "Do you understand what that means? 'Even ash of Ages gone, may grow a wood, a world, a home?'"

"I think so." His tone said he didn't, despite his words; words of a child trying to appear wiser than he was, ashamed of his own ignorance.

You could hear the smile on her lips and the twinkle in her eyes. "Well, in case any of our rabbit or raven friends in the garden don't, I'll say anyway."

He was too old to believe that foolishness, too young to own up to his own. So he let her speak, and in listening he learned. "Even from ash—the stuff of nothingness—can come the stuff of somethingness, with a little time. It's the way of the world, Tärin. Of ours, of others."

He lit up. "Other worlds Da' has been to, too?"

You smiled, answering, "Others Da' has been to, too."

"Aëros!" They both turned, eyes alight. Her voice held the slightest rasp, a subtle sultriness under all the spring sweetness, a wit and wryness sewn into the seams of world-weariness she worked hard to hide. But you saw those seams, saw all of them, all of her, and loved her for everything you saw. She was your person; you were hers. Your Aūriel, her Aëros. She saw your shadow in her periphery and turned, giving you her eyes, her smile, her vulnerable, enduring love.

She leapt into your arms. You breathed her in—lemongrass, lavender, mint leaves. You smelled like…well, like you'd been on an adventure: like old smoke drifting from dying embers, like worn muscles and weathered skin, like heavy rain had been your only shower. She didn't mind. It was a familiar scent. It was you.

"Da'!" Tärin. His shifting-silver mane reflected father and mother both, his face hers, his eyes yours—solemn, curious, keen.

"Aha! Aūriel, Tärin! How I've missed you!"

"We've missed you too, my love." Her words whispered in your ear, your soul, filling you with sorrow and joy. Love, a thing of duality.

Tärin took off running as he remembered something he was proud of. Then he remembered he had to tell you what it was first. "Da'! The range!" He frowned, focusing. "My arrows!" He stumbled, frowned deeper, focused harder, too roused for the measured thought of the man that was waking within him. His mind still ran away from his words as swiftly as most men run from both. "I have to show you something!" Near enough.

He wore a bow over his shoulder—yours. The earliest of your own artifice, not well made, but well-worn. You doubted if a day had passed where it hadn't seen the range. He was so proud of it, for it was an artifact of his father, a thing all sons long for, indifferent or ignorant to its imperfections. Sons do not see such things until they are fathers themselves. Such is the slow way of wisdom.

"Tomorrow, son, I promise. It's dusk, and I have to speak with your mother."

He stamped, pouted, rolled his eyes. Youth.

You waved him along, laughing. "Run on!"

He huffed, and relented. His will was hardening, but yours was stronger still and he bent beneath it, defying it only with words. "You're just making excuses because you'll fall asleep after you finish, old man!"

"Tärin!" Aüriel did her best to bite back her own laughter, red embarrassment rising into her cheeks and the long tips of her ears, which peeked through slits in the brimless knit cap she hardly ever went without wearing.

"I'm going, I'm going!" He darted off, ducking under vines and leaping over hedgerows as he went. He ascended a trellis, dove from its crest, was gone. Your son, threaded through.

"Your wit is showing in him, Aëros." She sighed, wistful. Her eyes held all the shifting hues of an aurora, flickering and iridescent, twisted with threads of teal and turquoise and bright, burnished gold.

Your smile met your eyes—silver moons, full then, long ago, now fading crescents, hollowing away. "You say that as if my wit isn't the reason you married me."

She stole your smile for herself, wore it with familiarity. "I married you because you don't fall asleep after you finish."

"Is that right?" You wrapped yourself around her, pulling her close, eye to eye, delicate. Then you tugged her knit cap down over her face, flustering her. "You'll be on your way to disappointment swiftly then."

You scooped her up, walking to the stairs, toward the bedroom. She giggled, squirmed, and relented, nestling into your arms. She lifted the brim of her hat back into place and looked up out of one aurora-hued eye, wondering. "What'd you need to tell me?"

You kicked open the door, tossed her onto the bed, leapt after. "It can wait."

She laughed as you tussled, the wistfulness in her eyes finding its way into the crooks of her mouth, the whisper of her words. "I would be happy if I died today, my Aëros." It was her promise, the oldest of them. A promise that would seem strange to most. A promise that endeared her evermore to you.

"As would I, my Aūriel."

You fell into one another—you, wearing the smile you wore when first you met; her, the smile you would see her wearing at her death.

Aëros blinked, returning to the waking world. The Shadow returned too, standing before him, eyes meeting his. Silence. He spoke, hesitant. "Was that now? Was that *just* now?" He shook his head, knowing. "No. That was... long ago. But..." What he'd seen was memory, mostly...

The smile you would see her wearing at her death.

It was nonsense. It was nightmare. Yet there, nested within it, was a wretched feeling of familiarity. His eyes fell to the ring on his left hand, joining his soul to his Aūriel's. It was the key to his promise, to his journey; the key to many things. It was of worked Argynt, the silver metal weaving about his finger like the roots of an underwood, a narrow band of wyrmstone worked throughout it, hoarding the moon's silver light like a dragon its trove, refusing to reflect it. It was inscribed with her wisdom, written in the language of the First of the First, taught to her by him, her husband, the Wayfarer—last of the Last of the First: *Always forward. Always on.*

He often found himself muttering the mantra in his mind, as if afraid that silence would steal its memory away. *Foolish.* So long as he had the ring, he'd keep his promise to return to his family. As a man, not the shadow of one. He wondered to himself again if he'd said farewell. His home wasn't far. A few days' trek. *I have time.*

No.

Aëros measured the Shadow, the wretched feeling of familiarity now warring with a feeling of wrath towards the wraith and its obfuscation. He ground his teeth, growled. Madness brought the Shadow, and the Shadow brought memories. That would seem a boon to one who was forgetting—it was not. Regardless, he knew the Shadow was right. He'd said his farewells. *I won't feed my madness. I won't submit to hysteria.*

The sea rolled into the cove, and the Wayfarer watched the waters tilt, heave, hammer into the half-moon as if their only desire was to sweep over the cliffs and drown the thing they were protecting. Arkym. A place of protection itself. Aëros knew that even drowned, the memories of that island, of his friend's internment on it at his behest, would remain vivid. They would linger, and in the end, were likely to be the last thing he would forget. The mind had a way of holding onto its grief.

Arkym marked the beginning of his betrayal. Dún—a crypt in the midst of the necropolis named the Barrows, where the bones of his friend were buried in a sepulcher of carven crystal—was the end, far off, far away.

The Shadow spoke, shearing the silence.

Move on.

The Wayfarer considered the beginning, and the end. His journey would take him from here to there, from Arkym to Dún, just as his betrayal had. For it was there, in the grave of the man he named friend, the man bound up in the meaning of his madness, that the memory of *how* and *why* rested. It was, of course, buried in his mind too. But it could not be retrieved without first standing where it was formed—or so the Shadow said.

It made sense; in returning to the place of the first thing forgotten he would return to the rest. He could only hope a fool's hope until his journey's end, and it was far yet, his way long and winding, with much betwixt and between here and there.

Here the Wayfarer stood on the cliffs of Crescent Cove, the Verdant Fells stretching out behind him—the western grasslands of hills and valleys, peaceful, serene, unfurling their vastness far beyond sight. A star was falling within the night, drifting from the forever-shattered moon, radiating pale, silver light. It wisped over the Fells and vanished, finding rest in the darkness beyond the southwestern horizon, in the direction of his destination, in the direction of Dún. He turned from the sea, the asylum, the beginning, setting foot and mind toward the end.

The Shadow strode ahead of him, its silhouette stalking through the dark, darker still. Grass rolled underfoot, gentle on his soles, bare as they always and ever were, weathered to roughness from a lifetime of adventure. Spring rain stirred in the eve, thin and scattered. He drew up the hood of his Shräud—a cloak drawing night down around him, the material threads of its fabric woven with the immaterial threads of Dräu, making him difficult to discern. Not invisible, but as a shifting, shapeless shadow on the edge of perception, easily missed. It was of his Aūriel's artifice. He found her scent on it even now: lemongrass, lavender, mint leaves.

11

Though night encircled him, he drew a crystal-framed lantern from Nowhere and illuminated it, limning his silhouette in silver and hiding him from the dark. Lúmoths drew around the artifact, fluttering, adding their natural light to its own.

The Wayfarer walked, went on, was silent. Silent so as not to disrupt the night-song of the Fells. Silent to search for answers in the miasma of his mind. Silent to mark the stride of the figure that was stalking him; there was more in this world to worry over than madness.

Haze thickened overhead, veiling moon and stars and darkening the Verdant Fells until they were half-hidden. The Wayfarer dismissed the betraying radiance of his lantern, the lúmoths dispersing as its light faded and the dark swallowed him.

As expected, the figure leapt, predator seeking prey, finding only empty air and the thick thud of dirt as he hit the ground with a grunt, the Wayfarer evanescing in his grasp, a shimmer of shadow in the dim moonlight.

The rogue scrambled to recover as a hail of arrows rained around him, pinning him in place. The arrows flickered with a black, luminescent light, lingered for a moment, then vanished into the Nowhere from which they'd been drawn. "Aëros! It's Thrace!" the rogue roared, sounding more impudent than predatory.

Thrace. Aëros—the Wayfarer—worked the name over in his mind. An image materialized from the few threads of memory left, an image of a friend, more a brother. *Thrace... I...*

"Weary of your threadbare illusions, Aëros!" the man named Thrace grumbled. "Weary of you altogether, as it stands!"

Aëros spoke from a hollow atop a hill next to the path his phantom had lured his friend along. "Threadbare?" He revealed himself from his hideaway and rekindled his lantern, lúmoths returning round him. "It's your wisdom that's threadbare, full of the folly of repetition. You should know better than to trust what you see when you seek me."

The man scoffed, spat. "Was there really a need for the arrows? You knew it was me long before I leapt."

Aëros shrugged, stowing his bow Nowhere. "I didn't." It was the truth. He'd known someone was stalking him, found the pattern of movement familiar, but he didn't have the memory to place the familiarity. He didn't admit it. "I might've taken you for Nomad, what with how you seemed to come from Nowhere itself."

"Do *not* conflate me with that incomprehensible inconvenience of a man." Thrace glowered at his friend, then bent the expression into the remnant of a smile. "You're just getting old and losing your wits." Aëros let silence hang, unsure of a response. "Come down!" Thrace spoke for him. "We've not seen each other in an Age and I'm welcomed as a beast of prey!"

The night-song of the Fells faded, awaiting the Wayfarer's reply. "And how, as you skulked in the shadows, did you seek to welcome me?"

"With an embrace!"

Aëros' eyes wore his skepticism well. "You've got dirt on your face."

"Oh, fuck yo—"

Aëros leapt from his perch, landing soundless beside the man who was familiar but forgotten. He reached out, offering a hand. "Thrace." As he pulled the short man to his feet, the lantern lit his features: green eyes, pale skin, faded hair, wry grin. Body corded with the tight muscle of a knight errant. He knew him. Knew him well. Something shifted in the darkness of his mind. Something felt off-kilter in the way his friend held himself. Something was different, didn't belong. He dismissed the sense as paranoia. "It's been a long time, Old Wolf."

The man, now remembered, pulled Aëros into the embrace he'd promised. "Too long, Old Raven. Far too long." His eyes shifted, wondering. "Where have you been?"

Aëros smirked. "Somewhere sometimes, Nowhere others."

Thrace huffed. "Don't patronize me. How long have you been back?"

"I'm not sure I am."

Thrace knocked his knuckles against Aëros' head. "Unraveling in there?"

Aëros looked to the Shadow only he could see, its mouth crooked, head tilted, wondering the same, as if it didn't already know. He banished it to his periphery. "A few threads, yes."

"No excuse. You sent no letter, no disembodied head, no whore in a butter-crumb cake. Nothing."

Aëros' brows knit together. "You're being dramatic."

"I'm not being dramatic enough!"

"Are you drunk?" Aëros leant in to smell his friend's breath. "You're drunk."

"You're mistaken." Thrace summoned a bottle from Nowhere, twirling it by a cord. "I've drunken; I'm not drunk. Yet." He unstopped the bottle, took a pull, and as swiftly as he'd summoned it it returned it to Nowhere. "Don't change the subject. I was starting to think the whispers were true."

Aëros' eyes narrowed, silver irises dimming, wondering.

Thrace waved the wonder away. "You're here, that makes the whispers whisper only."

Aëros studied his friend's eyes and saw in them the truth. He knew well the eyes hide nothing; the soul of the one who looks through them is always there, showing all they ever wanted to say, even against their will, if one only knew how to look. He worked out what the whispers were without need for explanation, and agreed with Thrace that they were whisper only. He was here, now. Unraveling, but not undone. Not yet.

As Thrace's eyes betrayed his worry, Aëros' betrayed his weariness. Thrace met them, read them, and looked through them to the sea beyond, realization solidifying into something halfway between concern and frustration. "What was that you said earlier, about the folly of repetition?"

Aëros' weariness shifted as he struggled for an answer. He knew Thrace knew why he was here, wasn't sure how to explain. But to his relief, his friend seemed to decide it didn't need bringing up. Not now.

Thrace smiled and gestured off into the Fells. "The Waypoint isn't far. We'll settle up some rooms and we can-"

"I can't."

Thrace leveled a curious eye. "Not even the night? Or part of it? I'll let you off before dawn. You can afford that at least. I haven't seen you since..."

Aëros hesitated, finished for his friend. "I don't remember either." He sighed, relenting. *What's one night?* The Shadow crept out of his periphery, its disapproval plain, eyes urging him not to linger. He smirked in spite of it, looked to his friend. "Aye. I can afford that."

Thrace slapped him on the shoulder. "How kind of you to cover the tab."

Aëros' smirk shifted sly as he made three knives appear from the same Nowhere as his lantern and Thrace's bottle, each somersaulting as he passed them from hand to hand. "Wager for it?"

Thrace spoke with the swift dismissal of a man who remembers well at least one folly he's not willing to foul up again. "Last time I ended up owing you a barrel of cider, three score aūrums, and the corset of the Warden's wife."

Aëros laughed, hearty and happy both for the memory and the ease with which he could recall it. "The last was a joke. I didn't mark you for her sort."

Thrace puffed out his chest and thumbed his suspenders. "Neither did the Warden."

The laughter of the delinquent duo lilted in the night as they strode towards the Waypoint. But such happiness was a faint warmth. The Shadow strode beside them and spoke its warning, reminding Aëros of his promise, chilling the revelry in his soul even as he wore it in his eyes for the sake of his friend.

Move on.

Or wither.

Chapter II: Mischief
• Stirring of Spring •

The Waypoint was nested between two narrow hillocks on the primary thoroughfare of the Fells. It was wooden, stout, and incredibly unimpressive. Murky glass windows and a single crooked entrance leaked warm umber light into the evening. A sign repaired to the point of disrepair marked the entrance, stating that the hovel it hung from was in fact the Waypoint Tavern: famous, infamous, alive. It was the oldest tavern in the West, if not in all of Eave. Some said it was as old as Eave itself, old as Eaē. Aëros knew better, knew that some things were beyond age. Some things were more than the material they were made of; they were the essence of an idea itself. The Waypoint was the distillation of all the taverns that had ever been, were now, would ever be.

It was the sole tavern on the trade route between the seaports and the villages knotted around the Fells, needing only its position and reputation to draw in the wealth and the waifs that walked from sea to inland and inland to sea. The Waypoint drew nobles and commoners, seafarers and landsmen, heroes and villains— everyone from the most singular of society's outliers to the most mundane. It kept draughts strong enough to strip the metal from even the most wayworn of livers, imported fare familiar and foreign, and offered the best in the business where debauchery, depravity, and delinquency were reckoned.

Aëros and Thrace rounded a bend, swaggering, and the tavern appeared before them. The night-song of the Fells died beneath the din that bellowed out from the amber-lit relic of an inn, swallowing the scent of dew and mist and fresh-fallen rain, spitting up sweat and swill and something that could only be loosely described as arousing.

It was a scene torn from a story, the primal desires of man its motif. Every vagrant and vagabond was a character in the tale being told, each a drop of blood in the tavern's otherwise petrified frame, imbuing it with life.

It was in the shape of the Waypoint's one and only doorman, Broawn—a behemoth of a man, whispered to be the kin of giants—that the blood of the tavern leaked into the night. Aëros wasn't certain, but he felt the whispers were probably right.

Broawn leaned half-hidden in a nook, his face halfway between a glower and a grin. He stood sentinel, the sole peacekeeper for the ruckus, row, or racket that wasn't the sort to settle itself swiftly.

Aëros considered the times he and Thrace had been at the heart of such barroom brawls. Most often it was his own instigation that led to them, but he never worried over Thrace fleeing from the fight. In fact, his friend was far worse than a coward. He was cocksure, prone to plunge headlong into the fray, with thought or without it.

Regardless of their past mischief, the Waypoint refused no one entry, no matter their misdoings or madness. Aëros approached, his shadow trailing behind him, *the* Shadow already leaning against the tavern, watching.

Broawn's glower-grin lifted as Aëros and Thrace stepped from the night into the tawny tavern light, filtering through cracks and murky windows. "Ah, the delinquent duo returns." He laughed, deep and rumbling. "Mischief's been light, come to weigh in?"

"Consider us feathers." Aëros reached out in greeting, pointed to his vagrant companion with his other hand. "Consider me one, at any rate."

"Aiming to avoid mischief?" He looked the two up and down, memories drifting through his eyes. "You?"

The Wayfarer's silver eyes glinted, betraying him. "Aiming doesn't mean you make the mark. But it helps."

18

Broawn's laugh rolled out again as he grasped Aëros' hand, smothering it in his grip. "Well, we'll see if your will's as straight as your shot, then." The sentinel shook, let go, and turned back toward the tavern. "Not that it much matters either way, you're both welcome at the Waypoint. Come in and make merry, mischief or no." He stopped just short of his post and looked over his shoulder. "Though, Thrace, perhaps no mischief with the maidens. They were fighting over you this morn." The looming man let out a worn, ragged breath. "Again."

Thrace grinned, making no promise with word or without.

Broawn saw his future in his silence. "Well, Six String asked me to mention it. Your choice in the end. Mind your face." He stopped, squinted. "You've got dirt on it."

Thrace's grin turned scowl as Broawn stood clear of the doorway, waving him and the Wayfarer within. The duo drifted into the pungent, tawny smog of the tavern. They took five steps, and heard the sentinel already busying himself with a pair of twins grappling on the floor, his smile brimming as he knocked their two heads together so hard even they couldn't make out who was who when they were right side up again.

Tavern maidens bustled from patron to patron as they took and served food, drink, mixture, and flesh. They were beautiful. Dangerously swift-witted, too. Thrace never seemed to notice—or to care, as was more his way. One lass noticed him, however; she ran up, kissed him, then hauled an open hand across his face as their lips parted. She was serving another table before Thrace could blink.

Aëros grinned and prodded his friend's cheek. "Dirt's gone." He gestured to the lass. "A product of poor self-restraint?"

Thrace turned up his nose, caught the scent of something foul, and turned it back down. "I know not the meaning of the word."

"I'm well aware." Aëros continued teasing his friend's cheek until Thrace smacked his hand away. He aimed the troublemaking thing instead toward a secluded, high-backed booth in the far reaches of the tavern, gesturing his intent to take it. Thrace agreed, and the duo pressed their slow way through the familiar raucousness of their fellow patrons. They had both been a part of it many times before, would hopefully many times again. Aëros found a wistful, warm sort of comfort in knowing that there were some things that stood still in time's flow, unchanging. The comfort was an illusion, of course. *That's all reality is, at any rate, an illusion, a story we tell ourselves.* The thought passed into Aëros' mind, and with it came a sense of distortion, as if the world, the Waypoint, shifted. Changing after all. He dismissed the thought and the sensation. The Waypoint stood still. That was that. Sometimes it was better to pretend.

A flagon hurtled through the air, smashing into some unfortunate drunk's skull who had nothing to do with the reason for the throwing. Two men barreled through the crowd, fists flailing in a wild, pathetic attempt at a brawl. Dicing tables appeared from the smoke and smog at random, card dealing, knife throwing, more. A few played pinfinger on tables and bartops, deepening the already pocked holes scattered across the sticky-slick wood. A gambling game wagered by the player on themselves, knives leapt between outstretched fingers as wit went for a walk, to be found again when the game was given up. The game came with a song, its lyrics grating the air as the knives danced to the tune:

Oh! One, two, three, four, five,
Come watch me with my knife,
There's liquor in my veins,
And blood that gives me life!

This knife does like to dance,
The liquor likes to lead,
Across the table runs their love,
My fingers set between.

Their courtship runs its race,
Together we shall see,
Whether they will wed,
Or whether I will bleed!

The blade is sharp and swift,
The liquor warm and wise,
But I the fool can never know,
Just how fast they can fly.

For their love shall never end,
This song forever go,
Until all time has met its death,
Or nine is all I know!

The final number differed depending on the experience of the player—experience marked by what they'd lost rather than what they gained. Few of the wandering-witless ever made it around the tune a second time, certainly not a third, and if a fourth or further came about, it was only ever due to a forgetting of what count the game began with.

Aëros and Thrace turned away from the hearth-hall of the tavern, passing rooms housing guests and the company they'd purchased for the night. Men stumbled from their dwellings shirtless and shouting for more food and drink, and some for more women. Some of the women lurched out demanding better men.

Another flagon whipped through the air, hurtling toward the same unfortunate drunk as before. This time he was prepared, and caught it, downing the dregs. Some of the draught spilled over Thrace as it passed. He tasted it, considering it with sage wisdom. "Sygbräu."

"Sun's Brew," said Aëros. "Not my taste."

Dice rattled. Knives chipped away. Women moaned. Men cursed. Someone knew nine. The delinquent duo found their table and settled into the nook, secluded from the hearth-hall and the heart of the night's reverie.

Aëros' mind went back as he looked about the tavern, at all the revelry and fortune—good or ill—and mischief. He could remember when he'd been an instigator of it himself. *How long has it been since?* He saw the Shadow wandering through the crowd. No one else paid it any mind. No one else could. So he pretended he couldn't either. Not here. Not now.

A barmaid sauntered over for their orders. She was flustered, fiery, in a hurry. "What'll it be?" Her smile was warm, but her eyes were tired and rimmed with impatience, flickering flame and cinder.

Aëros chuckled at her ire. It was embers compared to his Aūriel's. "I'll have a pint of Resin, three dozen oysters, and a loaf of the cinnamon bread with cinnamon butter. Thank you," he said, and meant it.

She looked to Thrace, hesitant. There was something else in that look besides impatience. Aëros saw it well. Thrace grinned. "I'll have you, if you're on offer."

She scowled, amber light limning her fraying, wild-red hair. "You've been with more women than a rumor, Thrace. You're only after me because I'm the only thing on the menu you haven't tried."

Aëros heaved over in laughter. Thrace sat back, pouting. "A Sygbräu then, if you've got any left lingering, whatever's darkest if you don't," he said, giving up. For now. The barmaid gave him an affectionate smile, gestured something obscene, and scurried off.

Thrace lifted himself up from the back of the booth. "That's Cassidy."

"*Never trust the softness of a woman's skin if her eyes are hard,*" said Aëros. "Your words. Maybe your father's? Probably a saying handed down your line since before Arök fell from the moon and bound the world together."

Thrace looked back in his memory, unsure of the origin himself. "Your point?"

Aëros gestured toward Cassidy. "Oh, the hypocrisy."

Thrace spread his hands, indifferent. "Speaking of hypocrisies, how's the woman who loves you despite yours? Neither her nor Tarin were around when last I looked in."

They weren't? Aëros smiled, veiling the desperation of a man trying hard to convince himself he remembered well something he was forgetting. "She's well."

"Ah, Aëros," Thrace said. "It ain't natural for elven blood to have that much wit bound up in all the beauty." His fawning was gilded around the edges. "She could swoon a dragon with a look alone."

Aëros' eyebrows knit into disbelief. "Are you pining for an elf?"

"It's admiration of a beautiful thing," said Thrace. "Not pining. I know well enough not to grasp a living flame. You, on the other hand, strip stark naked and leap barefoot onto the coals."

Aëros laughed, feeling the dry, wooden floorboards of the Waypoint beneath his bare and weathered soles. "So say you. Pining for an elf, so I'll say when next I see her."

"Do not." Thrace shuddered. "She'll melt me to withered bone and pale, pitiful ash, she will."

Aëros considered the truth of his friend's words, pitied him. "I'll add my silence to your ledger of owed favors." He pretended to count it out on ten well-experienced fingers.

"Wyrmshit," said Thrace, knowing Aëros too well. He was rarely silent about anything. "But wyrmshit aside, Aūriel is well, so Little Raven must be too?"

Aëros' smile brimmed, prideful, hiding the uncertainty in his words, his distrust in his own memory. "Finding mischief and misadventure where no one else is wise enough to look."

Thrace gestured at his friend's general existence. "The fruit doesn't fall far."

Aëros nodded. "I only hope it grows to be a stronger tree."

"Without doubt." Thrace agreed, frowned. "Thinking of your family is bitter reminder of my own solitude."

Aëros raised a skeptic's brow, and Thrace pulled a grin from his frown. "A reminder of how fleeting it is!"

Groaning, Aëros rolled his eyes, his soul rolling with them. "Requisition some interchangeable women, a cart, and open a traveling troupe of ill repute if solitude is so dear to you."

Thrace's eyes lit up, tawny tavern light flaring in their core. "How much do you think that would cost?" He rifled through a hidden pocket as if to purchase the idea then and there. Instead he drew out a mixture pouch, dumping its contents into a rolling paper for a smoke. It was ashroot, his preference. He rolled it, bit off the end, kindled it with a thin thread of Iné, and drew. He never carried his purse in his coat. Aëros had stolen it too many times for him not to stumble over the wisdom to hide it elsewhere. Not that elsewhere made a difference from anywhere; not to Aëros.

Thrace blew smoke over the table, adding to the tavern smog. Aëros inhaled the residue. Bitter, stringent, unfamiliar—*wait*. He looked at some of the dregs of the mixture, fallen on the table while Thrace rolled it. "That isn't ashroot."

"No," Thrace peered through the smog. He sounded surprised. "You know I don't smoke that soot."

I do? Aëros shook the thought away, knew better than to let it lead him to its inevitable conclusion. "Ashroot or otherwise, I'll spread some on your grave for you."

Thrace withdrew the smoldering coffin nail and glared at it, a taunt. "You and I both know I won't live long enough for this to kill me."

Aëros exhaled, breathing away his friend's death. "You're getting on in years, you know."

Thrace's smoke shrouded him, but his contempt was clear as fire in a field. "That's a threadbare thing to say, Aëros." He pulled

24

his contempt into a grimace, leaned in, and whispered, as if his words might wake the dead. "My da' and his da' before him will rise from their graves to drag me down themselves before something so subtle as smoke or time drags my bones into the dirt."

Aëros eyed his friend's smoke. "You'd probably prefer beheading, wouldn't you? You lunatic."

Thrace grinned. "That is indeed my preferred ending," he said as he dragged his death, words heavy with smoke. His brow bent and he looked up, as if searching for something he should have known, then realizing he'd never known it to begin with. "You?"

Aëros measured his friend, his own mind. "Age, if I can help it."

Thrace slammed his hand onto the table, dropping his smoke into a puddle of something he wasn't brave enough to pull it out of. "Age?!" He slammed the table again, unsetting it from its rivets. The tavern silenced, staring; Broawn watched, waiting. "AGE?!" He flustered, guffawed, made strange noises meant to be words. He rolled another nail, kindled it, drew smoke and dared the dirt to take him. "You, *the* Wayfarer, Walker Betwixt and Between Worlds, Slayer of Death, wants to meet it because of AGE?!"

Aëros' mouth went crooked with his ego, self-satisfied with his many names, all well-worn and well-known. All but the last. *Slayer of Death.* That name he thought better buried. He knew it augured where the conversation would go. The things it would begin to dig up, which could only be half-hidden from his friend.

He sat still, blinking in the wind of Thrace's outburst, and shrugged, small and certain. "I've had an exciting life. A quiet death won't be a mournful end."

"What a heap of—" Thrace fell silent, grimacing as Aëros stole his words with a glance. The few patrons watching from the sidelines gasped. The Wayfarer let the illusion of the weathered beauty he'd once had—the illusion he wore at all times—fall away, revealing the horror he had since become beneath. The truth of him was a web of scars wrought from the trials of adventure. A riddle of deaths avoided, succumbed to, revived from. His mouth was littered with suture marks long scarred over; the left half of his face was nearly missing, stitched together by sinew and ragged muscle; his left eye was clouded, seeing and sightless simultaneously. The massacre trailed down his neck, continuing over his body, lash marks and stab wounds and scarification hidden by his clothing. What his face showed was more than enough to imagine what was unseen, how short his rope had become.

Thrace closed his eyes, turning away, still grimacing. He raised his hands and shook his head. "If you say so and will it! Now hide that horror away!"

As swiftly as it vanished, Aëros' beauty returned, the image he presented to the world, a veil for what he hid. He wore a few scars openly, thinking them distinguished. Three marks down his left cheek, talons from a small drake. One running over his left eye, just missing his sight, or so he showed, the edge of an arrow just nearly avoided. He glared at the gasping patrons, then laughed as they turned away, burying themselves in the crowd, horrified. Thrace waved his hand up and down Aëros' general existence. "Didn't your da' ever tell you to wear armor when you're fucking with things that ought not be fucked with?"

Aëros laughed again. "He did, even gave me a fine set too."

"Well, make sure to leave it to me in your will. I at least have the sense to make use of it." Thrace looked to the wall beside him, at a wanted poster pinned there: crisp parchment, fresh ink; his own face painted across it, notarized by the Warden of the West. He drew on his smoke, found it spent, and grimaced again. He lit another, inhaled, smiled.

Aëros gestured to the sketch. "How's the Warden's wife?"

Thrace pointed to a room. His teeth flashed, wicked, remembering. "Ex-wife."

"That why you're painted up like a woman of comfort?"

"Who knows?" Thrace gave a noncommittal grunt. "Not like it matters. I'm too useful. It's by my hand and the blood of foolhardy politicians that the roads in the West are laid."

"You'd think after the first dozen assassinations they would look to find a foothold elsewhere." Aëros spread his hands. "But then I suppose the road elsewhere is laid with the blood of foolhardy something-or-others too."

Thrace slid his eyes from his friend to the picture on the wall, tearing it away. "At least I resemble a man this time. They always draw me as a ripping elf. I think they confuse me with you." He pointed to the wooden post adjacent to their table, saturated with wanted posters calling for his head. "What sort of threadbare degenerate can't mark a human from an elf?"

"You've Ayl in your blood, after all."

"Aye, a thirty-second, if that." Indignant. "You've probably the same amount of Ken in yours. A thirty-second ain't enough to show the taint."

"We're all blood-diluted half-breeds." Aëros gestured to the tips of his ears, far longer than Thrace's, longer than most elves' nowadays. "It's six to a half-dozen, and I think you look rather fetching as an elf."

Thrace stifled a snort as he tossed the Wayfarer the poster. "Here, have it then. You can look at it when you're lonely on the road."

Aëros made to toss it aside, froze. Thrace was missing a scar in the picture. He looked to his friend, finding him missing the scar in life. The scar of an arrow gone errant, gone awry out of Aëros' own hand. "Thrace, what happened to—"

Something whistled past Thrace's head and pinned the poster back on the wall. A drunk across the tavern hollered a heartless apology. He was throwing knives at a target. He missed.

Thrace conjured his bottle—now dry—from Nowhere, stood, and launched it at the man. Aëros glared as it careened through the air, then sighed and pulled the knife from the wall, whipping it at

the bottle. It caught its cord, pinning it to the painted target the
drunk had missed on the other end of the tavern, glass swinging
sober below it. *Wyrmseye.* The drunk cheered, his mates cheered,
the tavern cheered, someone screamed, knowing nine.

"Why go and do a thing like that?" Thrace glowered at Aëros,
disappointed. "The fool had it coming."

"*Feathers.*"

Thrace pointed at his bottle where it hung from the target.
"You see that?" He shook his head. "That's why no one plays with
you. When was the last time you missed?"

"I don't remember."

"That's why no one plays with you."

Aëros quirked the corner of his mouth up. "Tärin doesn't miss
either."

Thrace dragged himself back into his seat, sullen. "To ash
with the Aröaē line."

"Eventually," said Aëros. He pointed at his friend's smoldering
smoke. "But probably not before yours."

Thrace breathed out, smoke billowing from his mouth. "A
vice for you, a vice for he, and a vice for me, with sanity found
betwixt the three."

Aëros blinked. "That doesn't make any sense."

"Well, what sense is there in your dialogue on dithering with
death or vice that leads to it." Thrace released another plume of
smoke from the corners of his mouth, drawing it back in through
his nose. "You're prone to wander off into some region or realm or
world where the wager's wise you won't return. The dragon-
sickness might not be in you anymore, but I still see the memory of
it in your eyes." Thrace paused, some recognition running through
his mind; some memory of a question left unanswered, half-
lingering. "Why were you at the Cove? Where are you wandering
to now that has you in such a hurry?"

Aëros furrowed his brow, a name echoing in his mind. *Slayer
of Death.* The conversation had made its way, dug up what was

better buried. He hesitated. It wasn't that he didn't know the proper lie to tell, it was that he knew Thrace would know it for a lie as soon as he told it. He saw that Thrace read everything he needed to in the silence, anyway. "Dún."

Thrace darkened, his eyes burning into his friend's, darker still. "You're no better than Arök swallowing his own tail. Something something the 'folly of repetition'. Move on, Aëros. Move on."

Move on. The weight of the words collapsed on him. He'd heard them enough from the Shadow to get the point; he didn't need to hear them from his friend too.

Thrace's words waxed grim. "Why are you going back? Why Dún? That crypt holds nothing not better left forgotten."

"Seems it's the one thing I can't forget." The intensity binding Thrace's eyes to his friends did not lessen, coaxing words from the Wayfarer he wished to leave unspoken. "I don't know why I'm going or what I'll find. But I have to go all the same." It was a partial truth. What could he say? That something only he could see told him to? Was leading him there even now? He could tell him that. Thrace would understand. *This is no one's burden but my own.*

"You're heading somewhere and you don't know what you'll find." Not a question. Thrace's voice rippled with something between anger and sorrow. Aëros feared it was pity. "That's how adventure works. If you knew, it would just be an errand. What started you onto it?"

Aëros heard the echoes of forgotten things in that question, taunting him. "I'm not sure." Another partial truth. He didn't know *why* his mind was leaving him.

Thrace stooped over the table. The lantern overhanging it flickered, indifferent, scouring his features as he searched his friend's eyes and found in them something that did not belong to the Aëros he knew. "The dead have nothing to do with the living. Not anymore."

Aëros looked to the Shadow through the edge of his eyes. It drifted into an empty booth, ever vigilant, ever present. It watched, a guide, an ill omen, a crooked warden with a crooked skeleton key. It named him.

Slayer of Death.

"A man's will does not die with the man," said Aëros. "Forgetting it won't rid the world of it. Or myself."

Thrace swallowed hard. "Athair is rotting, bones buried, soul severed. You shattered his little trinket of unlife. He's gone. You killed him."

Athair. There it was. The name of a madman—the name of a friend, killed, betrayed—spoken, stringing round Aëros like a rope from a gallows tree. "Yes." The words came slow, as if admitting the truth of his betrayal was a disturbance to the world. "But death never meant dead to him, Thrace. He was born of it, surrounded by it. It was worked into every seam of his being. Whether his sickness drew it round him, or it drew out his sickness, death was his domain. Something calls me to his grave. It echoes from the Barrows, from Dún."

Thrace's words grew cold. "He's not alive, Aëros."

"No," Aëros agreed. "He isn't. But something of his will lingers in this world. I know it. Just as I knew what his will was— what he was. Knew it when we were young. Saw it in his eyes then, even if I didn't know what to do..."

"You did what you could, did more than anyone had a right to ask of you." Thrace saw the sorrow seeping out of his friend, wished he knew how to dam it up. "What he is—what he was... It's almost a tavern-tale. *Was* a tavern-tale until he came along. There isn't even a word to name it."

Aëros' eyes grew hard, certain. "I found two. In another world. "*Psyköpathy. Sociopathy.* They mean much the same thing, are by

30

most measures interchangeable. There are degrees of each. Athair is—was—the most extreme."

Thrace swallowed. "Two words. What sort of world needs two words for what Athair was."

Ours. The thought flickered in Aëros' mind and died there.

Thrace waited a long while before speaking, but he did eventually speak. "Whatever is left of Athair's will is in you alone, Aëros. If it calls you back to his grave, it calls from within yourself." A wraith of sorrow, of that terrible pity, glinted in his gaze. "I hope you can free yourself of it, my friend. For your sake. For the world's. For it will be far poorer without you."

Aëros let the pity, the sorrow, slide away. Thrace grinned, shook his head as if shaking himself out of some trance, weary with the weight of their words. "What is your route?"

Aëros crooked his neck side to side, sighing. "I'm making for the forest, then on through the Dragongrave. Maybe the Things Betwixt, if I must."

The lantern lit Thrace's surprise. He laughed, thick with contempt. "You mock me for finding distraction in death, yet here you walk with it at the lead. Hypocrite." Aëros gave no indication that his hypocrisy bothered him. Thrace grumbled. "Why bother with the forest? The boneyard? What will walking bring you that you'd lose by just ripping open a Rift in reality and stepping through?"

The Shadow looked over, forcing itself fully into Aëros' awareness, its eyes holding his. "I can't."

"Can't?" Thrace shaped the word as if it didn't fit his mouth.

Aëros nodded, shadows cascading over him and his words. "I've forgotten how."

"Forgotten?" Thrace tilted his head, smoke hanging limp from his lips, almost falling out. "How can you forget a thing like that? Nomad might flicker between worlds at random, but you did it by design."

Silence.

Thrace shook his head, sighing. "You really are going threadbare, aren't you?"

Aëros dragged his eyes from the Shadow's. "Even if I could open a Rift, I don't think I'm meant to for this journey."

"Meant to?" Thrace bristled, irritated, tossing his smoke aside, spent. "Since when has *meant to* meant a thing to you?"

Aëros shrugged. "A wayfarer is a foot-traveler. The journey wills I walk as one. There's no urgency." *Wyrmshit. Wyrmshit. Wyrmshit.*

"If there's no urgency, then take the long way around. Avoid the forest, rim the Wyrmspine, walk the pass, dally where death doesn't dwell."

Aëros heard Thrace, but his words were far away. He was staring off into the crowd, into a booth, thoughts numb to the advice of his friend. Thrace followed Aëros' eyes to the booth. "What are you looking for?"

Aëros stared at the Shadow that only he could see, sitting in the booth that appeared to all others vacant. "Something I don't remember losing."

Thrace grasped his friend's face with both hands, forcing his focus to him. "How many times do I have to remind you it was in the east, to a Rōvaraē woman. I gambled it for you and lost, and I don't think you're going to find it in Athair's grave." He frowned, considering. "I hope not."

The Wayfarer swatted his friend away, smiling. "Fuck off."

"So, no Rifts." Thrace worked the wonder over. "Even after the forest and the Dragongrave, you can't reach the Barrows without one. No Barrows, no Dún. Your ego may be mountainous, but it won't loft you over the Aegis."

"No *new* Rifts."

Thrace's eyes focused, alighting on his friend's meaning. "Ah, so the wood and the boneyard."

"An arrowshot to Arythos, yes." Aëros looked to a window and beyond it, beyond the Verdant Fells, to where his road would

32

darken—the Wōadglōam Forest; the Dragongrave and the great scar that ran through it called the Ashen Vale; Arythos, the fallen kingdom; and above its ruins the towering silhouette of the Wyrmspine, a mountain range of slumbering stone wrought from the corpse of the wyrm Arök, where what Thrace had forgotten hid from the world, waiting. *The Wayshrine.*

Aëros saw it, even from this distance. Not with his elven sight, but with his mind's, his memory's. A permanent, unfading Rift, woven into an archway of crystal, perched atop the peak of the mountain.

Thrace lit another smoke, face filling with conviction. "I suppose I'll be coming with you then."

Aëros turned the corners of his mouth up, his smile grateful but disavowing. "No." He looked again to the Shadow. "This isn't a fellowship. This is one I walk alone." *I wish it were otherwise. But I will not risk you or anyone for something as selfish as my sanity.*

"But—"

"No." Aëros' will was unbreakable, forged in the primordial flames of wayworn stubbornness.

"Why? At least let me walk with you to the Wayshrine." Thrace pressed on. "You know what lurks in the forest. You know what awaits souls like you—lone and foolhardy—in the Dragongrave. You will find need of aid."

"Perhaps," said Aëros. "But if I do, it will find me in my need. Not before."

Thrace scowled, resigned. Cassidy returned, her arms bristling with fine-smelling fare. She set supper before the delinquents, and they thanked her as she hurried away. Thrace shook the scowl from his face, knowing the point it aimed to make would miss its mark. He grabbed his stout, darker than dark, and raised it for a toast, all he was left able to do.

"Well," he began. "To death, Aëros. May it flee before you on your journey. May you find it at the end of your days in your bed, quiet, peaceful, ready for you as a well-paid woman."

The Wayfarer smiled and lifted his own flagon to clash with his friend's. The duo tipped the drinks back and drained them—to mischief and fair fortune, to foresight and hind, to adventure and its spoils. *No treasure this time around. No trove or artifacts or wisdom. Just my sanity. Dull.*

Aëros and Thrace set their drinks down with a thud, and began working their meal away over reminiscence of their youth, recalling stories both scandalous and solemn as they sojourned in their past. Aëros added to those he remembered, and let Thrace recall those he didn't. As the night waxed to its latest hours their conversation dwindled, time walked, and with it the Wayfarer went.

"I'd better be off to wander," said Aëros, the tavern crowd now thinned to a few lingering souls shackled to their stupor.

Thrace's eyes were reluctant, the green now dulled by smoke and drink. "Aye. I suppose the night's grown old."

Aëros stood, then paused as he remembered something. "Just one thing before I make my way."

"Oh?" said Thrace. "What's that?"

Aëros snatched a knife from Nowhere and hurled it at Thrace's bottle, still hanging limp from the post he'd pinned it to. *Wyrmseye.* The glass exploded, breaking the settling silence of the tavern, fragments twinkling in the amber light as they skittered over the floor. Broawn peered in from the entrance, glower-grinning.

Thrace's brow rose, amused and indignant once again. "Fuck happened to 'feathers'?"

Aëros smirked. "For old times' sake."

Thrace stole a sliver of Aëros' smirk for himself. "Ah, fuck off and farewell, Old Raven." His solemnity waxed. "Do not let Athair take from you in death what he failed to in life."

Solemnity waned again, ever a lesser thing. Thrace stood and held his hand outstretched. Aëros met it, pulling him into an embrace. "Farewell." He looked at the maiden Cassidy as they

34

parted, recalling another something nearly forgotten. "Do mind your face."

"Bah!" Arrogance. "She'll be mine before dawn."

"Thrace," Aëros' eyes twinkled with the 'I've seen into your soul and returned with the truth' twinkle they'd developed in the womb. "She was always yours. Her love was in her ire."

Thrace's eyes balanced between understanding and the fear of it. "I know."

"Ah." Aëros had come back with every truth. If only his own were so easy to find as others'. "You love her too."

Thrace faltered, looked away. "Fuck off."

Aëros looked at the poster painted with his friend's face, looked at his friend, and told himself not to think on what was missing, or consider why. He flipped an aūrum onto the table, to which Thrace tipped a thankful salute.

The Wayfarer turned to make his way from the tavern, did not look back, waving over his shoulder as he leaned into the night, alone. A shadow walked in his periphery—*the* Shadow. The only companion he did not long for the company of. The only companion he could not do without.

Night ascended to its apex, and the Wayfarer walked in the silver light of shattered moon and falling star, a fractured whole and the fragments of its fracturing. The Fells surrounded him, rolling hills of shadowed green and running streams that reflected the firmament above. His lantern was darkened and stored away, the lúmoths fluttering free from its imprisoning light.

Free. He considered illuminating his lantern again, hiding from the darkness, drawing the creatures to him. His own prison would be easier with fellows. It was tempting to take them with him. To take more than them with him. *Is that the consideration of a madman?* He thought not; only the consideration of a selfish one.

He waylaid along the base of a small fell, beside a smaller stream, setting the smallest of camps for the night. A thin rill of wind ran past him, drawing the sweet scent of the Fells with it, drawing the scent of something else too, something spoiled. His face knotted up as he wondered what it was, then remembered. It was him.

He wasn't sure how long he'd been on his journey, but his reek told him it was enough for him to be long past his prime. He examined himself. His clothing was weatherworn with the stains of adventure. It was a familiar smell, a familiar look; he was a wayfarer after all. *The* Wayfarer. He walked a hard, weary, wayworn road. A road that repaid tenfold what it took, if one was willing to wager against discomfort, loneliness, and death. Payment came in discovery, in knowledge: lost artifacts and languages; forgotten peoples and forlorn lands; new skills, new wisdom, new tales to tell of it all. He was a Wayfarer, and a certain scent was to be expected. His Aūriel never argued otherwise, ever eager to help him ease the weariness of the road away. She was once a wayfarer too—a wayfaress, she would say, smiling—but she was far less selfish than he, retiring her wanderings when Tärin was born.

A familiar longing ran through him. A grief, a hope, all wrapped up in his promise to his family. *I will be home soon. I will return to you. Whole.*

The stream ran silent, deep enough to wade in. He stripped and slid in. Alone. The water caught the sheen of the moon, and he looked to it, to Valrävn—the raven constellation grasping the celestial in its talons, cradling it as it died. It was failing, for the moon was shattered utterly, a hollow thing. The stars in the sky were the tears of its doom, the residue of its war with the wyrm that had once slumbered within it, fragments of betrayal speckling the firmament.

Eventually the moon would fade fully. It would take Ages, and Aëros would be long dead, but in the end, as was the way of all things, it would ash away, scattering its silver dust into the weft and warp of memory. Another might take its place, in time, risen from the ashes of its ancestor. He mused on the words of his Aūriel, written in the song she sang for him—the song *of* him. *Even ash of Ages gone, may grow a wood, a world, a home.*

He finished washing and drew his waywell from Nowhere, filling it with water from the stream, the threads of Vätn woven within the artifact purifying whatever was poured within. He drank, then lay himself along the verdant slope and measured the sky, watching Valrävn desperately clutching, watching the moon dim, doomed.

His eyes fluttered, weariness creeping up from his bones, but he did not desire sleep. For he did not sleep as most men might; his mind lingered somewhere betwixt and between stirring and slumber, a hypnagogic state rising out of his elven ancestry, his blood threaded nearly full through with the essence of the First of the First, a rarity after Ages of interweaving. When he dreamt, he was aware, lucid, walking through the halls and hollows of his inner self. When he was sane, this was a boon, allowing thought and consideration even while resting. Now that his mind was abandoning him it was a curse, forcing him to see how empty the halls had become.

But though he did not desire sleep, he had no choice but to take it. He was unlike most men in many ways, but like most men he was still in thrall to fatigue. As it mastered him, and the night-song of the Fells lulled him, he settled into the womb of slumber, comforting until darkness came, and with it dreaming.

Chapter III: Dreams, Memories, Nightmares
• Dreaming of Spring •

*T*he ferryman's vessel vanished in the mists *running over the river separating you from the rest of the world, leaving you both stranded; or so you pretended, too young yet for true adventure and the dangers it measured men against.*

You and he walked side by side over the deadlands, disturbing them, undisturbed by them, seeking their heart, arriving there on a path you knew well. This was Athair's home, after all. Raised here with the gravekeepers, taken in by them at his birth. You saw how he avoided the trees, dying and few though they were.

There were none here in the heart of the Barrows. Here there was only a mausoleum, or a ruin of one at least, its mystery drawing you both to it time and again. Dún. As then, as now. Its mystery took the shape of a doorway set into the ground, sealed up, shut away by a solid slab of intricately hewn stone. There was script running along its arch, illegible with the wear of Ages. You explored the ruin, fascinated with the ancestral nature of it; he explored it, fascinated by another aspect entirely.

He was standing over the doorway, studying it, mind working, wondering. "Aëros?" He'd looked to you in your youth. For friendship, for guidance—for someone who would understand him. He looked to you now, standing atop a crumbling wall, a ruin with no remembered past, no importance in the world, a ruin that would become everything.

You looked down at him as you teetered on the rim of the wall, roof caved in to your right, three stories down on either side. "What is it?"

"Well, you know how…" He trailed off, uncertain. You knew what was unspoken. Your mother had explained, and you understood, though you didn't agree.

"You won't go away forever." You fell back on your haunches, meeting his eyes and holding them. "Your folks are just concerned is all.

They want to make sure that if something's wrong, you'll get help making it right."

"Yea…" He tore his eyes away from yours, trusting you, but not whatever he held within himself. It spoke to him, told him otherwise. You didn't know how to overrule it; how to mean more to him than it did. He knelt above the doorway, running his hand over the script, staring.

Something heaved and rumbled. A frame far past ancient and tempted too often by the foolishness of youth gave way, crashing down. He spun around hard and found you gone; the wall on which you'd perched a wall no longer. "Aëros!"

He sprinted to you, hauling away rubble and debris. Murky light from the misted sky filtered through the dust of Ages as his eyes searched, seeking, desperate.

Something stirred; someone coughed. You heaved yourself up from the mess, hardly injured. He dug what he could off of you, and you shifted through the rest like a shadow, smirking.

"You fool," he said.

"Aye." Your smirk brought his own to him, familiar. "Thanks for rescuing me, the damsel."

You both laughed, hard, laughed with the naïveté of two boys who'd stood on the rim of death and returned; one who almost fell over, the other willing to leap after. The laughter cut off—something screeched in the cavernous ruin, screamed, desperate and terrified. The two of you froze, looking at one another. The screech came again, agonized, crying for help. You both scrambled towards it, fumbling to a halt in the center of the ruin, standing just before the doorway in the floor.

A mother raven danced around a nest—her nest—frantic. It had fallen as you had, and the eggs within shattered, embryos pouring out, dead. One chick, however, was born alive. Its body was broken, and it writhed, suffering.

"No…" You knelt down to the nest, mother raven screaming at you now, reaper of her motherhood. You looked at it, and its screams softened *into some sorrowful, horrible chirp, then fell silent beside the nest, knowing as you did what needed done.*

The chick squirmed in the nest, soaked in the death of its siblings. There was no easy way to do what you needed to, so you did what you knew would cause the least suffering to the bird. You lifted a stone from the pile of rubble, leveled it above the head of the chick, and pressed down with every bit of strength you had. The stone sunk to the ground with ease. You sunk with it, sobbing, the mother raven silent, watching.

You gathered yourself, wrapping your self-loathing and anger into a knot, and setting it aside to unravel later, when it was time. You would not hold it forever, only for now. For now, you built a small cairn over the corpse, some small token of reverence for the first life lost by your foolishness.

A shadow loomed over you, a friend, someone to confide in, someone who would understand. You turned, meeting his eyes, expecting to see a reflection of what yours held. A reflection of sorrow, of anger, of blame, of pity.

There was no reflection, only a smile. A smile wreathed with interest, excitement, arousal, crooked with the hints of insanity. You knew then what he was. What there wasn't even a name for in your world. Not yet.

"Athair!" You woke from your dream—your memory—your nightmare—screaming.

Aŭriel startled awake beside you, then gathered herself, seeing you breathing heavy, sweating, eyes widened to their limits, seeking what fled as you woke. She understood in an instant. "You're safe." She smiled and kissed your cheeks, your forehead, your lips, holding you. "You're safe."

You calmed, breath slowing, heartbeat quieting. A loud rap shuddered through your home; someone was on your threshold. You looked to one another, curious, concerned, and went; her to Tärin, you to the door.

You willed your lantern alive, hiding from the darkness swarming around you. The door loomed, waiting, silent. You opened it. There was no one. Just the empty night of a late evening or early morn. You looked, found what was left for you on the doorstep, and collapsed to your knees in horror.

She found you huddled over the threshold, breath as ragged as when you'd awoken. You clutched something, a dark, thick stream running through your fingers, pooling beneath you.

"Aëros, what is—" She broke off as she saw it. She didn't know what to do. For the first time in her life she looked helpless, because for the first time she was. She fell beside you. "Aëros—"

You were trembling, weeping, laughing. Tears fell, but your eyes weren't sorrowful, they were wild. You were a shadow of sanity, unrecognizable. She recoiled more at you than what you held. Catching herself, she drew up to you, held you, tried to reason away the madness, but found no words.

"It's Athair, Aūriel. He— Arkym—" You choked off, her scent filling you: lemongrass, lavender, mint leaves. You breathed her in, and all at once you broke. She enveloped you in her arms, holding you together as Thrace's disembodied head dripped blood into your home.

<hr />

"Da'?"

Tärin entered your study through the secret passage between the walls. He'd been searching for you, having found his mother in the garden, sitting and gazing in a distant way. He knew something was amiss. You weren't at the range like you'd promised, or in the garden with Aūriel, or on the roof with your eyes looking into the past of faraway adventures. That meant you were here. You didn't hear him enter or call out to you. You were too busy dealing with the horror of the night. Doing your best to set to rights what had gone so horribly wrong, making a plan for when it grew even worse, as you knew it would.

He was at your side then, watching you as you muttered to yourself, your eyes still wild, hair in disarray, silver ink spilling across your desk, over the ideas and plans and desperate efforts to decide the course before you. "Da'?"

His voice, so near, drew you out from within yourself. It returned your focus to the waking world, to your son, whom you'd forgotten in place of your grief, your rage. Seeing him looking at you with concern watering his eyes, you knew your mistake; knew too how to rectify it. You smiled half a smile and straightened yourself up, not wanting him to see you as you were, even though it was as anyone would be given the circumstance. You could not wash that sort of blood from your skin, that stain from your soul. Not in such a short time. "I'm sorry, Tärin. My mind…went away from me this morning."

His eyes were bound to yours, studying them, seeing the hurt there, knowing something was coming that he was not yet ready for. He knew it, because he could see that neither were you.

You hardened your will, buried your grief in your bones to be felt later, and stood, tussling his hair. "You have something to show me, if I remember rightly?"

He grinned under his mess of silver locks, and nodded. "Yes!"

Tärin led you out from the study, out from the house, into the garden. He turned, smirking a familiar smirk. "You're the predator, old man!"

You found yourself wearing the same smirk as you watched him dive through a hole in the hedges that formed one wall of the labyrinth. You dove over, unable to fit through, and fell hard on his heels as he traversed the architecture of wood, stone, and hedgerow, working his way and yours ever-so-surely toward the heart of the maze. You had him once, caught between two stone pillars at the hidden end of a corridor. But he figured out the escape, leaping between and up one pillar to the other, until he was over and into another corridor. You smiled, proud, and met him at last in the heart of the maze, where wooden targets were scattered high and low in the shapes of shields,

43

men, beasts, monsters. You'd built it for him, but he'd added plenty of his own artifice since. He was so excited to show you what he'd learned.

His heart smiled brighter than his eyes, his arrows tumbling from his quiver as he turned, half-skipping. They were new, quiver and arrows; he'd made them for himself, had even done his own fletching. You weren't there for that, but you were here now, and now is all there ever really is. "Da'! Remember how poor a shot I was?"

"You were never a poor shot, Tärin," you said as you passed under the archway into the range. "You hit wyrmseye nine out of ten arrows."

He grinned. "Bah! Wyrmshit!"

Wyrmshit? You laughed, surprised. Thrace had been around. You didn't mind. There was a time for cursing the same as there was a time for anything. Thrace wouldn't be around anymore, of course. You would have to tell him that. But now was not that time. Not yet. You didn't want to tamp his spirits, steal his focus. He was so determined to impress. He loved you so dearly, for you were a father worth loving, a man worth measuring himself against and up to.

He nocked his arrow, so similar to those you once fletched for yourself, drew, loosed. In a blur, he followed the first with a second. The first hit wyrmseye over a hundred yards out, the second trailing its wind and ripping it through down its shaft.

"Well fu—" You caught yourself before the word fell out. Tärin grinned. Thrace had been around after all. Wyrmshit was the least of it. You grinned yourself. "You robin'd the arrow."

His face wound up, confused. "Robin'd?"

"Split one arrow with another."

"Why robin'd?"

Your mind went back to an adventure long ago, in another world, another reality. There had been many. "Greatest marksman I've ever known. First I ever saw do it. Robin was his name."

His confusion waxed defiant. "Wyrmshit! You're the greatest marksman!"

You smiled. "There are many worlds, Tärin, with many men greater than me at a great many things." Your words were strung with

44

humility, somewhat sincere, somewhat untrue. Humility was, in the end, a more convoluted form of arrogance. He saw the essence of that wisdom and kept what he saw for himself, for measuring, adding it to the wisdom he'd already begun to find on his own.

You saw it there, a trove hidden in his eyes, and a pang of desperation leapt in your heart—the fear of a father desperate to hold onto the innocence of his son. For what is wisdom but the death of innocence? You mastered your fear, knowing you could not prevent what was waking within him, only guide it. "Would you like to come with me tonight?"

He drew back, skeptical, his head crooked in curiosity. "Where?"

"Hunting." You looked beyond the hedge, beyond the walls of Arythos, beyond the Dragongrave, beyond the primordial woodland, to the furthest edge of the Verdant Fells, the furthest Tärin would ever go in life. "Would you like to come?"

The pride he'd shown at robining an arrow was an ember compared to the flame that flickered through him now, his eyes gleaming with excitement. "Yes!"

You nodded, reveling in his joy, even as you felt dreadful within. What you offered him was a knife, and with it the severance of the last thread of his innocence. You knew its necessity, and hated yourself for knowing it. "Prepare what you'll need. We'll leave in the evening."

Aüriel called out from the villa. "Supper's on!"

"We're heading in!" You gestured to Tärin, beckoning him to put his bow and quiver in order and come along.

"Wash, and make sure Tärin washes too!"

Tärin looked at you, eyes rolling.

Wash? You'd reeked the night before, and she hadn't cared. You smelled of adventure and adventure returned from, and that was all the scent she needed. Tärin saw that, and decided that if your scent was good enough for you, good enough for his mother, then his would be good enough for him and whatever love he found in his life too.

Still, the mothering instinct drove her to redundancy. Wash. The instinct of a son drove him to insolence. The instinct of a man who

45

*knew better drove you to advise. "She'll know. For your sake, wash."
You found her redundancy charming, and his insolence familiar.
Distance will do that.*

He spoke in what he thought was a whisper. "She won't know."

"I will too, Tärin! Wash!"

You both flinched.

*"Ears like a ripping raven." Wyrmshit? Ripping? Maybe it was
good that Thrace wouldn't be around for a while. The thought died a
bitter death. He'd never be around again.*

*"And wrath to sleep Arök." You grinned, knowing the flame of that
wrath, that passion. "Come, the sooner we eat the sooner we can head
out."*

"Da'?" His eyes waxed curious.

You shuffled him forward. "Yes?"

"Will Arök ever wake up?"

*You looked to the forever-shattered moon, falling to its death in the
dark, to the silhouette of the Wyrmspine, running into the distance.
"That depends."*

*He followed your eyes to the celestial, to the mountains, to
everywhere he wished to go in life. "On what?"*

*You smiled and met his eyes, seeing your reflection, seeing his.
"Whether his dreams are more pleasant than the waking world."*

<hr />

*Supper was wonderful. After Tärin excused himself, she stood to clean,
and you stood, wrapping your arms around her. She held onto them as
you held onto her, and you watched Tärin go together. He climbed
through a window, sauntered up onto a ledge, and dove over a banister
into his room.*

"I'm taking him hunting tonight."

*She looked up out of the corner of her eye. "Do you think he's
ready?" Her words were hesitant.*

"He's a straighter shot than I." You knew well that wasn't what she meant.

"I don't mean with the bow."

You released her and spun her around to meet your eyes. "He needs to know about Thrace. The hunt will help ease that pain when I heave it upon him. He needs to understand. What death is. What it is to take a life…"

Memory of the night past flashed through your mind, and hers. You were right, and she knew it. You both wished you weren't. She watched your eyes grow distant, the silver in them dimming. She took your face in her hands and drew you back to her. "Thrace's death is not your fault, Aëros."

You broke her embrace then, setting distance between you, unable to bear the tenderness, the pity, the falsehood. "Yes, it is. Everyone that has died by Athair's will has died because of both the choice I made and the choice I failed to make."

She strode over to you, a bit of anger in her step, anger that you would pull away from her when you needed comfort. She wrapped herself around you, her own eyes streaming silver. "You made that choice for the love of your friend. Made it hoping he could be redeemed. The only other choice was not a choice at all. Not then. Not until—"

"Now." You finished her words. They were your burden, the choices made and the choice yet to be made yours to bear. They were not for her to weigh herself down with. Only you. Only ever you.

She felt the thought run through you, and whispered her promise to soothe. You were her sentinel. You pulled her tight, breathing her in, stroking her hair, braided and banded with silver. You echoed her promise with your own. She was yours.

Chapter IV: Aurora
• Dreaming of Spring •

Aëros heaved in breath, eyes distant as he awoke and the dreams, or memories, or nightmares faded. It was the midst of night, and the Shadow sat before him, watching. It stood, the intent in its eyes unspoken. *Move on.* Aëros' thoughts splintered and sped, desperate to make sense of what he'd seen, of its purpose, of the Shadow's will, of his own.

He thought of Thrace's death and felt an urge to rush back to the Waypoint, but subdued it, knowing not to feed his hysteria, no matter how much the part of the dream that was nightmare *had* felt like memory. One he'd witnessed. One he'd lived. One he'd preserved, forgotten. He hadn't. It was false. An illusion of insanity. It meant nothing.

The furthest Tärin would ever go in life. There was hidden meaning layered into everything he'd seen, layers of madness, of impossible events and horrifying possibilities. His eyes were hollow in the night, racing east to west, replaying what he'd seen, trying to work out the riddle of it all, of the narrative the Shadow was revealing, the story he was being told, or perhaps reminded of.

The Shadow held its silence, lingering, staring ahead, urging him forward, urging him on. His eyes fell to his ring—the key to his memories, his promise; the key to many things. *Always forward. Always on.*

He looked to the horizon, not with his elven sight but with his mind's: to the eastern border of the Fells, the shores of Vimaray, the coast of black sand and monolithic arches of weatherworn sea-stacked stone that hemmed it. He looked beyond those waters to the furthest reaches of his world, further still, somewhere his madness couldn't reach him.

No.

There was no freedom in flight. His mind was the home of his madness, and he could not flee from himself. He could not turn back. He could only move forward, no matter what his journey brought: memory, nightmare, worse. It seemed madness lay both before and behind, but to move forward was to find it of his own will, and to turn back was for it to find him. He knew which was worse. His ring shimmered in the night, illuminating the promise it held. Aëros nodded, knowing, and went on.

⸻ ◆ ⸻

A thread of gold light streaked the horizon, twining night to day as one fell to dreaming and the other awoke. Morning was here, and with it Aëros walked, having stored the makings of his camp away in the depthless, hidden pockets of his Shräud, each woven from the threads of Aūr as its illusory nature was woven from the threads of Dräu. They held instruments for survival and artifice: tools for digging, cutting, navigating, hunting, and foraging; a hammock woven from the fibers of a wōadglōam threaded with Aër, needing no anchor to hang aloft, floating freely; and many other artifacts and oddities besides. He ran the raiment through his fingers, feeling the half-illusion of it, the memories worked into its warp and weft.

He crested the grassy knoll he'd slept beneath, the fullness of the Verdant Fells rising to meet him at its summit. Endless leagues of dewdrop grassland swathed the rolling hills, coursing on to the Wyrmspine as it hemmed the lowlands, the mountain range running northwest and then southward along the outskirts of the West like the twisted spine of a coiled, resting serpent. Tavern tale held that the mountains were indeed a wyrm—Arök, first of the first of all things of thought, that which dwelled within the hollow of the moon, shattering it on its waking so long ago and falling to Eave, sinking into the land and the sea, wrapping itself around the world, holding it together, bound head to tail as it settled into a weary slumber. Tavern tale only, or so most thought. Aëros knew the truth, kept it for himself. Not every secret the world held needed knowing.

The runoff of the serpent sired the great basins of the Fells, the waterways of the lea-lands. Aëros walked over wild hills and settled flatland where farmsteads stood aged and worn, following the thin streams and strays of the waterways, wandering into glen and dell, where silent trails were tread by roaming beasts.

It was along these paths Aëros went, keeping off of those tread by Ayl or Ken. For while the primary highways of elves and humans were easier to traverse, they meandered, stealing time otherwise preserved by keeping as the raven soars or the vesta seeks—so long as one had the waycraft to navigate the wildland.

He stole a strand of wheat from the swath running beside him, twirling it in his teeth as the Fells' day-song lilted in the air. The sun sat unfettered in the firmament, its rays temperate, the wind fair, the trail soft and swift to follow. It was a perfect day, and he appreciated it, knowing it was one of few left for him. Of all the days he'd lived, those that were perfect were always the most fleeting. They came soft and silent, and left just the same. The memories of them were always hazy, limned with gilded, wistful nostalgia. Or so he imagined. His memories weren't hazy; they were gone.

"*Far into dusk their trail does go...*" He spoke to nothing, and followed the words with the whistled melody of his Aūriel's making, the song the Shadow had drawn from his memory, the song she named the Hymn of the Wayfarer, knowing well how to please his ego.

Nightingales alighted beside him, drawn to his singing, harmonizing with their own. The song went on, and the night went with it, streaks of color found in flame and flower petals threading the twilit sky as the shadows of the world softened under the growing dusk. The sun almost fully westered, weariness finding its way from the Wayfarer's bones, he saw his path was nearing a split, the diverging trail falling into a vale he was sure would hold a small pool at its base. It was down this path he traveled, his song dissipating as he descended.

The trail he followed was fresh, a herd recently passed. *Vesta.* He knew this track. It was old, worn by the beast's ancestors, worked deeper and deeper into instinct with each generation. The lithe, sinuous beasts once wandered as far as the westernmost vertebrae of the Wyrmspine, but that land was a waste now, arid and desolate, with nothing for them. *Only for me.*

He set a smooth pace along a thin stream, finding that it fed into the pool he'd known would be there. It drew up out of the grasses, hidden by their height, stealing only a little of the dying moon's light and the waning day's dusk for itself.

Dropping himself against the sharp slope of a nearby hillock, he dug through the hidden pockets of his Shräud, seeking provisions—and found scraps, realizing he'd forgotten to purchase stores at the Waypoint. He shrugged. The Fells were bountiful, and he remembered his waycraft well enough. *I hope.*

Silver and gold streamed through the pool, stolen light catching on the scales of the fish swimming aimless and unworried within. The Wayfarer glided over to the pool's edge and knelt beside it, his silhouette cascading over its surface as the hues of dusk gilded it with gold. He set his will on the shadow of his silhouette, the threads of Dräu weaving to his will, fooling the fish beneath the pool's mirrored surface into believing that he was somewhere he was not.

Fresh silver flashed into the water—his ring, shaped with the needle of his will into a needle itself, far finer than an arrow. He thrust it through the pool like a dart on the wind of his will, taking his marks swiftly, their death immediate. He drew them from the tarn, ring running through each like a silver thread, stringing the catch together like a necklace. He watched the shadows of the fish swing beneath him, melding into his own shadow as *the* Shadow watched from afar, stalking along the other edge of the water.

Ignoring the wraith, he set the fish down and willed his ring back into place. He reached into his Shräud, withdrew a stack of birchwood from Nowhere for a fire in the tree-barren lowlands, and wove a thin flame from the threads of Iné to set the oily wood alight. His dinner seared swiftly, and he enjoyed it as he watched nightshroud take back what daylight had stolen. Yet even as darkness loomed, the world was ever bright, lit by the shattered moon and the star-flecked sky. Another fell, burned up, faded away.

A streak followed the star, running through the night, an aurora awakening, weaving through the darkness with threads of teal, turquoise, silver, gold. It reminded Aëros of his Aŭriel, her eyes the same hue as the tear between realities flowing overhead. It taunted him with freedom he once knew, a distant thing now, like an addiction passed into unwilling sobriety. He gestured towards the stream of light, and in his mind the aurora moved, threads of Aŭr hearkening to his will. But that was only in his mind, a mastery he once knew and knew no longer, forgotten. The Shadow stared up at the shimmer in reality and gestured to it as he had. It rippled, flowing. He glared at the wraith, and it gestured to him, as with the aurora, and as the heavenly lights shifted with the Shadow's will, so too did he. The memory drew over him, drew up from within him.

It was a night as many nights before: you and Athair, camped out beneath the dying moon and its falling stars on the Verdant Fells. Interposed between the stars ran an aurora, its elysian light mingling with the silver of the moon, the nightshroud of darkness. You'd stalked a vesta and taken it swiftly, prepared the carcass, and set a thin thread of Iné to build into an open flame, wood drawn from Nowhere. You had a bag with no bottom, your Shräud having not yet been woven into existence, your relationship with Aūriel young, your understanding of the threads of Aūr younger still.

"That's quite a clever tool you've made for yourself," said Athair as he stoked the fire, gesturing to your bag. Your relationship with him was old now. You were no longer children, Dún far away, your innocence further. You were growing into men, growing wise. Learning more of the world, yourselves, one another.

"It's crude." You held the patchwork thing aloft, studying the primitive effort. "There's so much I have yet to learn of these threads. I'm stumbling around their edges, but I can't seem to fully grasp them."

He was staring at it too, admiring it, finding it quite remarkable. "A tear between realms."

"Between realities," you said, somewhat distant, distracted. You lowered the bag and met Athair's eyes. "I've discovered something else. Something that might help me understand. Might be beneficial to you, too."

His brows lifted, curiosity plain. "What is it?"

You smirked, almost vaunting as you reached into your bag, your tear between realities, and withdrew a small black pouch, embroidered with silver stitching and held fast by a silver clasp. You tossed it to him. He opened it and stared at the iridescent mixture within, colors shifting and shaping like the aurora overhead. It was a pouch filled with clairvoyance, near-omniscience, foolishness. He looked up, understanding still distant.

You drew a book from your bag, the beginning of a life's work, a guide to reality as you were coming to know it, to discover it. You opened it and quoted a passage recently written. "Sylysæ: a mixture of preserved moss extracted from the floor of the Wōadglōam's heartwood, saturated with an arkaēn distillation of deathspiral and nightshade nectars. Grants Tîraē, or "Sight," as translated from the elder tongue, defined as the ability to perceive the threads of reality with the mind's inner vision, allowing increased comprehension of the fundamental composition of self and other."

54

"Sight?" Athair smiled, approving. "I like the sound of it. You named it Sylyscybe?"

"Sylysæ," you said, correcting him. "It's a psychoactive mixture. Extraordinarily potent. My experiments with it are what led me to this." You held up the bag with no bottom, your first fumbling attempt at working reality to your will. "What you have in your hand is a refined effort. I'm expecting it to reveal what I have left to learn."

"I wonder what it will reveal to me." Athair's words were distant, your attention on your own wonders, detached from his. "How do we use it?"

From Nowhere you drew two worn traveler's pipes, tossing one to him. "Half for you, half for me."

He pinched his share of the mixture into the pipe and threw the remainder to you for yours. The fire had fallen to a steady flame, warming each of you as you lay back in the high grass of the Fells. The night filled your vision, silver twinkling, aurora rippling. You put your pipe to your lips, kindled Iné, and drew.

The Sylysæ flared, vibrant, iridescent colors flickering, burning, burning, burnt—ashing away on the wind. Your senses sharpened instantly, awareness stretching out: awareness of self, of the world, of each in respect to the other, of each in respect to the whole; the one; the Tapestry; Eaē. You felt the essence of what composed both you and everything that had once existed, existed now, and would ever exist in the time yet to come. As the prism of your perception reached its peak, you saw the nexus of existence: a finely woven web of all worlds, realms, realities, and timelines—the Tapestry, as your world called it.

Focusing, you narrowed your newfound Sight, setting it on the world without, curiosity your guide. With it you saw your world in a refined light, saw through the darkness of the night, the darkness of your ignorance. The aurora shifted overhead, a river in the sky, a ripple, a—

Not a river. Not a ripple. A rip. A tear. A rift between worlds, between realms, between realities. Your eyes widened as realization overwhelmed you, wisdom creeping in. What you'd stumbled into, woven into your bag of holding, had been above you this whole time.

You gestured to it, set your will upon it, seeing the threads that composed it, the threads that composed the fabric between worlds, the very essence of the Tapestry, of Eaē, understanding them—the threads of Aūr. As your understanding shifted into place, so did the aurora shift with it, widening in accordance with your will, to your bewilderment and your wild, childlike joy.

As swiftly as your Sight had come, it slipped away, the effects of the Sylysæ wearing thin. Yet the new knowledge that came from it remained, a new comprehension, new wisdom. The dawn was peaking over the horizon, the mixture having stolen your perception of time. You sat up, grinning like a madman, eager to share your discovery with your friend, oldest and nearest. "Athair! I understand!"

The distance between you yawned into a chasm as your eyes found his—found them staring into the eyes of the vesta you'd killed earlier in the night. Found the vesta staring back, standing, its underside slit open from when you'd dressed it, organs removed.

"So do I." His voice was still distant, even with your focus upon him. It was quiet, contemplative, almost innocent. "Isn't it wonderful?"

His eyes did not leave the vesta's, fixed on what he'd discovered, what he'd done. Neither did yours. The excitement of your discovery was devoured by the horror of Athair's.

The aurora of memory faded, the aurora overhead—the aurora of now—flowing in its place. "And now I understand no longer."

Aëros stared at the aurora, the longing he felt overshadowed by the sickening sense summoned by the memory it was bound to. He drew a long, weary breath, his weariness older still. He ignored it, tamped out the fire, and unshrouded his bow from Nowhere. Or rather his blade, not yet a bow. It was a thing of hidden secrets. Like him, it was sometimes one thing, sometimes another. When he willed it, it was a dagger, a long, vicious, sinuous blade. Its edge was unbroken, its inner frame hollow, diaphanous, forged from thin threads of Argynt woven into fluid patterns, the ethereal metal feather-light and steel-strong, shaped like the crescent remains of the forever-shattered moon.

Threads of wyrmstone wove through the artifact the way it wove through his ring. They ran from talon tip to blade, tapering into a grim edge so polished it seemed wet, along which ran a script of runes—old, primordial, of the First of the First. Aëros read them, but never spoke them. Not to anyone. They were his and his ancestors' alone to know.

There was a name for the sort of weapon it was in that ancient language: Tüllkühn—Trick Weapon. Rävnyr, 'Moon Fang,' was this artifact's personal, ancestral name. Aëros knew it as neither Tüllkühn nor Rävnyr, but Löekeh. A name not from the First of the First, but from a language of another world, another reality. The name of a mythical troublemaker, fabled for his mischief and misadventure. It fit the weapon as it fit the one who now wielded it, as any artifact of legend should.

Aëros set his will on the weapon and revealed the mischief within it. The threads working its hidden artifice unraveled, the dagger shifting, the hilt becoming a riser, the blade limbs, a string drawing out from a hidden hollow. Not always a dagger, but sometimes a bow as well.

He slung Löekeh over a shoulder, and set to following the trail skirting the pool, knowing the vesta who made it were near. He decided if he couldn't find rest, he would at least find provisions for the restlessness to come.

He flicked his traveling pipe and mixture pouch from Nowhere. The pipe was a simple one of dark wood, the pouch aged leather with the cartography of Eave tooled onto its face. He stared at it, the vision of a small black pouch with silver etching overlaying it. He shook the image away, unraveled the pouch, and packed his pipe. Lighting a thread of Iné along the tip of a finger, he kindled his vice and drew. The mixture was aromatic, soothing—wōadleaf, a blend hailing from the largest old-growth forest in Eave, the

Wōadglōam, which thrived on the western rim of the Verdant Fells.

Most forests of the West were nascent, threading the coast of Vimaray and the skirts of the Wyrmspine. The Wōadglōam was isolated, old, primordial. He was looking forward to sojourning in its heartwood, visiting an old friend who dwelled in that mythic hollow, even if he could remember little of him but his smile, welcoming and weathered. The memory of it drew out his own.

Smoke billowed about him, silhouetting him in silver-grey. He turned, and saw the Shadow walking along the far side of the bank, meandering in mimicry. Any thoughts he might have had faded into a wisp of obscurity as he rounded the base of a hillock, the vesta herd appearing in a clearing just beyond. He knew this field as well as he knew the trail that led him to it; an ancestral resting ground the elk-kin knew by instinct, threaded through generations.

The herd was sleeping in the tall grass, lúmoths flickering around them like little dreams drifting from the animals' settled minds. Aëros snuffed the embers of his pipe and returned it to Nowhere as he admired the beasts, their white coats catching the silver of the moon and the many-hued streaks of the aurora, the runic patterns marking their fur shimmering like lost letters of a long-forgotten language.

Crouched in the high grass, arrayed in his illusory Shräud, stealth threaded into his every movement, Aëros' sound and silhouette were hidden from all discernment. A buck rose from its rest to drink, finished, and lifted its head from the stream, lithe, branching antlers winding behind it as if swept by wind. It looked directly at him, knowing him with the same instincts that it knew the field in which it rested. Knew him and did not flee. But though it knew of his presence, the way in which it saw him seemed strange, as if it didn't quite know what he was. It stood there, prey, looking toward him, predator.

"*Do not fear death, Aëros.*" His father's voice echoed out of memory. For a moment he thought it was his own voice, the threads of ancestry were so similar. "*It ends no more than life begins. The Tapestry is eternal, infinite, and by the nature of infinity all things— animate or inanimate, living or dead, now or then—are without end and without beginning, are threads in the fabric of Eaē. All that was, is, and will ever be.*"

The memory left as he set the string of his bow beneath his eye as if he'd already nocked an arrow. As the string flexed, the shadow of an arrow materialized against the riser—the last of the weapon's wonders—and with it, another memory materialized in his mind, a memory he did not summon, holding him hostage.

"*Do you see them, Tärin?*"

It'd been a few hours since you and he stepped over the Rift into the region of the Fells where the vesta roamed, a gentle wind all the disturbance left behind as the seam between places stitched back together, sealed. He'd found the herd on his own. You'd seen it first, but he found it on his own. You were proud.

"*I see them, da'.*" *He focused with the eyes of a raven or a wolf or a wyrm—predatory.*

He was learning his waycraft well. He understood the threads of stealth and stalking, of reading how the story of a wild place has unfolded over time. He wove each into a fabric of knowledge in which he draped himself, wove himself into the story of this wild place in such a way that he seemed to have always been a part of it.

He drew an arrow from his quiver and made to set it beneath his eye. You held out a hand, forestalling him, your other hand holding a bow. Löekeh. "Would you like to use it?"

His arrow lingered, bow half-drawn, his eyes flicking between it and yours. He shook his head. "No. I have to do this with mine."

You nodded, and hid Löekeh Nowhere, understanding. "Someday I will no longer have need of it. Then it will be yours."

He smiled, the child within him desperate for that day to come, the man that was waking within him knowing it would when he was ready. He trained his focus to his arrow, his arrow on his mark.

"Wait for one to give itself," you said. "You know where to aim, you know how to breathe, you know how to loose."

You saw which would die, wondered if he did. Of course he did; he was your son, after all.

The hours walked, and you waited. He was a child, but he was patient like his father. You were his hero—his legend. The beast presented itself; Tärin held the bow drawn. He hesitated, but didn't lower his arrow.

"Da'?"

"Yes?" You knew what came next. Innocence.

"This is hard."

"Yes." You recalled this bit of wisdom well. "It is rooted in us to distrust death, to fear its coming, to others or ourselves, by the hand of others or our own. But it is a fear rooted in innocence, not in wisdom."

His brow bent. "What do you mean?" His arrow did not waver, the string did not slacken.

"There's something my father told me when I stood in your place, and he in mine." His eyes brightened. Gran'da Aröend was more a myth than a man, a myth that had given rise to the legend—to you.

"What was it?" Such enthusiasm.

"Do not fear death." Your father's voice echoed out of memory. You heard how much it resembled your own. "It ends no more than life begins. The Tapestry is eternal, infinite, and by the nature of infinity, all things—animate or inanimate, living or dead, now or then—are without end and without beginning, are threads in the fabric of Eaē. All that was, is, and will ever be."

Tärin was silent, working the wisdom over.

"Do you understand?" You weren't sure if he did. You couldn't remember if you had at his age, either.

"Yes." He saw with sight that foreshadowed the man he could have been. *"But I still feel sorry for it."* There you were, in his words, his intent. *"Will that ever go away?"*

"No." No lies. Not now. *"But the words help remind us of the deep truth of things, even if our heart feels otherwise. You don't need to kill it, Tärin. I just wanted you to understand."*

A star burned across the sky, falling for innocence. Tärin released his sorrow, his sorrow with his breath, his breath with his arrow. Wyrmseye.

The Wayfarer exhaled, releasing the memory with his breath, his breath with his arrow. Not quite corporeal, not quite ephemeral, the spectral dart flickered with a brilliant black luminescence as it trailed through the soft winds. *Wyrmseye.* As the vesta fell, Aëros' worry rose, his confusion. *He saw with sight that foreshadowed the man he could have been?* He saw the Shadow, standing where the vesta had been watching him, watching it. "Could have?"

Silence.

"This will only worsen before it improves." It was not a question. There was no wondering, only knowing. *If it improves.*

Shifting bow to dagger, Aëros set Löekeh in its sheath, passing his hand over it to return it Nowhere—a swaggering flourish, unnecessary for weaving, a display of vanity typical of an Arkaën. The artifact vanished, veiled by the threads of Dräu, tucked away like shade into shade.

His stride sleeker than shadow, softer than silence, Aëros glided over to his kill. The vesta's death was swift, painless. He knelt beside the fallen beast, its soul departed, the threads of Anima unraveled. He looked it over: full grown, long-lived, large enough to serve him well into his journey. He stroked the beast's shimmering mane and whispered something in his ancestral tongue, knowing it would hear. It gave its life, and the world

61

moved on. Aëros would give his own someday, and the world would move on then, too.

He dressed his kill, breaking it down to fit within his Shräud, storing it Nowhere, weightless. He turned away from the field, and continued on the path, leaving the herd to their dreaming, grateful for their sacrifice.

Crimson and gold, the sun had just crested the horizon as Aëros pulled the first of the vesta meat off the spit for breakfast. The remainder he kept Nowhere, in a place where it could age and dry unspoiled. He ate his fill, did not let himself sleep, remembering the night before, remembering Thrace. It might be he was as likely to face nightmares while awake as while dreaming, but it wasn't a risk worth the reward of rest. He could bury his weariness in his bones for a little while at least. The Shadow stood beside him, and a thought passed through him, wondering: *If wisdom is born from the death of innocence, what then what does the death of wisdom bring?*

Silence.

Chapter V: Waystone & Wanderer
• Stirring of Summer •

The sun was sliding through noon when the Wayfarer reached the peak of a fell that rose far above its kindred as it gathered over the grasslands in its length. It was named the High Fell, and a waystone marking the convergence of many trails capped it, ivy writhing over its weatherworn faces, suffocating the stone, desperate for survival. It was a way-marker, a guide for eyes greener than the grass underfoot. Aëros' eyes were old, greying, seeing far. They led him along the road of the old trade route, grown over and untended in its disuse. Led him up the High Fell, to the waystone, to the man sitting beneath it, hunkered in its shade, staring west, toward the wood.

"Hello, Nomad." Aëros strode up beside the man. He was a wanderer, wrapped up in a dark hooded cloak, weather-stained and weatherworn. A silver walking staff leaned against his side.

The man looked up, his hood falling to reveal a face worth sculpting in stone, fair enough to have been sculpted from stone itself, familiar enough to be considered friend, even if that friend could also be considered folly. "Aëros!" The man's face beamed, eyes glinting. "What a surprise!"

Aëros tilted a brow, crooked. "I would say the same, but I know better."

The wanderer's own brow went crooked, head tilted. He looked at Aëros, at the path from which he'd come, to the path ahead, leading on to the forest, and farther. "Where are you heading?"

Aëros' eyes fell on the road ahead. "To find what I've lost."

Nomad nodded, as if that made all the sense he needed. "Where will you find it?"

"The Barrows, Dún."

Nomad whistled, uneasy. "Wretched place that." He stood up, staff clicking on the stone as he took it in hand. "Why don't I join you for a stride? No harm in a little companio—"

He vanished, flickered out of existence.

"Inconvenience of a man indeed." Aëros recalled Thrace's description of the wanderer, sighed and continued on his way, thinking little of the exchange.

From the summit of the High Fell Aëros could see the outskirts of the Wōadglōam, yawning in the hazy light. They were dark, decaying. He would have to pass through to reach the heartwood, the last of the wood left alive, where its soul lingered, where a friend of the forest and a friend of his still dwelled.

As he descended the slope of the fell, the forest slipped away beneath the horizon of grassland, hidden by distance, lurking. He drifted on in silence of both thought and speech, the Shadow roving before him, leading him on, leading him astray, leading him to the one mystery in all reality he, the Wayfarer, could not unravel with his will alone. He watched the wraith strolling through the high grass and heather ahead, the sun unable to illuminate it, unable to reveal the mystery it was itself wrapped in. Only the end would unravel all. But first, the Fells, and soon—the forest.

◆

A week walked between the High Fell and the Wōadglōam Forest. Aëros walked with it, keeping his mind occupied with the labors of survival. Rove. Eat. Rest. Rove. Eat. Rest. He'd been able to smell the scent of the forest since he'd left the Waypoint. Not on the air, but in memory. Once, tavern tales had spoken of its magnificence, of how one might mistake its shimmering canopy for a verdant sea at a distance, if not for the monolithic trunks lofting the eaves, raising the sea into the winds rolling down from the Wyrmspine.

They were aureate tales, grand, true as soil underfoot—mythic, fabled, and still unable to sum the forest's beauty.

But those tales were of a time before Athair, before the catastrophe he brought, remembered today as the Devouring. Now dark enchantment and defilement threaded the outer rim of the forest, lingering as a pestilence slow to die. With the rise of Athair's horrors the tales of old fell away, their message of majesty replaced with words of warning, of fear, of a wood warped and wild.

Aëros rounded the base of a narrow corridor of knolls, and stopped hard as the outskirts burst up before him, fetid canopy rising, the sweet scents of memory replaced with the saccharine stench of the dead and the dying. The rim of the wood was thick with the warning of worse within, a heavy mist veiling what that might be, wafting no further than the woodland's edge, moaning with a fey voice to keep away. It was a voice used to being heeded. Nothing of the forest entered the Fells. Nothing of the Fells entered the forest.

The Shadow was of nothing but madness, and so walked forward, readily, unthreatened. It turned, waiting, offering a warning of its own.

Move on.

Or wither.

Aëros was the Wayfarer, Walker Betwixt and Between Worlds, some part of all things. Not now, perhaps, but once, and though he'd lost the mastery he still walked with the arrogance of it. So, ignoring the wood's warning, heeding the Shadow's, he passed over the threshold. The darkness within the wood recoiled as he entered, bringing with him his own darkness, foreign, and more horrifying still.

The day was cloudless, open and blue, the sun bright and piercing. Not here, of course, but somewhere. Here in the outskirts even the sun seemed to sicken and die in the murk of the wood, a dense miasma coating and confusing depth and distance with its bleak, haunting haze, swallowing what little light filtered through the festering canopy above.

Monolithic trees lofted into the ashen greyness, polluted bark peeling from petrified trunk, limbs leafless, crumbling to grey senselessness as they fell to the fen beneath. The lifeless trees loomed over heaps of withered and warping underwood; small beasts scurried through the refuse, born in darkness and in darkness thriving, scavenging with wild hysteria in hopes of not being themselves devoured. Here things that should live could not, and those that should never have come to breath drew it, ragged, desperate, hateful.

Aëros' initial strides into the ailing wood were the hardest to manage, for the underwood was marsh, every step a wetland trap, forcing him along a path far from straight, his head aching from the black water's noxious, saccharine fumes. Patches of the wood were sparse, seeming safe, almost inviting in the ease through which they could be tread. He knew better. They were barren for a reason, for the weak ground that composed them would give way beneath any more weight than the dregs of leaf-litter atop the thin rooting holding it together. If one found themselves falling through the forest floor, they usually found themselves falling to their death.

In a healthier part of the wood, he might have roved through the eaves, leaping from limb to limb. He pressed his hand to a tree, testing its strength, and stumbled as he passed through the brittle husk, which dusted to ash at his touch.

Turn back, the mists moaned.

Death alone dwells here. The silence of some beast half swallowed in a pit of tar.

Athair's will,

Slithering up from the swamps of your unconscious,

Will devour you.

As it has devoured this wood.

Unless you move on from it.

As you move through this world,

the wraith warned.

Aëros halted and swung around, finding the Shadow striding unhindered through the mire, watching him in all his suffering slowness. "So you can speak without riddle?"

Silence.

Aëros growled, teeth gritted, eyes sharp with frustration. "Speak on!"

A foul wind groaned in the air, shaking trees into ash, ash into memory. Aëros followed the motes as they fell, finding that memory, the Shadow stepping forward, stepping in.

> *... All memory scrawled upon a page,*
> *All fable passed from Age to Age,*
> *From ash to ash and shade to shade,*
> *A shade of dreamer's distant days,*

> *For even ash of Ages gone,*

67

May grow a wood, a world, a home.
Where tale and myth may find yet still,
A youthful and foolhardy will.

To follow those wayfaring ways,
To know now and forever say;
Far into dusk their trail does go,
Far into dusk their trail does go…

She sang to you, holding you in her lap as your hammock held you both, swinging in the eaves. A memory of long ago, long before. It is simple, it is sweet, in it the essence of everything you had, everything you wish to preserve, and will never remember should you succumb.

Your journey darkens now, Aëros, your journey begins its descent, down into the depths of this world, down into the swamp of your soul, the mire of your mind. Raise the aegis of your will. Heed the wisdom of her words.

For even ash,

Of Ages gone,

May grow a wood,

A world,

A home.

The memory flickered, fell away. *Athair.* The name echoed on the dead winds, echoed in his mind. It tied everything together—his journey, his madness; the rope around his neck. He held the Shadow's eyes, and the Shadow held his.

Silence.

Passage II: Descent

"So much of what those of the past desired to know, those of the present care little to remember."

— *Aröend Aëon Aröaē, the Greymantled Diplomat*

Chapter VI: Humanity
• Stirring of Summer •

Night swarmed into the forest, day fleeing as the last of its bleak blood ran out from beneath the eaves, fearing what awoke in the dark.

Aëros strode on despite the darkness, knowing well what awoke in the eve himself. He lit his way with his lantern, its silvery incandescence barely piercing the dampening murk. It cast a crescent of sanctuary around him, the things in the night creeping just beyond the threshold of its radiance, following, watching, waiting.

At times the forest was deathly still, the sound of Aëros' own breath and step like slow, steady waves breaking in the quiet of a hidden cove, even under the muffling of his Shräud and his hunter's stealth. Then the silence of the wood would shatter into a shrieking chorus. Prey fled predator, predator fled things more sinister still, until all were eventually overrun. The death throes of the fallen chilled the marrow in Aëros' bones, revealing a primal instinct not even he could suppress, forcing him to halt his stride and ease Löekeh from its hidden sheath, listening.

First came the wails of the doomed, pleading and woeful as they ran. Then the thud and tumble of a run cut short, and the awful, slithering sound of flesh being stripped from bone. The wails became screams, blood-curdling, the sounds all living things make when they come to understand that they've found their end. An understanding that it is lonely, it is dark, it is painful. Bones snapped—a sharp, hollow, echoing sound. The screams softened, back to wails, to pleas: for help; for mercy; for the pain to end.

Aëros listened to the pleas but did not heed them. This was not a place for pity. He waited for death to find the dying, waited for death to move on. When it did, so too did he.

The night progressed. Death came often, keeping him focused on the outer world, distracted from the one within. He preferred this. Death was a distraction from madness; not forever, but for now.

⸺ ◆ ⸺

Day came and Aëros bemoaned it, for the night-stalkers fled with it. His mind relaxed, drifting. The drear and murk that masqueraded as sunlight slithered through the withered eaves, slivers of grey too weak to reach the underwood. Day was safer, so he stilled himself, waiting for night, waiting for death.

He made camp, settling in the heart of a small ruin, a remnant of the first to dwell in the Wōadglōam, worn to fractured stone pillars and collapsing arches long before Athair infested the wood. There were no walls, no roof, no protections. He threw up his hammock, the free-hanging nest serving well to hold him aloft the rot, in the heart of a ruin, in the grave of a memory. He collapsed into it. A limb snapped from the eaves above, careening towards him. He dove from it just before he found death in the day.

Move on.

Says the widow-maker.

Aëros looked to the Shadow, standing beside the fallen limb. It was smirking, verging on a smile. He rolled the soul in his eyes as he pulled his hammock from beneath the limb, shaking free the debris and setting it again for resting, this time beneath somewhat thinner eaves and smaller limbs. He knew they were still large enough to kill him. He swung there, beneath the dying eaves, and slipped into sleep. He didn't mean to, but his weariness didn't care.

"This place never seems to age." You stepped from the ferryman's skiff onto the shore of the necropolis.

"I think it mocks us." He followed suit, laughing, a friend that neither distance nor difference could take from you. "Congratulations again on the little one, Aëros. I'm thrilled for you and your Aüriel. She'll be a wonderful mother." He looked at you, smirked his familiar smirk. "You'll be some sort of father, I'm sure."

You laughed, hit him on the arm, drew something from your Shräud and handed it to him. "Here."

It was a lantern, forged from beautiful black metal, its design slightly eldritch, its light a deep, radiant amethyst. He took it, marveled over it. "What is this for?

"A gift," you said, smiling. "To welcome you home."

He took a piece of your smile for himself, and tucked the trinket away. "You didn't need to."

You dismissed the thought with a gesture. "Nonsense. You're my best friend, and you're here, and that's worth celebrating."

"This is new." Athair took the hem of your Shräud in hand, looking it over.

You smiled. "Aüriel's artifice."

He pursed his lips, approving. "She's far cleverer than you, Aëros."

"She knows it too," you laughed. You swept an arm out before you in the general direction of everywhere, and wondered, "Why here?"

Athair's eyes slimmed, mischievous. "I told you in the letter, I have something to show you. Something I've discovered."

"Discovered?" Curiosity raised your brow.

His voice waxed hesitant, furtive. "I haven't been entirely truthful, Aëros. I was released a season past. I'm sorry I took so long to write you. I just…"

A season past? You'd told the psychiatrists to inform you ahead of his release. "I understand." His time in the sanitorium weighed on him.

73

It was a gentle place, its patients gentle themselves, quite unlike those he would eventually meet at Arkym. But it took a large swath of his youth from him, and he felt that lost time through you, who'd yourself been free to do and go as and where you willed. Sensing this, you shifted subjects from his madness to the fruit of it. "What sort of discovery?" He looked at you with eyes that said you should remember. You did, but hesitated to say it. "What the Sylysæ showed you."

The sod was damp underfoot, the mists soaking the soil to its bones, and your bare feet to theirs. Soil soon shifted to stone, Dún rising in ruin to meet you. "What's here, Athair?"

"Solitude," he said, more meaning beneath the word than he bothered speaking. He'd always had a flare for the mysterious, another feather of friendship. He was leading now, leading you along a path walked many times before, to the place you saw the first worrying thread of him that thrust distance between the two of you.

You worried still, even so long after your worry began. For you still saw that thread woven into the crook of his smile. Not worn away, but worn in, worn willfully. But friendship, genuine friendship, demands worry, concern, the desire to help, to support. To do otherwise would be to abandon, to betray; or so he would have you believe, given time.

He entered the ruins of the mausoleum and led you to the doorway set within the floor, sealed up by a solid slab of grey stone, warding off the curious, the foolish. His smile stretched, the thread stretching with it, and set his will over the threshold. The stone slab evanesced, a void opening into a stairwell, stairwell spiraling down into a crypt; a barrow; Dún. He passed within, waving you along.

You stood before it, and looked beside it, to a small cairn of stone no longer standing. Disturbed. It had been many years since that day, but you found yourself wishing the little grave had remained untarnished, as the memory of it had in your mind. You stooped, rearranging the stones back into form, realized the bones you'd once buried were there no longer. It had been a long time. Age makes ash of everything. You finished the cairn anyway, burying the memory; of a little raven, of that day. You swallowed your wisdom, your worry, and followed him down.

74

A thud sounded behind you, the slab returning from Nowhere, throwing you into utter darkness. You drew out your lantern and willed it to life.

"No!" Athair shouted, willing your lantern to death. "No light. Not yet."

The darkness halted all vision. Still, you knew his eyes were peering into yours, yours holding his, fixed. "Why?"

"You'll see." He broke your hold, one of the few in the world who could of their own will, and continued on into the dark.

You stood for a moment in that pitch black, and walked for many moments more—down, down, down into the depths of the barrow, down into the depths of Dún. You led yourself after the sound of his footfall, and when his footfall stopped, you heard a stone slab sliding in its place, followed by the sound of soft, muffled wind. "Now," he said, voice shaking with enthusiasm. "A little light."

You obliged, lifting your lantern, letting the faintest ray escape, a sliver cutting through the crypt like a thief's lantern. You did not understand what you saw.

There, in the heart of the room, was a sepulcher of stone. The lid was slid aside, the source of the soft wind within. Within it was a small mass of darkness, like a living shadow. It writhed as your lantern light fell over it, recoiling but remaining in place as if bound, screaming a faint, pitiful, painful scream—not wind after all.

You doused your lantern and held Athair's eyes through the darkness. "What is it?"

"A Shaēd." His tone was prideful, excited, filled with what you feared. "This is the fate of An'kou if they never pass on, if their Anima lingers too long with the living. They lose themselves, grow hateful and fearful, and in their hate and their fear twist into—" he lit his own lantern, his new gift, casting light into the hypogean crypt, lashing out at the thing that wanted only to dwell in darkness, undisturbed.

"Athair, let it be. It's suffering." You bent low, studying it despite your concern. "Why is it so small?"

He bent down beside you. "A soul is only as large as its body was at death."

75

"So… this is—"

"The Sylysæ showed me many things." He spoke before you, not wanting the thought finished. "I can call lingering Anima to me, move it from one husk to another, store it to preserve it. But I cannot unravel it, cannot undo what becomes of it if left to linger too long." His voice took some hope from your own, mimicked it perfectly. "Yet."

You looked up, looked to him, uncertain. "Preserve…it?"

He raised the lantern you'd given him. "In trinkets, in objects. It seems to preserve the soul, indifferent to whatever comes of the physical form. Like the Shaēd here, bound to the world, body long decayed."

There was silence for a long while, your eyes and his wound up with the Shaēd, with the weight of its implication. It was a different weight for each of you, a different implication. A tension grew in the silence; he broke it before it could build to dizzying proportion. "Let's head back, Aëros. We've cast light here long enough."

"I…" The light of Athair's lantern winked out. "Alright."

Athair slid the lid of the nameless sepulcher back into place, sealing the amalgamation of name-lost souls within. You ascended, leaving the Shaēd, the crypt, Dún behind. His voice echoed in the dark of the stairwell. "Aëros?"

You didn't stop, continuing up, away. "Yes?"

"What do you think?"

A pause, brief. "What were you hoping I'd think?"

Athair held back, unsure, tentative in his response. "Hoping? I'm not sure I was…"

"You should be cautious with this, Athair. With what you're working towards."

He grunted, agreeing. "Promise me you'll keep it between us? For now?"

You heard the worry in his words. A worry of being sent back. You shared it, setting your love at war with your wisdom. "I promise."

"I don't want to go back."

"I know," you said. "I don't want you to, either."

It was late, and the bed was warm, comfortable, holding you and her and all the weight of what you held within yourself, sharing it now, evening the load. "After we parted, I left for the sanitorium."

She pressed against you, showing you she was there, with you, for you. "What did you find?"

"Ash."

She waited, spurring you on with her silence.

"Burned to the ground. Rubble and ruin."

"He..."

"I found his psychiatrist holed up in some rotting inn, witless. I nearly had to kick his door down to get him to speak with me."

"How did you?"

You set your will on the threads of your being, shifting them into shadow, as a wraith, evanescing into the threads of reality, demonstrating how far you'd come with what the Sylysæ showed you. You coalesced, finding her admiring the mastery of a man she herself mastered. You smiled, bittersweet, threaded with sorrow. "All he had to say was half-muttered and raving. It was enough to wager on what happened, though."

"Athair."

"His mind is descending into some abyss I do not know how to wade through. What he showed me in that crypt..." You held your thought, unspoken, for she saw it, knew it as you did. Your eyes linked, knowing all the other held, for they hid nothing. "His understanding of what he's discovered is spiraling into genius, and I'm afraid only fell things will come of it."

"There's nothing you can do to help him?"

Her words were a knife in a wound you'd left festering far too long. A wound self-inflicted. You felt anger building in you at her, but caught it before it spilled over, knowing it had nothing to do with her. "Whatever Athair is, whatever it is he has, he was born with. Or born

77

into. Or both. He came into this world surrounded by death on all sides. At some point I have to reconcile myself to the truth that it is also within him, a part of him."

And you remember well how he was born into this world. You looked back after all, opened a Rift, and peered into the time before him, while he was still just a round showing in his mother's womb. Here, a memory in a memory, lest you lose one within the other.

She was in the Barrows, kneeling over a headstone, eyes wet, the flowers she brought with her the only vibrancy in the drear, dead landscape. It was someone dear she came for. Perhaps a parent. Perhaps a lover. Perhaps his father. You'd searched for that headstone after, could never find it. As if it only ever existed in her mind, and now only in yours.

The graverobbers grabbed her. Men of the Fēl. She was the only other prey in the necropolis as easy to pillage as the dead. A lone, pregnant woman, distracted by her grief, lost somewhere in her sorrows.

It was a vile act, and for that villainy they eventually suffered. But not before she suffered. Not before they were finished. Before they strung her up, sobbing, pleading, not for her own life, but for her baby, her unborn child, him.

A gravekeeper found her swinging some hours later. You watched him hobble up to the gallows tree, swaying. He tilted his head as he tried to understand what he saw through the low-lying mists, hurried himself breathless as he realized and ran to her.

Too late. Far too late.

From a rope of fiber she swung, and below her, in the bloody mire of her death, a stirring, panting life bound to her by a rope of flesh. Born of death. Surrounded by it. Is it any wonder he was moved to master it? Any wonder what he would become? As if he had not always been from the very beginning. Death was his domain. Death was his dalliance. Death was his to do with what he desired.

The memory nested within a memory ended, returning Aëros to the one that summoned it.

"There is one thing I can do." You stood, breaking Aūriel's embrace, and walked to the window, where moonlight was running rivers over the Fells, racing out to the sea. "I'm having him committed to Arkym."

Realization slid slowly into place. She closed her eyes, understanding your pain, bearing it alongside you.

"No one leaves the asylum, Aūriel. Not ever." She came to you, held you, your only comfort. You looked out, far away, to the betrayal before you. "Not ever..."

———————◆◆———————

Aëros awoke, staring up, swinging softly in his hammock, shoving the sickening sense the nightmare left into his bones. In its place came the sense of being watched. "Wonderful."

The Shadow was sitting cross-legged on a stone wall, staring, silent. He sighed, swung out of his nest, folded it up, and tucked it away Nowhere. It was time to move. Night was drawing down. He yawned and fell into stride, wondering when his watcher would wander along.

He walked awhile in the growing darkness, instincts sharp, awake, alert. As the last of the little daylight died, his lantern light flickered into existence. Its silver rays peered through the shadows, the silhouettes of skeletal trees shifting in and out of its aura, revealing a wall of eyes amidst the towering trunks, ringing him, glinting just beyond the trinket's reach, unwavering as they watched.

Löekeh appeared from Nowhere, string taut, arrow nocked. Aëros stared, unsure if the eyes that stared back were predator or prey. As a pair drifted from the dark, he found they were neither. He found they were dead.

"An'kou." Aëros breathed the name—cold, detached, almost apathetic. The thin thread that kept him from apathy came from the memory he'd just risen from, the nightmare, the whatever it was. He sheathed his bow, spoke to the soul, to those that remained beyond the reach of his light. "You won't find what you seek with me."

The lone soul lingered, its body ethereal, woven of a grey miasma, sharing only a slight resemblance to the life it once was. Whether Ayl or Ken or other was impossible to guess, the shaping of a body barely discernible beneath the haze that draped it. Aëros could tell only that it was the soul of a child, for it was little. He realized he also knew it was a boy. How he knew, he knew not.

He watched it, wondering what it wanted. "Why reveal yourself to me?" Perhaps it was just curious over a living thing in this place of death. It drew close, seeing him, searching his eyes as he searched its, and in them, he found something familiar.

Hello, little one.

Aëros swung around. The Shadow stood beside him, eyes holding the An'kou's, the An'kou's holding its. As the little soul stared, searching, its posture seemed to shift from the slump of sorrow to the rigidity of recognition. It and the Shadow stared at one another a while longer, something shared between them which Aëros did not understand, broken only once the An'kou turned away, rejoining its haunt beyond the sanctuary of light.

"He sees you." Aëros looked the wraith over, studying it. "Does he think you're one of them?" The idea slithered through his mind, uneasy. *No.* He thought, looked at his hands, his flesh. *No, of course not.*

Aëros began again to move through the forest, lost souls lingering just beyond his sanctum of light, encircling it, encircling him, the Shadow walking alongside, saying nothing. Not in the deliberate way that it had so far, but in the way that said its consideration was on other things. It was searching for something.

He was searching for something. The An'kou were searching for something. The blind following the blind following the blind.

<hr />

Aëros walked with the ring of An'kou through the night, walked with them and the sounds of death the night brought with it. He walked, undisturbed, until morn came, dawn sending death to dreaming, revealing the spirits from their haunt. They did not fade with the day. The dim, bleak unlight merely illuminated them and their grey, searching sadness. He studied them in the light, finding something else in their eyes he did not expect but was not surprised by. Hope.

Their hope was a comfort in the nervous calm of day, even if he didn't understand it. He breathed, found a stream of fresh air lifting through the underwood. He looked, saw a single ray of warm light cascade through the thinning canopy. He listened, heard the beast that would run him to his death.

As a shadow on the edge of perception Aëros walked, Shräud melting his silhouette into chaos and disorder. It veiled his form, muffled his step. Yet there were things that needed neither sight nor sound nor scent to mark him. He was a living thing where only the dead and dying dwelt. There was danger around him, the sort that was swift, cunning, indifferent. Desiring no end but his own.

The air waxed rotten, the gloom swallowed the light, and the howl—old, hateful, ravenous—ripped through the wandering mists, shaking them apart. Aëros dropped low, Löekeh unsheathed once more. The howl echoed again, closer, the An'kou vanished. *Even the dead fear this place.* Yet here he remained, not minding the distraction.

He snaked through the underwood, slithering through the refuse like a serpent, eyes like a wyrm's, sharp, seeking. The sounding of his death knell came in distorted, echoing bursts, howling that might be distancing or closing in, difficult to tell. He knew the thing that hunted him needed no sense to seek him. He was alive in a wood of death, standing out even under the illusion of his Shräud. If he still possessed his mastery, his understanding of the threads of Aūr, he could pass through the wood undisturbed. But he didn't, and as he came upon a clearing with a single tree at its heart, he knew that neither had he fled the beast that hunted him. No. He'd led himself right to its den.

The tree was a monolithic thing, once the sort for which the forest was named: a wōadglōam. Now it was ash, withered and ruinous and petrified. An immense hollow was cleaved into the base of its trunk, descending into darkness. There was a time when the tree had been a beacon of life for the woodland; now it was a tomb.

The skeletal remains of a knight hunched before the hollow, armor-clad and bowed over the hilt of his hulking sword. Mold and moss and petrifaction made the corpse a statue, a shrine in memory of itself. Aëros knew the knight; the wolfish armor and heathen greatsword were unmistakable. He knew the howl the same. They were a pair, after all. Partners.

The howl roared out from the depths of the tomb, and Aëros' adrenaline soared, instincts screaming, muscles corded and recoiling as the wolf—or what was once a wolf, now consumed by the will of a madman and the corruption he'd left behind—stepped from the great hollow of the tree. The tomb. The grave. A monolith of loyalty, friendship, betrayal.

"Sif."

The name staggered Aëros. The great wolf was a forest guardian, an ancient sentinel of the ancient woodland. No longer. He saw the madness in the beast's eyes—predator—and reeled around, understanding that he might very well have found his journey's end before he'd barely even embarked on its beginning. He knew what came after understanding: rent flesh, splintered bone, pleas—pitiful, pathetic, unanswered. Sif hurled herself forward, sundering tree and stone as she sped after him—prey.

The wolf was a monstrosity. Her coat, once silver-white, was drab and decaying, tattered and tearing away. Large patches had fallen from rot, flesh and bone exposed. Her eyes, black as moonless night, betrayed the defilement of her soul. Her maw dripped ichor, her howl was wet and pained, and a dark mist leaked from her wounds, causing that which it touched to age, wither, and crumble. Athair's will had taken her, devoured her, driven her mad. Aëros was once a friend; now he was not even food. Now he was simply something to kill.

He could not fight this beast—he would, if he had the skill, for her suffering was a sorrow undue the gentleness of her life. But he didn't, and so he fled, trusting his grace, his elven blood running him like wind through the hollow trees. Were the wood healthy, he'd have glided upwards, swiftening from vine to vine, branch to branch, ascending to his advantage. But the wood was dead, dusting away beneath even his feather-light step, and did not care if he died with it.

Tracing his way through the underwood instead, half with agility and half hysteria, Aëros reeled around petrified trunks, cut ragged turns about jagged stone, and dove through crumbling ruins, desperate to use Sif's immensity to her disadvantage as she crashed through the chaos of the wood.

It worked—barely. He maintained his distance from the wolf, but that was only a hundred paces, and the underwood was shifting to wetland, making his footing faulter, his stride slow. Yet on he strode, no other options open to him, silver hair streaming in the wind of his speed. Sif was swifter; she was gaining. *Eighty paces.* The wood was thinning. *Sixty.*

Aëros felt the touch of death on his shoulder, scented it on the breath of his hunter, heard it in the guttural rumble of her hunger. *Twenty-five.* The forest was fleeing him, offering him to the wolf, emptying itself to make room for his death. There was nowhere to turn to, too little time for an arrow, too little focus for illusion. All he could do was run. *Ten.*

The forest was nearly absent, the trees far apart, the ground growing weaker. *Weaker?*

Aëros understood in an instant. He could do nothing with his understanding. The ground bowed, sank, and disappeared beneath him. He was falling. Down into darkness; into an abyss; into the maw of the forest, devoured.

———————◆◆———————

Aëros plummeted into a pool of water, his bare feet striking sediment. He leapt up, thrusting himself to the surface.

The hypogean basin was dim, dimmer even than the overwood, for it was here, in the roots, that the blight Athair had left behind clung most desperately. Aëros' sight adjusted to the unlight as he strained his ears for sounds of Sif. He heard nothing of her, only debris falling from the sinkhole above, drawn down into the water, drowned in it. His eyes found focus, finding Sif, the great wolf having herself at last found death.

She had fallen onto a ring of stalactites erupting from the water, her body suspended by the spears, impaled, lifeless. Her black blood leeched down her tattered coat, running to the water in thin, revolting rivulets. She was gone, Anima departed. Whether her soul would pass on or remain behind, lingering, he could not guess. He hoped her free from the suffering of her life, hoped her soul would find peace in death, finding those she longed to see again. He hoped, even as he thought of the An'kou, knowing such a fate could befall any living, and felt sorrow. Breath shuddered into him, living breath, and he felt sorrow recede, leaving relief in its place.

A scream ripped through the cavern, running his relief away. It was not the howl of a predator, but the plea of prey, and it came from a woman. It was distant, echoing. He found that he knew its voice. *Aūriel.*

"*Aëros! Aëros, please!*" the voice called out to him, slowing his heart. *No. She's at home, in the villa, with Tärin.* The thought did nothing to ease the dread in his heart. He looked for the Shadow, found it standing atop the water, before a narrow fissure in the cavern's sheer walls, dividing them. The pleas came from the fissure. He held the wraith's eyes as the voice cried out. No memory nor nightmare came. *This isn't you.*

Dread deepened. He eyed the walls that rose overhead; roots and rock bound the dirt together, simple to ascend. The scream came again, painful, familiar, more terrified than ever—clearly a trick, an illusion. The fissure was dark and deep, visible only by the contrast of its utter darkness with the mostly-dark cavern.

It devoured him as he passed over the threshold of lightlessness. He thought he felt the eyes of the Shadow hollowing into him, a sense of disapproval, and turned to see the wraith walking behind him along the water, darker even than the deepest darkness surrounding him. But no, he found that the disapproval was his own, the wraith's emotion one he did not understand, though if he guessed he would say its eyes held a sense of urgency, a sense of urging *him.* He thought back to the An'kou, the little soul, to what passed between it and the Shadow, and how he did not understand that, either.

The current drew him on, the screams came again, and again. He told himself it was an illusion of this wretched woodland. He thought of Sif, of her death, of her peace, of the An'kou, and drowned the idea in the water. Darkness surrounded him as he headed down the passage, towards the screams, towards his death, knowing well there would be no rest for him should he find it.

Chapter VII: Death
• Stirring of Summer •

Aëros swam the passage as a blind man, feeling his way through the darkness. He heard the rush of water against the walls with each stroke, felt the current pulling him along, pulling him down. The unlight of the underground river forced him into his mind's eye—the only one with sight in the dark, weak as it was becoming. He found himself within, standing on the rim of insanity, the threshold to the asylum that held all he'd forgotten. *Come.* It called. *There is room here for you yet.* He growled, wrenching himself away from the precipice, withdrawing his lantern and casting the darkness away, casting himself back into the waking world, hiding himself from the nightmare within.

The crystal frame of Aëros' artifice, the light the artifice of another Arkaēn, the lantern did not sputter in the water, revealing the passage true as he traversed it. At times the waterway appeared bottomless, his imagination running wild with sunken things lurking below. At others it rose to dunes of mired sediment, allowing him to walk, to rest. The underground waters constantly forked, running off into many side-channels, his way only kept true by the screams calling out for him, luring him on.

An hour went by, two, time lost touch with meaning. The pass went on, winding, twisting, black root riven through black stone, black water running over black abyss. A light appeared in the distance; not a reflection of his own, but a natural light, peeking into the tunnel, taunting him. It grew as he closed the gap between it and himself. He swiftened his pace, bringing himself back into the open forest beyond, dismal though it might be, death waiting, calling, singing its siren song.

The waterway shallowed, and he picked up into a sprint as his stride struck sediment. He met the grey of a nearly spent day and welcomed it. The scream welcomed him too, filling the open air.

Aëros found his death and studied it, descrying the shape of it: the form, the elegance, the beauty.

He stood in a waterlogged trench, encircled by steep slopes of rotting undergrowth. They could be scaled with relative ease, but all hope of escape fled his mind. Before him, in the heart of the trench, stood the woman—or rather, what had once been a woman—to whom the scream belonged. He could not distinguish much beyond her tangled hair and frail frame, for she was long-dead, her corpse a mockery of life. She could have been anyone, even his Aūriel. He knew she wasn't. He was right. It didn't matter.

The woman hung in the air like a marionette, strung up by writhing, branching tendrils. The slender withes slid from a torso that stood twice as high as the Wayfarer even as its shoulders curved and its mass bent forward beneath its own weight. It loomed over the corpse, forced a final scream from its unhinged jaw, and summoned roots from the underwood to grab hold of it, dragging it down into the fen, returning the puppet to its store. Its tendrils withdrew into its chest, and it propped itself up from its slouch, revealing its immensity in an intentionally vaunting display, swinging in place with a lithe, hypnotizing grace, like an aged tree in a heavy wind.

Skeletal and covered in craggy, flowing bark, its body was a mass of moldering vines, roots, fungi, and humus, dripping with the same thin black mist that seeped from Sif, desecrating and withering all it fell upon. Its form was sleek despite its harrowing size, perched not upon legs, but on a bundle of interwoven roots growing up from the underwood, writhing about like a serpent's underbelly.

An exposed ribcage at the core of its hulking frame enclosed its sickly organs, beating in rhythm with its hypnotic sway. Two arms extended from its torso, gnarled and knotted, each ending in an array of sinuous, serrated talons. Keen and aquiline, the creature's visage drifted from side to side, slanted eyes staring, sickly green, deep and old and primordial as the roots of the world. Aëros saw well what was in them, the same as what had been in Sif's: Athair's will come to collect the toll of his betrayal.

This was once a Drúan, a forest spirit, like Sif, though of far older ancestry. Now, it was a Lësh'unn, fallen, twisted, riddled with corruption. It preened over him, and he saw his death in its gaze.

It tilted its head, seeming curious, then—deciding it was not—opened its mouth, the long, horizontal slit stretching, growing beyond the limits of its jaws, revealing row after row of fangs bathing in corrosive ichor.

It screamed, a horror that was of the world but did not sound it. It was melodious as an arrow over string, as sickly as rooks and ravens tearing sun-sickened flesh. Its roar rumbled through it, louder as it moved through the mire, tearing its way forward, claws shredding the refuse of the fen as it fell upon the Wayfarer before he could draw even thought.

Aëros' instincts worked faster than his reason, and he tumbled into the shallows as the Lësh'unn ripped past him. It spun around with overwhelming speed, forcing him to falter as he lurched away from the talons that slit a wide arc in search of him. He struggled to find breath and blade while his adrenaline raced, drawing Löekeh from its shroud between gasps. The Lësh'unn lunged—he leapt, foot on talon, darting from it with its own momentum, putting distance between himself and his death, arrows flickering from his bow as he fell through the air, each shaft errant, the serpentine beast slithering between them with unnatural ease.

Land, roll, leap. Aëros kept his eyes on his death as he evaded it, but the rim of the trench in his periphery, hoping for a path he'd missed. There was none. He was hemmed in with the Lësh'unn; he could not run as with the wolf. He would fight, die trying though he might.

The Lësh'unn was swaying again, measuring the Wayfarer, judging his speed and his threat. Aëros almost took his periphery away from the rim, but found it lingering as a single grey apparition faded into view along the edge. It was familiar. The young An'kou; the young boy. The little soul loomed over the precipice of the depression, its eyes a duality of sorrow, and—confounding Aëros—hope. He followed them, and understood.

The An'kou's eyes fell upon the Lësh'unn. The trickster that lured Aëros in with the corpse of a woman and the cries of fear it forced from her rotten voice. A voice it had stolen along with her life. He knew where he stood, and why the little, lone soul lingered above, eyes sorrowful, hopeful for what a living man might remedy in a place where only the dead dwelled.

It's his mother.

A root erupted from the fen, ripping Aëros' attention from the lost soul as he dove from its reach, rolling through the black water. As he tumbled, he released another hail of arrows, whistling the sound of death as they sped. Every single shaft struck bark, thumping as if striking a dead tree. Every shaft but one.

The one passed through a space between the Lësh'unn's ribs, near to piercing one of the organs within. It missed, but the creature's reaction of horror told Aëros all he needed of its weakness. The Lësh'unn flinched hard, reeling back, even though the arrow only found its bite in the inner bark of its chest, harming it not at all. Enraged, it roared, its splintering maw spewing ichor as it dove, crushing the Wayfarer—or rather, the phantom he'd left behind in the wake of his arrow-storm.

As the illusion vanished the Lësh'unn realized the deception, but not before Aëros reappeared from the shadows and hooked around its midsection, driving Löekeh's blade up through a space in its ribcage, shredding the organ his arrow had so narrowly missed.

The Lësh'unn recoiled, flinging Aëros away as it howled in pain. A geyser of dark ichor erupted from its inner hollow, immolating its own body as it poured from the wound within. A line of soot-black flame smoldered where the black blood fell, the creature's carapace smoking as boils blistered and cracked beneath the flames, bursting and spreading the embers into an inferno that began to consume it.

In its terror it dropped to the mire, laying itself atop the stagnant waters. The fen welcomed it, absorbing it as if to cradle and soothe its pain. The arena silenced as it vanished, though silence did nothing to lighten the miasma of the fight, still thick in the air. It was humid, heavy as an unexpected breath in the dark, leaving Aëros alert, waiting for his death to return, to take him at last.

He stood unmoving for what seemed an Age, the stillness deafening as his ears strained to discern any sign of the fallen spirit. No sound but that of his own running blood and rough breathing stirred the world. Death was, in the end, a silent, lonely thing.

A geyser of foul water and smoking embers drenched him as the Lësh'unn erupted from beneath, taking him from his wits. Its talons sunk into his side. *Deep. Too deep.*

He roared in agony, falling to his knees as the Lësh'unn reared its jaws in a display of dominance: predator over prey. It bowed its maw above him, salivating. Aëros heaved on the talons impaling him in a pathetic attempt to expel them. As he stared at them, he found he was not thinking of how they were inside of him, mutilating him, but of how they had torn through his Shräud. How he would not be able to repair it, for it was of his Aūriel's artifice, and he had not her skill with weaving together the threads of the material with those of the immaterial.

"Threadbare fool..." he muttered as he looked into the hypnotic gaze of the thing that held him, blood sputtering from his mouth as he spoke.

The Lësh'unn's maw descended upon him, its breath stifling as he tried to focus. He looked to its chest, prone, to the organs beating just beyond the ribcage that exposed them. He had to be precise, he had to be swift, knew that Löekeh would be no use.

91

He wove the needle of his will through his ring, shaping it into a needle itself. He thrust the barbed dart into the Lësh'unn's inner hollow, willing the fluid metal to twist, tear aside, severing organ from root in a smooth, skillful stroke.

Silver flowed back onto his hand as a waterfall of ichor poured from the wounds, incinerating the Lësh'unn's viscera like flame on aged parchment. Its maw contracted and its aura of dominance turned to submission as it fell back, its sinuous talons sliding from Aëros' side as it collapsed into a heap of its own death. Its throes were quiet, its breathing slowing to gasping stutters as the flame devoured it, the last of its Anima departing in thick, smoldering smoke. Prey.

Aëros collapsed in the fen alongside it, a mixture of his own blood and the Lësh'unn's ichor pouring from his wounds. Predator.

"Fuck—" he stammered as he toppled into the shallows of the mire. He blinked, sight blurring. He saw the Shadow, standing, staring. Not at him, not at the Lësh'unn, but at the An'kou, drifting from the rim of the trench. It passed down the slope, over the waters, to Aëros' side, and sat beside him.

This is not his death.

The An'kou looked up to the Shadow—sorrow, hope, trust. It looked back to Aëros, bowed its head, held it there a moment, then stood, went away, passing up the slope, over the rim, into the wood beyond. The Shadow watched it go, lingered as it left, at length returning to Aëros.

Aëros stared. "Not—" blood, vomit, exhaustion "—my death?"

Not yet.

Aëros sneered. Half of his face was sunk beneath the fen; half looked on helplessly into a dimming world. "Tell that—" he coughed, hacked, spit up his life "—to the fucking hole in my chest."

The Shadow sat beside him, a look of pity, a look of sorrow, a look of hope.

Move on, Aëros.

Move on from this delusion.

Blood trickled, lining the Wayfarer's crooked mouth, collecting in the water around him. The mire and mists drew out of his awareness. He was dying, and the Shadow sat beside him, the crooked warden with its crooked skeleton key, telling him he wasn't.

His own key shimmered in the water, wrapped round his finger, the key to his promise, a promise he would break now by his own foolishness.

Tärin, Aūriel...

His breathing grew ever shallower and swifter, his vision tunneling as his blood drained, dragging his consciousness out of him with it. His awareness slipped, and the illusion that masked the deaths of his past fell, his humanity revealed.

I'm sorry...

His breath staggered, each inhalation coming later than the last as his eyes glazed over and death took him further into her embrace, away from the shores of his own mind, to the shores of hers.

He saw the Shadow through bleary eyes, its form fleeting, flickering, fading as his own life faltered. It did not seem worried. As it thinned, another shadow drew up to it, familiar. *Little Raven?* It approached from the rim of the fen, making its way to him as his eyes closed against his will. His mind fell to darkness, and in darkness he dreamt: of a raven, a loving mother, a madman, death. He did not remember his dreams when he woke.

Chapter VIII: Effervescence

• Stirring of Summer •

*A*lways forward, *Aëros.* Aūriel's voice caressed him, comforted him. *Aūriel's voice...and...wind?* His consciousness rushed back, the image of the beautiful horror that killed him the first thing to return with it. He jolted up, seeking the Lësh'unn, sharp pain tearing through him as he inhaled, adrenaline cascading through his veins, sharpening the dullness that had overtaken him. *I'm not dead.* Pain lanced through his side where the creature's talons pierced him. He clutched the wound, finding strips of bandage in place of ragged flesh.

A breeze wisped over him. *The air.* It was no longer saccharine, no longer putrefied. It was soothing, steadying. *Delusion.* He inhaled again, more softly, expecting the acrid aroma of rotting undergrowth and fetid mire to strike him, but it was absent. In its place drifted the scent of new rain and old trees. He looked up from his wound and his eyes widened. He knew where he was; he *remembered* where he was.

Joy overcame him, and he made to throw off the quilt that warmed him and stand from the bed that rested him. Made to, until his wound sent a whip of pain through him, searing his blood and waylaying his will. His arms and legs were leaden. Not from travel, but revival, from his body's efforts to heal his death, his foolishness a too-common inconvenience. He collapsed, his head hitting a pillow as he struggled to maintain consciousness through the receding pain. He tried to bury it in his bones for later, and found he had to beat it down, forcing it into submission.

"Ah, ah. You're not so surefooted yet. You were dead, after a fashion." The voice, cheerful and hinting at sarcasm, echoed from an open terrace at the edge of the room. It was a window revealing the forest. Not the outskirts, but the heartwood, its viridian light inviting itself into the grey-wood room. It drifted in, mingling with the simple light of the sun, streaming down in shafts of yellow-gold through the upper eaves. Another death, another day.

Aëros' eyes darted to the terrace. "So, I *was* dead?"

"For a very long time I thought you were. But you're here, so it seems, as I said, only after a fashion. In this case, the fashion of *mostly* dead," the voice spoke, tinged with amusement. "Mostly dead I can fix. But you can still add it to your tally, if you like."

Aëros felt over his face, finding the illusion of vitality returned, the truth of his humanity hidden. He was alive, and so were his lies, to the self and otherwise. He looked up, finding the figure moving out of shadow, revealing himself, smiling as ever.

"Shaē." Aëros said the name as if to ensure the man it belonged to was truly before him. He barely recognized him, save for his smile, a beacon through the murk of his mind, drawing out his own. "My old friend. I am so glad to see you."

"As am I, Aëros." the druid's amusement shifted to worry as he came to Aëros' side, a gnarled staff in one hand, a smoldering pipe in the other. "It's a relief to see you alive."

Aëros studied the druid, etching his features back into his mind. A more even dilution of elf and man, Shaē's features were midway between the sleekness of Ayl and boldness of Ken. He wore an average brown tunic tucked into average brown britches worn over average brown skin with a mess of average brown hair set above average brown eyes. Yet despite his evident averageness, he was anything but. For he wore a smile so wide, so comforting, and so genuine that tavern tales told it wrought from the primordial essence of kindness itself, the fundamental thread responsible for all light, warmth, and joy in existence. His aura hummed with this innocence, urging the furtive heart to trust, the cynical to soften their skepticism, the solitary to admit companionship. His smile waxed curious as he stayed the pipe he'd been puffing, embers glowing. "What drove you into that fen, Aëros?"

"Sif." *Desperation.* "I stumbled on the Abysswalker's grave. It was her den."

Shaē nodded, his smile held a bittersweet sorrow as he spoke, eyes far away. "She never returned to the heartwood. She remained with her loyalty and her betrayal until darkness took her too. I've kept watch over her, though I could do nothing for her…"

The druid's eyes held a question he couldn't bring to words, hoping there was something Aëros had done for her, that she was free now, rejoined with her oldest friend and ally. Aëros answered with his eyes, affirming it was his hope as well. He moved on from his silence, on from the sorrow. "How did you find me?"

Shaē laughed over the naïve question. "I kept watch over Sif the same way I keep watch over all the forest—by looking where it tells me to."

Aëros peered out from the room, over the terrace, into the heartwood beyond, living, breathing, thinking. "I didn't know it could still speak with the dead parts of itself."

"It can't." The druid's smile lessened, something as unnatural as the blight that afflicted the forest. Smoke billowed from his pipe, the mixture crackling. "But it hears the pleas for help, and answers as it is able."

Aëros found his own frown falling as he looked on Shaē's despair, for as his joy brought all to levity, his sadness brought only woe. "Recovery is a slow battle fought with a steady will, Shaē." He caught his friend's eyes and reassured them. "Always forward, my friend."

"Always on." The druid looked to the Wayfarer, hint of a smile returning. "I have missed your silvering perspective." His expression waxed curious, as if remembering something obvious that passing over the threshold from terrace into room had taken from him. "Why the outskirts?" He held the Wayfarer's eyes, seeing in them his friend, but seeing something else too, something *other.* "Why are you here, Aëros?"

"I'm—"

Shaē waved the answer away, his pipe burning brightly as he drew. "That was going to be a lie." He fell quiet, the silence thickened. He spoke again. "There's something missing from your eyes, Aëros."

"I'll find it."

The druid's brows knit together. He tapped the Wayfarer's head with the stem of his pipe. "Is it not simply in here?"

Aëros laughed and swatted the stem away. He felt the sickening sense of what he'd lost but could not recall stir inside of him. *Not here.* "The memory of it, forgotten."

"So you search Eaē for the thing itself, to remind you."

Aëros shook his head. "Only our world."

"Our world..." The druid looked the Wayfarer over, and his posture went rigid, eyes unmoving. "Where in our world?"

Another lance of pain tore through Aëros' side, another grimace marred his face. "The Barrows," he said through gritted teeth. "Dún." *A grave. A sepulcher. The bones of a madman.*

"You say Dún and mean Athair." Shaē's voice was plain, the pain well hidden, the fear for his friend less so. "Why?"

The Shadow. Aëros looked for it, and there it was, cast along the wooded walls of the room. He was unsurprised. He was alive, so too was it. "A wager," he answered. *Curiosity, need, fear, the complete lack of another option.*

"A wager." Shaē saw his friend's curiosity, and the need just beneath it, and the fear beneath that. He exhaled a ribbon of smoke, settling into acceptance. "You will need a long rest before you are well enough to continue."

The Wayfarer smiled, appreciating the sense of being understood, worried over, but ultimately unquestioned. "How long have I been bed-ridden?"

The druid looked up, as if seeking the answer scrawled on the ceiling. "Three weeks," he said at length, finding it in the warping age-lines of the wood.

Aëros rolled a shoulder, measuring his pain, the ache in his body, his bones. "Sounds right."

"You've drifted in and out since. The side effects of the tonic I've been administering keep you mostly asleep." The druid pointed to a series of crystalline flasks set atop an Arkaēn's Kiln. "I've only just begun weaning you, this is the first you've been fully awake since I found you."

Aëros looked at his side and rolled his arm, testing the injury. It bit, muscles spasming, and he groaned. "How bad a shape am I in?"

Shaē inhaled, pursed his lips. "Well, your wound won't kill you."

"But?"

"But I wouldn't be in a rush to leave the forest just yet." Shaē cast his eyes over his friend, some curiosity or wonder or confusion hiding within them. "The injury will linger a long time. Might not even mend on its own."

Aëros weighed his friend's advice, considering. "But it won't kill me."

"Not directly, no." said Shaē. "But I urge you against leaving. There's aid yet for you here. I suppose it all depends on how great your hurry is."

Great enough that I cannot stay. Great enough to linger here in fear of continuing on. Aëros knew he must go, but was more than willing to let the wound serve as excuse to stay.

"I can afford to tarry a little while," he said, lying. To his friend. To himself. The Shadow stood stalwart, knowing the lie for what it was, knowing everything.

Do not—

"You are a dear friend, Shaē. You do and have done so much for me." Aëros smiled as he interrupted the Shadow, unwilling to abide its omniscience. The wraith glowered. Aëros' smile melted into a frown as a horrific howl rumbled out of his stomach.

"Seems I've yet more to do, you feral deer," said Shaē, laughing. "I'll fetch breakfast. Stay in bed."

Aëros sat silent as his friend turned on his heels. He couldn't argue against hospitality here even if he wanted to; Shaē was too stubborn a host. So, he settled in his bed to wait for his fare, and distracted himself with a study of his bedchamber.

Set within the hollow of a wōadglōam, no hemming, hewing, or felling had played a part in its creation—the arboreal domain of the druids was woven into the trees as they grew, a harmless effort that made the forest only more beautiful for it. There was neither seam nor jointing nor nail nor plank, the whole of the room merely twisting and warping with age in kind with its host.

Within the winding walls ran a mosaic of carvings that were not carvings, forming thin and flowing scrollwork. It appeared natural, as if the wood of the walls had willed the art into creation itself. That wasn't true, of course, for it was indeed a work of artifice and will, of those who awakened beneath the eaves of the forest when it was in its adolescence, the First of the First, the ancestors of the Ayl.

The walls through which the scrollwork ran were a soft and shifting grey, illuminated by the sea-green light of the forest. The radiance drifted in over the terrace, drawing Aëros' attention out to the heartwood. It was a sea of wōadglōam—monolithic, primordial, each twining about the other, their luminous lifeblood running through veins of liquid crystal, the pulsating sap the source of the Ara's light, the memory of the petrified and ashen brethren in which Sif made her home all the more bitter for the beauty it once was.

But the outskirts were healing, and in time would be as the heartwood again—a mythical place of fable and Age-ancient tavern tale. One such myth spoke of the forest's birth: when Arök broke free from the moon, shattering it as it fell to Eave, it drew the ash of the celestial down with it, luminous and vital. From the ash grew the first of the wōadglōam, an Archtree, the first of the Ara, of all life on Eave, filling the emptiness, its location lost to time, known to Aëros in a time where he could still walk between the Ages, lost to him now in the asylum of forgotten things.

Still, he recalled the tale, and it in turn recalled for him the words of his Aūriel's wisdom. *Even ash of Ages gone, may grow a wood, a world, a home.*

He loved the Wōadglōam Forest above almost any other wonder he had walked with, or world he had wandered, or reality he had moonlighted through. He held the Wayshrine alone above it, though that was not wholly a fair thing to do, being that his own will was that which wove it into existence. The hidden refuge reflected his own artistic aesthetic, mirroring mountain, sea, and woodland in a way that revived the feeling of seeing the grandest thing of one's life for the first time, every time he visited his sanctuary betwixt and between worlds.

Still, the Wōadglōam Forest was the root of his woodland loves. It soothed him, invigorated him, wreathed him with its tranquility. It was a place of harmony in which he could shadow himself away from the woe and want of the outer world.

Shaē once asked him why he would not come to dwell in the woodland. He'd wondered over it himself and came to a simple answer. *"The woe and want of the outer world are not of the outer world's making, but my own,"* he said. *"The forest is a refuge, a sanctuary. I may dwell here for a time unburdened by my worries and desires, but in the end, if I came to live here, a part of it would always be to hide myself from them. I don't want to taint the truth of this place with falsehood, its purpose confused with my own."*

"Breakfast's up!" Shaē stood in the doorway, a large platter of food in one hand, a pitcher of turquoise liquid in the other, and a smile more pleasant than aught else curving his face.

Aëros' own smile warmed. "After three weeks, I may need a second." He adjusted himself in his bed, ignoring both the pain in his side as he took the platter from his friend, and all formality as he set to devouring it.

The fare was of honeyed boar belly and hickory-smoked eggs, sour blood oranges and roasted garlic cloves, salted apple jam and toasted cinnamon bread with soft cinnamon butter—a favorite. He ate his breakfast without tasting any of it, and the second after that too. Shaē watched with a self-satisfied smile as the meal settled in his friend, lulling him into a content and comfortable sleep even as the day just began its waking.

Shaē stood, speaking softly over his shoulder as he went. "Rest easy, my weary friend. Perhaps you will find what you are searching for somewhere in your dreams."

Chapter VIX: Tonkori in the Moonlight
• Stirring of Summer •

Aëros did not dream. The Shadow did not disturb him. It was late in the evening, or perhaps very early the next morning, when he awoke. The light streaming into the room no longer mingled with the rays of sun, instead roving through the darkness undiluted. Sleep dulled the pain of his wound, but his weariness lingered. He looked over to the nightstand beside him, and found a pitcher. The liquid within hummed with the same viridian light as the forest, swirling with shimmering silver. It was the sap of the wōadglōam, the lifeblood that flowed through their crystalline veins, drawn from their weeping withes, served raw.

A chill spiked through Aëros as he pulled a draught of the pleasant sap down, its flavor something like the shiver of mint leaves, the acidity of lemon, and the sweetness of pear, all tinged with a fourth, unknowable sensation Aëros had long ago thought of as the taste of silence. It wasn't that the taste was missing, as sound would be in silence, but that it was subtle, as silence could often be. As the silence of smoke billowing in the wind. As the silence of the inner mind, present only when it was not considered—gone, like a startled bird, if it was. Like the silence of the wōadglōam, witnessing Ages form and fray in the fabric of eternity, the woodland alone remaining, a soundless sentinel of all that was and would be, their soundlessness bound to their bones, their blood, their bark, their sap. The taste of silence, setting a silence within the Wayfarer, bringing to him some measure of a tranquility he'd not felt since...

A breeze blustered into the room, drawing his eye to the forest, drawing into his breath—the scent of silence to match the taste. He rested the pitcher of wōad-sap back on the nightstand, its contents swirling in currents of shimmering silver and soft, shifting greens.

Settled in his full stomach, he found his ears lifting as the strum of strings and song drifted in over the terrace, stirring the silence with sound. The music resonated from somewhere in the eaves of the ancient woodland, drifting slowly into the room, air humming with its gentle melody.

Still aching, Aëros lifted the quilt from his bed, tired of being tired. He slid his feet onto the floor and rose, the wood cool on his bare feet as he made his way to the terrace. His eyes sharpened with both the light of the wōadglōam and the slivers of silvering moon, one born from the death of the other, or so the fable spoke. He looked out on the night, veins of viridian light twisting up the monolithic trunks of grey wōadglōam, threading through the eaves from limb to branch to the slender withes that were their leaves, lifeblood weeping from them with the memory of all the seasons they'd lived.

Aëros inhaled the night-air of the forest: clear, deep, soft with the scent of freshly fallen rain, and rain now falling from the clouds bound beneath the canopy, the forest's vastness giving rise to its own weather. The breeze came again, chilling, and he looked about for something to warm him. He found his Shräud hung up, and reached for it, remembering as he did the wound it had suffered in kind with his own. He draped it over himself, finding the torn threads patched, the seam sewn shut, its illusion not unraveled; but unraveling, fading, weak.

Shaē had done what he could to mend the garment, but the thread and cloth he used to heal it would not in turn heal the threads of Dräu. It was a skill only Aūriel possessed, a wound only her hands and mind could mend. To his fortune, the hidden pockets leading to Nowhere were still intact, the threads of Aūr from which they were woven unharmed, allowing him access to his near-infinite hoard in that liminal space betwixt and between worlds. Still, the Shräud's unraveling was a heavy burden, that burden another catalyst to see him to his journey's end, to see him back to the woman who wove it, the woman he loved. The memory came subtly, gently, as if he were an injured animal and it a tentative touch, intending to ensure a festering wound did not seal up on itself, cautious not to dig too deep.

"I have a surprise for you, Aëros." She smirked her 'I've seen into your soul and returned with the truth' smirk, and drew out a present wrapped in leaf and twine. You loved surprises, for it was rare that you found one, and she knew that well. She'd made this one with her own hands, own will, own wisdom. You smiled and drew the twine and leaf away, revealing her efforts to etch that smile out of the grim stone that so often held it. It was a wayfarer's cloak, woven not only from thread of cloth but thread of Dräu. Hidden hollows of limitless depth lay within, woven of Aür—her own understanding of what you'd taught her, her own artifice of what she'd taught herself. "I call it a Shräud."

She'd studied your life's work in between studies of her own, and learned more swiftly even than you. She was brilliant. Your eyes widened, amazed, and your smile spread with your love. You hugged her and kissed her as you whispered your promise. "I would be happy if I died today, my Aüriel."

She smiled and whispered in kind, "As would I, my Aëros."

The memory left, and as far as Aëros could tell, no part of it was nightmare. Still, soft as it was, it left the familiar ache, same as all the others, echoing up from the asylum. Caught in the duality of bittersweet nostalgia, he buried the ache in his bones, easy enough for its subtlety, and continued on, Shräud wrapping him, weariness hidden from his awareness.

He leapt from the terrace to the immense limb beneath, soundless. The limb twined about others, reaching into the distance far from sight. Rain scattered on the weatherproof surface of his Shräud, keeping him dry as he searched for the music that

105

drew him; but he found it had subsided, lost to the gentle winds rustling through the eaves.

Sitting, he shuttered his eyes, laid his head to the limb, and listened. He drew a deep, unconscious breath, and another, and another, his mind wandering through the seams of the forest, searching. He found the flickering lifeblood of the trees as it went, the threads of Aūr that composed it obvious, if untouchable; saw the patter of rain strike the lifelines from above; felt the scurrying of wee beasties; and finally heard the strum of music reverberate once again, sensing it ripple through the forest as it developed into song, lilting through the trees.

> *Melody faithful, now melody play us!*
> *Wind-sea and wave-sea, and tree-top belay us!*
> *The stars are a'fallin, the moon is all shattered!*
> *The silver is streaking, the raven's the sadder!*
>
> *Swing mellow faithful, now swing mellow with me!*
> *Light is the leafless, low-lying the way-lea!*
> *The shade is below, with the gloom of the mourning!*
> *Good-hearted the faē, folk listen for the morning!*
>
> *Strumming strings sounding, and strumming strings seamless!*
> *Woven and wand'ring and slumbering dreamless!*
> *The winds in the woodland the winds in the willow!*
> *The wōadglōam will rest him like cold under pillow!*
>
> *Melody faithful, now melody lay us!*
> *Wave-sea and wind-sea, and tree-top betray us!*
> *Bones are a'rattlin', while bones are a'restin'!*
> *Lullaby! Lullaby! Soft and so settlin'!*

Hush all you songbirds, now hush all together!
Notes in the wind-waves, and notes on the feather!
A strumming, a streaming, a song not to tarry!
Rest all of you weathered and worn and way-weary!

Aëros opened his eyes as the words faded and the notes stilled, the light of the wōadglōam pulsating in rhythm with them. Standing, he followed the light towards the music's source. He drifted slowly at first, savoring the sight of the wood through which he wandered as if it were his first time seeing it. But as he went, he swiftened his going, his aches distant, the forest soothing, the urge to move a deep remnant of his agile ancestry.

With renewed vigor he climbed, weaving through the labyrinth of limb and leaf like thread through a needle. He ascended, and saw the end of the eaves approaching as the final boughs grew near. With curiosity guiding him, he leapt through the last layer of leaves, leaving the gentle mists and soft rains below as the clear night welcomed him above.

The view from the heights was boundless, as if it were a painting pulled from the dreaming of some master artisan who, even for their mastery, was incapable of breathing life into such a work unless within the unconscious realm of sleep. The canopy glimmered with the viridian light of the sap filtering up from below, mingling with the moon's own cascading, silver radiance. The twining light formed a sea of roving, prismatic waves as the warm, wild spring winds whorled over the woodland.

Aëros was not alone in the overwood. Small, skeletal forest spirits peered over the top of the canopy, surfing in the waves of wind running over the eaves, afraid to venture fully from the forest, curious enough to tempt part of themselves at least. There were thousands of them, flickering and fading in and out of existence, expressions veiled by masks of bark, leaf, twig, and moss. Kodama, Shaē named them, spirits lingering on the boundary of life and death, fading into the realm of one and out of the other at will or at random—that the druid did not know. Neither did Aëros. They were not as the An'kou—souls suffering in unlife, bound to the waking world by some unfinished act or desire—but something other, something different from and yet kindred to. They were translucent, limned with the light of the wōadglōam, drawn to the ancient forest, birthed by it, as the ancestors of all life on Eave had been. It was not so in all worlds, the Wayfarer learned long ago. In some life came from the sea, some from the stone, some from realms he knew not the name nor understood the nature of. But in this world, life came from the forest, born from the ash of the shattered moon, drawn down with the wyrm in its fall.

The Wayfarer stood atop the canopy, amidst the chatter of the Kodama, listening for music. He found it, and found that it had softened, losing itself in the open air of night. Atop the eaves hung a set of swings woven of limb and vine, suspended from a series of branches reaching above the roof of the forest. On the lowest sat Shaē, staring off over the woodland with a faraway gaze, strumming an instrument with which Aëros was unfamiliar.

Aëros approached the druid, his steps soundless on the leaves. He took a seat atop the canopy near enough to listen but not disturb, watching as Shaē plucked out the sound of his strings. The melody melded with the cadence of forest and night, drawing Aëros in as if he was a part of it—and indeed he was. For the resonance he felt was that which tethered all things to one another: him to the forest, forest to the sky, sky to Eaē, Eaē to memory. *Memory.*

He fell into it, even if he did not draw on it. It appeared, dancing over the waves of the woodland-sea, he alone its audience. The Shadow stood beside him, a crooked warden with a crooked skeleton key, a crooked narrator of a crooked story it insisted on him witnessing, implying a meaning to its madness.

"Thrace is dead, Shaē."

He didn't know what to say. His smile was thinning, like mist under morning sun.

"Athair will come for you," you urged him, drawing his eyes to yours and holding them, pleading. "He'll come for everyone."

Betrayal begets betrayal. Shaē understood. There was no blame. He knew what you knew, knew what Athair really was under the mask of humanity he wore. What he would inevitably do, regardless of reason. You'd made a decision. The only act the equal of treachery would have been inaction itself; indifference; apathy in the face of adversity. He shared that philosophy with you, a feather of friendship, your minds and wills linked in that one way among many—but not all.

"I can't—won't leave," he said, and this was a place where your wills diverged. "I will warn the rest. Those that will stay will be welcome, and will defend this wood." He tried to prop up his smile, but the supports splintered, fractured, fell away. "This is all I have left. This is my world, my home, my family."

You did not argue, did not respond with words at all. You simply looked on in sorrow, until his smile broke free from his own despair, demanding yours from you. You clasped his shoulder and bowed your head, heart heavy in spite of—or perhaps because of—the love within it, and left: him to his home, you to yours.

Shaē did not die that night, but he died before you ever saw him again. You did not know if it was swift, or if he was kept alive far too long, twisted and tangled until his smile wrung the other way around, his misery unnatural. Would he still resemble himself? As Sif still resembled a wolf, the Lësh'unn a Drúan? Or would he be warped beyond recognition? No matter. You have no memory of him as he was when he ended. You buried much, and in his case and others you buried memory where you had no bones. You couldn't weave a corpse from ash. Not even Athair could do that—wouldn't have granted such a gift even if he could.

You do have a memory of the forest though, the inferno, the pillars of smoke rising into the winds like a mountain of grey, fluid stone. You saw it from the roof of your villa; it was time to depart the Fells. It wasn't safe there anymore. You'd take your family and head to the home of a friend in Arythos—the last remaining sanctuary for the living in the West.

"A somnambulant strider of moonlight, I see." Shaē spoke, drawing the Wayfarer's thoughts back from the distance that held them. "I've seen that faraway look before, Aëros. Seen it through my own eyes, and others'. You were somewhere else. Somewhere unkind."

Aëros heard his friend, though his focus was still displaced, his breath arrhythmic and stuttering, shallow. He turned to look at Shaē, thoughts still reeling. When he met the druid's eyes, his mind calmed, comforted with the truth that what he'd seen was madness. Shaē alive before him, smiling as ever. "Your music drew me from my dreaming."

Aëros looked at his friend a long while, as if ensuring he was truly there; watched the rise and fall of his chest, the pulsation of the woodland as it too breathed, druid and forest in rhythm, each in rhythm with the world, with Eave, with Eaē, harmonious. He measured his own breath, discordant in its disharmony, remembered how once it had risen with the world's, fallen with it. *I'm even forgetting how to breathe. Forgetting how to be a part of my own world.*

Shaē watched Aëros watching him, watched his thoughts as they came, and went. If Aëros had been watching the druid's eyes he would have seen his thoughts, too. Would have seen how they searched him now that he was awake, alive, seeking for something that was missing, or seeing something that didn't quite belong. Aëros would have seen the threads of this search weave neatly into a realization. The druid smiled, a somber thing that did not belong, then let it fade, and with it the thought he'd resolved. It was not a thought he should share, a revelation not meant for him to reveal, but for Aëros to discover on his own.

Aëros met Shaē's eyes as what had been in them evanesced, and found them smiling sincerely, which made him smile himself. He pointed to the instrument resting beside his friend. "That's new."

Shaē nodded, head bobbing, enthusiastic, not as if there was any other way he might nod. "It's from the Crescent Isles, a tonkori. I thought it might do to learn an instrument."

The winds picked up, running over the eaves. Aëros grazed his hand through the forest-sea as its tide rippled around him. "It's a fine night."

"It is," said Shaē. "Fitting for a pipe." At his word, he withdrew two: one from his sleeve, one from a nook in his staff, set to rest beside the tonkori. "A gift." He handed the Wayfarer the pipe from his staff.

Aëros took it carefully, examining and marveling over its detail. It was wrought from the twisting grey wood of a wōadglōam, inlaid with masterful impressions of roots and vines and tendrils threading themselves through one another. The design grew up from the bowl, fading into the shaft as it ascended the stem, intertwining over and within itself, sleek and elegant. "You made this?"

Shaē laughed. "Indeed I did! Wrought from the withe of a wōadglōam fallen from age. I meant it as a gift for you once you returned. It's been a long while."

The Wayfarer's smile brimmed as he turned the pipe over, considering it and many things besides. "Thank you, my friend."

The druid withdrew a leather pouch and opened it, offering its contents to Aëros.

"Wōadleaf?" Aëros asked as he reached for the mixture, its sweet, sharp scent clear as the forever-shattered moon hanging overhead.

"It certainly isn't Sylysæ." Shaē winked, knowing well the many vices and many curiosities of his friend. "Drawn from its soaking three days past, perfectly seasoned. It's artisanal, if I say so, and I do."

Aëros was already packing the pleasant mixture, tamping it tight, grinning at his friend's eccentricity. "So say I too."

The druid followed suit of Aëros, packing his own pipe and flicking a small striking stick against his leather pouch to set it alight. He held it up to the bowl and inhaled. Aëros lit his own with a thread of Iné, and soon both pipes flared to life, smoke billowing.

A warm current filled the open air, caressing the eaves, whirling loose leaf-litter and iridescent pollen up in its mistral. The druid and the Wayfarer let their conversation drift, instead sitting quietly for a time, talking not at all to each other and thinking little to themselves.

"I've missed the forest." Aëros spoke, knowing that to let his mind wander freely was foolish. His words were soft, wistful; nearly a whisper.

"Your woes weigh heavy." Shaē gestured for his friend to join him on one of the swing's many tiers. Aëros obliged, perching atop the seat set above and aside the druid's own, looking down as his friend spoke wisdom. "Burying sorrow is like burying water, Aëros. It simply seeps into the soil and up into everything that grows from it."

A small silence followed on the wind of the words; small and swift-going. "The wōadglōam bear their sorrow beautifully," said Aëros.

"Immortal ancients drifting through the Ages as the world around them falls and rises from the ash of others," said Shaē, a whisper himself. "Sorrow is all things of such permanence can know." He looked to Aëros, not through his eyes but through his thoughts. "Not so unlike you, Walker Betwixt and Between Worlds. You have seen Ages the same as the Ara. In truth, you have seen more than even the forest could dream of, in a fragment of time too small to process it."

112

The Wayfarer stared straight on into the night, a thread of smoke drifting through his pursed lips, leading his hesitant words. "Do I seem so sorrowful to you?"

Shaē was staring on now too, searching for the depth in the night; of his friend's words, of his own. The forest fell silent, listening. "What do you think Thrace would say to all this?"

"*Fuck off.*"

Shaē roared approval. "Wyrmseye, my friend. Wyrmseye."

Aëros dropped to the seat Shaē sat upon and they overlooked the woodland together. "This forest would be whole, healed, had the other druids remained."

Shaē shrugged. "Even if they had not returned to the Isles, there is not much they could have done." *Returned? Too kind a way to say ran, my friend.* "There is little I myself can do."

"You are doing something, though." Aëros' words were proud, urging his friend to take such pride in himself. "You made a choice to stay; they could have done the same."

"They could have. But it is not my place to judge their actions. That is something they must do for themselves," the druid said. Words for his own comfort, his own convincing, though he would never confess it.

"Well, what of your action, then." Aëros dragged the sweet smoke out, let it pillar away in cascading rings. He watched the druid, searching his features. "Do you regret staying?"

Shaē's face shifted with a smile and a bewildered laugh. "Of all who might ask me that, I would think you alone would have the answer without needing it given."

Aëros said nothing, searching his mind, his memories. Maybe he knew once, but no longer. Perhaps he'd never known at all, as likely as aught else.

Shaē saw Aëros' inner thought play out in his eyes and sighed. He inhaled smoke, exhaled, inhaled air, and spoke. "To regret is to fetter ourselves to the past. To blind us as present and future drift by, until those too have withered into what has been—into a past you cannot remember for never having lived it when it was present. A waste." He was not smiling; he was neutral, searching, struggling to understand, to find the wisdom in his own words. "As for the answer to your question, perhaps I shouldn't expect you to know it. I have yet to reconcile it even with myself." A glimmer of warmth split through his neutrality in the shape of a thin smile. "Though if anyone could see into someone's soul and find the truth of it, I'd wager on you before the person themselves."

Aëros looked away from his friend, back over the forest, to the sky, to the stars that fell from the forever-shattered moon, clutched in the talons of Valrävn. "The wise are ever fools of their own wisdom. Easier to pass on than walk with, I suppose."

◆

The Wayfarer and the druid remained atop the eaves for hours, drifting through conversation as their mixtures burned and the night grew old. Eventually the sun peeked over the canopy, and Shaē decided that it was time to rest. He looked over to his friend, finding him already fallen to his fatigue, dreaming.

"To bed with you," said the druid as he whistled a note down into the forest. The wōadglōam hearkened to him, vines and withes working in harmony to deliver the Wayfarer to his bed, gracefully lowering him through their dense labyrinth. Soon he lay in his room, resting on the feather mattress, silver quilt drawn about him, lulled into a rejuvenating sleep by the cradling song and silence of the forest.

Chapter X: Sinew of the Soil
• Stirring of Summer •

"*A̤eros.*"

The Wayfarer's eyes shuttered as his mind wandered out of its inner silence, dreamless once more. Shaē stood at the foot of his bed, smiling as ever, gesturing for him to rise and ready. The Shadow stood beside him, watching, but distant from its usual intrusion into his thoughts. Perhaps it sensed his fatigue; perhaps it was just bored with him. Perhaps wondering was pointless, which he settled on as most likely.

Shaē smiled as Aëros woke, and spoke softly. "They're ready."

Aëros stretched his neck, his back, his everything, joints snapping into place. "I'm grateful, even if it took so long for them to come to a conclusion."

"Drūans are of the trees. Old, and slow." Shaē looked out from the window into the wood. "And trees take a long time to say anything, and anything worth saying takes a long time to say. Or so they'd tell you."

It was not the morning after his journey to the forest canopy, but many hence. Aëros' wound was healing, but healing slowly, the limit of Shaē's skill long since reached. So, the druid called upon those few with greater skill than his own, in hopes that they could salve what he could not. It was time for Aëros to move on. He stood—or tried to—only to crumple beneath the pain of his wound.

The druid reached out, helping Aëros stand. "Easy, friend. They haven't healed you yet."

Aëros winced as he righted himself. "The pain is reminder enough."

"Soon to be a distant memory."

The Shadow stood beside the druid, watching. Aëros smirked. "Soon to be forgotten, more like."

Shaē laughed. "That's the spirit!"

The Wayfarer fell in behind the druid, and they passed beneath the arch over-setting the stairs, the corridor lined with veins of sap, illuminating the stairwell ahead, steps falling into darkness, winding down and around the inner hollow of the wōadglōam that held them, dreamlike and near-eternal in its immensity.

Yet near-eternal is eternal not, and at length the pair of friends reached the end of the winding descent. They passed over the threshold and out onto a terrace that encircled the trunk of the tree, entirely open to the heartwood. Even after descending so far as they had, the underwood was still shrouded from view by a well-woven tapestry of limb and leaf and weeping withe.

This middling level of the woodland held but one new wonder—the druids' kingdom in the trees, made Ages ago when the First of the First still walked 'neath eave and shade. Arkaēns, cartographers, seamstresses, woodwrights, taverns, inns, homes, hostels, villages and cities, scattering until sight could no longer descry them. It was a hidden sanctuary in the midmost region of the wood, wrought for all fair folk seeking refuge from their woe and want for a time. A home for many, a home for none. It was abandoned, left for the wind and the beasts and a solitary soul too kindly to leave a wounded thing untended.

Aëros' eyes and his thoughts falling on Shaē and his suffering and the journey he followed. *I'm sorry for holding you in mine for so long, my friend.* He wore a smile halfway gone to sorrow, grim and self-spiteful. Shaē noticed, did not impose. The friends fell into stride again, leaving the vagrant kingdom to its rest, descending a stairway ringing the rim of the wōadglōam's grey trunk. It spiraled down, down, down, passing into the under-layers of forest, the underwood arriving like a half-remembered dream in the day.

A thick carpet of moss blanketed the forest floor, luminescent and shimmering like the eaves above, waves of viridian light running on as gentle wind pulled the soft bedding in its wake. Adolescent wōadglōam sung out from their deep, running roots, swaying beneath the wisdom of their elders, while small, curious Kes scampered and winged about, flickering in and out of sight amidst the dense underwood, wondering at the appearance of two visitors from the overwood above.

Leaves fell, draff drifting down, for though the heartwood was eternal, it aged like any other forest, all trees shedding branch, bark, and leaf after a time. But though the Wōadglōam was a forest, and behaved as a forest, it was old, ancient, wizened. When the draff of age fell, it did not layer atop itself, did not litter the forest floor.

A wood wyvern, not much bigger than a twig, leapt onto a leaf that was falling, extended its leathern, feathered wings, and flew to another, and another, until it landed along the trunk of a wōadglōam, watching, chirping with curiosity.

Aëros watched the leaf the wyvern began upon at last land, watched as the barest edge of it met the barest edge of the moss, watched as the light of the moss traveled through the leaf, outlining its veins, the leaf evanescing, lingering for a moment as glowing flecks of radiance, until the radiance itself fell back to the moss, drawn down and gathered into the roots anchoring the soil; old as the eldest wōadglōam, old as the moon's death, as the ash from which the woodland grew.

"Arök serves as the bones of the world, the Ara's roots as the sinew of the soil. Arök binds the world, the Ara binds his bones." Shaē's words echoed from memory. "What perishes here gives life anew, as in any forest. To live is to bring death, to die is to bring life, two ends of a single essential thread of existence. From ash a forest, from forest ash."

The Wayfarer mused on his friend's words, on the cyclicality they themselves offered, circling the words of his Aūriel, circling him, his journey. He set his musing aside, for his belief in the cycle

117

was the foundation of his philosophies, no longer requiring careful consideration. The world went on, always would, as would he, until he was ash—which was his hope, or until he was a husk, hollow—which was his fear. He would find his doom at his journey's end; would choose it, if he was able. For now, he was still in the midst, following the druid through the underwood, the iridescent moss soft on his soles and his friend's, bare as they each always and ever were, like-minded with many feathers of friendship between them.

The world beneath the eaves was serene, the Ara seeming to slide out of their path as they went, easing their passage. The veins of the forest lit their way, outlining the moody underwood as it flowed along the trunks of the wōadglōam, running and rising into hidden canopies above. Water—a small stream by its sound—ran somewhere just beyond sight, calm and unhurried. The two wanderers rounded the base of a wōadglōam, a distance words could not measure, and the waterway appeared. They fell in alongside it, following it upstream until the sun was a few degrees before its zenith. Small though it was, the stream seemed to siphon all the forest to it, beasts both familiar and foreign gathering around its banks.

There were those that roamed both the woodland and the world: vesta and night-wolves, silver-ravens and moon-owls, lúmoths and nightingales; and those that dwelled solely in the Wōadglōam Forest, rare even in their home.

Kodama pattered along the embankments, fading in and out of life and death, meandering mischief lurking behind their unassuming innocence. Some prodded at Shaē, climbing up and onto his shoulders and staff, one sitting itself upon his head, cross legged, head tilting side to side as the druid trotted along. Others mocked and teased the other beasts, tugging at them, splashing them, riding atop them. Most made fools of each other, knocking those too close to the water's edge in or blaming this antic or that on another when their mischief went too far.

Forest giants lumbered about in contrast to the impish spirits, thoughtful in their passive meandering. Grey and hulking, their flesh was like bark, evolved from Ages of life in the woodland, their bloodline adapting and intertwining with the Ara as many in the forest had, the Drúans the eldest of such mixing. The giants kept to themselves as they drank and wandered in search of whatever it was the blind searched for. For they were indeed blind, though sightlessness was never a hindrance to their goings, always mindful of their weight and their wander, always gentle.

The embankment of the stream was a revel of life, and Aëros would miss it ere long. But that was the way of the Wayfarer: to move on in search of things that had themselves been moved on from; to return to those left in memory; to leave them behind as he went on so he might in turn learn to miss them, for in longing he found lay the greatest love. He held many vices, the wells of his humanity vast, a bone-deep desire for wistfulness, nostalgia, reminiscence hoarded most precious of all.

The stream wandered far, but far Aëros and Shaē walked, and at length its source revealed itself. A ringed shrine of nine Age-ancient wōadglōam encircled an underground spring, its hypogean flow running up into a shallow mere, clear as crystal, running on into the waterway.

The pair passed into the grove. The wōadglōam that hemmed the pond were primordial, even as far as their kind went. In the base of each trunk was a large hollow from which warm light thrummed out into the sanctuary.

"This is..." Aëros faded off as he looked around the enveloping haven, as he felt the heartbeat of the forest pulse through him, his own arrhythmic with the world's.

"The heart of the heartwood; home of the Drúans," Shaē finished for him, eyes bright, wide, taking in all that surrounded them.

Aëros smiled. "I was going to say wonderful."

119

The glow thrumming from the hollows of the trees brightened, and out stepped the Drúans in unison, as if they were but the same mind shared between separate bodies. Six spirits from nine hollows. Aëros marked the difference, despaired for a moment, then set it aside, admiring those who remained.

Drúans seemed at first very much like any Ayl, Ken, or other upright sapient might: perched on two legs with two arms to match, a torso to fix them, and a head for wisdom to hide in. But in truth their resemblance to elf, man, or other stopped at such generalities.

Their skin was like flowing bark, grey and sleek, and between its twists and turns and cracks and clefts a soft glow like that of the wōadglōam radiated. Their faces were angular, keen, beautiful, and from their heads tapered long vines in some semblance of hair. They stood tall and moved slowly, like the forest giants, and with grace, like the vesta. They paused momentarily as they left their homes, appraising the day, the druid, the Wayfarer. If they had objections, they were unknown. They strode to the water's edge and waded in. The pool was hip-deep on Aëros and Shaē, but only so for the Drúans as they knelt, beckoning with a simple gesture for the two elves to join them in the deepest heart of the heartwood.

Aëros hesitated, for the image of the Drúans wavered, and in its place appeared the Lësh'unn. The two were not different beings, but reflections, one the shadow of the other. Each Drúan held a Lësh'unn within them. Every living thing held such a perversion of self, an imprisoned inner darkness, taking only the grim influence of some corruption or wicked circumstance to tear it free.

Aëros considered this as his vision flickered between Drúan and Lësh'unn, considered it as he considered his own shadow. Considered *the* Shadow, appearing out of his periphery beside him. His own doppelgänger, his own inner darkness, or inner madness—its nature still a mystery at which he could only wager.

Whatever it was, it was not the same as the Lësh'unn, which meant it might be as it claimed—salvation—or something far worse, far more insidious for its deception and its subtlety.

Regardless, remedy or ruin, it was not important now, nor was the Lësh'unn, for it was not here. Here there was only Shaē, the Drúans, himself, and his wound. He turned to the druid, and Shaē led him forward into the basin, into the innermost hollow of the heartwood. The water shivered through him, its rejuvenating threads mending him of weariness he had not even known he suffered, so long buried had it been. He and the druid joined the circle of spirits, two children in the midst of elders.

The Drúans looked to the druid, who offered his warming smile as an embrace. They said nothing, but Aëros could tell they too were glad. No living being—so long as there was the thinnest thread of warmth somewhere within them—could resist the sincerity of Shaē's soul.

Shaē motioned to Aëros, to his injury. It was apparent, blood leaking through the layer of cloth applied only the night past. The Drúans set their attention on the center of the pool, an image of a Lësh'unn shimmering into existence between the misty rays of sunlight scattered there. The sentinels gestured to the simulacrum, asking if what it represented had caused the wound. Aëros' eyes told the tale, and the Drúans' visages fell grim over the shadow of their kin. They whisked away their image, turned back to the Wayfarer, and bowed.

"They're apologizing for the Lësh'unn," said Shaē. "And thanking you for helping it."

Aëros narrowed his eyes, confused. "Helping?"

"Yes," said the druid. "The Drúans are as the Ara, dwelling in a state of dreaming and stirring. By slaying the Lësh'unn, you freed it from its curse and set its soul to dreaming. Soon it will again stir and rejoin its kindred in the grove. Though soon to them may be many Ages to us."

121

Aëros thought back to Aūriel, to Tärin, to his home—to his promise to return. For now, he returned only the Drúan's bow of gratitude. They rose and gestured for him to wade to the center of the pool. He removed his bandage and passed through the water to the mere's heart. There, just beneath the surface, was a stone plinth large enough to rest upon. He understood without need for explanation, sliding onto the slate-grey slab and laying back.

He looked to the Drúans as the water settled at his sides; their heads were sunken upon their breasts, the gentle glow that hummed out from the core of their bodies seeping from their fingers like sap from the wōadglōam. The liquid light cascaded into the water, rippling out. The Drúans wove the glimmering water into a gossamer sheet, guiding it over Aëros' wound as a second skin, the salve glowing a pale gold as it warred with the corruption within him. It seared his senses to apathy, separating him from his pain and all other feeling as the infection screamed to the surface.

Rot slithered out from the wound and into the mere in a streak of black ichor. It writhed in the water, gathering in on itself as if it were the culmination of many minds, each desperate to escape its death, willing to sacrifice one another for the selfishness of their own survival. But it was a vain betrayal. The Drúans' will was too great for the small thread of darkness to withstand. It dissolved, becoming small, radiant flecks of light, reabsorbed by the woodland, purified, at peace.

Before Aëros' senses returned, he was whole, the mending over, the sheet of healing water sliding back into the pool. He lay still, panting softly as his awareness of the world drifted back to him. Slowly, tentatively, he lifted himself from the stone slab. He looked to his side as he righted himself, finding rejuvenated skin in place of a wound. Even the lesser injuries of adventure he'd gained along his journey had been mended, the faintest hints of scars remaining, delicate reminders of wounds that once were but were no longer.

Aëros looked to the Drúans, intending to thank them again, but stopping short as he caught a strange concern in their eyes. They were not looking at him, but beside him. He followed their gaze, finding the Shadow perched there upon the plinth. His brows furrowed, bewildered. *They can see you?* He looked back to the Drúans, measuring their gaze, unsure if that was true, or if they could merely sense the wraith, another thread of darkness, clear as that which festered in their home.

The Drúans lingered in their look for only a moment, before concern shifted to pity, and pity to respect as they bowed their heads again to him, and to Shaē, and turned back to their hollows and left, their ability to heal him not great enough to mend the wound given himself and forgotten.

"How do you feel?"

Aëros had lost himself in his thoughts, but Shaē's voice summoned him back. He took a piece of his friend's smile, and stood from the dais, revealing the reminder of a wound that once was but was no longer. "Restored." He was swaggering, nearly an instinct for him. Once it was a sturdy sense of self-confidence; now it was a mask meant to deceive. He felt brittle inside, a hollow thing, a withered husk, like the petrified corpse of the wōadglōam in which Sif had made her home of loyalty, of betrayal.

"Wonderful!" Shaē leapt in the water, excited, sincere, brimming as ever. He didn't see Aëros' eyes—solemn, pensive, strung up in the gallows tree of consideration. It was only a sliver of a thing, after all, and Shaē couldn't see what the Drúans could, his nature too pure to perceive such subtle shadows of self on his own. The Drúans could be Lësh'unns. Aëros could be a madman. He doubted Shaē could be anything other than Shaē.

"Come, we'll celebrate your health!" Shaē grasped Aëros' shoulder, overwhelmed by the happiness of his ignorance. He led him from the grove, almost dancing as he went. "We'll have one last meal before you move on with your journey!"

Aëros saw the gilt around the edges of Shaē's world, and felt the black around his own thin ever so slightly. He smiled, crooked though it was.

———————————◆———————————

The two friends enjoyed their supper slowly, savoring both it and their last hours within the company of one another. Shaē prepared a parting feast fit to rival royalty. The table brimmed, laden with slabs of vesta; fresh breads; flame-charred fruits; and of course, wōad-sap in draughts deep enough to drown a dry sea.

They feasted and made merry as the sun fell and dusk drew over the forest, and from dusk until night wove its way through the sighing leaves, and from night until the sun stirred from its dreaming and peeked again through the awakening eaves.

As dark waned and Aëros' journey neared waxing, he rose a glass in gratitude, reverence, farewell. "To all of our tomorrows, my friend; let them be always brighter than we expect them to be today."

Shaē lifted his own glass and smiled. "Here, here!"

Chapter XI: The Little & The Lost
• Stirring of Summer •

Aëros passed from the heartwood in silent, swift stride, the beauty of the inner hollow slowly fading into its murk-ridden outskirts. He found his departure uneventful, quiet. Nothing disturbed him and nothing dared think to. He wagered that the darkness was acting in self-preservation, sensing what happened to the thread of itself woven into Sif and the Lësh'unn. Fearing him, it left him be. Regardless of why, the forest's boundary arrived swiftly, and as he passed beyond its embrace he turned, a fleeting look the last memory he would keep of the forest as it was, the threshold veiled by a grey mist, shrouding the darkness that lurked within.

The darkness took a last look at him as well, happy to be rid of whatever he was, sorry for its foolishness in disturbing him in the first place. It was glad he was gone, so it could die its slow and silent death at the hands of the forest's sentinels.

Darkness looked away. So too did Aëros. Yet as he turned, he caught the silhouette of a familiar apparition haunting the precipice just beyond the wood. The little An'kou, alone no longer. Another stood behind him, hands holding his shoulders, tender, loving. They looked at him, the boy and his mother, and in their eyes, Aëros saw gratitude, hope, sorrow. All three for him. Behind them all, somehow a twining of each, he saw a fourth thing hiding, something familiar, but unknowable, for it did not belong to him.

He watched the lost souls, searching for understanding, and realized that they were watching him too, all of him: a man, and his Shadow. He turned to see the wraith standing beside him, seeing more than him; the hidden thing was meant for it, its meaning shrouded in mystery to Aëros, as everything surrounding the wraith was.

Aëros watched the Shadow, watched the An'kou, as unspoken things passed between them, as the silent conversation came to its end, as the lost souls turned at last back into the forest, fading into their rest, lost no longer. He considered the words he'd given the An'kou when first they found him. *You won't find what you seek with me.*

"The wise, ever fools." He put his back to the forest, eyes seeking what was to come, leaving behind what had passed, moving along, moving on. Silent and alone.

Behind him, the Shadow lingered, looking, longing. It was a moment only, but a moment long enough to tell its tale, hidden in the silhouette of another's, buried beneath tales past, present, and an end yet to come. The wraith fell in with the wake of the Wayfarer, leading him not from behind or before, but from within, and beside.

Chapter XII: Augury
• Dreaming of Summer •

Bones. **Bleached, overgrown,** from entire ribcages the size of small mountains to shards whittled down to serrated points by the weathering of Ages, rolling out before the Wayfarer, separating him from the ruins of Arythos and the Rift atop the mountain in which the base of the fallen kingdom was hewn.

Like the Verdant Fells, the Dragongrave was a grassland, though that was where the likeness left off. There were no hills, no knolls; only meadow, bones, and deep, jagged fissures scarring the land, impossible to ford for their immensity. It was, after all, a graveyard for dragons, a relic of a war between them.

The boneyard was a silent memory of an Age far before those who named themselves First of the First came to wander the world, the moon newly shattered, the land shaking and upheaving as Arök—first of all wyrms—shifted in new, uneasy slumber. In that Age the dragons ripped the roots of the world and reaved one another as they sought the precious stones of their grandsire's hide for their own hoards. The Dragongrave was the greatest remaining remnant of that war, serving as reminder of the only sliver of wisdom that greed ever earns the greedy: those who die with most—die.

Since that time the dragons diminished, their numbers near none, those that survived living out their last days in caverns far removed from the world where other living things walked. The boneyard drew at times their ancestors, their sires, first to descend from the line of Arök—the Wyverns and the Drakes. Whether they came in mourning for their descendants, or for a reminder of their folly, none but those mythic Kes knew, their kind far and few as well, relegated to tavern tales and Ages gone.

Standing before the Dragongrave, Aëros faced a choice: to pass over, or below. To go over the boneyard meant long, winding routes skirting the edges of the deep ravines and fissures, drawing out his journey. But to go beneath, through the world under the graveyard risked confronting those who dared dwell there.

The Ashen Vale, as it was named, followed trade routes well-worn before the fall of Arythos, before the Devouring made the Dragongrave a barrow for Ayl and Ken as well. Those still remaining amongst the memory of war lived their lives in search of the hoards over which the dragons died for, hidden in the deep places beneath the boneyard, the greed of the wyrm-kin running in their own blood, men though they be. Men who in their avarice betrayed all loyalty for the weight of a coin, distrusting of and dissonant from the threads that held the seams of society together, riddled with the taint of dragon-sickness. They were feral; they were foul; they were the Fēl.

So too were they the simple choice, between the safe, dragging path of grasslands and horrifying inner thought above, and the narrow, unbroken route riddled with the disquiet distraction of death below. If the Fēl proved too great a trouble, there was always a shortcut Aëros knew of. The Things Betwixt. But it wasn't likely he'd need it, and he feared it even if he did. The Shadow didn't seem to disapprove of his choice, which told him nothing of whether or not it was a good one. The path would come as it would, so he continued on as it did, stepping forward, heading down, descending, foolish and foolhardy, humanity stringing him along and Shadow striding beside, silent.

Chapter XIII: Bones
• Dreaming of Summer •

The overworld of the Dragongrave disappeared as Aëros descended ever down, down, down. Beneath the fragmented ridgelines rising above him like teeth—jagged, starving—sinking into the maw of the Ashen Vale. Devoured.

Unable or unwilling to grow in the shadow of the great scar, the fertile grasslands of the boneyard withered in its underbelly, the Wayfarer's stride shifting from soil to dark, ashen-hued stone. Though summer had begun its dreaming, its heat still lingered, strong and stifling. Aëros wiped beading sweat from his brow, felt it running in rivulets all over him, collecting in his eyes, his hair, the crook of his mouth. He was arrayed in his Shräud, but did not consider removing it. Its illusion remained damaged, weak, but its hue was still deceptive, allowing him some subtlety in the dark ravines and fissures of the Dragongrave's underworld.

Far, farther, farthest; the path drew on, down ridges of great black and grey stone, the still, silent walls rising overhead, blotting out the high sun of midday. They stretched and thinned without reason, wide as a city thoroughfare, slim as a thief's alley. They looked as if they could be the shelves of an ancient river, carved by its running. In a way they were, but the river ran with greed, giving no life, leaving only a withered husk as it dried, a hollow canyon, a scar in memory of what once was but was no longer.

His route was the trade route of old, on which Arythos once thrived, that purpose a thing that was also no longer. He knew the route well, had walked it often, each journey calm, eventless. There were men who roved in the depths of the Vale even then, searching for treasure, but their influence was regulated, kept above the line of banditry by the sentinels of Arythos for the sake of the traders and travelers they protected.

That was before the Devouring, before the fall of the great kingdom, of the world west of the Wōadglōam Forest. Now the Vale was regulated by the Fēl, outlaws at the edge of the world. If he was fortunate, Aëros would not cross them on his road, for the Fēl had no purpose in surveying it, knowing none were fool enough to walk its length, knowing that the dragon's troves lay nowhere near it—the very reason for its founding as a trader and traveler's passage.

But in the end fortune favored the wise, and Aëros was foolhardy. He knew it, the world knew it, and soon the Fēl would know it too.

———— ◆ ————

The first six days in the Vale were uneventful. The heat rose with the sun, swelling, stifling, making his every stride a labor. When day died and night drew on, the heat faltered, a brittle, hollow cold mantling the stone in its place. So Aëros walked during the liminal hours between each, ate poorly when he settled down, slept well when he settled in—his hammock holding him aloft the stone, quilts warming him when the frost of night tried to creep into his bones.

It was the seventh day that nearly killed him.

It was temperate, a time between the moon's slumber and the sun's reign, the undercroft of the Vale dark only due to its depth and distance from the surface world. The sense of unease came as it always did—with little warning—for it was instinct, and the instinct itself was the warning. Something shifted in the way the air hung around him, his hair lifting as if tugging him toward the disturbance, the constant sound of wind tunneling through the Vale somehow different, hesitant, waiting.

Up the walls of the scar he climbed, rising into its ridges, passing layer after layer of stone webbing and winding between the walls, binding them together, creating a labyrinth in the heights, like the bones of some ancient beast, buried.

High, higher, highest he ascended, keeping a wyrmseye on the scar, gliding with a raven's grace from one perch to another. His instincts swelled as he climbed, thrumming in him. It wasn't a thing taught—the knowing of one's own doom—only learned through experience of many almost-deaths and some mostly-deaths. The more often the knowing appeared, the more natural its augury became. He saw nothing, heard nothing, felt only the primal instincts hidden within him snap awake, sharpening his awareness of the world, honed by repetition of use.

Ash ringed him as he halted his ascent somewhere in the mid-ranges of the ridges, stories above the undercroft, stories below the Dragongrave. Still, he heard nothing, saw nothing. He stooped onto a bridge that bound the ridges of the scar together. He traversed it, stepping with silent stealth, Shräud blending him into the stone as it undulated and twisted beneath him, sharp, thin, severe spines protruding from its sway at regular spaces. His hand lighted on one as he passed, and the stone sheared away in his grasp. He studied the shard. Its symmetry was marvelous: rounded at its peak, tapering to a wicked point beneath. He blew dust and weather from it, revealing a layer of iridescence. He held it still, glittering in the dark, blending with the ashen stone, his eyes opening, understanding that what he held was not a stone.

It's a scale.

Aëros leapt, drawing Löekeh from the hidden sheath of Nowhere and shifting blade to bow as talons ripped through the air where he'd been. He leapt away, found more approaching from the side, leapt again—too slow. They wound up in his Shräud as it trailed before him in his backwards dodge, shearing through the tear Shaē had only just patched, completely unraveling the raiment's illusion. He cursed, and leapt away from another flurry. He landed along the wall of the ridge, catching himself on a sliver of stone, pulling himself up, a perch a raven alone could alight on.

131

With an arrow nocked beneath his eye, flickering with black, luminescent light, he waited.

Dust gathered around what he'd disturbed, its eyes all that pierced the ashen cloud, meeting his. Suddenly they shuddered, surprised, confusion running through them as Aëros' pair of eyes became many. He shimmered, divided into phantoms, mimics of his stride, his form, his grace and going. He wove the needle of his will through them, threads of Dräu obliging, scattering along the walls of the Vale, the winding stone binding ridge to ridge, throwing the beast hidden by dust into a frantic anxiety, uncertain, bewildered.

Aëros held his arrow, though his perch was now perch to an illusion, his own higher, safer. He watched the beast's eyes race, meeting each of his phantom's, meeting his. He held the eyes as the dust floated and fell. When it faded, revealing the beast, he laughed in wonder, lowering his bow, arrow disappearing soft and deathless as he slid Löekeh's string slack, his phantoms evanescing, needless.

"Bone drake," he said as the beast coiled around the opposing ridge, groaning as its claws sunk into the ashen stone it hid itself against and within. "I really am going threadbare."

Stone splintered and fractured, falling, crashing into the darkness of the undercroft below. The dust of Ages trickled from the curves and ridges of the ancient beast as it limbered the inaction of intentional stillness away. Aëros watched in fascination the half-ancestor of the dragons, wreathed in an illusion of stone as he'd once been wreathed in the illusion of his Shräud.

The bone drake's body appeared to be layered by an external skeleton, a skull resting atop flesh, its own skull beneath. In truth, its outer hide *had* once been a skeleton, the bones not its own but another's, bones of ancestry, fused to its hide, petrified with time. Females wore the bones of their mothers, males the bones of their fathers. This was a male drake, its colors bleak, wearing the bones of its sire like a knight wore the armor of his own. Whether out of

132

reverence or resentment, out of binding or betrayal, no scholar knew. Aëros considered this—from the perspective of a father; from the perspective of a son. He wore the bones of his, Tärin the bones of him. He wondered what came with the bones. Was it the wisdom of age? Or the failures? Was there a difference? What bones of a son were his father's? What bones of a son were his own?

Aëros stood now, the instinct of death threading him, wondering if Tärin would grow as familiar with it as he was, as arrogant. He stood, knowing down in the deepest hollows of his ancestral memory that the answer was yes, yes of course. Tärin would learn those instincts, had already begun. To consider otherwise would be the self-deceit of a father fooling himself into the hope of his son's safety, as his father had fooled himself, as all fathers did. He considered again the perspective of a son, of his own father, of the drake before him, of the death in the stories beneath him. It set him at ease, a single thread of certain sanity amidst the fabric of his madness, warm, comforting.

The drake's serpentine head rose, seeking, searching. It writhed, a low rumble thrumming in its chest, shivering the stone, the muscles beneath the bone hide tensing, coiled; ready, afraid. The drake was no predator, a gentle thing merely surprised by a foolish elf. In its fear its own instincts leapt alive, scenting death on him: of the vesta fed him by his friend; of the vesta he himself slew in the Fells; of Sif; of the Lësh'unn; of Athair. All the lives he'd taken, lost, and still had left to reap; the death of his sanity; the death of which he reeked. The drake stilled itself, seeing that he was still, sensing that though he was both responsible for and harrowed by death, he neither sought nor reaped it aimlessly. The rumbling softened, disappeared, the tension in its body relaxing.

"There, there. Hush, hush." Aëros shifted on his perch, eye to eye with the ancient beast. "I am only passing through; a fool in a foolish place to be." He pointed ahead, to the far edge of the Vale where he would leave the boneyard behind and enter into ruin,

133

into mountain, into memory. "I have a long way yet to go. Farewell."

He made to descend, then halted, instinct of death screaming at him. He looked to the bone drake, measuring it, and saw that its own instinct hadn't left either. His eyes sharpened and widened as his thoughts swiftened. "Why were you hiding?" His realization crystallized, understanding weaving neatly into the fabric of his instinct. "Fool."

The drake roared as an arrow punched between the riveting of petrified bone-plate, ripping through its back, its craggy maw chipping in its wrath. It was not the flickering luminescence of an arrow drawn from Nowhere, but the simple fletching of feather and wood and knapped glass. Aëros' eyes flicked to the ridgeline above and saw silhouettes against the dimming sky. The drake saw only him, felt only its instincts.

It lunged, piercing through the air like an arrow itself, diving toward him. He dove, dropping a story to a thin bridge of stone, many stories beneath. The drake was recovering, searching for the one it thought sought its death. Aëros crouched, hidden behind a spire of stone, no longer hidden by his Shräud, measuring the ridgeline, watching the silhouettes trace their way along it, searching themselves, hunting. *No, not hunting. Poaching.* He set his will to work, intending phantoms. There was no time; the sky overhead was already flecked with death. *Fuck.*

Arrows tore down into the Vale. Aëros leapt away, descending another story—two—three—errant shafts clattering against the stone overhead. The drake crashed down above him, eyes finding his in their fall, burning with the hatred of betrayal, the nooks and niches of its armor riddled with well-placed arrows. He swore as the beast dragged the stone down around him, dragging him down with it.

Wyrm and Ayl tumbled into the undercroft together, the beast railing out, seeking death, the elf conflicted, seeking to avoid it. The drake's tail lashed, whipping through the air, a visceral point tipping it. Aëros pulled himself taut, spinning away as he fell, the undercroft speeding towards them, ground crumpling under the weight of the drake is it crashed down. Aëros landed soundlessly, rolling out the little momentum he carried, falling like a feather from an arrow's fletching. He knelt, poised, dust pluming up around the drake, masking it.

The air cracked, the drake lunging from its veil, maw gaping, tail flicking forward. Aëros leapt up, placing foot on tip, leaping again as it passed beneath him, somersaulting forward, opening from the tuck, landing on the snout of the drake, mounting it, Löekeh wielded, arrow drawn, nocked, level with the beast's eyes, hesitating. He searched them for some measure of peace, hoping for some proof that if he withdrew, so too would it. But he saw only its fear, and knew that neither hope nor will would remedy anything now.

He stood sidelong, bow drawn as the arrow wisped through the air. Not an arrow wrought of black light, but of feather, wood, knapped glass. He heard the slithering sound of slit flesh as it tore across his neck and passed by, ripping through the drake's eye. He stumbled back as a second arrow rode the wind of the first, splitting the shaft down its center, severing the drake's brain stem. He watched it pass, watched it robin the first, and thought to himself: *Wyrmseye.*

The drake writhed, spasmed, fell still. He fell from it, clutching his throat, collapsing into the darkness of the undercroft, his mind in turn collapsing into the darkness of itself. Not from blood loss. He knew what that felt like—the Lësh'unn his latest lesson. *A paralytic.*

Limbs limp from the toxin, consciousness fading, Aëros caught the drake's eyes, the strange look of lifelessness in them reflecting the hollowness of his. In that hollowness he found his fear of death, not for death itself, but for what he'd leave behind, for what he might become, was becoming already.

135

He was not dying now, not as he had been in the muck and mire of the wōadglōam's outskirts. Now he was merely disappearing into the darkness of his mind. It was swallowing him, devouring him. From the periphery of that darkness walked the Shadow, a guide to uncertainty, a shade of insanity, leading him away from the madness of its making, or perhaps further on, a reminder of what he'd lost, of what he'd lose, leave behind if he did not make it to the end. It knelt beside him, pulled his hand from his neck, and showed the promise woven into the flesh of his finger, the promise death would break, the pain that would bring. He stared at the ring, at the Shadow, at the reflection in the drake's dead, empty eyes, seeing only one thing for certain— himself.

Chapter XIV: Orphan
• Dreaming of Summer •

Aëros groaned as he awoke. *Awoke.* He remembered the Vale; the drake; death. But there was no death, not for him. He was not on the other side of that veil. He was here.

Where?

Darkness.

His eyes opened. The darkness did not leave, but it lessened. It was night, the sky overcast, weak moonlight struggling through. His vision was murky, as if seen through streaked glass or muddled waters. His hearing swam. All his senses were muffled. With his dim sight he saw a faint flicker of warm light, around which shadows roved. A faint sound echoed through the deep waters of his grogginess—the sound of fools reveling.

He focused on his limbs; they were leaden, each motion of muscle restricted and aimless. He willed movement into them, and found his arms were outstretched, manacled to chains lashed somewhere above him, and his legs bound together, forcing him to his knees.

Sight and hearing slipped back, the threads of his thoughts weaving together. The murk faded to his periphery, blinding only what lay beyond his immediate sight. He measured the open-mouthed cavern in which he was prisoner; the rusted chains coiling across his arms; the fools rounding the fire beyond, smoke billowing up, drafting in; the silhouette of an old man squatting before him, measuring him.

Aëros' watcher blended into the world like the dust of ages, surprising him as he seemed to materialize from that dust. He blinked, wondering if the old man was just a hallucination caused by the paralytic mixing with his madness. When the man remained, he decided it did not matter, and tried to speak. His throat was dry and cracked. He choked, coughed, tasting the iron of blood dried to his throat. He remembered the arrow, the sensation of skin opening across his neck. The wound ached, felt tight, the telltale discomfort of newly sewn sutures, of another almost-death healing. Significant, but not lethal. He would wear this one without illusion, a sign that said, *I walk with death.* Which in turn would say to some, *stay away*, and to others, *come and get me.*

A new light flickered into creation; a tawny lantern. It limned the cavern, the gaol, casting shadows in its clefts and crevices, its hidden hollows and hoary webs. The old man cradled it, his silhouette revealed, watching. He was cloaked and barely visible in the weak light, his own crevices and hoary webbing making him seem kindred to the cavern, as if wrought of the stone himself, hidden in it like the drake.

Aëros' eyes widened, roaming the camp, questing, then grew sorrowful as they found their fear. There, rotting beneath the roof of another cavern, lay the hide of the bone drake. His anger stirred. There were too few of the gentle creatures left in the world, far too few to be so pettily poached. They were timid beasts, hunted to the point of extinction. He felt the blood in him roil, felt his teeth grinding, felt the paralytic wearing thinner and thinner. When he found freedom from it, so too would he find freedom from these gaolers, these fools. Eyes fettered to the deceased drake, Aëros tried to speak again to the old man, now in the murk of his periphery. Again, no words escaped; only pain.

The man stood and stepped forward, careful to keep a cautious distance from the imprisoned beast. As he drew up from the shadows and brought the light nearer his face, the crags of his age solidified, revealing not just an old man, but an elder: weary, prideless, grim. He was missing an eye, but did not need both to see.

"Patience." His voice sounded like a river-worn stone looked—smooth, passive, wise for its wearing, slightly muffled beneath his long, tangled beard. "Here." He lifted a waywell from his belt, tilting it into Aëros' mouth. It was cold, musty. It helped.

"You're Fē—" Aëros sputtered, hacking.

The elder's mouth twisted up into an unreadable expression. He offered more water, drained some himself. "Fēl. Yes."

Kill them.

Aëros looked for the Shadow, and found it sitting on a stone around the campfire, another silhouette against its blaze, as if kin to the men who reveled around it. It was staring into the flames, then turned, and stared into him. *Kill them.* The words weren't the wraith's. They were his. This comforted him, and the Shadow looked back into the embers of the fire, knowing.

The elder spoke. "I'm not surprised you know us. Likely know all the other questions that start with the first letter of the first of your names, too." He smiled, wily. "Wayfarer."

Aëros turned his eyes back to the drake. "You didn't have to kill it."

The elder frowned and shook his head, disappointed. "You're saying that out of guilt. Your fault we even happened across it."

"You were poaching."

Another shake of the head. "We were hunting; luck has it we ended up hunting a drake." He gave Aëros a deliberate look, meeting his eyes. "Don't think luck brought you into the mix, though. Not for the drake at least."

Aëros considered the elder's words and found himself agreeing. His anger *was* for himself. The drake was safe—hidden well. Even his elven sight hadn't descried it, yet it was his footfall that disturbed it, revealing it in its fear of being found and its kind made fewer. It hadn't been Aëros' arrow that took it in the end, but it might as well have been. Its death was his fault, his burden. He raised his eyes to the drake's, and though they were lifeless, he held them, speaking to them. *It's a worthless gesture, but I'm sorry.*

"I wouldn't have had it this way," said the elder, his own regret clear. He looked up; to a murder of rooks and ravens circling the encampment; to the other men, running around the campfire in the ignorance of youth. "The young pay no mind to death. No concern or consideration for it." He turned back to Aëros, his eyes speaking before words even met his lips. "Wayfarer. Wanderer Betwixt and Between Worlds," he paused, deliberately, letting the silence hone his next words to a fine edge. "Slayer of Death."

Aëros smirked. Not in pride, but in challenge to the doom that last name seemed to set on him.

"Or the Devourer's Bane, if you prefer."

Aëros' smirk widened, answer enough.

The elder leaned back on his haunches and lifted his chin. "Is yours the confidence of the wise man or the foolhardy?"

Aëros laughed softly, and spoke, softer. "Is it ever anything other than both?"

The elder thought for a moment, smiled, then wandered back to the mouth of the cave and squatted on something dark. "These men don't much care for your names. Most of them haven't even heard of you." He gestured to the rabble behind him. "I fear even if they did, they wouldn't know better. Wouldn't know to respect myth when the maker of 'em wanders in."

Aëros shrugged, chains rattling, shoulders rolling uninhibited, muscles loosening, warming up. "My names don't mean or matter much but to my own ego and arrogance."

The elder gave him the sort of look a grandparent gives their grandchild when they've caught them at something their parents— the wisdom still not in them—never have. "We both know that's only a half-truth." He leaned forward. "There's some who know you all too well. Some," he leaned forward further, "to whom those names hold more worth in ransom than a dragon's hoard."

Aëros' smirk shifted into a sneer. "True. My wife is one."

"Aūriel," the elder mused, a statement of certainty, no threat in the naming. "She has more tales rimming her life than you do, Wayfarer." His smile was brimming. "I know there's an empty socket under that illusion of a pretty face. I know those who took it

140

sent it to your Aūriel with a ransom request." He leaned in, looking side to side with his own solitary eye, whispering. "I heard she drew the last images that eye saw out of it, seeing all too well where you were being held. The gang who sought to ransom you found their bones torn and scattered in more ways than the dead littering the fields above our heads."

Aëros acknowledged the truth of the ridiculous story, believing it, even though he had no memory of it but for the hollow of one sightless socket. The elder looked at him, grinning. "You've my respect for wedding a woman who can see everywhere you've been just by reading your eyes, Wayfarer."

A long moment lingered between them, as if they were each waiting to see if Aūriel would appear from Nowhere with the wrath of a woman listening to two men whispering over her. When the moment passed, it passed into laughter, the mingling mirth of men knowing the terrifying wit of their women in mutual empathy. Aëros' smirk curled back into its habitual place, knowing that no woman's wit, wile, or wisdom would ever match his Aūriel's. Still, he let the old man enjoy his fantasy.

The laugher of both fell from its rumble, faded, evanesced into comfortable silence. The prisoner filled it. "There's a skinweaver in the east who pays well for elven blood as pure as mine. Isn't often he's able to get his hands on the life essence of the Last of the First of the First. His crew calls in at Crescent Cove every fortnight. I'd refer my ransoming to them."

The elder nodded, as if assured of something he'd already known well, and stood, revealing what he'd been squatting on: a small chest. He unlatched the lid, opened it, and drew a piece of raiment from its hoard. Aëros' raiment. Aëros' Shräud. The elder lifted it as if it were a thing of reverence, an artifact belonging to a myth. It appeared now as little more than a grey, weatherworn cloak with no notable feature. The drake had shorn through its threads, unraveling its illusion entirely, revealing him from his hiding even as he revealed it; the only difference in the revelation being that it ended with him breathing, and the drake skinned. He flicked his eyes to the carcass, then flicked them back to the Shräud. It was unrecognizable as the artifact it truly was, unrecognizable save for the fact that it came cloaking the myth for whom it was made. He realized it was patched again with thread and cloth, as Shaē had done, and found it strange.

"I did my best to mend it," the elder said, lofting the cloak. He pointed to Aëros' neck. "Did my best to mend you too. Not much skill with needle and thread though. Not a physician, seamstress, nor Arkaēn." He looked the patchwork over, the simple stitching, and shrugged. "Shräud. Such an archaic word." He pointed at the Wayfarer, the elf, the Ayl, last of the Last of the First. "Means shadow in the old languages. Which is what those who seek to divest you of your freedom mean when they say you're 'like trying to catch shadow in a dark room.' Or so I've heard said from the same sort who told me of your damsel most distressing."

Aëros' eyes glinted, amused both for himself and for his Aūriel. *Damsel most distressing*. He knew she'd like that. "And so your words loft the monolith of my ego and my arrogance, already colossal, ever higher. If you add any more to the mountain, you'll need a sherpa to summit it."

The elder placed the Shräud back into the chest, walked over to Aëros, and knelt down, eye to eye, at a safe distance. "Never was a fan of mountains. Learned young what they can take from a man. Know well enough not to climb yours." He looked over his shoulder, looked at the revel and raving circling the fire, the youth and their ignorance, looked up to the rooks and ravens, circling, and looked back at Aëros. "Know enough to know your names and that I'd do well to mind them. Fair, foul, false, and some too true to find anything but fear in."

Aëros held the elder's eyes as he held the burden of his madness: with something between reverence and hatred. There was no dragon-sickness in them like there was in most men who stalked the Dragongrave. Just the memory of it. A youth long passed into wisdom. "You don't look afraid."

"You don't look frightening." The elder swallowed in unconscious unease. "I've heard many whispers of you, Aëros. Many tavern tales."

"I'm certain."

The elder studied the Wayfarer, searching. "Some have you dead for a long while."

Aëros' eyes narrowed, searching himself. "Do I look dead to you?"

The elder narrowed his own eyes, and stroked his beard down to its tail, finding the answer at its end. "Parts of you, yes." He stood up, and turned before Aëros could respond. "Doesn't matter. Let these fools learn of you if they must. It might be youthful rashness wins it out over you, but I wouldn't wager on it. The rooks and the ravens will be pleased regardless." He turned back and met Aëros' eyes for half a heartbeat, as if reassuring himself of something, the one—sightless but seeing—lingering a little longer than the other.

Aëros might have asked what the elder saw in his eyes. But he knew, knew the man had seen it as soon as Aëros awoke, for the eyes hid nothing, if one knew how to see. Still, if Aëros had asked, the man would have said, *They've got the look of a man who's forgotten himself and far too many other things besides.* He'd say, *I won't have any part in helping you remember.* But he didn't need to say these things; instead he simply shouldered a pack and strode over the threshold of Aëros' gaol into the night, lantern flickering at his side as he went, speaking words other than his eyes would have said. "Farewell, Wayfarer. Until we meet again."

"Farewell," Aëros echoed, the word a whisper, given in reverence. The lost lantern light left Aëros in darkness, and through it he looked to the Shadow. *Let's be done with this. Let's not linger, isn't that right?*

Silence.

Aëros was swiftly regaining sensation in his body, his hands and fingers yet to awaken, still slumbering, even now. But it would not be long. So, he waited, and while he waited, he watched.

First of all the things he noticed was that the elder had left the chest behind. He understood what that meant, but didn't understand the reason; didn't try to. His attention slid to the night beyond his cavern, beyond his gaol, to the men circling the flames as if in mimicry of the rooks and ravens circling overhead, scenting death on the updrafts. A sliver of moonlight beamed down through a break in the overcast night, the rain in the air hesitating. The ray illumined the camp, if camp it could be called.

Sat in a hidden nook worn out of the ridges by wind, weather, and age, the encampment's only egress was an arch splitting the encircling stone ridge in two. Its only lodging stood in the form of two shoddy shacks built from bone, surrounding the flames the Fēl themselves surrounded, the campfire more a bonefire for the fuel that fed it.

Some men were drinking, some dealing cards, some throwing dice, some playing pinfinger. Aëros' mind filled with a memory of his friend's words: "*A vice for you, a vice for he, and a vice for me, with sanity found betwixt the three.*" It filled with the memory of his reply next: "*That doesn't make any sense.*" He wondered who'd said that, knew he couldn't remember if he tried.

It appeared the men did not care to mind him as he was minding them. He was bound and could not flee. They could enjoy their revel, their night, and deal with him on the morrow. Once he would have simply walked as a wraith from the fetters of his bonds. His way out would be harder now than it would've been then, but it would amount to the same thing in the end. He smiled as sensation returned to his hands, as he set his will on his ring, his key to many things, freedom found.

His eyes widened almost to the point of tearing, pupils dilating even in the dark, devouring it, betraying the hollow in his heart carved out by a new, horrific realization.

144

Pain, dull, aching, impossible to miss now that he was aware of it, radiating from his left hand, masked before by the paralytic. He shuffled his fingers—thumb, index, middle...

His ring finger was missing.

No, that was unimportant. Fingers could be replaced. His ring, his soul, the key to his promise, to the memory of it, could not. His finger had grown into the roots and hollows of its artifice, time binding it to his flesh. It was gone. His head lashed up, gaze piercing forward, tearing through the darkness like an arrow through a wyrm's eye, perceiving the men ringing the flames. The Fēl had taken it—finger and all.

Kill them.

The voice in his mind was bestial. It left him, echoing out in a horrible scream. "WHERE IS IT!" He lashed forward, joints cracking as he heaved his way toward the threshold of the cavern, the threshold of his gaol, memories not yet lost flashing through his mind's eye, desperate to remain, to be remembered. "*WHERE IS IT!*" His teeth gnashed, his wrath restricted only by his bindings, rust dusting from his chains as he railed against them.

Fear raced alongside his memories. *What if they've sold it?* He realized they hadn't had time to do so. *What if they've lost it?* He stirred, seeing his gaolers for what they were in this moment: drunken fools traipsing round an open fire, careless, carefree. The idea was galling, but what was lost could be recovered. *What if they ruined it, the engraving, the promise?* This was the one eventuality he could not rationalize away, could not bring himself to bear. *Always forward. Always on. I'll forget. I'll forget. Aūriel. Tārin.* "WHERE IS IT! WHERE IS IT! WHERE IS IT!"

His Shadow was standing before him now, knowing his thoughts, saying nothing. Aūriel's words echoed in his mind, repeating so as to not be forgotten. *Always forward. Always on. Always forward. Always on. Always forward—*

"WHERE IS IT! *WHERE IS IT!* **WHERE IS IT!**"

He was seething, breathing hard, ragged, hollow. His head was bowed, limbs limp, sweat pooling around him from his rage. He knew, somewhere beneath the panic, that he was being foolish. Succumbing to worry and woe would not free him from this prison. It would not return him to his ring. He tried to turn from the raging, primal emotion. Tried to take what little wisdom lingered within him and wrap himself in it for sanctuary, and found humor therein. *For nine is all I know!* He tried to calm himself, tried to keep the wrath buried.

It boiled over, again and again and again, bursting from its burial, refusing to rest, to wait, and so—

"WHERE IS IT! WHERE IS IT! WHERE IS IT!"

The ache in his left hand flared, the terror of what it meant searing, the thought of what he might not get back, what he might forget, what was taken from him, and who had taken it, repeating over and over and over again.

Kill them.

The Fēl were order-less, honor-less, anarchic. The strongest killed with strength, the weakest killed with wile, the daftest killed with luck. They were fools. They were rash. *They will all die, forgotten.*

He realized his eyes were shuttered, slammed shut. He heard a noise in the night. It was murky, like when he'd first woken from his paralysis, and he realized he'd merely retreated within himself, the outside world muddled as he tried to bury his mind within his mind. His hearing sharpened, elven instincts acting without being willed. He heard yelling, grumbling, the sounds of irritated men stumbling to the source of some disaster. Beneath these sounds he heard the source to which they ran, as his mind returned to the waking world, as his eyes peeled open. He heard himself, screaming. *"WHERE IS IT! WHERE IS IT! WHERE IS—"*

A hand struck him, knuckles dragging across his jaw, and in the muffling of his madness he heard the faint voice of a man telling him to *shut the fuck up*. He blinked, focused, found the eyes

146

of the man level with his. He was kneeling, tapping the side of his face as if to stir him from his mania. "Oi!" *Tap-tap-tap.* "What the *fuck* are you on about?" *Tap-tap-tap.*

Aëros stirred out of his madness, focusing on the man. *Tap-tap-tap* went his hand. "You fuckin' there mate?" went his words, his voice all gravel and grit, filled up with arrogance. *Tap—tap—* Aëros bit down on the hand, tearing away a chunk of flesh as the man yanked it away. The *tap-tap-tap* became a *thwack-thwack-thwack.*

Aëros' head spun, eyes rolling back to kilter. "You know, you shouldn't pull away from a bite. You're supposed to lean in and—" *Thwack-thwack—*

Another man reached out, stopping the strikes. Aëros fell into focus, and found it was no man, but a boy, no more than twelve. *Near old as Tärin.* "Bäs—"

The man—Bäs, it would seem—tore his hand from the boy's grip, scowling. The boy flinched, faltered, and fell back into shadow. Bäs turned back to Aëros, grinning horribly but keeping his distance, careful not to stumble into the embrace of a man on the verge of insanity, like a wounded animal forced into a corner, desperate and determined that if it was to die, so too would everything around it—friend, foe, or otherwise.

The boy walked over to the man, calm, cautious, and stood beside him, watching Aëros watching him. The other Fēl still stood round the bonefire, dark silhouettes under dim moonlight, surrounding dying embers and flickering coals, watching with hard, silent eyes as the rooks and ravens circled above.

Bäs, the boy, and the men settled in darkness all measured Aëros while he measured them. He saw each of them, every detail: from their outer trappings to the selves they were each so desperate to hide from discernment. The eyes hid nothing, the soul within them always. Theirs were the souls of the forsaken, the lost, the unwanted. Aëros knew them well. They were kindred to his, after a fashion. He wondered what they saw in him.

Kill them.

It was a disparate group, fragmentary, nonsensical, a mosaic of lost men unfit for society by their own saying so. Skin both swarthy and ashen; eyes both weary and tireless; scars; wounds—open and sealed; lost limbs; finery and poverty; hatred and indifference; the naïve and the not-yet-wizened. The Fēl.

Move on.

The Shadow skulked around the men, stalking, looking over their shoulders as it looked to Aëros, following the same ominous, ouroboric path as the murder of black birds above.

Aëros was speaking, whispering. Bäs leaned in, listened. "Where. *Is. It.*"

Aëros lunged as far as his bindings allowed. Bäs recoiled and stepped back, avoiding his prisoner's gnashing teeth. *Thwack-thwack-thwack.*

Aëros' head fell limp. "You must be fuckin' threadbare." Bäs was breathing heavily, adrenaline raging. He gripped Aëros by the chin, dragged the Wayfarer's eyes to his, then found his stare held by them, dominated by them even as he was free and Aëros imprisoned. He disregarded the sickening sense of subordination and drew out a familiar blade. *Löekeh.*

Bäs' grin was verging on manic. "Where's what?" Metal touched flesh as he held Aëros' own weapon to his throat. "This, maybe?"

"Bäs!" The boy reached out, trying to rein in the arrogant man's fury. *The boy's an orphan.* Aëros didn't know how he knew that, only that he did. Then he realized the boy reminded him of someone. *Athair.* Orphaned himself, the same age as this boy when the raven died. Aëros looked at the man before him. *This is his father.*

Bäs recoiled, slamming the back of his hand across the boy's face, sending him sprawling over the chest still sitting at the mouth

148

of the cave. *Or father figure.* He spun back and squatted to Aëros' level, Löekeh poised, hand searching beneath his shirt, drawing out something on a chain. "Well then…" The weak killed with wile, and it seemed this one had wile in plenty. "Maybe this?"

The arrogant, youthful, naïve man lofted what he hid beneath his shirt, its metal bloodstained, teasing it, saying no more of it. The moonlight glinted onto it, swallowed up by the wyrmstone woven throughout. He treated it like a trinket, a thing of worth no greater than the metal it was forged from. Aëros stared at what the man saw only as wealth, seeing himself a key: to his promise; to his memories; to many things—freedom the apotheosis of all.

Bäs swung the trinket before Aëros, too far. He was arrogant. He was naïve. He was young, and the young paid no mind to death. Only the wizened, the rooks, and the ravens.

The boy leapt from the ground in stubborn fury, wrathful, and shoved Bäs from behind, a son wearing the bones of his father, bound up in them and too young to know it. The arrogant man's eyes widened as he lurched forward, lurched over the rim, lurched within reach.

Aëros lunged, biting down on the ring. He bared his teeth like a wolf's, ring concealed in his mouth, chain bit beneath fangs, holding the weight of the arrogant, ignorant man on its length, predator and prey. The clouds opened, the rain fell, rooks and ravens descending with it, and then—

Darkness.

Chapter XV: Things Betwixt
• Dreaming of Summer •

"*I told him of Athair. Of Thrace. He won't leave.*" The Rift binding the forest to your bedroom flickered soundlessly, disturbing little more than the threads of reality, a gentle wind the only lingering disturbance. It shimmered and knit back together, the seam in reality sealed.

She made room on the bed, her silver hair brilliant in the moonlight filtering in over the terrace. You walked over and lay down. She pulled you close, held your eyes with hers. "*Did you expect him to?*"

A tear ran. She brushed it away, smiling, bittersweet. "*No,*" you said, the word heavy. "*But I hoped.*"

You looked away from her, out over the terrace, beyond the villa, to the forest, to the Dragongrave, to Arythos. "*We'll take refuge in Jä's villa. We'll be safe in the kingdom. It will hold against the horde. At least until I can speak with Athair and reason with him.*"

Reason? A frail hope. You knew he was beyond that. Athair was coming, and hope wouldn't forestall what he would bring, reason wouldn't prevent him from bringing it. It was your betrayal that began his war on the world, and by betrayal would it end, hope pouring away.

She pulled you back to her, kissed you. "*I would be happy if I died today, my Aëros.*"

Smiling, you echoed her. "*As would I, my Aūriel.*"

"*If the worst should happen,*" you said, solemn, "*Jä will lead you to the Rift atop the mountain. Your song fits the lock woven into it. It'll open for you.*"

She nestled into you and held your hand, feeling over your ring, touching her own to it, the roots of each melding with the roots of the other. "*Do you remember how we met?*"

You laughed. "*Aūriel, how could I ever forget?*"

Aëros stared at his ring as the memory faded, the warm sense of having remembered polluted by the sickening sense of something forgotten, festering with all the little unnerving narrations the Shadow added, reminding him that his madness was tied to his memory, memory to madness, a fabric of insanity. How they were tied, well, he'd beaten that question into the mires of redundancy. 'How' would be known at the end, his first and only priority to make it alive, for to make it in one piece was a feat he'd already failed at.

His missing finger ached, clotted and dull. His neck was tight, the skin poorly healed. The rain fell overhead, gone from a downpour to a patter, drawing his dried blood into the desiccated stone underfoot. He salivated, and spit red onto the Ashen Vale. *Thirsty?* Joints creaking, he limbered and fell into stride, resuming his journey where the Fēl had held it up.

The Fēl. When the dawn came, he'd already been up and away, seeking the old trade route. He tried to recall how he'd escaped his capture, remembered only the arrogant man dangling his ring before him, his son's betrayal, and then—darkness. It seemed the darkness had taken the memories, his rage sending him into a dissociative fugue. Whatever happened, he'd been able to flee, and without a trace of the Fēl on his heels. Apart from his wounds, he was safe. He wondered if the entire event was a hallucination, but the throbbing pain in his finger and throat said otherwise.

He lifted his marred hand, studying it. He'd recovered his skeleton key, sitting now upon an artificial finger formed of the Argynt that in turn formed the ring, his will shaping the enchanted metal into a simulacrum of each, his promise not yet forgotten, now truly a part of his flesh, metal though it be. The false finger worked as well as any of bone and blood, and would make for a decent chapter once the story was through.

A shadow walked in his periphery, his shadow, *the* Shadow— studying him. He turned to it, and found its eyes roving through his, searching. He heard a caw from above, and saw the same rooks and ravens from the Fēl encampment circling above him. They were intelligent beasts, as smart as any seven-year-old sapient. They often hunted with wolf packs, serving as the wolves' sight over the landscape, seeking prey and leading them to it, developing a symbiosis between predator and scavenger. Staring at them, he wondered which they thought he was: predator, or scavenger, or prey.

* * *

Aëros tarried only once in seeking the trade route, to cleanse his slit throat and to cauterize the root of his ruined finger. He assumed the elder had stitched him up, as he had his Shräud. He'd done a decent job of each, and the wound would at least heal well enough. His finger was something else, a piece of himself lost. He found some sick sense of pride in it, and thought back to the humor he'd found in the Fēl's encampment: *For nine is all I know!* Nine no longer, the song now singing eight for him forever after. He didn't mind.

Thus mended, it took him less than a day to find the old trade route in the center of the Ashen Vale. He'd been walking along the midmost layers of the scar, following the stone bridges binding wall to wall, sliding along narrow ledges, like a bird of prey, searching, the rooks and ravens overhead, circling. He was cautious, keeping a focused eye out for suspicious stone or signs of men. He found neither in his going, but still had a way yet to go before he met the western egress of the Vale.

He had two choices before him once again: to continue on the old trade route, or to take his shortcut. The latter would be safer, swifter, soon to arrive at. But it would also be silent and solitary, leaving him alone with himself, his mind, and his madness.

It was a hard choice, but the Vale had been the easy one, and he'd nearly lost everything to it. He knew he'd indulged his

153

humanity enough, that if he kept testing it eventually it would fail him. So he descended to the gutter of the Vale and headed slightly off the trade route, making the hard decision.

Half a day walked by as he searched for the shortcut, knowing it was near, if memory served him. He laughed at the thought, scanning the walls of the scar as he went, searching for the tell-tale sign of ever-so-slightly discolored stone which would betray the hidden threshold.

It was a secret he'd discovered in his youth, long before he could walk through the worlds as he willed, longer still before he'd lost that mastery. In a way it was a foreshadowing of him finding such knowledge in the first place, his curiosity as essential to his nature as Shaë's kindness was to his. That nature led him to many discoveries, some newfound, many long forgotten. This one was of the latter, a hidden passage hewn beneath the Dragongrave even before the grasslands took on that mantle, by a people Aëros himself knew nothing of, even before his forgetting began. He chose to leave some secrets secret, the world more wonderful for its mysteries.

The ouroboros of curiosity brought him what he was looking for as the sun was setting, the shadows already softening and the day's heat fading to brittle, boreal cold. He stopped in a place that seemed placeless, as like to any other part of the Vale he'd yet passed. But only to the unskilled and unknowing eye, to the eye that did not seek for something that it should not expect, knowing that was where something often was. The sun slid another degree below the horizon, the subtle shift in light revealing a slight discoloration in the shape of an arch set against the wall. Aëros set his will on it, the stone shimmering, soft and ethereal, a silver outline etching the discolored arch into a doorway. As the threads woven into the stone unraveled, the outline brightened, refined, revealing a painting of the Wyrmspine, its peaks set beneath a sea of stars falling away from the forever-shattered moon, Valrävn clutching it as it died.

Flickering, flaring, fading, the doorway shifted from stone to nothingness as if the stone had never been, the entrance to Aëros' secret revealed as the gate departed to Nowhere for a time. He stood a moment before the opening in the stone, the opening into what he named the Things Betwixt; its true name, if it had one, long lost.

It was a hypogean network of interlinking passageways that ran the entire breadth of Eave, a labyrinth under the skin of the world, stretching beneath grasslands, mountains, forests, even the sea. He'd mapped much of it, and much more was still unknown to him; he remembered what he'd recorded of what he'd explored, knew the route to the doorway on the edge of the Vale, opening out onto the Dragongrave. Or so he hoped, assuming that if what he recalled was delusion, the Shadow would steer him from the false course. Assumption of anything wrought from madness was itself mad to make, he knew, and made it anyway. If his journey was to end in a labyrinth in the hollows of the world, all the more poetic for when he finally lost himself within the labyrinth in the hollows of his mind.

Still, none knew of the pass but he. It would be free of distraction, of death, seeing his body to the next chapter of his journey in turn. What it would do with his mind, in its silence and solitude, he ignored, knowing it would not do to dwell. He passed over the threshold of a hard decision; fearful; foolhardy; final.

Chapter XVI: Reminder of the Rim
• Dreaming of Summer •

The Things Betwixt welcomed the Wayfarer, the stone doorway reappearing behind him, returning from Nowhere. He thought he heard the cawing of rooks and ravens as it closed, a fading cry of disappointment, but let the thought fall away, unimportant.

All light blinked out as the doorway closed, sealing him in darkness. He might have illuminated his lantern, its silver-white light more than enough to see by, but it would have been redundant. Warm light flared to life from the Things Betwixt's own lanterns, running along its corridors. The light allowed him to see far, but not as far as the passage ran, failing to reach his eye from such a staggering stretch, casting the furthest point of the corridors into a void. It reminded him of the darkness of his inner mind, swarming around him, waiting to devour what was left. He was safe from death here, but he was not safe from himself.

Aëros roamed the hypogean maze, wending his way along its meandering path. The lanterns flickered a steady pace as he passed, moving the air, air moving the flame. His footfall fell just as rhythmically, keeping time with the shivering glow. Breathing became a conscious effort, the only sound apart from his step and the odd rumbling of Arök's bones as the world shifted above, beneath, and around him. The Things Betwixt were not pristine, many passages leading to rockfalls and cave-ins, as many dead ends as there were ways to lose oneself in the labyrinth, a dead end a doom one could find even in the midst of a corridor if one no longer knew their way. Thirst. Hunger. Exhaustion. All as lethal as a wolf, a drake, a man.

On he went, the darkness receding before him, swallowing up where he'd been, lanterns flitting, footfall pattering, breath steady, bones of the world rumbling. The corridors and passageways were unchanging, with equal darkness before and behind, provoking a sense of endlessness, and the desperation endlessness draws up from the deeps of the mind. The silence was stifling, the solitude enslaving. He tried desperately to keep his focus on his path, on the passage, but its hypnotic sameness forced him ever into the complexity of his thoughts; his mind's desire to think, to wonder, to consider too strong to repress without external distraction.

He fell into his mind at times, his going autonomous, his focus on his inner self, the thing he once reveled in so proudly and now feared more than anything else. In it he stood, perched on the rim of his unconscious, looking down into its dark, abyssal depths, listening for the echo of things in the asylum, watching as the few flickering threads that remained continued to unravel, dragged over the rim, forgotten.

There was a memory of his childhood, his father showing him the proper way to string a bow. *Between the legs, stable on the foot, leverage the limb, loop the string, let it lax.* There was the time he'd been caught pickpocketing a ring from a man who'd himself pickpocketed it from a gentle florist, and had his face carved up for the failure; he was shown by his mother how to wear an illusion of beauty to hide the truth of the massacre beneath, the value in appearance explained by her, while also explaining the value in knowing that the face he wore in the world would be different for everyone he met, but to never forget who he truly was beneath.

A memory of Aūriel passed by, the first time he ever saw her, walking through the Dragongrave on the outskirts of Arythos for no reason other than for curiosity's sake, passing through meadows of high grass and heather, the moon setting silver silhouettes over her and the fields as she sang softly to herself and the nightingales that winged around her. He saw in that memory her smile, her eyes, her silhouette, a small silhouette walking with her, hand in hand, walking into the weft and warp of forgetting, into the smoke, the ash, the smell—of blood, of death. Thrace's, Shaē's, the sickening sound of slit flesh slithering over a blade, screaming for

158

help, for hope even as hope drained away, screaming for her, for him, for everyone, for anyone. Aūriel! Tärin! AŪRIEL! TÄRIN! AŪRIEL! TÄRI—

Aëros heaved himself out of his mind, staggering to his knees in the corridor, the wind of his fall sending the lanterns sputtering. His mind did not care—it reeled out of him, the memories echoing through the corridors, laughing, crying, screaming, sobbing, all calling to him, for him, to remember. To remember. To remem—

"NO. *NO. NO!*" He stumbled forward, picked up into a sprint, screaming into the void. "*NO! NO! NO!*"

He covered his ears, trying to blot out the voices, but he couldn't. They came from inside him. They were *his* voices. His memories. His nightmares. His madness. "*NO! NO! NO!*"

The lanterns rushed past him, light leaping in his wake, darkness fleeing before him, terrified of the darkness he carried within himself, blacker still. He ran, heart pounding, muffling the rumbling of Arök, his footfall and his breath ragged and panicked. Ran until the voices were all-consuming, with no reprieve of silence between them, the monotony of the Things Betwixt giving them substance, the horrors hidden within him giving them momentum, building, growing, trying to drag him in, drag him down, devour him. Here was where his journey would end, in a labyrinth in the bones of the world, in the labyrinth of insanity his mind had become. A wraith, forgetting the world as it was forgetting him, wandering witless.

It's alright.

The Shadow spoke, almost impossible to hear, soft in the calamity of his mind.

Aëros.

It's alright.

Its voice grew, not louder, but greater, the voices in his mind softer, muted, muffled by the Shadow's gentleness.

It will pass.

Aëros' sprint slowed to a jog, a stagger, and then a halting, haggard stop. He opened his eyes, not realizing he'd shuttered them from the world without, trapped within. He looked around, his breathing returning to normal, even if it was arrhythmic with the world's. The voices were gone.

Watching the Shadow watching him, he felt the threads of many emotions tugging within him. Most were those that had appeared when the Shadow did, simply summed up as distrust mingling with disdain. The others, set in the shade of the rest, he could not define. He knew only that they were responsible for what he now felt: gratitude.

The wraith responded as it so often did, with silence, even though Aëros knew it felt what he did, knew his appreciation and his loathing both.

He focused, moving on from the ordeal, finding that he did not know how long he'd been running. Minutes. Hours. Days. It didn't seem to matter. He'd arrived where he intended to be. Somewhere in the midst of a familiar passageway, stone running on into blinding darkness both before and behind. He set his will on a wall beside him, marked by slight discoloration, and as the entrance into the labyrinth had shimmered and faded, so too did its egress.

The doorway unraveled, and light from the outside rushed into the corridor even as he rushed out to meet it. The stone sealed itself behind him, the Things Betwixt once again an empty, forgotten relic of a forgotten people. He was on the western edge of the Dragongrave, the doorway set in an immense bone rising out of the grasslands like a spear, itself set in a crescent row of similar jagged fossils, hidden by fitting in. When Aëros was young and knew no better he would say they were teeth. He now knew better, and still said that they were.

Beyond the spires of stone ran roughly a league of barren plains separating him from the ruins of Arythos. The ground was scorched, blacker than the stone of the Ashen Vale. It was not the burning of dragon-fire, but of men, a wasteland on which their war had been waged. The ruins of Arythos were distant, bleak beneath the sun, grey clouds rolling in from the Wyrmspine, the fallen kingdom set in the base of the tallest mountain in the chain, the spine of Arök; first and greatest of all wyrms, if myth was to be believed.

Behind was the Dragongrave, the Vale beneath, the true entrance to the trade route somewhere to the north of where Aëros had ended up. He headed towards it, seeking to rejoin the path, for it would lead him to the ruins, and the ruins to the mountain, the mountain to the Rift sitting in silence at its summit, marking the beginning of the end of his journey and, he hoped—knowing it was a fool's hope—his madness.

———◆◆———

The ground was black beneath the Wayfarer's feet, his bare soles discolored by the soot, so thick was the charred reminder of the Devouring, even so long after its end.

Unlike the Dragongrave, the plains were bare, nothing to break their monotony, barren of life and the creations life wrought to entertain itself. Wind, tunneling down from the mountain passes, ran wild and uninhibited over the flatland. It lifted the ash, throwing Aëros into walls of it as he went, swirling black dust engulfing him, darkness surrounding him on all sides, better than the darkness of his own mind by far.

161

At times the wind would quiet, revealing Arythos as it drew ever closer. Its outer ward was immense, running for leagues in either direction, shrinking in its distance. Once it had been a bulwark rising stories above fertile grasslands, standing sentinel for the greatest kingdom in the West. It was rubble now, immense only in the length of the scar it left behind, sentinel to nothing, to no one, the land barren, as devoid of life as the plains before it.

Still, when the wind settled and a small pillar of lonely smoke lifted up from the threshold of the fallen kingdom, masked by a few charred and caving walls which once stood as a guard-gate, he did not pause in surprise or wonder. Did not slow to consider. Did not worry over something living in a place no living thing had a right to be. After all, he understood that sort of audacity well.

Chapter XVII: Rooks & Ravens
• Stirring of Autumn •

With the smoke came sound in the shape of a song. Aëros couldn't remember having heard it before, knew how little that meant about whether or not he actually had. He continued toward smoke and song, listening as each rose over the ruins, taken by the wind.

...I am a lone wayfarin' stranger,
I seek a land where silence calls,
A lonesome road there leads my footstep,
A lonesome road I weary haul.

I walk beneath the falling starlight,
I travel with a cradled moon,
My mind gone back to youthful twilight,
My mind wrapped up in hazy hues.

I see nightshroud is drawing 'round me,
I look beyond a darkling sea,
A ferry fords the waters roiling,
A ferryman with simple fee.

There on the shore of coal-black sand dunes,
There where the road begins its end,
I walk with wisdom shortly fleeting,
I walk on down the steep descent.

Where step falls slow and sight starts dimming,
A weary ache stiff in my bone,
Here walks one soul as those before him,
Here walks one man all on his lone.

Lonesome the road 'til lone its ending,
A quiet place for quiet thought,
Rest found at last from olden twilight,
Rest found at last I weary sought.

...I am a lone wayfarin' stranger,
In a far land I silent call,
To mark the way for those behind me,
To mark the way their foot must fall...

The song, new to Aëros, found that place of rest itself, ending. The voice that sung it he found familiar. "First I've heard that," he said as he stepped into the camp and let himself be known.

The elder sat atop his pack, feeding flames with fallen timber, watching as a silhouette materialized through the smoke into the Wayfarer. He smiled, unsurprised. "It's an old one. Very old." He gestured to a mound of rubble on the other side of his fire, offering a seat.

"Didn't think I'd see you again so soon." Aëros measured the elder and his smile, and took the seat. He held up the patched part of his Shräud. "Thanks for this."

The elder waved the thanks away. "My name's Grimnyr, by the by."

Aëros leaned forward, warming his hands on the fire, day dying and night shivering into place. "Grimnyr," he said, nodding as if intrigued. "That name isn't of this world."

The elder's beard tugged up with his smile. "No, it isn't."

"I've been to the world it's from." Aëros watched the elder, searching. "It means hanged man."

Grimnyr scratched his jaw. "Is that right?"

Aëros saw the hint of a smirk forming beneath the elder's grey whiskers, and shared a hint of his own. "What are you doing here, Grimnyr?"

"Oh, you know." The elder shifted on his pack and adjusted his cloak, keeping the new cold at bay as the sun dipped below the mountain. "Felt like the right place to be."

Aëros looked around, at the charred plains behind him, the ruins before, the emptiness of each, and the Wyrmspine rising over it all, foreboding. "Thought you didn't care for mountains."

"Ah well, where you'd care to be and where you need to be are so often separate places."

Aëros' eyes narrowed, the silver in them sharp, glinting. The Shadow came to sit beside him, stretching itself out to the fire.

Grimnyr watched Aëros' eyes trail away, acknowledging something beside him. "What do you think of fate, Wayfarer?"

Aëros' eyes flicked back to the elder. "In what regard?"

Grimnyr was smiling again. "In regard to whether or not you believe in it, I suppose."

Aëros studied the elder, wondering over this game of riddles answered and unanswered both. "Of a sort."

Grimnyr's smile dimmed, apparently not pleased with a non-answer this time. "What sort might that be?"

Aëros, ever stubborn, didn't yield. "In that cavern, in that gaol, you named me Walker Betwixt and Between Worlds."

Grimnyr added another piece of fractured tinder to the fire, twirling it in the coals, pushing them around, sparks scattering. "I didn't name you that, but I called you it."

Aëros brushed a few errant embers from his Shräud. "You know what I'm able to do."

"I know of what you *used* to be able to do, yes." Grimnyr gestured around him, to the ruins, the rubble. "If you could still do it, I don't think I'd have company right now."

Aëros watched the elder's eyes, one good, one gone; watched the knowing in each, and wasn't surprised in the least. "You understand how it works?"

"Of a sort."

Aëros raised his hands, bowed his head. "Then you have your answer."

Grimnyr pursed his lips. "But I don't have yours."

Aëros slumped, sighed. "Yes, I believe in fate. But not as most mean it. Not as some force twisting us along at a whim, at random." He shook his head. He seemed to be talking more to himself, or repeating some past argument he'd rehearsed with an imagined partner a thousand times over. "Everything that was, is, and will be, are composed of the same threads of reality, linked. When one is woven, or frays, or knits back together, all others are affected. That is fate. Infinite, but predictable: a paradox, unless you can see the pattern."

The fire cracked in the pit, wood crumpling in on itself, falling to ash and embers. Aëros was watching the flames dance in the coals, running on and dying, burning up with life. Grimnyr watched too, and spoke to the answer he'd rooted out. "I know many men who would argue against you. Even if you opened a Rift to a kindred reality and let him argue with a kindred version of himself."

Aëros stood and walked over to a fallen beam, kicked it in half, then tossed each half into the fire. "I've ripped the threads of the Tapestry from seam to seam. I found one truth: reality is an opinion. It can be disagreed with. Even mine. But as with opinion, reality is difficult to see beyond."

"What is it you see now?"

"An old man asking old questions." Aëros sat back down, stared. "You?"

Grimnyr looked Aëros up, down, through. "A young man afraid of answers. Drawn to find them all the same."

Aëros considered that for a moment, thought of where he was and why, and laughed out loud. Grimnyr paid the stroke of madness no mind. Aëros' laugh died a bitter death. "Do you know what the word 'wayfarer' means, Grimnyr?"

The elder pointed to his own feet, bare as Aëros'. "Foot traveler."

Aëros pointed at the man, at his mind. "So I once was, so I have become again."

"Even ash of Ages gone, may grow a wood, a world, a home."

Aëros' finger went limp and dropped hard, his eyes filling with anger. "Where did you hear that?"

Grimnyr picked up pointing where Aëros left off. "You mumbled it in your stupor back in the camp." His eyes ran over Aëros' hands, nine fingers of flesh, one of ruin. The knowing in his eyes ran the color of curiosity, and he spoke it. "You escaped."

Aëros measured the elder, wary. "You knew I would."

Grimnyr grinned, and gave a short laugh. "Might have wagered on it, if there were wagers to take." His grin fell away, fell serious, and he leaned in. "What happened to the Fēl?"

Aëros grunted. "You ask like you aren't one of them."

"Am I?"

"You walked with them."

Grimnyr sat back, sinking into his pack. He looked up, and pointed to a flock of black birds circling around the pillar of rising smoke. "Rooks wing with ravens; both run with wolves."

Aëros knew the birds were still following. He'd felt them as he crossed the wastes, had no idea how they'd kept track of him through the Things Betwixt. "One isn't the other, true. But their purpose is the same. Judgment falls on the action."

Grimnyr looked down from the birds. "So, Wayfarer, what judgment found the Fēl?"

Aëros looked back in his mind, searching for the memory, finding only the asylum beneath, taunting. "I don't know."

Grimnyr smiled. "Don't you?"

The elder's smile met his eyes, both dark. One was the dark of the void, of nothingness; the other, the dark of age. Aëros found himself held by them, uneasy. "I don't remember."

Grimnyr, the elder, closed his one good eye, nodding as if understanding. He stood, pulled up his pack, and pulled from it a black pouch, embroidered with silver stitching and held fast by a silver clasp. He offered it for no comprehensible reason, no certain reward. "Would you like to?"

Aëros stared at the pouch intensely, knowing, deciding. "Sylysæ." It was not a question, because what the elder held was a thing of answers only: a thing of revelation, of remedy, of ruin.

The Shadow stood rigid, its gaze flicking between Grimnyr, the pouch, and Aëros, as if trying to reconcile the three together, as if seeing something it had until then missed, and still didn't fully understand even as it saw. It forced its way into Aëros' awareness, warning.

It would be unwise.

Aëros heard the Shadow, didn't disagree, didn't take his eyes from the pouch. "I shouldn't."

Grimnyr did not reply, did not try to coerce, did not withdraw the pouch. The Shadow loomed.

You. Are. Not. Ready.

Aëros knew the truth of the Shadow's warning, even as it warred with his want, forged from the confidence of the foolhardy. The mystery of his own madness was itself maddening, and the Shadow's rare and riddled words were no salve. He knew what the elder offered could unravel the riddle of his forgetting, knew also that it could very well unravel him.

The elder saw the want win out over wisdom in the Wayfarer's eyes, and tossed the pouch through the smoke, a helping hand. Helping in what way, well...

Grimnyr drew a pipe from his pack, a gnarled, stained, wayworn thing, as petrified as the ruins around them. "That's seen better days," said Aëros.

Grimnyr held his pipe up, good eye running over the wood, seeing all the memories worn into it. "It's seen many." He looked to Aëros, wondered of him, "Have any wōadleaf?"

Aëros pulled a pouch of the mixture from his Shräud and tossed it in turn—a fair trade. "Plenty, if you need more."

Grimnyr shook his head, hefting the pouch. "More than enough." He pinched the mixture into his pipe, kindled it with a thin thread of Iné, and took a long draw, exhaling rings. Each met the fire's own smoke, vanishing as they joined, dying into the wind as one.

Aëros held the pouch of Sylysæ with the ease of someone familiar with its weight. It had shown him much in his life, given him the mind to find more, expanded the fabric of his curiosity and his understanding so completely that it was one of the few senses of self that lingered, refusing to unravel, to be forgotten—for now.

As much as his curiosity had given him, so too was it his greatest risk, thrusting him into the unknown, the unexplored, the uncertain. Sylysæ was a catalyst of curiosity, an answer to many mysteries, the cost being the loosening of one's mind, its threads. When the fabric of self was strong, this was only ever a tool for greater understanding: of self; of other. But if the fabric was fraying, near threadbare, it could very well unravel what was left. There was no way of knowing what effect it would have on him. He could only hope. As ever, it was a fool's.

He unclasped the pouch and stared at the iridescent mixture within, colors shifting and shaping like an aurora. It was a small amount. It was enough. He thought of its components, its effects.

Sylysæ: a mixture of preserved moss extracted from the floor of the Wōadglōam's heartwood, saturated with an arkaën distillation of deathspiral and nightshade nectars. Grants Tíraē, or "Sight," as translated from the elder tongue, defined as the ability to perceive the threads of reality with the mind's inner vision, allowing increased comprehension of the fundamental composition of self and other.

It was the first analysis ever made of the mixture, a note of his own discovery, the first to study the threads of Aūr, to seek the wisdom they held, the only one ever to weave them to his will. They were the threads of reality, and he tore them apart and stitched them back together to walk betwixt and between his world and any other as he so willed. It was euphoric, addictive. It had been long since he'd fed his desire, for he'd forgotten his mastery, and his journey had not yet brought him his need.

He loved the threads and loathed them, a forever echo of the duality that raged within him. The love was for the freedom they granted. The loathing was for something he could not recall—had forgotten—the seed of his madness. The Shadow saw it, down in the depths of the asylum, but could not release it. Not even with its skeleton key. Not until Aëros was ready. That was why the Sylysæ was unwise: for he wasn't. He was a fool, and the wraith knew with painful familiarity what a fool was willing to do for answers. It grasped his eyes with its own, holding them, or perhaps held by them, the difference thin, if there was any at all.

You will find your answers at your journey's end.

You will find them as you were meant to find them.

Given a little more time.

Endure.

The Shadow was likely right. The mixture could very well fray his lingering sanity threadbare, send what little remained over that dark, abyssal rim of forgetting. But he'd barely made it this far, death a constant companion. He would find it again ere the end, wasn't sure he'd avoid it. He was never sure, only ever hopeful. It was a distraction, but it would be no salve. Memories of the An'kou flickered behind his eyes, memories of what Athair had shown him so long ago, the Shaēd in the dark crypt beneath Dún.

A small flame flickered into existence atop Aëros' index finger, its light mingling with the campfire's, casting his face in shifting shadow. Now graven with sorrow, with fear, now crooked with a smirk; the duality of his humanity warring within him.

His pipe appeared from Nowhere, that which Shaē had given him, the Sylysæ barely a pinch in the bowl. He lit it and snuffed out the flames in one motion—the one atop his index finger, and that burning in the pit before him—leaving him and the elder in darkness, the only light that of the moon and the embers smoldering in their pipes. The Shadow still held his eyes, and he its, each bound up in the other's, bound by something Aëros did not understand, but might, given the time.

This. Is. Unwise.

Aëros laughed as only an insane man might, and spoke to the Shadow, indifferent to his company, knowing his company was indifferent to him. "I'm heading to the grave of a madman in hopes of finding the cause and cure of my own madness, based on the word of a wraith only I can see, while everything I have ever been is swiftly slipping away, forgotten." He raised the pipe to his lips, eyes wild with hints of insanity. "Is this what the death of wisdom brings?"

You will not understand.

"We'll see."

The Sylysæ flared, vibrant, iridescent colors flickering in the pipe, burning, burning, burnt, ashing away on the wind. Aëros' senses sharpened instantly, his awareness stretching out—of self, of

171

the world, of each in respect to the other, of each in respect to the whole: the one; the Tapestry; Eaē. He felt the essence of what composed both him and everything that had once existed, existed now, and would ever exist in the time yet to come. He saw their nexus—a finely woven web of all worlds, realms, and timelines laid bare by the simplest of strands, reality reaching its loftiest prism of perception. Focusing, he narrowed his newfound Sight, drawing it inwards, drawing it over the rim of madness, down into the asylum.

It was deep, a pit spiraling down, down, down, into darkness that was the essence of itself, pure and primordial. Below—far, far below, in the deepest part of that pit—was the seed of his madness, imprisoned. He knew this, even though he couldn't see it. So he descended, seeking it, first passing other things, other memories forgotten.

Some were soft, pleasant:

The time Tärin caught a rabbit with his bare hands, bringing it up to Aūriel and himself, wondering if it could be his pet. Their startled reactions, laughter, explanation that it didn't seem like the rabbit—squirming and frantic—wanted to be anything but wild.

He and Thrace exploring the ruins of Askerot—the grand athenaeum of the First of the First. Of their flight as the Old Wolf mistakenly knocked an old decorative sword down a well, the sound echoing through every grand corridor and ornate hall, stirring the goblins squatting there awake and into frenzied pursuit of two fools with no business in a place where the ancients had grown wise.

Shaē, Aūriel, and himself, sitting in the boughs of a wōadglōam, watching forest giants lumber by searching for companions, the mating ritual of hide-and-seek, not so unlike his own search for the woman who would become his wife, his love, his dearest friend.

These memories and more he was glad to recall, making the descent worth the risk. But his curiosity led him, and darker, deeper things waited for him in the asylum of hidden self. He found them, found things he'd forgotten even before his madness took root, forgotten on purpose to hide himself from himself, hating what he buried.

The time he'd stolen near five hundred aūrums from Jä, a friend as old and close as Thrace, or Shaē, or Nomad. Aëros had been young, stood too tall upon the perch of his arrogance and self-interest, had taken the coins because Jä came from plenty. He knew his friend would have given him the wealth freely if he'd asked, but his pride was too great. Why ask for something when you have the skill to take it without being seen? The answer came with the stolen coin: to preserve your honor, your code, your soul. He hadn't kept the gold long before returning it, the guilt too great. But neither had he revealed himself to his friend, even to this day, so many seasons hence.

His betrayal of Athair. Watching his oldest friend restrained, shackled with chains of Argynt, shadowed away to Arkym. The duality of his love at war with his logic, brotherhood battling his understanding of what his oldest friend was, had always been, would always be.

When he broke things off with Aūriel, before the ring, after the promise. He was young, uncertain of his desires, his wants, and she of hers, the relationship strained between two people coming into their own, learning themselves, and unable or unwilling to learn the other at the same time. Still, it shocked her when he ended it, came like a storm unseen in the night. Time passed, and he reconciled himself with his foolishness, reached out to her and set things right. But the wound was raw, untended, the threads of the relationship fraying, and it wasn't long before Aūriel ended things of her own accord. But time heals all wounds, and as she so wisely said: even from ash of Ages gone, may grow a wood, a world, a home.

Down the spiraling pit he went, deep into the black abyss of his hidden, unconscious self, guided by his Sight. He passed memories that made him feel full and alive for the first time since his forgetting began, and passed others that made him pause, overwhelmed with sorrow, pain, and self-loathing. He continued on only because his desire to uncover what he'd buried—what had begun his descent into insanity—was too monolithic to turn from because of something as pathetic as his own past mistakes. That was until he came upon the memory of the Fēl. It thrust him to his knees, holding him in a place of recognition, of reconciliation, forcing him to see what he was becoming; had perhaps always been.

It was threaded as those the Shadow showed him were—with a sickening sense of familiarity in something that should have felt foreign, something he had no recollection of preserving. But this time it was not the wraith that showed it. This time he could not dismiss it as a symptom of insanity, as hallucination. This memory was a memory in truth, and in its truth was utter horror, the Shadow there beside him, narrating.

You were bent, bowed before the men that imprisoned you, thinking you only a man, not heeding the myth, the whispered tales of those older and wiser. Betrayal was how this began; betrayal was how it would end. You sneered, the key to your freedom grasped between your teeth, held with the ferocity of a feral beast. You yanked, links of chain scattering, your ring returned to you. You stood, blinded by wrath, by rage, by a hatred you thought long worn away.

The Fēl were still, amazed, snared in their confusion. You held up your hands, ten fingers, unshackled and unfettered. Nine of flesh—one of argⓔnt. You set your will on the false finger, and demonstrated why such a trinket was worth more than the metal it was forged from. It threaded through the air, shifting shape into your ring, shifting again into the form of a key—skeletal, limitless.

Their eyes widened, the dream melting away, their somnambulant stares shattering as reality sped back to them. Realizing what was happening, not knowing how they would suffer for their failure to foresee it. Youth paid no mind to death—only the wizened, the rooks, the ravens circling, knowing a predator even if it did not know itself.

You evanesced, dividing, a dozen phantoms scattering from where you stood. The Fēl fumbled in wonder and fear. Another dozen appeared, and another, and another, only one the trickster who wove them. The phantoms filled the narrow space, feigned attacks and pursuit. The Fēl parried and evaded, hurled and hollered, swung and swore. They fled only from illusion, slew only illusion. One man came close to sticking the true trickster with a spear, but you were swift to dodge as another phantom took your place. You made use of the mayhem, collecting your raiment from the chest, reveling in the spoils of your gambit. Vaunting. Swaggering. Cavalier.

It was good old-fashioned physical comedy, the likes of which even the great Tramp, Kaēton, and Pasha would admire and marvel over. They were distracted, utterly, freedom easy to take in the chaos. But still— 'Kill them.' *I looked to you, wondering.*

Is your need so great?

"Need?" *You turned to me, and considered the thought.*

It will heal nothing.

"Will it harm?"

Silence.

As abruptly as the phantoms appeared, they vanished, leaving the Fēl frozen, confounded, leaving you standing before Bäs, Löekeh poised in his hand. You laughed—growled, wicked, wolfish, feral—and every man in the camp but him and his son fell dead, their silhouettes slumping, dying in darkness, forgotten.

The deaths came too swiftly for Bäs to register, his mind unraveling as it tried to process. They had to die, but you are no torturer. You'd used your ring, wove it with the needle of your will into

175

a needle itself, thrust through the air on the impetus of your wrath, striking arteries—messy, but efficient. You preferred to use Löekeh, preferred to keep the symbol of your love unspoiled by bad blood. But Bäs still held the blade, and besides, it wasn't you who had tarnished your ring with blood; or so you convinced yourself.

The needle hung in the air before Bäs, his head spinning like an owl, taking in the lifeless corpses of his fellows, stopping on his son, who like his father was grasping at understanding, the only other soul left living.

"You and yours threatened to take everything I had left." You stood before the arrogant man, gesturing to the needle of your will, weaving it back into a false finger to wear upon your hand, the weight of the dead making it no heavier for their reaping. "In doing that you wagered the same against yourselves—and lost."

Bäs' head whipped around, back to you, his rage great, but lesser than yours. He leapt, lunging for you with your own blade, and stumbled back as you divested him of it, any skill he might have mustered muddled by his anger. You thrust him to the ground, all will gone out of him as he knelt before you, staring, eyes pleading, his son behind him, watching. "Don't hurt the boy."

You stood over him as he'd stood over you. You, fettered by chains, him, fettered by fate, by the doom of his actions. You lifted his chin with the tip of Löekeh's edge, binding his eyes to yours. "I have a son, near the same age as yours." You shook your head. "They are both children, but in his mind yours is ancient with abuse. Isn't that so?" You gestured over his shoulder to the boy. "You owed him more. You owed your son better. You kept him in this wretched life, and there's only one way for him to escape it."

"Please, don't—" His words caught in his throat; pain swallowed back down into his heart. You needed no words of assurance, for you saw the truth of what this man was—what sort of father he'd been—clear in his eyes, and beside it, the regret he shouldered, bowing him under its weight. He was just a man. Same as you. You didn't care.

As he had no words for you, neither had you any for him. Löekeh arced, twisted, was still. You held the blade low, the artifact of your ancestors dripping scarlet. He slumped as the life rushed out of him, as you rushed to his level, forcing his eyes back to yours, predatory, maskless, the horror of you revealed. You drew him close, whispering. "Soon you will cease to exist. Your memory will fade. From the minds of those you loved, from the minds of those who loved you, from those who hated you, those you might have known yet, had you chosen a different path. Everyone—your son above of all, freed finally from the chains with which you bind him."

His eyes burned with hatred, sorrow, fear, the last of his life leaving him. As his head fell forward, you peered over it, to the boy, to his son, having seen perhaps twelve summers, never to see another.

The boy you looked at was now a corpse, knelt before you as his father was, mirroring him. His neck lay open, like his father's; in his lifeless hand was a knife, dripping scarlet. In his eyes, he held a look of unalloyed fear, of having stared into a horror, and instead of letting the horror reap him, had reaped himself. An easier fate—or so his fear had convinced him.

In an instant all the wrath and rage and hatred boiling over in your blood burned away, replaced by a deep, hollow well of sorrow, the sense of having lost something, of gazing on a sight that should have felt foreign and finding it familiar. The memory of another transposed itself over the boy, the memory of your final betrayal, of a friend dead by your hand, of Athair. Not as he was when you slew him, but as he was when first you saw what he was, so long ago, in the ruins of Dún, in the ruins of your innocence. The memory flickered away, leaving the corpse of reality before you. Not a man that might well have deserved to die as a boy, but a boy. Innocent, guilty of nothing but the company he was forced to keep.

You stood there, before your massacre, wondering if there was any difference between you and Athair. He had been bound within Arkym, and within the sanatorium before it. Call him a patient if you like, but you knew he was a prisoner. He escaped. Did what any desperate animal would do. Like the drake. Like you. Birds of a feather. Who were you to judge? To serve as executioner.

In fairness, this was not your intent. You would not have harmed the boy. He was too young to be foul. But that wasn't always the case, was it? Athair was foul from the womb. An irredeemable wretch. Or was he? Would it have made a difference? Did it make a difference with this boy? As with the bone drake, his death was your doing, your fault. Nameless, forgotten, blood draining away, drunk by the cracks in the cool, ashen stone, you watched the boy die. You left him, rooks and ravens circling above, ominous, ouroboric.

You rationalized what had happened. That this bloodbath would have been the seed of madness sown in the boy, that the trauma of it would fester, rotting, dragging him into the same abyss that is swallowing you, devouring your memory and soul. You know not what sowed the same seed in you—or rather know and will no longer admit, the first of all things forgotten—but you recognized the seed in another all the same.

This was better. In a way his death was his freedom from the torture of his life. He would not have to fight, as you fight, to retain his sanity, to preserve what he told himself was himself—or so you told yourself. You believed none of it, and still don't, even now.

You might have lost the last of yourself then. But in that moment your wounded hand thrummed, drawing you back to it, back to your promise. In that moment the world seemed to shimmer, as if becoming something that could be seen through, illusory, shifting and ambiguous like a dream. You felt something inside you vanish, dragged over the rim of insanity, tossed into the asylum of your hidden, unconscious, unknowable self, another thread frayed, forgotten.

As you stood atop the narrow, rooks and ravens overhead, only a faint glimmer of bonefire smoldering beneath, not recalling how you'd arrived there, you wondered what it was you'd lost, then decided it wasn't important. You shrugged away the wondering as pointless. You were free. But you and I know you are far from it. Far indeed, with such a long way yet to go, and no guarantee that when the end is met and freedom is found, you will have the will to do what you must to take it. Your time is thinning, your sanity shearing, what little of you is left wearing swiftly away. You have gone far enough into yourself, stop here, go no further. Not now. Not yet. Not until the end.

The memory—for it was memory—fell from awareness, settling in the lingering, half-hidden place of the mind where all memories lurk, waiting for recollection. It left a residue of bewilderment behind, of disbelief. But Aëros couldn't deny it. *I killed them.* He had, and he'd forgotten. It wasn't delusion brought on by madness; his forgetting of it was. For after all, his madness was a thing of forgetting. His mind burying itself within itself without him realizing it, bound in the asylum. He considered the implications. If this memory was true, then...

His remembering proved that what he'd lost he could recover. The proof came at cost, his sanity the less for its finding, yet the finding of it strengthened his will, his belief that he could find the end of this thread of insanity, and sever it. He need only remember more, painful though it would be, his suffering the seed of salvation, rooted to the seed of his madness.

He was still within himself, still in the darkness of the asylum, the Shadow beside him, watching, calling him out on his wyrmshit. He met its eyes, desperately trying to peel back the layers of his ignorance, to unravel the wraith's riddles and the mystery of his madness to which it was tied. He saw the threads that fettered him to the wraith, and bound it in turn to the things hidden within his own mind. It was a shadow older than the form that cast it, an enigma even with the near-omniscience of the Sylysæ's Sight. He reflected on the words of the only one amongst the Fēl wise enough to run from him—the words not spoken, but held in his eyes, remarking on what they saw in Aëros' own. *They've got the look of a man who's forgotten himself and far too many other things besides.*

Aëros heaved himself up and hauled himself forward, will set, stubborn, determined to understand, to remember. Not when the Shadow said so, but when *he* willed it. He staggered forward, further down, the Shadow watching, eyes wide. It was unable to restrain him with anything other than words, and those passed unheeded.

Limping forward, Aëros descended, down into the pit of his unconscious, desperation driving him forward, driving him down, shuffling in the darkness of his own mind, searching for the first thing forgotten. He passed memory after forgotten memory, horror after buried horror, until he found himself at the bottom of the pit, standing before a sepulcher at the base of his mind. He knew it well. A sepulcher of carven crystal. The sepulcher he would find at his journey's end, here now within the asylum of his mind. He reached out, touched it, and was swallowed up, devoured. Not by nightmare, but memory, nightmarish though its hue. As the Shadow had warned, what he saw he did not understand.

Aëros saw himself standing in a world buried beneath dunes of ash, suffocated by smoke, devoured by darkness. Before him was a sepulcher, *the* sepulcher, carven crystal, housing the bones of a madman. But it couldn't be. The sepulcher was beneath Dún, beneath the sealed doorway, waiting at his journey's end, the truth of his madness bound to the bones in that grave. He thought back to the Fël, to the memory he'd buried and replaced with a lie. He looked to each memory, each sepulcher, each world, and wondered which was truth and which was lie, or if they were each one, both, or neither.

The him in the world of ash spoke, and he realized that neither the sepulcher nor his other self were alone. He stood not before one grave, but many: hundreds, thousands, so many they vanished in the distance of the ashen dunes. All were stone, all but six, wrought from crystal. He was bowed over one in the midst of them all, five others encircling it, five other souls encircling him, himself the only living one among them, something familiar in the eyes of each.

Aëros watched himself speak, to the souls, to himself, to nothing—he wasn't sure. *Farewell, for now. I will return. I promise.* He watched tears fall, watched as his other self slid the lid of the central sepulcher away, set himself inside, sealed himself away, watched as a faint iridescent light flickered from within the grave, flared, and faded away.

A familiar ache erupted in his chest and carved its way through his bones. Not the him in the memory—the nightmare, the whatever it was—but the him that endured it. The deep, dull, horrible ache of immense sorrow, of grief, of loss. It crippled him, the memory fading but the ache remaining and sharpening into pain, the thread that was a root to the truth of his madness pulling him down, dragging him further than his mind could manage, severing his sanity thread by fraying thread.

He was hollowing away, suffocating, his vision tunneling and fading to black, echoes in the darkness of dread and loathing—of himself, of his curiosity, of everything he could not understand. He was drowning in his own mind, drifting away.

Drifting.
Drifting.
Drifting.

And suddenly he was rising.

He was wrenched up out of the asylum, leaving him stranded as he had been, upon the rim separating him from his madness. He was lesser, sanity held together by far too few threads. He looked up. *You.*

The Shadow stood over him, sentinel.

This was unwise.

181

Aëros felt the world shimmer, as if coming out of a dream. He was back on the threshold of the ruins, night shrouding all, the elder sitting, smoking. He saw Aëros return, and stood, shouldering his pack, whispering as he went, just loudly enough to hear: "Farewell again, Wayfarer."

His smirk crooked with pain, Aëros fell back into darkness. Not the darkness of insanity, but of slumber, his audacity taking its toll, the Sylysæ wearing away, wearing him thin, wearing him down. It was not a peaceful rest, for in it he dreamt: of ash, of ache, of what he'd forgotten and could not understand. Not now. Not yet. Not until the end, as the Shadow said.

Chapter XVIII: Inconvenience
• Stirring of Autumn •

"Aëros." A voice, distant, thin and echoing as if spoken from the halls of some endless labyrinth. It was murky, muddled...familiar.

Aëros snapped awake. It was day, and Grimnyr was gone, the rooks and ravens gone with him. There was a new fire in the pit, a small one for cooking, mostly coals, thin flames and thinner smoke trailing up into an overcast sky. There was some meat searing over a stone, and some wild onion too. Not scavenged from the ruins or the wastes, but from somewhere else, by someone else. He looked up, and found that someone on the other side of the smoke in place of the elder.

A wanderer sat wrapped up in a dark, weather-stained and weatherworn cloak, a silver walking staff set at his side. The man looked up, revealing a face familiar enough to be considered friend, even if that friend could also be considered folly. Birds of a feather.

"Nomad," Aëros groaned, weary and weighty, and stood, stretching in the morning haze, his bones snapping into place. "Where'd you flicker in from?"

"A desert. Some other world." He scratched his chin. "I think. Deserts all look the same after a while, one world or another." He paused unexpectedly, continuing with an even more unexpected thought. "I was walking with a fellow there who had the same searching look in his eye as you. Like he'd forgotten something important."

Aëros watched his friend for a long moment, words lingering in the air, then turned away and began walking towards the ruins, towards the mountain, towards the next chapter of his journey. Nomad scrambled up, retrieving his food and his walking staff and falling in beside the Wayfarer. Aëros looked at him, and asked as he went, "Was this fellow searching for what he'd forgotten too?"

Nomad took a bite out of his onion and offered some to Aëros, which he gratefully took. He pondered his friend's question. "I think he was going to kill it, actually. He wasn't very pleasant."

Aëros stopped in his stride, considered his friend's words, and then strode on. Nomad kept pace, and kept speaking. "It's been an Age since I've seen you."

"No, it hasn't."

The wanderer stuffed the meat he'd been cooking—which hadn't really cooked and was mostly raw—into his mouth, and washed it down with a draught from a waywell. Its flow slowed to a trickle, and he upended the water vessel over his mouth, draining what little was left. "I guess I was in that desert longer than I thought."

Aëros drew his own waywell from his Shräud, filled with wōad-sap before he'd left the forest and Shaē behind, and offered it to his friend.

Nomad took it, grunting his pleasant surprise at the sap and drinking more than one would expect the vessel could hold. Finished, he looked to his wayfaring friend, wondering. "Aūr?" Aëros nodded, and Nomad tossed the waywell back to him. "You'll have to make me one."

Aëros put the waywell into a pocket in his Shräud, returning it Nowhere. "It's Aūriel's artifice, you'll have to speak with her."

"Ah." Nomad marked Aëros' Shräud, another of Aūriel's works. Noticed its patchwork repair, its ruined illusion. Then he noticed Aëros as he was, looking ruined himself: eyes sunken, seeking something lost; finger missing, replaced by Argynt and will; neck torn open, sutured no better than his Shräud. "The road to Dún hasn't been kind, I see."

Aëros passed over the threshold of Arythos, passing into its ruins, the tallest mountain in the Wyrmspine rising before and over him, summoning him to its peak. "Some parts weren't. Some parts were."

"Shaē's well, then?"

184

"Brimming." Aëros' eyes dimmed. "Will you be with me long?"

"You know I have no idea." Nomad came up beside Aëros and looked into his eyes, at his wounds. "They're healing poorly."

Aëros felt his throat with his ruined hand, and watched as what his foolishness had brought him the night before flickered in the half-hidden places of his mind; remembered, incomprehensible, horrifying. Aëros met the wanderer's gaze—green and gold—with his own—silver and sunken crescent moons, once full. "But they are healing."

"Nasty scars."

In that moment Aëros let wane his mask of beauty, the massacre beneath unveiled. He revealed his humanity for but the briefest of moments, only long enough to demonstrate his indifference to the newest additions.

The wanderer waved, gesturing for the Wayfarer to put the web of almost deaths and mostly deaths away. "Point taken, point taken."

Aëros replaced the truth of himself with his mask, and continued walking.

Nomad followed. "Where is Aūriel these days?"

Aëros looked inwards with his mind's eye, finding the answers murky and more than half-forgotten. "Enjoying the summer at our villa on the Fells with Tärin."

He gambled his sanity each time he spoke of something he had no memory of: not a lie, but neither the truth. A fantasy; a falsehood; an illusion. He felt something shift uneasily in the asylum as he told his imagined tale, felt that it might reach out and devour him for his audacity in trying to recall what it held and he was not ready to remember.

Nomad turned his head up, scenting the wind, reconciling some confusion. "Aëros."

"What?"

"It's autumn."

185

Aëros scented the wind himself, and found the crispness on it that betrayed the season, betrayed his forgetting. "So it is."

Nomad flickered from existence and returned a moment later, the hem of his cloak aflame. He beat it against the ground in a fury, exasperated. "That was not a pleasant place." His breath came hard, energy spent. "Women with cloven hooves and forked tongues." He shrugged. "Not the worst of places either."

Aëros rolled the soul in his eyes and strode forward, Nomad following. He'd follow until he followed no longer, whenever that might chance to be. "It's been a long time since I've walked here," he said as he and the Wayfarer traversed the ruins. "It's so desolate."

Aëros leapt onto a thin stone wall, balancing along, surveying the rubble Arythos had become. "It has been and will remain so for a long while to come. Athair's will seeped into this land, and unlike the forest, these ruins can't restore themselves."

Even ash, Aëros.

Even ash.

Aëros stopped mid-stride and looked at the Shadow. The memory came.

You, Aūriel, and Tärin made the journey to Jä's. A swift passing from one threshold to another, a Rift opening in your home and leading to his. You were sitting atop his roof now, looking over a letter newly received. Delivered on the featherless, bone-bare wings of a familiar raven, scrawled in a familiar script. 'Arkym,' it read, and so to Arkym you would go.

Tärin found you there, overlooking Arythos. The view stretched far, past the kingdom's walls, into the fields before the Dragongrave. The fertile soil was soaked through with blood, and a pillar of flame leapt up from the forest. You ignored it, drawing yourself back to the

fields, their red tinge not given by the dawn. The greatest part of
Athair's horde waited there, a stone-still shoal in a sea of crimson.
They'd come so swiftly, passed over the West like wind. They were
waiting now: for the living to wither, to weaken, to fade. They were
dead—or undead, rather. They needed no water. No food. Nothing of
living need.

"Da'?"

You heard him ascending the trellis but pretended not to, hoping he
would leave you be, hoping he would remain with his innocence. But he
was wise, growing wiser. Your doing, you knew. He'd done so well on
the hunt. Your thoughts toed the line of pride and regret as you gestured
for him to join you, setting the letter to ash with Iné, the memory of it
all you needed. Arkym. Athair.

You caught his eyes as he stood beside you. They hid nothing. Not
his understanding, not his fear. He saw yours too, still red around the
rims. "Tärin, I have something to tell you. Something hard. Thrace—"

"I overheard you and Mom." His words slowed, unsure of himself,
of what he was saying, of what he felt of it. "I know." He caught your
eyes again, and in them you saw sorrow. Not for Thrace, not for Shaē,
not for himself. For you. He was looking out beyond Arythos, to the
forest. The sky was rolling blue as the sun burned the dawn away. He
looked back to you, his father, wondering. "Is Shaē alright?"

You nodded, knowing it was a lie. He knew it too, knew there was
a place for lies just as there was a place for truths.

Your eyes slid away from each other, both finding the moon, going
pale in the daylight, and watching as a pair of stars fell from it. One
burned up before the other. Neither made it over the horizon, lost
somewhere in Nowhere. "I'll be away for a while, Tärin. Not long, but
a while. You'll be safe here. Jä will see to it."

"You're going to find Athair?"

Find him? You thought of the letter, the word, sent by him,
summoning you. "Yes."

"Do you know where he is?"

You nodded. "I think so."

"What'll you do when you find him?"

Kill him, *you thought.* "Reason with him, if I'm able," *you said, a lie relative to your intent, your hope.* "If I can't, then I don't know," *the truth relative to reality, for you feared killing him was beyond your ability, beyond anyone's by this point.*

He squatted, the posture of a predator in search, like a raven, his eyes keen, seeing what waited in the fields. "They'll come soon."

"Yes," *you said.* "But not today."

It was the truth. You couldn't have known then how close it was to being a lie, but you would.

He said nothing else; you saw he was verging on tears. The tears of a boy not yet a man, and tears of anger at that fact, anger at the inability to do more.

You reached out into Nowhere, summoned Löekeh from its shroud, and shifted blade to bow. You held it out, offering it to him. He did not reach for the bow, but neither did he hesitate as you placed it in his hands, an artifact of his father, a symbol of pride.

"It's yours now, Tärin. I do not need it. Do not want to need it for what I have to do. I'm giving it to you, and everything that goes with and has gone before it." *His eyes widened, unsure of what this meant. You held them with your own, tried to help him understand.* "I hope you will have no need for it but practice. But that's only a hope, not a promise I can make." *His eyes saw yours, saw the meaning in the memento, in your words; he heard them in the deep places of his heart where a son longs to know his father's pride. You smiled, softly, sadly.* "I hope one day you'll forgive me."

Tärin's expression warred between sadness, excitement, bewilderment, fear. He pulled the string taut, an arrow flickering along the riser, aimed towards the crimson fields, and held it until the dawn burned fully away, until his arm wearied and fell, a tear alongside it, falling, perhaps, for innocence.

"Are you alright?" Nomad was watching Aëros, paused midstride atop the wall he'd been walking. He'd withdrawn his weapon, his bow-blade, and was staring at it.

The memory faded. Aëros returned from the rim of insanity, returned Löekeh to its shroud, resumed his stride. "Yes."

"No, you're not."

"Doesn't matter," said Aëros. "It's a problem only I can mend."

Nomad gave a short laugh. "That's what you say about every problem."

Aëros smirked, silent.

───────◆───────

Wanderer and Wayfarer continued on through the rubble of the ruined kingdom as the sun arched above them, hidden by the overcast sky. They wended their way through the remnants of old bakeries and smithies; toy-makers', carpenters', and glass-workers' workshops; of homes, schools, taverns, libraries, and even more remnants of society beside. Neither Aëros nor Nomad could make any of this out, of course, for all that remained of these places were simple foundations, living only in memory—in nightmare.

They stopped again only once, at the foot of an old villa, of which not even the foundation remained. All was ash. "This was my friend's, once. Jä. A brilliant Arkaēn. A better friend. Kept Aūriel and Tärin safe..."

Nomad walked up alongside Aëros, his silver staff clicking on the stone, a tool hiding a secret. "Where's he gone?"

"Left Arythos with the rest of the dwarves after the kingdom fell." Aëros laughed, and shrugged. "So he's either somewhere in the East, or up in ashes."

Wanderer shared the Wayfarer's mirth. They remained at the ruins for only a few heartbeats and half-hidden memories before the journey took them again, back towards the mountain.

Old minecart tracks led the way, Arythos having grown a great deal of its wealth from the rich veins of ore and gemstone running beneath the Wyrmspine—one of the original hoards of one of the original dragons, named Ankäthägäun, long dead. The tracks stood out in mockery of the fallen kingdom, their metal still pristine and shining despite the ruins, forged of Argynt, as most things of much use were once.

They found the maw of the mines in swift stride. And maw it was, for it was a dragon's mouth, gaping, six stories high and half that across. Not the mouth of Arök; that was sunken in the sea, his tail wrapping around Eave, meeting his jaws in the depths, bitten by it, binding the world together. Or so myth made of the wyrm.

The maw of the mines was hewn out of the mountain itself, a grand simulacrum of the dragon that once made it its home, hording its wealth, brooding over it. The Argynt tracks ran in, each traveling in turn down many shafts and corridors, branching away, an artery to the mountain's depths.

Mining equipment and the oxidized remains of raw ore littered the tunnel entrances, the image of miners having just finished a day's work petrified in time. Some of the shafts were sealed off, some collapsed in on themselves, but most were still open, disappearing into darkness. The sky overhead was darkening itself, both with the shadow of night and the threat of rain, the intemperance ushering wanderer and Wayfarer forward.

Nomad looked from side to side, shaft to shaft. "Which way?"

The Wayfarer strode into the entrance dead ahead. "Doesn't matter."

Chapter XIX: boom
• Stirring of Autumn •

"*D*oesn't matter." Nomad's mockery was as weighty and weathered as the stone that surrounded them. They'd entered the mountain, and—like the maw of the great serpent its entrance was shaped after—it had devoured them. They walked now through the darkness of underground caverns, their way lit by Aëros' lantern and intuition. The mines smelled of limestone and ironwork, wet chalk and dry bone.

"It doesn't," said Aëros. "I don't know the route through the mines, so any way is as like any other to lead me where I need to go."

The wanderer rolled his eyes. "We don't even *know* where we need to go."

"We? This isn't we, Nomad." Aëros begrudged that it was, in fact, we. At least for the time being. "At any rate, of course I do," he pointed to the ceiling of the cavern, and beyond it, to the summit, to the Rift. "Up."

"Then why does it feel like we're going down?"

"We are." Aëros' lantern hung in his hand, light so bright it hummed, scattering the dark. Its rays caught the Argynt rails and formed them into thin, scintillating rivers of light. "The dwarves were delvers. To go up, we must go down."

Nomad's head was crooked, considering. "That doesn't make any sense."

"Neither do you."

Nomad shrugged. "Fair enough." He would not argue that. "Mystery aside, how is it you don't know the way to the Wayshrine?"

Aëros sighed, the sound as weighty and weatherworn as Nomad's mockery. "The way is simple; you enter through the Rift.

The trouble is, I don't know the way *to* the Rift. I never walked it. I only ever meant it as precaution."

Nomad's eyes narrowed. "Precaution for what?"

"For something like that." Aëros pointed to the Shadow that only he could see, striding in darkness, darker than it. The effigy of his madness, of what he'd lost, forgotten, and was searching for. *I know you see it in my eyes, my friend. Everyone else does.*

Nomad grunted. "There's no other way?"

Aëros shook his head. "I wanted the Rift in solitude. The summit fit. It's the most remote place on Eave, inaccessible save by another Rift or by way of these mines. And as you can see," he gestured in the general direction of 'lost,' "even I can't navigate this labyrinth."

"Then just open a Rift."

Aëros rolled the soul in his eyes. "I'm done with this conversation."

"Someone's sensitive today." Nomad shrugged, and dropped the subject. He looked around, taking in where exactly he'd found himself. "At least this is a pleasant place to be lost in."

Aëros looked around and found himself in agreement. He and Nomad were passing through a warren, the massive cavern a nexus for the smaller shafts making up the arteries of the mines. So immense was it that Aëros' lantern could not illuminate it end to end, curtains of darkness hanging both behind and before. What the light did reveal, however, was a marvel, the mines a mixing of the Things Betwixt and the Wōadglōam Forest.

Like the labyrinth hidden in the ashen stone of the Ashen Vale, the mines went on for endless leagues beneath the Wyrmspine. More than once did both Wayfarer and wanderer find themselves in a shaft or cavern or warren that seemed regrettably familiar, their path looping on itself even as they made certain to avoid retracing old trails with every bit of waycraft they could recall. Frustrating as the going was, their annoyance didn't last long, fading in the wake of their admiration of the stone underworld.

Like the Wōadglōam Forest, the mountain grew roots of its own. They bound roof and undercroft together, undulating blue-black stone carved out by the slow will of trapped wind and hidden waters over the stretch of Ages. Veins of ore and seams of gemstone were folded into columns, branches of a larger central lode lost somewhere too deep in the Wyrmspine for hewing. The precious metals and stones were the lifeblood of the mountain hoard, light catching in them, flickering along the monoliths like the sap of the wōadglōam.

In the midst of one warren, Aëros stopped. "Let's rest, eat something." He kicked over two metal buckets filled with debris and slumped down on the butt end of one, offering the other to his companion.

"Appreciated." Nomad took the makeshift seat and evaporated as he sat, flickering back into existence a little while later.

Aëros was rifling through Nowhere in search of fare, paying no more mind than a question to the anomaly. "Where, and for how long?"

"The brig on some forsaken ship—" Nomad hacked and coughed, spitting up seawater. "—for an entire summer."

"Our summer?"

"I don't fucking know, mate." Nomad was drenched and smelled like salt air, spoke like a saltier sailor. "It was hot and wet and cramped and all I could see was an endless ocean through a porthole as tight as the captain's daughter was loose."

Aëros' brows lifted, hand held halfway in Nowhere, surprised. "What's an ocean?"

Nomad opened his mouth to answer, hacked out more seawater. "It's like a sea, but more vast."

Aëros' brows rose in recognition; his hand continued its search. "Ah, I've seen those before." He withdrew a few handfuls of smoked meat, a gift from Shaē, and offered half to Nomad, who accepted it with the hands of a starving orphan. Aëros thought back to the Fēl, the boy, Athair, then pushed the thought away, pushed it down. He considered looking to the Shadow, but decided not to give it the satisfaction. It already knew his mind.

"Thanksh." Nomad spoke around the meat as he chewed it. "They fed me fuck-all on the ship."

"Do you ever tire of that?" The Wayfarer swallowed and paused eating, waiting for an answer.

Nomad held a finger up as he pulled from his waywell— refilled somehow—to wash down the salt and the smoke. "Sometimes."

They sat in silence for a while, eating, drinking, readying themselves to begin again. Aëros watched his friend, knew he shouldn't be here. "Even if you're by my side now, you won't be when I reach the Rift, let alone my journey's end. You can't be. It's my burden, no one else's."

Nomad bit off another piece of flesh and chewed it slowly, thoughtful. "Don't worry. I'm sure I won't be here long. But I'll stay for now. Seems I'm not supposed to be anywhere else yet."

They returned to silence. The sound of eating. The sound of drinking. The sound of something echoing through the mines from somewhere beyond the reach of sight, hidden by the curtains of darkness surrounding them. Wayfarer and wanderer looked at each other, and peered into the shadows of the warren, ears straining. The sound vanished as swiftly as it had come.

"What the fu—" Aëros' elven ears twitched as the sound came again, louder, moaning through the stone.

Nomad stood, alert, though his ears were less keen. "What do you think—"

Nomad flickered from existence, and Aëros rolled his soul in his eyes. "Of course."

Again the sound came, groaning, still impossible to place, but closer than before. It was a terrible din, dragging Aëros' mind back to his nights in the wōadglōam's outskirts, predators rending the flesh of prey, prey begging, pleading. Nomad returned, clothing inside-out. There was no time for questions. The sound echoed again, and again died away. Closer. Out of place. The mine had few sounds—the slow drip of water, the trickle of thin, aged dust, the soft whistle of soft wind, the click of Nomad's walking staff, each subtle, unobtrusive. This was the grand sound of nightmares, the sound the mind imagined it might hear from dark places on the periphery of the world. Only it wasn't imagined. It wasn't nightmare. Not the Shadow's, not anyone's. It was real. It was here.

Nomad looked to Aëros. "Should we run?"

"Yes."

"We're going to wait and see what it is, aren't we?"

Aëros nodded.

The wait wasn't long, and when it went, it brought a man in its place. A large man. An *incredibly* large man, emerging from the darkness where nightmares crept. But he did not creep. He sprinted, hauled himself forward, bumbled through his strides. He was lightly armored, wearing only loose mail, some sort of bulky vest, and a square helmet. An assortment of odd tools and trinkets encircled his hips: picks, hammers, some strange device coiled up with a length of glinting rope and spike. He was hurtling away at breakneck speed, the sound pursuing him from behind, coming louder and louder, swifter and swifter.

Wayfarer and wanderer looked at one another in confusion, undecided. They watched as the giant man barreled towards them, heedless, only skidding to a halt a mere blade's length away, nearly tumbling over his own feet. Aëros made note of this, his will already set on drawing Löekeh from Nowhere. He cast his lantern over the stranger, wondering, finding him somehow familiar. The hulking man simply stood there, almost innocently, as the Wayfarer's eyes widened and his mouth unhinged. "Jä?"

The large man lifted the metal face-plate of his helmet, revealing a square jawline, a ragged beard, and blue-hued eyes beneath. "Aëros!" He gave a cheerful wave and slapped the Wayfarer on the shoulder, his gauntlets like kegs. "You should be runnin' now." He dropped his face-plate and sprinted away, hurtling in the direction opposite of what pursued him.

"Jä?!" Aëros turned in utter astonishment.

"Your dwarven friend?" Nomad turned with him. "Neither in the East nor in ashes, then."

Aëros' eyes were wide, bewildered, his head crooked. "How—" He didn't finish his question, for it was not a time for them. It was a time for running.

Hundreds of creatures, the size of stones, of boulders, of buildings, tore through the curtain of dark, pouring into the light, teeth gnashing, claws tearing into the stone. Wayfarer and wanderer took one look, turned on their heels, and hurled themselves after Jä, who was now barreling into a mineshaft. They barely reached him before the creatures bottlenecked in the tunnel, slowing their raging pursuit.

"Jä!" Aëros heaved the name out between ragged breaths.

"Aye, good to see you too, laddie!" the large man cheered over the hunger and hatred of the creatures. "But we'll reminisce later. For now, follow me!"

Neither Aëros nor Nomad needed convincing, smelling the rancid breath of the horde on their heels. The only thing holding the swarm at bay was the small shaft, its tight quarters hindering movement and number as the creatures stumbled over one another in their hunt.

"Get ready!" Jä shouted over the din.

Nomad shouted back, "Ready for what?!"

"Five!" Jä began counting.

"Oh, fuck." Aëros knew how well Jä could count down from five.

"Four!"

"'Oh, fuck' *what*?!" Nomad did not.

The dwarf held up four fingers. "Three!"

"Why are you counting down?" The wanderer threw his question at the Wayfarer. "Why is he counting down?"

"Two!"

Aëros pointed, shoving Nomad forward. "Just run!"

Jä looked at the four fingers he still held up, bewildered.

Boom.

The three adventurers could not see the explosion, but they heard it, the warren behind them torn apart, those creatures left within it crushed under the mountain's weight. The arkaēn reaction built on itself, becoming more and more violent as it sped towards its apex. The creatures in the tunnel could sense the doom of their kindred, the scent of death exciting them—until the shaft gave way, and their excitement turned to terror as they became another crimson stroke on the stone canvas, another muse for a mural of blood. It meant reprieve from death by devouring for the adventurers, in its place an oncoming death by living burial. Aëros wasn't sure what was preferable, though it wasn't as if he was being given the chance to choose.

The passageway turned over and over again, lit by Aëros' lantern and the disproportionately small oil lantern that swung at Jä's side. All the while the collapsing rock that trailed them swiftened, chasing their heels, seeking to paint them on the stone the same as the creatures. The mountain would eventually swallow them, but not yet.

Jä disappeared, Aëros and Nomad disappearing in turn as the dwarf yanked them into another shaft just as the old collapsed behind them. The new tunnel was a safety shaft supported by Argynt framework, standing proud against the explosion.

"Timed everythin' perfectly," said Jä, bent over, heaving and ho-ing, regaining breath. The effort it took him to do so, and the glare of disbelief that Aëros staggered him with, strongly disagreed with his calculations.

The Wayfarer examined the new passage, finding something missing. *Nomad.* His eyes widened, as did Jä's as their realizations met. Aëros hurled himself at the collapsed passage, tearing at the stone, screaming. "Nomad!"

Jä watched his friend unravel, put a hand on his shoulder. "Aëros, he's not gettin' ou—"

"What is it?"

Aëros and Jä spun on their heels as the wanderer flickered back into existence. He held a flagon of ale in one hand and a caramel apple in the other. He was tipsy and smelled of perfume and fine hearth smoke. Jä staggered in shock. "What the fook?"

Aëros collapsed as relief and fatigue flooded him, but Jä was already postured up again, pulling him to his feet. "Happy days, but isn't time to rest yet. And this is comin' from me, Aëros. You know how much I hate runnin'."

"Fook?" Nomad looked towards the collapsed passageway, took a bite of his apple, a draught from his ale. "Did we do that?"

"How many charges did you set, Jä." Aëros' tone demanded more than asked.

Jä scratched the back of his head, looking like a child caught eating sweets before supper, or a man caught in bed with his wife's sister. "Ah, well..."

BOOM.

The trio flew through the tunnel, winding around falling debris as arkaēn eruptions threatened the structural integrity of the mountain itself. Jä formed an awkward and apprehensive smile as he ran. "I may have miscounted."

Aëros kicked him mid-stride. "You've been miscounting since you learned numbers!"

The path to safety was short, and they dashed into it just as the auxiliary tunnel caved in, stone crumbling even as the Argynt framework stood fast. It was designed for cave-ins, not mountain-ins. They found themselves in another warren, as large as the last. The only feature that made them certain it wasn't the same was that it wasn't buried beneath stone. Wayfarer and wanderer stooped themselves over, hands on knees, as they drew fresh wind for what they'd spent. Jä collapsed to his back, sucking down all remaining air for his own fitful heaving.

Nomad looked at Jä, ragged and panting. "I think you have a problem."

Jä propped himself up on his forearms. "Aye, ya fookin' think?"

As the adrenaline of the event subsided, minds calming, Nomad regarded the large man for what seemed the first time, sizing up his behemoth frame. He stood a head and a half above him and must have weighed what both he and Aëros did together. "You're a dwarf?"

"Aye!" Jä punched his hands into the air with pride, forgetting they'd been supporting him, and hit the floor on his back hard, dust pluming up around him. "I'm as stubborn as stone and as rooted to it as the mountain."

"But your size…" The wanderer flipped a palm up and shook his head. "I know dwarves are stout, but aren't they supposed to be short?"

Jä went cross-eyed. "Have you not seen one before?"

Nomad remembered back to his conversation with Aëros, and shook his head.

Jä's brow rose, skeptical. "Well, some are, some aren't, same as every other breed of livin' thing. In my wanderin' I've met giants the size o' dwarves, dwarves the size o' imps, n' imps the size o' giants. And I'm not talkin' about how tall they were." He grinned. "World's a strange place."

Nomad flickered from existence.

Jä stared at the empty space where the wanderer was once but was no longer. "He do that often?"

Aëros rolled his eyes. "Only when it's inconvenient."

"Where'd he go?"

"Another time, another realm, another place in our own. It's always different."

"Didn't know there was more like you."

Aëros finally found his breath, and perched himself beside Jä on the floor, setting his lantern down between them. "He isn't."

"What's different?"

"I choose where I go. I imagine it, will a Rift to it, and walk through." Aëros stared at where Nomad was no longer. *Used to, anyway.* "He doesn't open a Rift, doesn't choose. For him it's random."

Jä laughed, booming, bellowing. Dust trickled from above, and he cut off, looking about, nervous. "So, he's broken."

Aëros drew his waywell of wōad-sap from Nowhere, pulled from it, stopped it up, returned it. "He tells women he's a mystery."

Jä scoffed. "So do you."

Aëros grimaced, then smirked. "I let them come to that conclusion on their own, wyrmshit as it may be. Too many of me for mystery."

Aëros' eyes drew distant, a sign he was musing. Jä rolled the soul in his own, recognizing well when Aëros was basking in the golden silhouette of his ego. "Many of you?"

Far too many.

The Shadow sat across from Aëros, pulling on the threads of a memory. In it Aëros saw himself sitting with his son, sharing the secrets of his work, his mastery, passing knowledge down the family line.

"There's more than one you, Da'?"

You nodded. "More than one of you too, Tärin. Many more."

His eyes were wide and full of wonder. You sat across from him in your study as you sit across from me now. It was night, the room lit by

200

candlelight and the illusory images of Dräu you'd been weaving to demonstrate your instruction.

"What's more," you continued, "is that we share a thread of ourselves across all realities that share a version of ourselves, and sometimes those threads overlap." You gestured to your head—to your mind. "You know when you feel you've seen something or done something or been somewhere before? When the world seems hazy and dreamlike?"

Tärin nodded.

"That's your reality overlapping another where you've already seen, or felt, or lived." You wove two effigies of yourself, one running, the other falling into its step, a fraction of a moment delayed, then overlaid the two, one slightly out of sync with the other. "In another realm they had names for it; déjà vu—I've seen this; déjà senti—I've felt this; déjà vécu—I've lived this."

Tärin watched the illusions run, enthralled. "Are there other versions of everyone?"

"Almost everyone." You saw the question blooming in his eyes, answered it before he asked. "His name is Nomad, and there's only one of him."

"Only one in the whole Tapestry?"

"Only one."

"Da'?"

"Yes?"

"Have you ever met another yo—"

Nomad returned, disturbing Aëros from his memory, Jä from the question that seemed to lead into it. The wanderer was sitting atop a white horse. Jä looked to the beast and the wanderer in turn. "I'm not cleaning up after him."

"This is Shad—" The horse whinnied and flickered from existence. The wanderer fell from his perch, striking the stone floor. Hard. "Agh!"

Jä roared with laughter as the wanderer writhed. "Any more surprises?"

Nomad wheezed as his wind returned. "Fook if I know."

The dwarf shook his head, looked at Aëros. "He is rather inconvenient, isn't he?"

Nomad grumbled, near to standing, assessing his surroundings as he rose. "What now?"

Aëros stood, clasped him on the shoulder. "Now we let the dwarf lead."

Nomad looked to the hulking man. "Do you know the way?"

Jä scratched his arse. "The way where?"

"The way out of here."

"This is a mountain, isn't it?"

Nomad squinted.

"And I'm a dwarf, am I not?"

His squint deepened. "Apparently."

Jä and Nomad stared at each other for an uncomfortable length of time, until the dwarf's mouth curled up and he laughed and whacked the wanderer on the back, sending him stumbling. "Find your kilter, mate. 'Course I know the way."

Nomad righted himself. More time passed. "Well, which way is it?"

Jä pointed to the collapsed tunnel.

Nomad's beautiful face contorted into something hideous. "I meant a way we can use."

The dwarf tilted his head like a confused beast. "Well, you should've said so."

Aëros laughed, agreeing. "You should have."

"There's another path, but it leads to the peak o' the mountain."

Nomad's face found his hand.

The Wayfarer answered for him. "That's perfect."

Jä bent a wondering brow at his friend, though it didn't take long for it to lift in understanding. "The Rift?" His eyes narrowed. "Why?"

Aëros picked up his lantern. "Got a place to rest?"

Jä took the hint. "Aye. It's not far, we'll be there in a flash 'n a bang."

Nomad groaned. The mountain groaned in response—the trio froze. Aëros looked to Jä, asking with his eyes if he'd miscounted again.

"Isn't me."

Another rumble, up from the depths of the mountain, up from beneath. The warren shook, and ancient dust trickled from its eaves.

Jä sneered. "Out o' the shade—"

"—and into deeper shadow still," Aëros finished, instincts flaring.

The rumble became a roar, the trickle a downpour. Something was coming up, up through the stone, up through the mountain. Stalactites careened down, spearing the floor as the adventurers stumbled to evade them. Boulders crashed and metal whined as the tremors grew and the cavern floor fractured, spider-webbing like shattered glass as the roof fell and what lurked beneath rent its way up.

The warren's undercroft erupted, darkness appearing where stone had once imprisoned it. The Argynt tracks alone retained their form despite the cataclysm, the metal the strongest stuff Eave could forge in the embers of its Ages. It was the tracks the trio caught as the stone fell away beneath them, and they heaved themselves up onto the rails as what had riven the warren apart appeared in the light of their lanterns.

It was a beast of antiquity; not the dragon that once lorded over the mountain hoard, but a descendant of Arök far older, dwelling within the stone, sleeping in the world's heart, the hollow core where tavern tales said another world slept in silence.

Aëros knew not of this other world, but Jä did, and knew the beast that came from it. Its name fell from his memory to his lips in his awe. "It's a wyn."

"A what?" wondered Nomad.

The *what* railed against the Argynt tracks. The metal was unyielding, but the adventurers were still shaken from their footing. Its head took up almost the entire chasm, the rest of its slithering, serpentine form arrested by the mountain's grip. Its maw unhinged, and its stalagmite teeth crashed into the metal in a desperate attempt to silence those who had disturbed it. It heard the adventurer's breath, their speech, their fearful hearts, but it saw nothing—having nothing to see with, the darkness blinding it long ago. It thrust again, bound up by the stone, the rails, it a thing of immensity, the warren not near immense enough.

"A stone serpent," said Aëros to Nomad. "We need to go." He looked at Jä. "You need to lead."

"Well I sure as shite ain't balancin' on these!" Jä nearly sat in a pout, barely able to keep himself upright on the rails with all four limbs supporting him. "Dwarves aren't meant for this faē-footed fookery!"

Aëros was already sprinting along the slender rails towards a solution. He reached a mine-cart just as Nomad caught up to him, the wanderer's agility rivaling his own. They heaved it forward, pushing it to their lumbering comrade.

"Aye, laddies! Now that's an idea!" The dwarf cheered as he pulled round explosives from his vest as if he were plucking petals from a flower, dropping them into the snapping maw of the wyn. They were small, leathern, and twine-wrapped. He called them his Spouses, and their arkaēn inferno was sticky and horrifying, immolating the stony carapace of the ancient serpent and melting its iron-black teeth.

The wyn recoiled as its fangs fragmented, shards ripping through its mouth. But it was a temporary distraction; its jaws were lined with thousands of concentrically undulating teeth, and a few lost made no difference to the death those left could reap. Its movement was limited, yet with each motion it carved the stone away, its scales serrated and grinding, widening the way, more and more of itself slithering through. The Argynt rails were the only thing it could not break. The mountain creaked as it thrust its skull into the tracks, again and again and again. As Aëros and Nomad kited the cart to Jä, the wyn heaved once more, hateful, terrible, and with its effort came a great groan as the stone to which the rails were riveted fractured, ever weaker than the Argynt itself, the supports splintering from their rooting.

"Haul it, laddies!" Jä hurled himself into the cart. "Straight on! Way out is there!"

The Wayfarer and the wanderer grunted as they threw their weight into their behemoth comrade, setting the cart gliding along the tracks. They each ran along one rail as Jä rolled before them, trying desperately to keep the cart from tipping as the beast below rammed over and over. With each impact the stone holding the rails fractured further, the supports screaming their death throes as the tracks buckled and dipped into the chasm.

"The shaft!" Jä stood and pointed as if he were the captain of a great ship. The wyn thrust again, throwing him back onto his arse, a reminder that he had barely any land-legs, let alone sea. The entire railway dropped five spans, wanderer and Wayfarer lurching back, cart turning up onto one side as it fell in and out of kilter along a single line of track.

"Fook!" Jä threw his weight hard onto the uplifted side of the cart, his companions finding their footing and yanking it down with him. It made little difference. More and more of the supporting struts snapped from their bracing, the rails dipping ever lower as the stone gave way. But the trio was not twenty spans from the shaft, and they knew they would make it before the tracks collapsed and the wyn took them.

The wyn knew they were wrong.

205

It lurched, it struck, the stone groaned, and the tracks gave way, their supports severed at last. The three companions were flung forward, the rails shearing from the walls of the warren as they fell.

Jä reacted the swiftest, drawing from his belt his strange device. He aimed it at the shaft and a flash later a length of Argynt rope had run itself through the stone, anchored by a spike of the same stuff. Nomad and Aëros grasped the cordage as it appeared, swinging into the chasm wall like birds finding their perch. Jä crashed into the stone like a boulder through a building, just barely hanging onto the device.

All three watched the wyn below, the rails caught up in the serpent's maw, forcing them open, vulnerable. Jä looked up to his comrades, his eyes flickering between bemusement and something else. Aëros recognized it immediately: *Madness.*

"Be back, laddies." Jä disconnected the rope from its mechanism, saluting as he fell.

Nomad, wide-eyed, moved to dive after the dwarf, but Aëros grabbed him. "He's seen far worse. Now climb, you're in the way."

Nomad had no words, his face wound up in bewilderment as he watched the dwarf plummet towards the wyn and surely his death.

Jä dove headlong into the serpent's maw, a grimace his only flinch as it roared, spattering him with its foul breath and spittle. He landed on one of its fangs, twice as large as himself, cracking it with the weight of his impact. He stood over its throat—red, fleshy, putrid, panicking in desperation. He laughed as he unwound his vest, revealing a harem of Spouses and arkaēn reagents sewn into its lining. Smiling, he lit a fuse and dropped the Wrath of Wives into the gut of the prone behemoth.

Another roar ripped out of the wyn, but it was vain, its doom sealed. Aëros felt a bit of pity for the creature, but it was no bone drake. It wasn't timid, wasn't gentle. So the pity passed, unburdened.

Jä took another length of rope and fit it to his device, firing it again at the shaft above. Nomad dove back as the spike ripped past his head. He and Aëros had already reached the shaft, and had been watching their mad comrade from its precipice. The grapple bit into the stone, and Jä climbed, the wyn left below as it struggled to wrench the rails away. Jä counted silently to himself as he ascended, waiting, waiting, waiting—

Nothing happened. Jä looked down at the wyn, writhing around, and shouted up to his companions, "I guess it's a du—"

BOOM.

Wayfarer and wanderer watched the wyn disappear in an inferno of black flame, its mass immolated by the heat, body boiling and evaporating. The mountain moaned as, deep within it, stone more ancient than time shifted from its slumber.

Flames licked Jä's boots as he hauled himself up the line, hand over hand, far too slowly. The explosion threw him up, launching him into the shaft, colliding with and collapsing on Nomad. He leapt up, eyes wild around the edges, eyebrows seared off, laugh booming as loud as the explosion, hair blown back, soot staining every bit of exposed skin. He looked over the edge to admire what he'd done.

Aëros joined his friend's mirth, losing himself in it, rolling around in the ash blown into the shaft. He slapped Nomad on the back as the wanderer righted himself, groaning. "See? I told you he'd be fine."

"Aye! Not a scratch on me." Jä held out a hand over the chasm below, flipping the good finger at the dead and dying beast. A shard of the wyn's tooth ripped through the air, cleaving finger from hand. The will of the living did not end with their deaths, and the beast's vindication was complete with Jä knowing nine.

"Fook!" the dwarf bellowed as a spurt of blood erupted from where his finger used to be.

Aëros held up his own left hand, flashing his Argynt finger, mouth crooked. *"For nine is all I know!"*

Chapter XX: Wed
• Stirring of Autumn •

Jä's cavern wasn't far. It was a square, sequestered space, an old storage area by its look and location. Its ceiling was a story high and the floor only forty paces or so from end to end, walls sheer and carved with ornate runes and iconography. Scattered about were light furnishings: a few bed rolls, some blankets, a fire pit over-stood by an iron spit at its center. The only oddity, aside from Jä being in the mines to begin with, was the haphazard stack of barrels and crates set against every wall. In the farthest corner was an Arkaēn's Kiln replete with decocting equipment for potions, poisons, elixirs, philters, salves, and the dwarf's main artifice: reactive arkaēn reagents, or in layman's terms: explosives. The crates were overflowing with his decoctions, some finished, most half-worked or spoiled, all strewn about the distillery just beside the cache.

"I see you've been busy out here in the midst of nowhere." Aëros took a seat on an empty crate after a very thorough search to ensure it was actually empty. He adjusted himself as the dwarf searched for bandaging to mend his mangled hand. "Why are you even here in the first place? It's a good thing you didn't lose the other finger, Kaēlyn would've killed you."

Jä hinted at a frown, and looked at his ruined hand, to the ring on the finger beside the one no longer there.

Aëros' brow furrowed. "What's wrong?"

"Kaēlyn and myself been tryin' to work through things, Aëros. Tryin'…" No longer a hint, Jä's frown was now a broad, direct statement. "I know it's been an Age since we've seen each other, and you don't get round to your sister much. But you really don't remember?"

Aëros watched his friend, disbelieving, then realized in horror that he was serious. He thought back to the memory of when he'd

209

broken things off with Aūriel, and felt the sorrow his friend felt. He stood up, walked over and hugged him. "I'm sorry."

Jä hugged him back, crushing him, squeezing the wind from his lungs. "Jä—" Aëros choked, struggling against his friend's strength.

"Oh." Jä let him go, scratched his head. "I really am glad you're here, Aëros."

Aëros smiled. "I'm glad to see you too."

"Anyway," said Jä. "Kaēlyn took an oath to protect when she became a physician. She wouldn't kill me over my ring."

Aëros bent a brow. "You believe that?"

Jä laughed, shaking the cavern. "Fook no!"

Nomad dusted off an overturned crate of his own, found the wrappings Jä was looking for, and tossed them over. The dwarf wound the dirty cloth bandage around his finger, placed some odd yellow tinder on the fire, and set it ablaze with a striking stick. He turned to the wanderer, offering a hand. "So, now that things are settled down, name's Jä Sonwúd."

Nomad took Jä's hand, his own swallowed by the burly fist. "Nomad."

Jä stared at him like he was stupid. "Aye, I get that by your tattered clothes and vanishin' act. What's your name?"

"Nomad," said the wanderer a little more curtly.

The dwarf spoke behind his hand to Aëros. "He really is broken, isn't he?"

"His name's literally Nomad, Jä."

The dwarf looked back to the wanderer, revelation clear as his mouth widened. "Ah. Well then, good to meet you, Nohome."

Nomad took the sarcasm as well as he took the dwarf's hand. "Same to you, Jä." He looked around the chamber, then to the single exit and entrance. "We're safe here?"

The dwarf nodded. "For now. But the ghúls'll be riled up from earlier, and they'll be huntin' for us. Specially after the ruckus that wyn roused. We'll be waitin' a while here to let 'em settle before we go headin' out again."

Nomad's crate was uncomfortable. As if there was any other way it might be. "Ghúls?"

Jä shook his head as he stared into the charring tinder. "For someone who dances between worlds, you sure know fook all about 'em. The fookin' things that tried to eat us! Scavengers that fed on corpses durin' the Devourin'. Hunger did 'em in the end though. They ate everythin' they could and turned to cannibalizin', becomin' even fouler for it. Wretched things."

Nomad stood, figuring it better than sitting, and walked over to the Arkaēn's Kiln, curious. "Why are you here with them then?"

"Bit o' fun." The dwarf joined the wanderer at the cache of explosives. "They fook fast and no one will miss 'em. Plus, it's nice to see the mines again. Many memories here. Sort only a grave stirs up."

Nomad jumped as Jä snatched an explosive he was about to fiddle with out of his hands. "It's not a fookin' toy. So," Jä aimed the conversation at Aëros, "You know why I'm here. Fook you doing?"

The Wayfarer thought for a moment, drew breath for the story he was about to tell. The dwarf held up a hand. "No. You know that if it takes that much wind to start it's already too long for me." Jä remembered his weariness. He saw something unfamiliar in Aëros' own, wasn't sure what to make of it, so didn't bother trying. "Been on too many quests with you already and they always go pretty much the same way. You drag some poor sod along—me—and we both end up battered, bruised, stabbed, hung-over, indebted, imprisoned, lost, inked, wed, or a combination o' all the aforementioned ailments n' more, with naught to show for it but a tavern tale and a trinket or two. I'll show you and Nohome here to the peak, but that'll be all the part I play in this one."

Aëros' mouth went crooked, eyes wry. "For once you're not exaggerating."

The dwarf laughed, bitter, resigned. "You're rippin' right I'm not! I can't even count how many times I've saved your arse."

Aëros threw an accusing finger at him. "That's because you can barely count to begin with!"

Jä ceased laughing and feigned indignation. "It's hard to learn numbers when you've only nine fingers to count on!"

Nomad squinted; Aëros cackled.

The wanderer looked at the Wayfarer and dwarf. "Did you say wed?"

"Aye," Jä agreed.

Nomad waited for the dwarf to go on, then looked to Aëros for an answer, then gave it up unclarified.

A rumbling echoed through the cavern—Jä's stomach. He took off his helmet, pulling out a block of aged cheese that was by all measures too large to fit in it, but somehow fit all the same.

"How did you..." Nomad trailed off as he watched the dwarf, realizing there wasn't going to be a good answer. "Never mind."

Aëros pulled some of his cured meat from Nowhere. *Going taste-blind to this stuff.* Jä grabbed more of the tinder he'd been using to feed the fire. "I've some meat of my own to roast," he said as he went in search of it.

Nomad looked at the odd yellow flame of the odd yellow tinder. "What're you burning?"

The dwarf tossed more of the kindling into the pit. "Ghúl bones."

Aëros frowned at the bonefire and its fuel, and then at the dwarf. "And the meat? What kind is it?"

"The dead kind." Jä propped up the iron spit and thumped a chunk of flesh onto it. It reeked, giving Aëros his answer, which he rather wished he didn't have.

"You know, I have plenty of smoked meat left." Aëros offered some to his friend.

"Well why didn't you say so?!" The dwarf snatched it up. "I've been eating this rotten shite for weeks."

The three adventurers fell silent as they ate, minds fixed on the flames, letting the warmth seep down into their bones, stripping weariness away. Aëros was surprised to find himself content, not lost within himself, not worried about it happening. Not worried about the memories. The nightmares. The forgetting. His promise. His madness. The bone drake. The Fēl. *The boy. He was just Tärin's age. I should've left. I should've walked away. That other world... The ash, the graves, the burning, the screaming, the death, the—*

A hand, open, slapped Aëros across the face, launching him off his crate and sending him tumbling into a pile of tools. He lay there for a moment, collecting himself, pain throbbing along his lower jaw.

"What the fuck..." He stood slowly, caught between the waking world and the one within. "...was that for?"

"I was talkin' to you and you disappeared on me."

"Where the fuck would I disappear to!" Aëros thought he heard the Shadow laughing at him. It was in the corner, leaning against the wall, smirking.

Jä prodded Aëros' skull. The Wayfarer flinched. "You disappear in here. You did it before. It's annoyin'."

Aëros grumbled to himself, remembered his memory with Tärin. *Agreed.* "What were you saying?"

"Time's walked." The dwarf wiped food from his patchy beard. "I reckon it's as safe as it'll get. Still, best tread careful-like and bring our luck with us."

Nomad grinned like an arsehole. "Have any to spare?"

"Aye." Jä pointed to the crates of explosives and gave a self-satisfied and sadistic smile.

The wanderer groaned.

Chapter XXI: Luck
• Stirring of Autumn •

J ä led the way with swift strides to the summit path, and as Aëros said, to go up they must begin by going down.

The dwarf explained that the two adventurers had been skirting the perimeter of the mine's heart, a great chasm in the mountain's core in which the dwarves had done most of their delving. They deviated from this ouroboric path with Jä's guidance, finding the great pit without issue from either the maddening labyrinth or the wicked things that found the madness a comfort.

"Long way down." Nomad peered over the lip of the chasm. It descended into darkness, as the warren of the wyn had. The light of their lanterns struck the shadow, silver for Aëros and gold for Jä, yet neither cut the barest sliver through its shroud. In its depths something stirred. Something that hated the light, suffered in it.

"Long way indeed." Jä kicked a pile of loose debris into the pit. They did not hear it strike bottom, if even there was one. "Know a fool who knew a fool who fell in once."

"Oh?" Nomad tried to imagine what that would be like. "What happened to him?"

"Still fallin'!" Jä mock-charged the wanderer, sending him backpedaling towards the chasm. The dwarf, roaring his ridiculous laugh, caught him before he found a fool's fate. "Ease up. We're almost to the summit."

Nomad dusted off his pride and looked up, the roof of the chasm hidden behind the same darkness as its undercroft. "You mean bottom?"

Jä stared at Nomad for a long, long while. "No." He turned and descended. Down, down, down into the depths of the mines, to seek the summit, to find his doom.

The path down followed a spiraling stairwell of stone carved against the walls of the chasm. Aëros thought it felt familiar, and remembered the Sylysæ, the asylum. Darkness swirled around him, the mountain's great roots of undulating stone anchoring the nascent overworld of Eave to its primordial underworld, like the threads of self anchoring his conscious mind to the festering pit of his unconscious, unknowable self. He cast off the parallel, knowing better than to let his mind wander, instead minding the descent, the stone, the work of the dwarves, the walls of the pit inscribed with their runes, craggy script running on before, behind, above, and beneath.

Alongside the roots that moored the mountain to the depths of Eave ran great, vertical lines of coiling Argynt rope. The cords stretched from the heights of the chasm into its depths, vertical highways for the clockwork artifice used to speed up and down the many strata of the mine.

They passed one of the lifts, and Nomad wondered why they did not simply take it to the summit. Jä paused and placed the most tentative of steps onto the machine, and in response the delicate gears that guided the mechanism disintegrated, rotten from an Age of disuse and disrepair, the platform careening down into darkness to find the fool in his fall. "Not everythin' can be made o' Argynt."

Nomad gestured on. "Continue."

Each layer of the chasm held a hoard of different treasures. Some silver, some gold, veins of sapphire and amethyst and onyx running through others, and at the farthest depths glimmered the lode of raw Argynt shared by every vertebra in the Wyrmspine. The trio admired the glinting trove as they passed, Jä's admiration deepest and truest among them, the memories he found filling him with pride and sorrow both. Pride for what he and his ancestors had built, sorrow for having lost it. The Devouring had taken it from them, and in their fall they were forced into a new chapter of their history—a chapter of enduring and vagrancy and uncertainty.

Still, the ancestry of the dwarves, high or low, was preserved in the minds of all their kind. Forged in metal, carved in stone, threaded through memory. A single poignant shard of this ancestry flared within Jä, an aged song. Melancholy as it was, he found himself singing its sorrow: for himself, for his kin, for the ancestors that rested in the mountain tomb, their ache soothed as he sung.

...Deep under bones of the world-wyrm,
'Neath stone and dark a soft sound stirs.
A rumble deep, a drowsing breath,
Down in the dark there something slept.

An ancient beast, of ancient tale,
Its serpent hide of stone-black scale.
Its brooding over treasure hoard,
Its greed to gold forever moored.

The last who lived through kindred wars,
In times far back, in years of yore.
Now sat upon its mounded throne,
Now as a thief in mountain hold.

Then came a few who stories told,
Were breed of men with souls long sold.
To carven halls of hand-hewn stone,
To whittling out the world-wyrm's bones.

Far west they went, far west they roamed,
In search of hidden hoarded gold.
Black were the lands long scarred by war,
Black was the mind of beast disturbed.

Down into dark the stone-men delved,
Their chisels carved, their hammers fell.
A rumble deep, a rousing breath,
Down in the dark there something crept.

Writing round its glimmering mound,
A stone-black serpent stone-men found.
Onto the beast the men did fall,
With blade, and axe, and hammer drawn.

The serpent reared with flaming ire,
Its wrath met by both son and sire.
Upon its hoard it held its weight,
Of gold, of greed, of cursed fate.

Bound blade met fang in darkness dim,
The mountain moaned a moan most grim.
Stone broken by the serpent's frame,
Stone withered by the serpent's flame.

The warren heaved a mighty sigh,
No men nor beast gave up their fight.
About them all the stone heaved way,
About them all the stone did lay.

Their greed, their want, their lust, their doom,
The men, the beast, the stone, their tomb.
All buried under mountain tall,
Their pride came long before their fall.

Within the mountain-dark is found,
The echo of memory bound.
Of secret truth in heart of men,
A serpent writhes, a serpent wends.

Desire round that gold is strung,
Like rope around a neck is hung.
'Neath stone and dark, there rests a curse,
Deep under bones of the world-wyrm...

The trio walked in silence as the song echoed in their thoughts, its grim murmur fading back into the stone from which it was hewn. It was the last pleasant memory the three would share in the mines. For the thing that stirred in the deep of the mountain dark was coming, coming, coming.

Aëros would be the first to hear it, not yet, but soon. Now he was merely the first to speak. "I didn't know you had such a voice," he said to Jä, his inflection halfway derisive, halfway sincere.

"Didn't always." Jä grinned, sly and wolfish. "Few o' the Rōvaraē lasses learned me long ago."

Aëros stole Jä's grin for himself and wrung it into a smirk. "Kaēlyn know about that?"

The dwarf chuckled, deep and rumbling. "Fook no! Was long before her. A smart man knows better than to tell his wife o' his past conquests."

Aëros clapped the dwarf on the back. "Aye, a smart man."

Jä scowled and Nomad laughed. Aëros' smirk shifted to a frown as he caught the sound of something in the depths of the chasm, a whispering like soft wind, his elven ears far keener than his companions'. His instincts stirred and sharpened into focus, finding the sound familiar. "Do you hear that?"

The wanderer turned, his own mirth stuttering slowly. "Hear what?"

"That sound." Aëros strained an ear over the chasm. "Like... wind."

"Wind?" Jä stopped too.

"Hush." Aëros held up a hand. "Listen."

The wanderer and the dwarf tried, heard nothing. Nomad shrugged his pack up on his shoulders and clicked his staff on the stone. "Aëros, you're hearing things and confusing them for something worrisome."

"Aye, Hobo's right." Jä agreed. "I don't hear a bloody thing besides the racket o' me own feet and the settlin' o' the mountain."

The Wayfarer scowled as the dwarf and the wanderer continued down the pass, Jä leading them ever onward, ever downward. But the whispering persisted, growing louder in Aëros' ear as they descended. He shook his head. "I'm telling you; there's something down there, and I think it's heading up."

Jä looked over his shoulder, swaggering in insincerity. "Maybe we woke Arök."

Aëros grumbled, then halted hard as the whispering silenced and, in its place, came the beat of muffled wings and a rumble like the sound a wolf makes before it howls. Aëros' mind fell back to the Wōadglōam. *Sif? No.* The sound wasn't bestial—it was old, primordial, something else. Jä and Nomad stopped too, looking back at Aëros, the Wayfarer looking at them, eyes glinting with satisfaction.

Jä held his lantern over the lip of the chasm, searching, and fumbled backwards as a great shadow flew up from the darkness, cast in the trinket's light, a silhouette in the shape of Arök's most avaricious descendants. The rumble became a roar, a scream—a death sentence.

"Dragon!" Jä's blood ran stone-cold. The scourge of his ancestors, the foe they'd felled to free the mountain from its greed, to hew into and hoard its treasure for their own. He lit a Spouse and hurled it as he backpedaled; the mines groaned from the force of the explosion. Stone crumbled and memories poured from the walls, the draconic silhouette racing over the debris, avoiding death as only the undead could.

Aëros knew better than Jä, knew this was neither dragon nor any other breed of wyrm. As the shadow shifted, mutating into the shape of a monstrosity composed of roots, of tendrils, a simulacrum of the beast that had mostly killed him, he remembered something he'd seen in the forest, in memory, in nightmare, a horror Athair had showed him.

Jä moved to hurl another Spouse at the creature, but Aëros grabbed him, arresting his arm mid-throw. "Jä! Douse your lantern! It's a Shaēd!"

"A what?"

"Douse your fucking lantern!"

Aëros willed his own dark, then ripped Jä's from his side and hurled it into the chasm, the pitiful flicker falling down, down, down into the depths of the pit. The Shaēd sped after it, and as the light was swallowed in the depths, darkness in turn swallowed the adventurers. The screaming softened and silenced, the enigma seeking the light that gave it substance, to destroy it for doing so, to return to the darkness in peace, disturbing nothing, disturbed by no one.

The adventurers waited, breathing. Aëros spoke through a whisper. "It's a Shaēd."

His mind went back to Athair, to the An'kou, to the wandering spirits of the Wōadglōam Forest. Here was their fate. Here was the fate of those slain during the Devouring, risen again by Athair to serve him, wights in his undead horde. Slain and risen, slain and risen, until their bodies were little more than shapeless heaps of rotting flesh, their souls left to wander, to suffer, fear and sorrow and contempt knotting and twisting until something new was born, something vile and vindictive, a horror bound to the will of the one responsible for its creation.

Now Athair was dead, the Shaēd masterless, aimless, the memory of each individual soul that formed it forgotten, bled into soil and devoid of humanity. It buried itself in the mines, the darkness its only sanctuary, suffering quietly in the womb of the world, alone. The world moved on, and here it lingered, wrapped in the pain of an Age long passed into ash.

Aëros pitied it and the souls that composed it, but knew there was nothing to do but let it slumber. "Go, while we have the dark." He urged his friends onward, downward, to the pit that would lead them to the summit.

221

"I fookin' hate when you're right," Jä said through a sigh. "Never hear the end o' this."

"We can't see a thing." Nomad wasn't wrong. The dark was a threshold they could push against but never pass beyond.

"Use the walls as a guide." Aëros didn't heed his own advice; he didn't need to. His ears could distinguish between the sound of the thick stone to his left and the empty chasm to his right. "We can't give it light to live in. It'll end us."

"Not if I end it first." Jä pulled out another Spouse, and for a moment the chamber was illuminated with the light of a striking stick intended to set the explosive to life. Aëros sliced the flame out with Löekeh's edge. Jä didn't argue. Its momentary spark revealed the horrible, seeking form of the Shaēd, slithering up the chasm walls as a mass of writhing tentacles and lidless, serpentine eyes.

"Hoh, fook that, through the dark it is," the dwarf whispered, acquiescing. "Will it hear us?"

"It doesn't care," Aëros' voice sounded in the dark. "It wants the light, not us. So long as we don't cast any, we'll be sa-"

Screeching, screaming, the sound of starvation. *Ghúls.* Out they came from their dens in the mountain. They knew the Shaēd well; they'd been hunted by it in the past, when light still flickered in lanterns yet to fade, when the murmur of Arythos' fall still echoed in the mountain's halls, not yet a memory. They sensed the horror awaken, feared it, and fled blindly, driven by instinct into its nursery, for in their instinct was also ignorant, bestial idiocy.

By ill chance the trio found themselves in the midst of the ghúls' flight, fiends pouring onto the stairwell from entrance shafts both below and above the adventurers, trapping them. The horde came too swiftly to plan against, and darkness would not serve against the ghúls as it did the Shaēd. So alight flared Aëros' lantern, its silvering rays glinting off stone, shadow, and the fearful visages of his companions until then hidden behind the dark, their shame for such fear apparent in the light. Had he not been trapped behind his own face, Aëros would have seen the shame reflected on himself. But with the ghúls on them, the Shaēd restored, he took no time to catch the reflection in his friend's eyes. Despite his efforts, death was a distraction once again.

The ghúls were surprised to come upon the adventurers—surprised and gleeful. Their fear of the Shaēd settled in the shadows of their minds as hunger overwhelmed them and they set to sate it. The trio found themselves pinned in place on the stairwell, each holding their own against the horde, fiends slaughtered by silver and Spouses and the hatred and suffering of a living shadow.

Jä took the lead, hurling explosives in no particular fashion, obliterating stone and flesh indiscriminately. A behemoth of a ghúl reared on him, and he laughed as he slipped off a gauntlet, revealing a knuckleduster beneath. He pulled back, wound up, and punched a hole through the fiend's chest, depositing one of his widows-to-be within. The ghúl tried to tear out its death, failed as the Spouse erupted, bathing the dwarf in ichor as he boomed with laughter.

"Careful where you throw those fucking things!"

Whether it was Aëros or Nomad who'd yelled it, Jä didn't know, his ears ringing with the ruin of his Spouses and the din of the ghúls' screeching. Still, whoever it was had a point. Useful as the explosions were, the dwarf's haphazard throws forced both Wayfarer and wanderer to fight around the chaos, diving awkwardly away or using the bodies of ghúls as bulwarks against explosions and shrapnel.

The arkaēn reagents served as more than a force against the ghúls, distracting the Shaēd as well, the anathema drawn to their searing flashes and away from the trio. Even so, the adventurers only made slow, halting progress, the cleared space too swiftly refilled by the horde, the dwarf's demolition offering at best a brief reprieve for Aëros and Nomad to play their part in the pathetic attempt to withstand the inevitable.

Aëros' lantern danced as he did, willing his phantoms to work, doppelgangers leading the horde astray. The illusions leapt, dodged, and threaded through the ranks, causing ghúls to strike out only to find the flesh of another. Those that followed the phantasms found their way to suicide, for the illusions leapt from the precipice of the chasm, fiends following to find their hunger sated in death.

While his phantoms distracted, he bled the leathery host with blade and bow and the key to many things willed into a needle of many deaths, carving the ghúls through as if they were of no more substance than Dräu. He vaulted, balancing between acrobat and assassin as he tore life and limb, reaping, slaying. He hooked Löekeh through the eye socket of one ghúl, leaping and using the anchor to twist himself up and over, cleaving through its skull and shifting blade to bow, feathering fiends with a hail of arrows so swiftly the skill couldn't be described as anything but mastery, the accuracy anything but art.

As if in duet with Aëros, Nomad joined the fray with the secret of his staff, a trick weapon hiding a length of bladed Argynt chain, terminating at both ends in small, sinuous scythes. It was named 'Güngnyr', the Swaying Staff, the sound of the word much like that of the blades as they whistled through the air. The blades blurred as the weapon patterned and twisted, trailing through ghúl flesh and ghúl bone with equal indifference. His acrobatics mirrored Aëros' own, grace shared between friends who'd spent long seasons under the same shattered moon together. He careened through the host, diving over and through their ranks as his blades sang a lusting, lecherous song.

The carnage created between elf and dwarf and enigma in the shape of a man was of genocidal proportion. Flesh was flayed, bone cracked, and ichor sprayed, waterfalls of black blood pouring out over the rim of the chasm. Still the horde came. It came, and it came, and it came. Drawing the adventurers to their doom, step by step, down, down, down into the depths of the mines, to the memories sunken there, down in its abyss.

Argynt tracks flashed in Aëros' white lantern light, horizontal runs forged to reinforce the primary shaft, suspended over the chasm. The trio could hold the descent no longer, and found themselves thrust out onto the rails.

The ghúls tore out after them, graceless, greedy, skittering over the bodies of their dead and one another. They trampled those that lost their footing and threw those in their path away, hurling them into the chasm where the fool who had fallen long ago awaited their company. Those that made it to the front of the pack fared little better, for they were clumsy and oafish things, the slender rails too lithe for them to mount long, and they tumbled down to meet the betrayed.

The trio arrived at the center of the rails, their rally against the horde lasting only seconds. The ghúls were a pittance of worry, for the Shaēd had not forgotten them, and seconds were too long a time to allow a thing shaped by light to last. The anathema needed no footing to find the rails, needed only that which it hated, that which it feared, and Aëros could not extinguish such fear before it fell upon him and his.

It washed over the few ghúls still clinging to the tracks, the fiends' skin rotting to flesh and flesh to bone and bone to ash so swiftly their death-cries echoed longer than their essence remained. The Shaēd glided over stone and corpse and rail, screaming with all the souls that composed it, with their agony and their suffering, hastening toward the adventurers, toward the light—and it was on them. Its form shifted, took on the silhouette of the wanderer, its shadowy limbs transposed into his weapon, chain and scythes railing out in search of death that would bring it darkness, and in darkness, peace.

Aëros tried time and again to extinguish his lantern, to welcome darkness; but for his light he was the Shaēd's primary focus, and he could not move his mind faster than the horror struck, so the radiance remained, dancing as he did.

His silhouette flickered along the chasm walls, showing his grace on the stone in pantomime as he glided away from his death. His silhouette dove, extending out along a rail as it caught itself on its arms, rolling into a sphere of shadow along the slender track, continuing its momentum as it followed the lithe strip of Argynt along the contour of its back. As it stood, it vanished in the shade of another shadow, its caster no safer for its vanishing, for he could not dwell in the darkness as his shadow did. Once, certainly, but not anymore.

Löekeh blurred, blade to bow, bow to blade, arrows and edge ripping through the Shaēd, tearing through its stygian flesh as it sped after him. It did not flinch, did not falter, did not care. It had him. It was swifter. For he was of substance, it of shadow, born of the former, moving ever swifter for it. He saw his death, his second or hundredth. *How many has it been?* The Shaēd's blades careened towards his neck. *Beheading, then.* He smelled ashroot, did not know why.

The blade clanged, never biting, struck down by that which it mimicked. Nomad was beside the Shaēd; he had saved Aëros. Aëros could not do the same for him.

The wanderer dove from the reach of his doppelganger—too slow. The shadowy scythes shifted and became fine points, ripping through him. He staggered at the impact, pulled himself free, and teetered on edge, grasping the rail as he fell, Shaēd above, death below.

A flash interrupted the solemn sound of silence before death, the sound of thunder and war. Jä hurled a harem of his Spouses, explosions tearing the Shaēd apart. It reformed, railing out against the dwarf, but so clumsy was he that he'd slipped during his throw. He fired a length of Argynt rope, and missed. The ghúls cheered as they fell, for now their prey fell with them.

The Shaēd turned back to Aëros, to the light, scythes swinging, singing, seeking. It lunged, and as it did Nomad hurled himself up, saving Aëros a second time, but not before the Shaēd's blades curled through the air, slicing just before the Wayfarer's throat, grazing his sutures, throwing him off-kilter; a strange sensation. He'd have caught himself easily, if only Nomad hadn't pushed him as he teetered, sending him falling, sending him down. He'd done it on purpose. *Why?*

The Shaēd watched him tilt over, lantern still lit, still lashed to his side, and set itself to leap after—too slow. Nomad slit the cord binding lantern to belt as Aëros fell and caught the glowing trinket in hand, holding it, watching the Wayfarer tumble away. His eyes were not those of a man who'd killed a friend, but those of a man who'd figured something out before him, reveling in it and swaggering with arrogance.

What did I miss? Aëros took time to think as he fell. Time to consider as the light of his lantern evanesced above him, his friend caught up in a frenzy of shadow. He fell through darkness now, the sound of wind returned, not a whisper, but a gale as it rushed past him, gusting over him as he sped headlong to his doom.

Darkness devoured him. He felt it in his periphery; the chasm's darkness, and something more—the Shadow. It fell as he did, down, down, down into the depths of his memory, the womb of his madness. Into the asylum with its skeleton key. The wraith dragged itself out of his mind, out of the asylum, dread drifting in the wake of what it withdrew.

Aūriel. Tärin. *That was all that ran through your mind as the kingdom burned around you, just like the fields beyond, and the forest beyond that. You could not fathom how swiftly it had fallen. You'd only just left in search; less than a day had passed. You knew it wouldn't stand forever, but you had no idea how thin the thread that held it together had become, to be severed by a gentle wind.*

You'd left just after midday, passing quietly through a Rift to Arkym, heeding the letter Athair had sent you, leaving Arythos behind, besieged, but at peace, none but Jä and your family knowing that you went. Or so you thought. Athair came in the night, his horde razing Arythos to the ruin over which you walked. You'd trusted his word, thinking all he wanted was you. You were right; but you do not end at the edge of your skin, the beat of your heart, the memories in your mind. He wanted all of you. He knew you would trust. 'Arkym' he'd written. A lie, playing you for a fool. A betrayal for a betrayal. When you realized your folly, when you ripped open a Rift to return, you did not return quietly, did not find Arythos at peace as you left it, did not arrive in time. Not for the kingdom. Not for anything. Anyone.

Wights wandered the ruins, dead littered the ground, red ran through the streets. You recognized some, dead and undead alike. You slew indiscriminately. Aūriel. Tärin. That was all that mattered. That was all that remained.

"Aūriel! Tärin!" Your screams shook the smoke and the soot from your path, and drew the wights and the beasts of the horde to you. You did not care. They were nothing, ephemeral, unworthy of your attention. You tore through them as you tore through the rubble of your home, searching, frantic, hoping that nothing was all you would find. Perhaps a sign of flight, a mad dash to the mines and then the Rift beyond, the contingency plan, Jä's heavy boot prints leading the way.

Jä. Stone buried him. You heaved it away, shielded him as ash blistered up around you. He was covered, cloaked in grey, in the wilting of death. He coughed crimson mist into your face.

"Aë... Aëros..." He saw you through the one good eye that remained, clotted as it was. You didn't know where the other had gone.

"Jä, Jä! Aūriel? Tarin?! Where are they?!" You shook him. He was dying and you shook him. As if all of it was his fault. You staggered as you realized your madness, you apologized, embraced him. You had to know. He was not as important as them. "Jä... please..."

"H—" More spasms, more blood. It arced up; you would never forget its scent, its taste. You saw him as he saw you now, through the

stain of his death. "He took them, Aëros. They came too fast. I'm—" His eye rolled back, his last breath came, and with it his final words. "I'm sorry…"

You opened a Rift, laying him in a bed he knew well, to be cared for by the woman who loved him, leaving him to look for the woman who loved you. Your wife, and your son.

The nightmare faded. Aëros was falling, shaking, soaked through with the sweat of horror and disbelief. *That isn't what happened. They fled when it fell. They escaped. To the Wayshrine. To safety!*

He threw his horror upon the Shadow.

You know that isn't what happened!

Silence.

Aëros sped down, down, down into the womb of the mountain, into the secrets of the stone, the secrets of himself, horrified.

Chapter XXII: Death

• Stirring of Autumn •

I'm dead.

   No.

The crash into the stone—*crash? No, that's not right. I just...*

Aëros landed on his feet, featherlight, as if he'd leapt off something less than his own height. He should have splattered.

What...

He was whole—or his body was, at least. He looked up. There was stone above him, light around him, limning his silhouette in...*silver?* He found its source: the light of the moon, pouring through a window, carved of stone, a terrace overlooking Eave.

Night veiled much, but had it not he would have seen the vertebrae of the Wyrmspine hemming the West on all sides save its easternmost edge, where the barest sliver of Vimaray's shores would have glimmered against the horizon. The ruins of Arythos rested beneath; the Dragongrave stretching in turn; the Wōadglōam Forest, the shimmer of its heartwood visible in the heights; and the Verdant Fells, his home in a coastal forest at the grassland's furthest edge. Southmost he might see the Aegis tearing up into the sky, the ward blockading the Barrows from entry by foot. Once he could have walked as a wraith through the reality of the stone. No longer. Now he must pass through the Rift, the Wayshrine, set atop the mountain—

Summit. Aëros thought back to Nomad, back to what he'd told him. *To go up, we must first go down.* He realized now what Nomad had figured out before him, realized the push wasn't betrayal, but guidance. His eyes widened. *Nomad. Jä.* His head whipped around, searching for his companions; he could not find them.

"Jä!" His screams were familiar, and he felt the ache of nightmare echo through them. "Nomad!"

His eye caught on something, dwarven in shape. A corpse in a corner of the stone-wrought room. *Jä.* His mind reeled.

"That isn't me, laddie. Only that fool who fell." Jä chuckled, his voice booming in the chamber. Aëros turned, finding his friend bracing himself in the window, looking out over the vista. He looked like a gargoyle, a menacing work of carved stone, grinning. "Fookin' Shaēd must've killed him."

Aëros beamed as he strode to his friend, but the smile faded as he saw his wounds. Blood oozed from his back, flesh cleaved from bone, ribs a sickly white in the pale moonlight.

"Jä," Aëros stammered, "your back..."

The dwarf looked over his shoulder. "Aye, seems that fooker got me good. Oh well." His face was pale, drawn. "Where's Nomad?" He returned his eyes to the vista. He was cold. The wind in the peaks ripped tears from his eyes, but it wasn't the wind that chilled him. There was no warmth in death.

"I..." Aëros looked the dwarf's wounds over. They were beyond his skill to mend. He thought back to the wanderer, left behind. He searched the chamber for him, but found nothing. "Another world... I'm sure."

Jä's bleeding slowed. So did his breathing. "Beautiful, isn't it? The elders really knew how to hew..." He collapsed, sinking to his knees, shaking the memories of his ancestors from the mountain tomb. "You're so alike 'em, Aëros, the dwarf lords o' old. So stubborn, like the stone..."

"Jä!" Aëros dove to him, supporting him, cradling the dying man as he might a newborn, gently. "No, no, you're alright. You'll be alright."

Jä grinned, beard lifting, bloody. "I can see you lyin' in your eyes, Aëros. It isn't a worry."

Aëros' eyes were indeed welling up with his lies, falling onto his friend. "You can't die, Jä. You can't."

The dwarf's grin widened. "Want to wager on it?"

Aëros shook his head. "Jä… I have to tell you…"

"I know, Aëros."

"You do?"

"O' course. I know you've always loved meh, settled for Aūriel."

Aëros laughed, hearty and full of all the memories he knew he'd forget. "No, you fool." He averted his eyes, embarrassed by his petty secret. "That gold… Those five hundred aūrums, I sto—"

It was Jä's turn to laugh, rumbling out even as he hacked on his death. "How many times are you gunna apologize for that?"

Aëros' eyebrows knit together, searching. "I…I never…"

Jä shook his head, a weak, pitiful gesture. "Forgiven you so many times I'd miscount if I tried to remember them all."

Aëros' smile grew bittersweet, knowing another thing forgotten when he found it. "You'd miscount even if this was the first."

Jä's bellowing laugh flattened. He breathed and he bled and the cold crept over him. His shivering slowed, and his eyes unfocused.

"No, no, no." Tears rimmed Aëros' eyes, red, hot, unwanted. "Not like this, you threadbare fool! Not because of me!"

You can save him.

Aëros whirled on the Shadow, sitting on the precipice of the window overlooking the world. *See! He dies here, now! Not as you showed me, not in that nightmare!* He thought this, but screamed aloud, "How?!" Jä choked, dark blood dripping from his mouth, unseeing eyes glazing over. Aëros looked at him helplessly, looked back at the Shadow, still screaming. "HOW?!"

The Shadow turned away, looking out over the vista of Eave, out into the night, to an aurora, a severance betwixt realms, between places and times. It flowed below Valrävn, clutching the moon in its death; flowed in mockery of what Aëros had once been the master of and was no longer, of what he'd lost, forgotten.

Aëros understood. "Show me. WRAITH! SHOW ME!"

The Shadow met his eyes again, something welling in its own, dried by the wind before falling.

It might unravel you.

"WRAITH!"

Aëros felt the Shadow draw into his awareness, his mind, step over the rim of the asylum, and plunge down. Down, down into the depths of his memory, his madness, tearing out another root growing from its seed. It was the mastery he'd lost. Not the understanding of it, but the instinct—the sort worn into one's being by countless repetition, becoming an unconscious effort. It was hazy, fraying, enough. It was all he could afford to remember of the skill, and even now it was likely too much. Regardless, he took it from the Shadow, weaving the threads of reality with the needle of his will.

A seam in reality appeared before him. It pulled apart, torn into a Rift the same hue as the aurora in the night beyond the window. The tear was wild and writhing, unstable, chaotic. It flared violently, as if angered by its own creation, but could not shut itself away, not while Aëros willed it open. Through it appeared a maiden, her eyes wide with wonder as the Rift opened before her too, connecting one place on Eave to another, leagues and leagues and leagues distant.

"Aëros?!" she cried as she saw him, knelt before the Rift as a shadow washed over him, his past deaths bare on his face, scars and wounds and memories of humanity unmasked. But her focus didn't linger on him long. He was not so important as that. "Jä?!" The dwarf's name fell from her mouth like the name of a thing she never thought she'd say again, layered with regret.

She passed through the Rift, leaving her medical ward on the other side of the world, and entered into the cavern atop the tallest mountain on Eave. She rushed to Jä in her worry, bewildered, looked to Aëros, horrified.

"*Mend him.*"

"Aëros?! How… You're supposed to be—"

"*MEND HIM!*"

Kaēlyn recoiled at his wrath, familiar, forgotten. A sister knows a brother well, after all. She hesitated, but Aëros' will was unwavering, and none could resist it once rooted, not even reality itself. She hoisted the dwarf up and dragged him through the Rift, returning the most important man in her life to her life, leaving behind a brother she'd already left behind, and would now leave behind again.

She set Jä on a bed and glanced back to the cavern at the end of the world, catching a fleeting glimpse of Aëros, knelt beneath the weight of his humanity, a silhouette in the darkness, a duality of wonder and horror.

"*Tell Aūriel and Tärin I love them,*" his voice echoed, something strange present in it, something familiar missing. "*I will be with them soon.*"

He did not see the sorrow that flashed in her eyes, the confusion, the disbelief. He heard only her words, her pity. "Oh, Aëros…"

Aëros felt the Rift evanesce as he released his grasp on the threads of Aūr, felt the instinct he'd used to weave it leave him, disappearing back into the asylum, forgotten again. He felt the fragmentation of his sanity, a sensation that once came as the exhalation of breath, now racking him with anguish so severe he could not draw back the air that it tore from him. His mind was devouring him. Again. His fault. Again. The dismal light of his sanity withered, black filling the edges of his periphery, darkness overtaking him. Again.

Chapter XXIII: Hollow
• Stirring of Autumn •

Aëros saw himself, alone. He was walking over dunes of ash, vast mounds of it, something slung over his shoulder, wrapped in soot-stained cloth. It was a corpse, and what little skin showed was black, rotting, unrecognizable.

The path he walked was long and arduous, roving over the hills of ash with no light to see by but his lantern's, the sky black, blotted out. He collapsed; the corpse fell, tumbling to the ground, rolling down the dune. He scrambled for it, falling over himself, caught it as it hit the bottom and cradled it, whispered to it, his words murky and muddled. He placed it down gently, lovingly, and began to dig, to carve, to craft. A grave. A sepulcher. The first of six. Of hundreds. Of thousands. Of as many as there were bodies to bury, even if the body was absent.

A far too familiar ache thrummed in his chest, both the him in the world of ash, and the him that bore witness to it. It was the deep, dull, horrible ache of immense sorrow, of grief and loss, yanking him over the precipice of his unconscious self, pulling him down into the asylum, towards the seed buried in its depths. It was the memory of his madness, the memory of its source. He stood before it, finding it buried in his mind as it was in the world; in a sepulcher far too familiar. A light flickered under its lid, iridescent like the shifting hues of an aurora, but muted, dull, withering away.

It's dying. Aëros reached out for it but found that he could not take it, his mind warring with itself, bringing him to the brink of memory, wanting him to remember, but fearing what would happen if he did. It was the final thread in the fabric of his forgetting. To pull it would be to unravel the mystery of his madness. He wasn't ready. Not yet. Perhaps never. He wouldn't know until the end, and this wasn't it. It was still the midst, and in the midst it was night, mountain wind blowing in over a window overlooking Eave, the shattered moon shining bright and unfettered in the firmament.

Aëros felt the world shimmer, as if he were rising out of a dream. He knelt before the window, overlooking a painted world, so beautiful it could be nothing but pigment on canvas. His body became a statue in that place, mind drifting from him as he fought to retain it, to grasp it and keep hold. But it was as if he were reaching for mist, evanescing in his fingers, threads so thin a gentle wind might sever them.

He looked around the chamber, at the streaks of blood left by his friend. *He's seen worse.* He felt the lie crumble within him, but told it all the same. The Shadow sat beside the stains, perched upon the window's precipice. It was staring at him, into him.

Stand up, Aëros.

Stand up and move on.

The Wayfarer's breathing slowed, his senses, his awareness, the fragments of his mind coalescing into some semblance of a splintered whole. The fragments were weaker, the fractures larger, the fabric threadbare and fraying. He stood again on the rim of insanity, smirking, his deaths hidden, his humanity his own to know and to shoulder. Sweat poured from him as he stood; his silver-streaked hair hung before him as he lifted his head and turned away from the painted world, turning towards what little was left of his journey.

He approached the back of the chamber, following the dwarven knotwork as it converged on a circular doorway hewn above a simple semi-circular stairway. Engraved into the door was an arch of elven design, familiar. *The Rift.* Around the arch circled a likeness of Arök, tail bit between jaws, an ouroboros, binding the bones of the world together as the Rift bound the threads of reality.

As he ascended the stairs, the doorway flickered away, shifting from stone to nothingness, putting him in mind of the Things Betwixt. Moonlight streamed in, mixing with snow and the cutting gale that carried it. The wind whittled his bones and bit him to his marrow, burying itself in search of the little warmth nestled there. It found only his weariness, and recoiled.

The cold was nothing. He ignored it as he stepped over the precipice out onto the path, the threshold behind him closing.

The Wayfarer drew up his hood, wrapping himself in his Shräud. He looked to his ring, its inscription, the words that had carried him so far, and would carry him the rest of the way. "Always forward..."

Always on.

Chapter XXIV: Wayshrine
• Stirring of Autumn •

The Wayfarer ascended the slope of a narrow mountain pass, each step weary but weightless, walking atop the drifts of snow as only his featherlight step could. The path to the Rift was easy, obvious, leading up through a narrow alley of ice, layers and layers building up over the Ages on Arök's spine, trailing like spears from its ridges. It was night, but it was clear in the heights, the light of shattered moon and falling star setting a silver shine over the snow.

Wind ran through the pass, sometimes gentle, blowing softly, just enough to lift the finest crystals of ice from the surface of the winter quilt, flakes forming into gossamer sheets. Other times it was a gale gusting against him, as if pleading for him to turn back. He pushed forward despite it, embracing the cold, the discomfort a welcome distraction as the distance between the summit and himself diminished. *Not far.* The Rift, then the Wayshrine, then the Barrows, then Dún, and then? *A grave, and the memory of a madman.*

The moon lit his way in place of his lantern, lost to the womb of the mountain. The silvering light of the celestial traced the snow and his frozen breath. It mingled with the aurora, a seam in the reality of the sky, lacing the darkness with teal and turquoise and bright, burnished gold. The snow shimmered with its radiance, limning Aëros' silhouette in the memory of something he'd once mastered, now forgotten, a relic of the mastery just before him, waiting.

Shorn flat, the summit did not stretch far. It was blanketed by snow everywhere but at its heart, where a dais hewn from the blue-black stone of the Wyrmspine rose from the silver-white quilt, a ruined archway of elven design rising in turn from it.

The Rift was decrepit, crumbling, covered in rime and hoarfrost, worn down by the wind and the snow and the indifferent will of the Ages. Aëros approached, ascended the dais, and examined the arch; the weathering of time, withering worlds to ash and from ash raising them anew. He whisked away the illusion, reveling in his cleverness.

The ruin shimmered and evanesced, the fractured stone replaced by carven crystal, glimmering with exceeding brilliance. Its scintillating frame inhaled the shattered moon and falling stars and the aurora running through it all, working them into its aura, pulsating with it as if breathing, each breath in rhythm with the world's, in harmony; Aëros' own breath arrhythmic, displaced.

Memories stirred in Aëros' mind. Not the sort forgotten, but the sort lingering in the half-hidden spaces of consciousness, waiting for recollection, or recollecting themselves, as memories so often did. He'd wed his Aūriel on this summit, and had set the Rift atop it as much for that memory as for its solitude. He saw her in his mind's eye even as he saw her on the Rift, etched into the crystal, the image of her and him on the same dais on which he now stood, sealing their love in the ouroboros of their rings, the roots of each melding with the roots of the other.

As he thought of her, he thought also of her words, her song, the Hymn of the Wayfarer. He sang it now, a sanguine melody woven of wistfulness, of reminiscence, of more than could be forgotten in a lifetime.

> *…Fair few still walk the ways of old,*
> *Those trails tread by foolhardy souls,*
> *Who wandered where none had before,*
> *Through grove, and moor, and silver shore.*
>
> *For in those elder days they say,*
> *To wander was the only way,*
> *In lands untouched, in lands unknown,*
> *In wood, and vale, and hall of stone.*

Their journey roved and wrought a word,
For leaf, for moon, for bone, for wyrm,
Each name a thread in stories told,
Each tale, each myth, worn ancient old.

Of dragons dark and brooding lone,
Of forest eaves 'neath dusken gloam,
Of havens hewn from argent white,
Of realms beyond the seams of light.

All memory scrawled upon a page,
All fable passed from Age to Age,
From ash to ash and shade to shade,
A shade of dreamer's distant days,

For even ash of Ages gone,
May grow a wood, a world, a home.
Where tale and myth may find yet still,
A youthful and foolhardy will.

To follow those wayfaring ways,
To know now and forever say;
Far into dusk their trail does go,
Far into dusk their trail does go…

The song faded into the night; memory lost on the winds. The Rift, to which memory was a key, flickered alive. The threads of Aūr undulated gently, calmly, starkly in contrast with those Aëros had woven to save his friend. *Save him? No.* He was wrong, he was right. He'd saved Jä, but he hadn't saved his friend. Regardless, that Rift was a testament to what his mind was now: a fragmented, shattered, ruined thing. The Rift before him reflected what it had once been, long before it began to devour itself and the Shadow slithered out to save him. *Or so you say.* The wraith was beside him, as it had been from his journey's outset, as it would be until his journey's end. He looked over his shoulder at the path he'd taken, finding his footprints missing, wiped away by the wind, barely a hint on the snow to begin with, any memory of him being there forgotten. He turned back to the Rift, the shifting hues of arkaēn light illuminating his silhouette as he stood before it, fading into nothingness as he passed beyond.

Passage III: Dusk

"To walk betwixt and between worlds is to relinquish the illusion of reality as a constant. It is a phantasm of perception, a shadow on the periphery of consciousness. A choice. A perspective. A delusion which, in our ignorance, we take as definitive. In sum: reality is an opinion, and it can be disagreed with."

- *Aëros Elwaē Aröaē; The Wayfarer's Guide to Ëae*

Chapter XXV: Memory of Mastery
• Nowhere •

Stepping over a Rift was a simple and unremarkable thing, like walking over the threshold of one's own home. But in that simplicity was where the wonder was found. To will open a seam in reality, to pass from one realm to another, the only marker for direction one's own imagination—it was a fancy of children, a fairytale idea. But not to Aëros. To him it was a matter of mastery; of study, of practice, of understanding.

Here was the apex of that mastery. Here was the Wayshrine, a child's fairytale fancy strung up in a perpetual twilight, trapped in an eternal dusk, a liminal time in a liminal place reflecting the liminal threads of its weaver's sanity. The irony wasn't lost on him. It was a hidden place woven into the space betwixt and between all of existence, a nexus tethering all realms, worlds, realties, and times. 'Nowhere' as Aëros knew it; Ânwyn as it was named by the First of the First.

Auroras streaked the twilight, binding realm to realm in this place between them all. A crescent moon hung in that sky, unbroken, rimming an aureate sun, each celestial seated in place, sinking below the horizon, which was rising and which was setting was uncertain. They were a part of the Wayshrine, and the Wayshrine was a part of the Wayfarer. He'd willed all it was into being, each thread woven with deliberate design, possible only in the unreality of Nowhere.

Under the intermingling dayglow and nightshroud stood a forest set in the heart of a motionless lake, the lake ringed by a range of unbroken mountains, peaks rising and sinking like the Wyrmspine. Only instead of the pale blue-black hue of Arök's bones, this was a serpent of shadow, the essence of primordial dark, stygian scales flecked with glinting gemstone.

A single pathway stretched from the haven that held the Wayfarer to the wood on the water, a mosaic of many carved crystalline shards, soft and pale, a sliver of space between each. The forest pulsated, glowing, breathing, and for the first time in a long time Aëros felt that his own breath was at last in rhythm with his world.

The forest was of wōadglōam, grown from seeds Aëros himself had taken to his haven betwixt realms and sown long ago. From the forest's hollow grew the greatest of the trees, a monolith of ancient ancestry, all others saplings in comparison.

He approached the forest, passing over the crystalline pathway from the Rift to the wood. Another haven ringed the forest itself, many other paths akin to that which he walked running from it. Those paths wandered to other Rifts, other worlds and other times and other places waiting through each. He would pass them all by but one. There was only one world for him to visit, only one place to return to. But not yet. Not just yet.

It wasn't long before the Wōadglōam loomed over the Wayfarer. He traveled inwards, to the innermost hollow of the heartwood, the mountains and the mere vanishing behind the forest's verge as he delved within.

The hues of the dusky sky laced the forest's eaves. Each lofty trunk was dark as anthracite, its lifeblood amethystine and old. It flickered up from root to sky, falling as it reached the canopy, dripping back down to the underwood below. Like the rest of the realm, the Ara of the grove lived in the twilight of life, forever balanced between autumn's stirring and dreaming, appearing very different from the Wōadglōam Forest, which was bathed in the hues of spring and summer, knowing no winter and only swift autumns.

A winged, serpentine shadow fell over him and the woodland, a shadow from above, flying swiftly on and vanishing. *The Shaēd?* No, not the Shaēd in its phantasm of a dragon, but an ancestor of the dragons themselves, descendent of Arök: a wyvern. It was passing through realms, through one of the auroras lacing the sky, innumerable seams for innumerable worlds, all interwoven here in this place of perpetual transition.

He twined this way and that through the forest he'd grown himself, taking no route in particular, unhurried. Time was his to take in this place betwixt realms, for it was a place where time did not dwell, and because of this neither did his madness. It was itself a thing of forgetting, forgetting a thing of memory, memory a thing of time.

The Wayshrine was a temptation for him to linger longer than he ought, a refuge for him alone. He'd taken no one here, not even his Aūriel. It was his selfish reprieve from the world, from everything and from everyone. There were other reasons to keep others away, reasons that had to do with the fragile kilter of one's own perceived reality, so easily torn apart when shown something like the Wayshrine. But he knew those reasons were lesser. He knew this was a place for when the company of all but himself was a burden.

Still, he knew the realm was a transient reprieve, a temporary salve. As he could not hide himself away in the Wōadglōam Forest, neither could he here. For though time was of no consequence, in the worlds beyond it continued to tick away, urging him to return—to his home, to his family.

Even if he didn't, even if he dismissed his life beyond Nowhere, he still could not hide from what he was merely forestalling. The Shadow still strode alongside him, meandering through the forest the same as he. His madness was muffled, but it was not gone. The wraith was a reminder of his unraveling mind, of what was to come when he met his journey's end, of what he would find there, what he would remember; what was already lurking within him, buried. He knew he would come to the end. But not here. Not in this place of distance and dissociation.

He turned his attention from the Shadow and his thoughts from his sorrows, to find that he'd come to the heart of the heartwood. The eaves of the eldest wōadglōam swayed over him, its roots and its withes reaching out in welcome. A wooded archway grew within its trunk, veiled by a ward of dark vines unraveling their inviolable knot as he approached, unveiling the entrance to a hidden sanctuary within the hidden realm: the Everglōam, as he named it.

A seclusion he'd woven within the hollow of the tree, the Everglōam served as a place of solitude, study, rest, and reflection. Pitch cloaked the hidden grove as he entered, but the darkness abated at his return, the sanctuary illuminating as it woke from dreaming to greet him.

Crystalline spires grown in harmony with the tree's inner hollow caught the light of dusk and refracted it, from sky and sap to spire and back, growing until the only dark of the grove was soft, translucent shadow. From the spires grew smaller workings of the pristine gemstone: a desk, a set of shelves, an Arkaēn's Kiln, a mirror, a ring surrounding a steaming bath set at the center of the sanctuary, and an ornate chest that seemed to be the center of it all. It was to the desk that Aëros made his way, finding it as he'd left it: laden with parchment, inks, tomes, trinkets, devices, and imaginings. It held a myriad of his works, his studies, and his burdens.

There was a tool that pointed northwards in another world but nowhere in his. A clockwork mechanism, its components tinkered with as it sat beside a blueprint of its functions. A to-do list set atop a plinth, its words blurred by a smear of spilled silver ink. A statuette of Arök he'd carved from crystal, set in a preening pose of grace and austerity, wrapping around a likeness of Eave's many fractured lands, tail bit between jaw, binding itself and the hollow world together. A small black pouch, embroidered with silver stitching and held fast by a silver clasp, filled with clairvoyance, near-omniscience, foolishness. He wouldn't partake again. Not until his sanity was settled. It sat on a book, though 'book' was too plain a word for it. He moved the pouch of regret onto his Arkaēn's Kiln, and lifted the memory from beneath it.

Not a book, but a grimoire, bound in Argynt, its title scribed into the ethereal metal, waiting at the heart of the artifacts, for it was indeed their heart—the tome holding their memory. He lifted it, lines of light scattering from where it lay. The title etched within its cover was elegant, and illegible everywhere but here, the text revealing itself only in the Wayshrine's dusk. As the melting sky poured over the words, the calligraphy shifted, and he read: *The Wayfarer's Guide to Eaē.*

It felt foreign to him, as if it were not his own hands that scripted and bound it. He unclasped the cover and leafed through the pages sealed beneath. It was an examination of the Tapestry, of Eaē—of how it functioned, what composed it, what existed within it. It was a work of his past, the writings of a mind undisturbed.

There were secrets within that would shake the foundation of reality for all learned men. Secrets no man need know. Secrets he'd discovered and forgotten, written before him, incomprehensible for all the understanding he'd lost to the dark corners of his own mind.

As he turned the final page, a loose piece of parchment fluttered from the tome. He grasped it as it fell, careful to be delicate, for it was a memory far more precious than the rest. It held a likeness of Aūriel and himself, a portrait she'd drawn of them both. Tärin had not yet come into the world when she'd inked it, but he was in it nonetheless. Aūriel was expecting—Tärin's round shape showing as both future mother and father brimmed with pride over their son-to-be. It wouldn't be long before even their names left him. He would find his journey's end before then, at least. But that was little guarantee he would keep what he had left upon its conclusion. Even less that he would regain what he'd lost.

He turned the memory over, singing in his thoughts her song, the Hymn of the Wayfarer. She'd signed it simply,

-   *I would be happy if I died today, my Aëros.*

As would I, my Aūriel.

He thought back to Jä's death, the one in memory—nightmare. To his final words: *He took them.*

Athair took nothing.

The Shadow drew out of his periphery, looking over the portrait in his hand, looking over him. Aëros' eyes lifted. The portrait flickered, the words of his Aūriel replaced by the words of another, the memory of a letter.

Dreaming of Summer
13th of Lúnastal
Third-day

Aëros,

My friend, first and foremost of all things: congratulations. When news came to me of your marriage, I was beset by dual emotions. It overjoyed me to hear it, for you and your Aūriel are by all accounts two kindred threads, for Ages untethered, now rewoven as when Eaē was young.

Still, overjoyed, I did not write you as I do now to express my happiness. For so too was I mournful, for not being there for you on that day. I felt removed, disjointed from you while stuck here. It was selfish. I admit it only because I know you understand that sort of selfishness yourself.

But now, on the day you announce your son-to-be, announce that you and your Aūriel have woven something new from the threads of one another, I can say I will feel no mourning; no detachment, no regret. For I will be there for him as I could not be for you.

The sanitorium has seen me fit for release. Even as I write this letter, the documents of my freedom are being signed, sealed, set in stone. I will arrive in port a fortnight from the date marked on this parcel. If you are willing, I would love nothing more than to see you upon disembarking. We have so much to discuss, so much time to recapture and recall.

Until then, my dear friend,

- *Athair*

P.S. I have something miraculous to show you. I'll say no more now—I know how you love mysteries.

A miracle, he said. The Shaēd was what he had to show you. A miracle. The sanitorium did nothing. You suspected as soon as you finished the letter, knew for certain once his miracle was revealed. There was nothing to be done. He couldn't be changed. You knew that. Psyköpathy—the word you discovered in another world. A suffering mind. He cared for you, but he saw the abandonment in you upon his return. You saw there was no hope for him upon his. Nothing to do. Nowhere to send him. Nowhere but Arkym.

You finished reading the letter, and for the hundredth, the thousandth time, tucked it and its memory away in Nowhere.

'For I will be there for him as I could not be for you.'

His words lingered in you, meant as apology, as self-sorrow, felt as wounds self-inflicted. You hadn't been there for him either. Not as often as a friend should. Life moved forward, binding you to its routine. Distance displaced your devotion, and made the detachment seem justified.

Dual emotions warred within you: your love of him, and your logic telling you what he truly was. What you'd never quite seen leave his eyes since the first day you noticed it, so long ago, watching you and your sorrow, smiling at the death of a little raven; the first of all things slain on that mound of doom, of death, of Dún.

You stood as at your journey's beginning, overlooking the rim of the sea, night washing the world, moon liming it all with silver. You were perched atop the Crescent Cove, the waves of the sea beyond so immense it seemed as if the world itself tilted with them, shaking the bones of the land as they struck. You focused on a small isle of stone at the center of the cove. An asylum. Arkym.

Not a place for common folk afflicted with common ailments of the psyche. No. It was a place for those rare folk whose nature it was to unravel: Ideas. Lives. Existence. A place where they could unravel nothing but themselves. It was an asylum not for the sanctuary of those within, but to spare the world without.

"Athair." You spoke into the wind. Spoke to yourself. Spoke to him, stranded, abandoned on that isle for years now. Years since you placed him there. Years more since the letter. He hadn't escaped yet. Hadn't yet drawn you back with a lie, hadn't begun the Devouring of the West. You stood, shut your eyes to the world, drew a long, ragged breath, and opened them to find the entrance of the asylum before you, a Rift flickering behind.

The wardens standing post startled and leveled spears at you. The outer sentries were well-trained, but not prepared for one such as you. Not that you meant harm. You dropped the hood of your Shräud and apologized for the abrupt appearance, producing a diplomatic crest given by the Warden of Arythos. The wardens of Arkym drew up their spears, set their focus on the large outer doors barring the first entrance into the asylum, and began the complex ritual of weaving to unravel the threads locking the gate. You smirked, set your will on your ring—key to many things—and set the key in the lock, turning, opening. "It's alright, I'll see myself through."

Flustered and surprised, they stood aside. You played the same game six more times, seven doors barring seven passages, each leading deeper into the asylum, further and further down into its depths. Each layer held those such a place was designed to hold; the deeper, the more desperate the need to hold them. You could have passed as a wraith through the reality of the doors, but you wouldn't. There was ritual to the descent. You'd only distort it so far, understanding the value in both respecting and disturbing tradition.

Seven doors. Seven layers. Each entrance more complex than the last. Until one more door stood before you. A last, given no number,

254

given no name. You set your ring within, unraveled the ward, and passed inside.

The room was well-furnished, an adequate study. Books lined the walls; inkwells, paper, tools, and trinkets littered the desk at its heart. The bed was well-made, the food well-cooked, the water clean. It was a homely place. But the shackles of argent binding his legs, the impossibly complex lock on the door, the seven before it, the isle of stone in the center of a cove at the edge of the world—all spoke to the prison it actually was. Athair sat behind the desk, alone, waiting. "I do not forgive you."

Behind you the door slid back into place. You stood, eyes bound up with his. "You think me that petty? That I would come seeking forgiveness?"

His eyes were flickering. A fire burned in a hearth at the edge of the room. "You came for something."

You swallowed, seeing a hatred in those eyes that was ruining you. "It's been a long time."

Athair nodded, to himself, to you, knowing. "How is Tärin?"

You held silence for a long while. Then you acquiesced to the request hidden in the question, opening a Rift, a raven's sight over your home, over the range, your son in the heart of it, bow blurring, arrows flying.

"Your son, threaded through." Athair was smiling, staring into the Rift, watching. "Does he know me?"

"He knows an idea of you." Your heart felt sharp as you spoke, strings snapping. "I won't tell him all of you."

"He'll learn before the end."

"Yes," you agreed. "He's far too clever to keep his innocence long. But it will be his own to learn in his own way and in his own time."

Athair looked away from the Rift; looked to you, your eyes bound up in one another's, in all the history shared there. "Do you wish I would fade away? The memory of me?"

Your voice hitched; you held it, let your words out without faltering as the Rift flickered and evanesced. "I wish all I had was Tärin's idea of you. I wish I didn't know all that's in you. I wish I couldn't see your soul."

His chains clinked as he leaned forward, widening his eyes. "It's all here, Aëros," he said, pointing to one of his large black pupils, dilating. "Always has been."

"Always will be," you said, grief and regret weighing each word.

"I know what I am, Aëros." He leaned back, straightening himself. "The word you found for me in another world. What was it?"

"Psyköpathy."

"Psyköpathy." He rolled the word in his mouth as if trying it out. "I walk past someone on the road, and I think to myself, 'Why are they alive?'" His voice dampened to a whisper, curious. "What is in them that makes them alive? Is it different from others? Different from me? I can't help but want to know. I can't help but find out. What moves the threads of our existence, Aëros? Apparently, that makes me strange, sick. To me it's normal. It's strange to me that everyone else thinks it isn't."

The grief and regret within you mixed with disgust, with that first sense of worry you had all that time ago, with the death of a little raven, smiled over. From there the vesta. The Shaëd. What next? "What you were working towards, you were working towards without thought of its consequences."

Athair sneered. "Birds of a feather, eh, Aëros?"

You held your face impassive, silent.

"I work towards unraveling death. You work towards unraveling the very threads of reality themselves." The fire in the hearth flared, flame catching in the black pools of his eyes. "Tell me, which do you really think has more consequence bound up with it?" His sneer shifted to snarl, he went on, not wanting your answer. "I sit here, bound. You stand there, free, seeking to settle the war between your logic and your love. To decide which is the right thread to work into the fabric of my fate." He smirked, something sinister slithering out, something you knew had always been there. "Do not worry yourself, old friend, Old Raven. I will settle the decision for you."

He glanced down, pulling your eyes with his, to the desk, to his hands. "I never thanked you for your gift, Aëros. For the lantern. For revealing yourself to me. A false friend. Here, for you."

There, in hands unfurled, he held a little, baby raven. The *little baby raven. Undead, bones stolen from the cairn you in your foolishness had raised, a dull green glow pulsing in the cavities of its eyes. It hopped forward, a skeleton strung together by the threads of Anima, living in unlife. It came to the edge of the desk and set something down. Three withered stalks. One of lavender, one of lemongrass, one of mint leaf. You read the threat there, the hatred, winning its war with love. It was his hate, not yours. Not yet. Not until the residue of his dragged you down with it; continues dragging you down, even now.*

Aëros put the drawing into the grimoire and placed the tome back on the desk, light scattering once again as it found its place with the other memories that lay around it. It seemed there was more to memory than time after all, and even if he wished to give into his fear, to dwell here in the Wayshrine and hide from truth, he could not. The Shadow would not let him.

He sighed, eyes catching his reflection in a crystalline mirror, standing beside the ornate chest. *Haggard* was the first word that came to mind. *Forlorn* lingered in its shadow. He was dirty, silver hair unkempt and wiry. His beard had grown thick, thicker than it had been in many seasons. His eyes were pallid, his skin drawn. The beauty of his elven features was in grotesque contrast with his withered stare, his mask veiling only his deaths. *A fitting look for one perched upon the precipice of insanity. Like a man with a rope around his neck and the forest floor just the right distance beneath him.*

Weariness cried out from his bones. He expected too much of his body, too much of himself. Setting his will to repose, he wandered over to the steaming pool encircled by the ring of crystal and stripping, throwing everything to the ground indifferently. Everything but his Shräud, which he hung with care, threads of grief replacing the threads of Dräu now ruined.

His everything ached as he lowered himself into the water, its warmth soothing as it slid into his bones, binding to them like sinew. It drew his weariness from him at last, seeping out, escaping

257

the misery of its master for a time. It would return when he finished; he couldn't lose it altogether. It was necessary. He hated it. He loved it, so lashed to his marrow it was.

The water drew the tarnish from his skin as it did his fatigue. The journey had riddled him with soot and sweat as well as sorrow. He let it all bleed away, and drew Löekeh from the realm to shave down to the stubble he was fond of—that his Aūriel was fond of.

Finished, he lifted himself from the pool, walked over the soft grotto sward to two pillars of crystal, and strung his hammock from neither of them. He leapt into its weave, swaying gently, cradled.

Slowly, sensing his exhaustion, the light that filtered into the Evergloam softened. The atrium of wood and crystal grew dark, the strands of light dimming as the eaves drew together, shuttering the twilit sky away. The pale, amethystine light of the sap alone lingered; pulsating, breathing. Lulling him into slumber, into darkness, and in darkness—dreamlessness.

Chapter XXVI: Bones of a Father
• Nowhere •

Ä eros drew up from his rest by the breaking of dawn, or what could be mistaken for dawn in his realm of perpetual dusk. The atrium above opened, eaves unfurling, the pale light of the Everglōam brightening. He slid from his hammock, stretched, and noticed the Shadow standing beside the ornate chest at the heart of the grove.

He stood slowly, thoughtfully. The sward was soft underfoot, the chest heavy in his mind. It was a chest of memories, an effigy to his past, holding memories he did not wish to forget, even if he no longer had need of them. They inspired reflection, reminiscence, nostalgia—the emotions he held above all others. He kept the artifacts of his life that would evoke those emotions here, for without them he feared losing the parts of themselves they were tethered to. Not to madness, but to time, to age, to the vastness of existence and the space of his mind. For in such an expanse it was easy to lose, easy to forget.

The chest was locked, like the entrance to the Evergloam, behind a tangle of threads only he could unravel. He set his will on his false finger, his ring, and it slid away, melting, reforming, and reshaping to fit his need. He passed it into the lock, turned it, unwove the tangle set to secure his hidden hoard from the world. The key withdrew and slid back into place on his hand.

He lifted the crystal-hewn lid of the chest, revealing its trove. The Shadow stood behind him, overlooking the chest as the light of the moon glinted off the dragon's hoard within, though that was perhaps not a fair comparison. It was greater than any dragon's hoard by far.

Artifacts and trinkets and weapons and raiment, currency of gold and silver and copper and dust, knowledge and fable and wisdom and foolishness, garb from the poor and the noble, art of abstraction and absurdity, memories of worlds far from his, from lives he'd lived within them, secondary to the one that ensnared him, the one that kept him, the one he longed to return to. The one he *would* return to, even as he shut all others away, in this chest, in the asylum. He would not lose it, he would not shutter it away; not within this chest, and certainly not within his own mind.

The hoard held something he needed. Not the foreign blade he'd taken from a world of eldritch knowledge—etched with runes, a work of scholars and Arkaēn's, its blade wreathed and melded with moonlight, as if guided by it. Nor was it the ring, its power withered and faded, an empty, burned-out husk. Nor was it any of the other wonders of his walks betwixt and between worlds. It was something from his own world, wondrous indeed, memories of pain and sorrow woven into its making, clinging to the past as night clings to darkness. It was armor; forged in a time long before the Devouring, forged for one far older than he, for his father, Aroënd.

It was a masterwork, wrought by an artisan long since lost to the vault of memory. Aroënd had given it to him when he was young—an artifact of a father, of pride. It was beautiful, and he hated it. He'd stowed it here, in the Evergloam, for when it came time to array himself with it. That time was behind him, having found too many things that ought not be fucked with on his journey already. He could hear Thrace's chastisement even now. Recalled their talk in the tavern. Still, he'd survived—mostly—and there was a fair stretch yet to go. Plenty of opportunity to add 'definitively dead' to his epithets of 'almost' and 'mostly.'

The Barrows was a kingdom for the dead, a quiet place. For the dead did not stir, their purpose being to rest, to rot, to serve as consideration—for philosophy, for introspection, for progress. Or so it should have been. Athair had stood above the buried kingdom, his very aura raising its kings up where he walked, drawing on their pain and their suffering to move them.

He was dead. But not all that he'd risen had died with him. There was a reason the Aegis had been erected, a purpose behind the monolithic ward of impenetrable stone separating the Barrows from the rest of the West. Some things that ought not to still walked in the deadlands. Some still stood sentinel over Athair's grave, remnants of his will. Aëros sighed and reached into the chest, withdrawing a remnant of himself.

Twæraēth—'shifting shadow'—the armor of his ancestors was named. Valrävn also, by the smiths who forged it, after the constellation holding the shattered moon together, desperate to hold on to a dying thing. Aëros did not miss the deep irony binding the name to the armor to him. Amused, he donned it, fitting him as if age had shifted nothing.

It was wrought of a wyvern's hide, hued with the iridescent and illusory shadows of dusk. Elven tracery etched its leatherwork and metallurgy, the designs joined by Argynt plates forged in mimicry of a wyvern's scales and feathering. The plates were leaf-thin and leaf-light, tougher than arrogance and longer-lasting than it too. Upon the hauberk's shoulders sat great pauldrons, the left shaped to deflect arrows as its wearer aimed their own from that vantage. From the hip fell slanting tassets, flowing like the tail feathers of a raven, guarding wyvern-wrapped leggings beneath.

Aëros found his reflection in the mirror, and thought of the bone drake, wearing the bones of its father as he now wore the bones of his. He hoped with a desperate, foolish hope that Tärin would never wear them himself. Not these, at least, so stained by blood and the memory of it. To any other—arrayed as he was in the armor of his ancestors—he looked the part a noble warrior, a destined hero, fated for wondrous feats and fables eternal. But his pride did not swell; his mountainous ego grew no greater. His raiment wasn't meant for such grand displays. In the end, he knew, neither was he. *I am a vagabond, a wandering itinerant, a waif. There is no hero here. Just a madman on a limb with a rope around his neck, afraid to die.*

Aëros stared at himself a moment longer, shut and sealed the chest, the conclusion of his journey weighing heavily on his thoughts. He knew brooding would not hasten its arrival, nor prevent what he would find at its end, whatever that might be, but still...

He felt ambivalent, a twining of curiosity and fear taking him as he considered what was to come; desiring an end to his madness, but uncertain what the cost of salvation might be. Regardless, there was only one way he would take, only one way he *could* take, and as it was from the outset, it was only ever the Shadow's.

The wraith stood beside him, the mirror devoid of its reflection. It was the essence of reflection itself, a perfect echo of the darkest hollows of his soul. An echo beyond worlds, beyond place, beyond time. Fragments wound up in the web of infinity, shared. To him it was still an enigma, confounding. Perhaps a hallucination. Perhaps something other. He knew what it was, deep down, in the tomb buried in the depths of his unconscious, unknowable mind. Might have even worked the truth of the wraith out without need of opening that crypt, recalling that first memory, the seed of his madness. He certainly had all he needed to do so.

Unnecessary. He would find the answer where it was meant to be found: at his journey's end.

Chapter XXVII: Rim of Return
• Nowhere •

He passed beneath the eaves of the wōadglōam, finding the many pathways leading to other realms, realities, and planes of existence. Some led to the past, some to the future, some to fragments of each. One led to a reality where all things mythic and mysterious had faded, existing in an Age of industry and science. One to a world composed entirely of sea—what Nomad named an ocean—the sapient life that dwelled there living their lives beneath the waves. One where the world was formed of arithmetic, numbers their threads, equations their weaving, mathematics the foundation of their reality. Some were similar to Eave, while some were governed by entirely different principles. Most held a myriad of indescribable oddities; some nothing at all.

The Rift that was his heading led to none of these. That which he now paced toward would lead him not somewhere new, but take him back. To Eave. To the Barrows.

He followed the path over the water, his reflection traveling on one side of the silent lake, the Shadow along the other. At its end stood the Rift, the seam between realms set in an arch of carved crystal. He did not hesitate as he approached; took no momentary pause for pensiveness or self-reflection. He could not escape his madness, could not run from it, could not hide. This was not a sanctuary from his affliction, it was not a home, but a waypoint along the road to return to it.

Always forward, Aëros.

"Always on." The Rift shimmered as the Wayfarer passed through it, his going simple, unremarkable. His silhouette flickered as the threads of Aūr knit themselves back together, disappearing from his hidden realm as the gateway closed, the Wayshrine left behind, suspended in memory, suspended alone.

Passage IV: Abyss

"Some believe the Abyss to be the void—the aspect of the Tapestry that is nothingness, emptiness, hollowness. Many simply permit the term to reference things of a dark and eldritch nature, or otherwise the unknown and the unknowable. The things one fears that exist just beyond the ability to understand. The depths of one's own mind, where the asylum of the unconscious lurks; a fragment of self rarely visited with conscious volition. But in truth, none know what this entity truly is. It has simply existed since the dawn of memory, a shadow older than the form that cast it, forever lingering in the depths of the mind, lurking just beyond reach, drawing the curious to places they ought not to be. To dark, soundless shores. To the madness drifting just beneath the surface of sanity."

– Athair Gwäth Ânnäthär

Chapter XXVIII: Repression

• Stirring of Winter •

Aëros stepped onto a shore, a river running before him, cold stinging the air. The Rift faded, sealing him between the waters before and the Aegis behind—the monolithic ward of stone impenetrable, binding the only pass in the Wyrmspine together, preventing any return to the lands from which he'd come. The only way now was forward, over the currents, to the deadlands on the far shore, the Barrows beginning where the river ended, hemmed by the ancient waterway.

He stood there on the shore of black sand, overlooking the black water, a signpost hewn from stone standing beside him. He brushed its ivy away, revealing the river's name, worn and barely legible to any who didn't already know it. *Styx.* He let the ivy fall back in place and looked out over the water, waiting.

The sound of his breath was obvious to him, echoing in his ears beneath his hood. It was arrhythmic, discordant with the world's again. The only other sound was the siren song of the river, beckoning him to wade in. He taunted it, bare feet just beyond reach of its grasping tide, denying it. He dared not enter. The surface was like slate, too dark to peer beneath, but even so he could sense the souls chained there, fools who'd tried fording the waters of their own will, intent on pillaging the dead; now trapped, forever searching for a shore they would never find. There was but one way to ford the Styx. Only one way to the Barrows. So he waited there on the river's edge, listening to its siren song, until the song shifted, no longer of the waters but borne over them.

It came from a silhouette, drifting forward, muddled by the mists, its outline slowly solidifying into the shape of a small skiff sailing through the gloom. Its approach was haunting, for no oars rowed it, and no one sat beneath its sail-barren mast. With each ell the song sharpened, until the last lines of its chorus swept to shore, drawing to its end.

> *...And so the river Styx does roar,*
> *A silent call upon its shore,*
> *All dead do hear its siren staves,*
> *A gentle hymn beyond the grave...*

The vessel halted in the water, lingering just past the breaking of the shore. Suddenly, the sail-barren mast twisted, a humanoid form, skeletal in its litheness, revealing itself from its unintended disguise.

Aëros drew back his hood and tipped his head in greeting. "Ferryman."

"Still here? After all this time?" The stranger's voice was brittle, feminine. She lifted her head just enough to observe the Wayfarer, looking out from beneath a shroud that seemed to swallow all light drifting under its beguiling veil.

Aëros smirked. "I could ask the same of you."

The ferryman crooked her head and raised a hand, unfurled in request, cloaked in the tattered ribbons of a beggar's robe, stained by ash.

Aëros rummaged through his Shräud, producing six aūrums from Nowhere. He tossed the ferryman the iridescent coins, the woman pocketing her fee without bothering to examine it. Aëros did not know what she used the currency for, nor did he care. It was the toll, it mattered only that he paid it.

The river sang as he vaulted over it, landing aboard the vessel. The dismal craft drifted from the shore as Aëros settled in and hunkered down against the chill in the river air. He looked to the ferryman, her dark form silhouetted against the mists, another of the world's enigmas he never came to unravel. First to arrive in the Barrows, the only gravekeeper to remain after all the rest left and the land was sealed up by the Aegis, she had simply always been.

Caretaker, overseer, and for the few times when the dead waters of the river Styx required fording, the ferryman too.

Against her shoulder leaned an old, sinuous scythe, its blackened blade etched with runes foreign even to Aëros. He knew only that the tool was ancient, primordial in its forging. The blade sat perched upon a shaft of petrified grey wood, a small lantern fashioned from anthracite crystal hanging from it, radiating a light of deep, black luminescence. It reminded Aëros of his own, slit from his belt by his friend, another death avoided. He felt the rope around his neck even still; wasn't certain there was a time where he hadn't. He looked at the ferryman, the waters filled with those whose rope had run out, and measured his own. *So little left.*

Aëros watched as the ferryman turned her head. She looked out across the waters, gaze fixed on something apart from the current. Aëros glanced to where her eyes fell and found the Shadow walking calmly across the river's surface. It strode on, peering through the mists, seeing the end of Aëros' journey, humming the Hymn of the Wayfarer either to herald it or in mockery; perhaps both.

Aëros looked away. The ferryman watched for a long while, until the silhouette of land coalesced beyond the mist. The Barrows. The vessel settled just before the embankment. Aëros did not tarry in his departure, leaping from skiff to shore, the Shadow drawing up alongside him. He glanced back to find the ferryman already gone, then turned forward, continued on, to the end.

There was a small strait of black sand before the fetid fields of the Barrows' burial mounds. Aëros' first step over the liminal space separating them was featherlight, shadow-silent, a whisper of all the secret stealth in his ancestry and his skill. The ground cracked beneath his foot, splitting the air like a whip through the immense silence of the Barrows; a silence vaster than his, unnatural, consuming sound and hating it. His step let the land know that yes, here was a living thing in a place where dwelled the dead, the buried, the long, long forgotten.

He held himself in that space for a drawn, weary moment; half on the shores of the Styx, half on the deadlands of the Barrows. Not out of fear, but embarrassment. He shook his head, rolled the soul in his eyes, and dragged the rest of himself over. The ground cracked again, and it seemed to him that the dead beneath the withered land groaned at the disturbance. But those who rested in the crypts of the forgotten no longer had any command over the waking world, not unless the waking world called them back. He apologized, ignored their dissent, and went on regardless.

The Barrows sprawled out, the edges of its map hidden, none threadbare enough to fill them in. Aëros wandered its festering landscape, through mists sliding over burial mounds, following the undulating hills in search of their heart, their hollow, the mausoleum and the sepulcher at the center of it all—Dún.

Thicker, darker, colder, the miasma grew as he crept along. It coalesced beneath him, coating the sickly heath, shrouding his steps and his way, the sun unable to disperse it, the celestial's light pitiful, struggling to break through its own mantling of fog. He marked something moving in the overcast sky, a murder of rooks and ravens, following, circling soundlessly. Predator or prey; he no longer wondered which he was to them.

The mounds rose and fell as Aëros passed over them, like a fever dream of the Verdant Fells drawn from the mind of some sick soul. Each hill was a mass grave for the dead of different Ages. Some held the remnants of the First of the First, some held those even older still. None told the tale of their delving; the deadlands seemed to have always been, as the ferryman that oversaw them. The Wayshrine was far from the only realm that could set the stable mind slipping. But as that was sealed away by a Rift, the Barrows was sealed away by the Aegis.

The Devouring had begun in the deadlands. Athair raised the lifeless from their burial mounds, the foundation of his horde. He drove his wights into the living world, willed them over the West like a plague. The Aegis was erected to prevent it from ever happening again, keeping the living out and the dead in. It served its sentinel purpose well. Still, the ward was a work of hindsight, unable to undo something only foresight could have prevented.

Athair's will lingered in the world, woven into the blood and bone of Eave, fading, but still there. The forest. The mines. The An'kou. The Shaēd. Aëros, so wound up in the will of the madman himself.

The Barrows rolled on for leagues, burial mounds rising and falling in the mists like the back of a great serpent writhing beneath the soil. It did not go on this way forever, and as the sun dipped below the horizon, the landscape shifted under its dimming light. The hills flattened, receding, vast hypogean crypts replaced with lonely gravestones, cenotaphs, sarcophagi, all their inscriptions worn away with the weathering of the Ages. Some of the headstones and burial markers were profound, crumbling and collapsing under the weight of their own grandiosity. Others were small, trivial things, standing still and true, steadfast in their simplicity, knowing the dead had no need to boast.

Beside the crumbling headstones stood patchworks of petrified wooden stakes driven deep into the rotting soil, perhaps markers themselves, and the desiccated husks of ailing trees. The branches of the diseased Ara were bare, their roots upturned, gnarled, writhing for water and sunlight, their drooping limbs a tangle of misery and bitterness for being brought to bear in such a diseased and dying land. The wooden stakes seemed to mock them, taunting them on to their death and inevitable fate as rotting wood, mire, humus.

Between the scattered grave markers and sparse woodland rose great spires of stone, vanishing into the overcast above like anchors to other worlds. As a child Aëros liked to think they were the graves of giants. As an adult he still did.

Through the memory of Ages no longer remembered the Wayfarer walked, the Shadow walking with him, guiding him as ever, to remedy, to ruin. As a great silhouette appeared through the haze, familiar even for his forgetting, Aëros knew that the wraith had at least guided him to his journey's end. Dún. The silhouette stirred something within him, down in his unconscious, unknowable mind, in the depths of the asylum, the seed of his madness, the sepulcher of his memory, screaming for freedom, for remembrance.

With each weary step the muddled outline of the dark structure sharpened, the screams growing, the asylum shaking with their fury, hammering in his mind. He toiled on, heaving himself forward, teeth grit against his suffering, mouth curled into a crooked snarl, ready to sever the threads binding him to his madness, to Dún. It loomed up, blanketing the Barrows in the shadow of his doom, for in that shadow wicked things lurked, aware of his presence, tired of it. The rooks and the ravens circled, ouroboric, scenting blood on the air. Another death, another distraction; but first, another nightmare.

You stood in ash and ruin, the world around engulfed in an inferno, Arythos ashing away in the flames. Watching the corpse of your last friend disappear behind the closing Rift, his last words lingering with you, horrifying. "He took them, Aëros. I'm sorry."

Sorry? They were your everything, and he lost them. How could he? Why didn't he fight harder? Why didn't I? Why wasn't I here? Why did I leave? Why didn't I take them with me? Why didn't I keep them safe in the Wayshrine? What have I done? What have I done... What have—

"Jä stood strong, Aëros." The voice echoed through the smoke, silencing your woe. You recognized it immediately. "Though it did not mean much in the end."

"ATHAIR!" You whirled round. "WHERE ARE THEY?!"

Athair laughed, his voice coming from behind. You twisted back, making to draw Löekeh from Nowhere, and remembered you'd given it away to your son, hoping he'd never need it, unthinking of the need you yourself would have. So you set your will on your ring as you whirled, shifting it into the needle of your will. It sunk into something, into flesh, ripping through it.

It was a wight. Some poor soul slain in the onslaught of Arythos, the sickly dull green glow of reanimation burning in its eyes, steaming off of it like heat in winter. It tilted its head, lips peeling back into a smile. It spoke, Athair's voice speaking through it, its mouth moving unnaturally as it transmitted the words from far, far away. "They're here, Aëros. With me."

You set your wrath in your will, your will in your eyes, and your eyes into the dead gaze of the undead wretch, speaking to the villain looking back through them. "I am coming for you, Athair."

Silver flashed as you willed your ring into a wide, paper-thin blade, whistling wet as you dashed it through the wight's neck, beheading it. The body dropped, its head rolling into a pile of refuse and ruin, the undead light of unlife flickering, fading, final. It came to rest beside something familiar. You moved a stone, a shard of glass, and found a bow. Tärin's bow—the bow he'd practiced with, the bow you'd made yourself and given him—buried beside his quiver and his arrows. You stooped, took the bow of your boy and his arrows, slung both over your shoulder, hoping they would be enough to do what you now had no choice but to do. Your ring flowed back onto your hand as you stood and turned round to face the Wyrmspine.

There before you stood a kingdom's worth of wights, staggering through the smoke. Friends. Strangers. Dead. Their mouths unwound, smiling, smirking, speaking. "I am waiting, Aëros," Athair sneered through his marionettes, then set the wall of feral death upon you, his three last words echoing beneath their howling. "Do not linger."

The horde was too many for a man to defend against. So you shed your humanity and evanesced into shadow, becoming shadow, walking as a wraith through the seams of reality, of Aūr, until you stood far above the ruined kingdom, looking down from the peak on which your Rift stood, silent and still.

You watched the flames consume Arythos. Felt those flames rising in yourself, feeding your wrath, building, burning, incinerating everything inside, until it devoured even itself, fading into a cold, empty, hollow cavern in your chest. You fell into the apathy, let it hold you, let it keep you. You could not let the fires of its making devour you, not now, not yet. You turned to the summit, to the Rift, to the place where time stood still, the one place in the world in which you could hide from it all. There was no hiding now.

A shadow fell over you, and shadow you became again as you tore open a Rift to the Barrows, to Dún. To your family. To Athair. To the end.

The nightmare faded. A raven cried. Another step, another breath. Neither were Aëros'. He drew Löekeh from Nowhere and shifted blade to bow, wrapped himself in the apathy the him in the nightmare had felt, ignoring the horror of it, the screams hammering on the lid of the sepulcher in the depths of his mind. He pushed forward, stride unchanging, eyes searching. The mists undulated, pulsating as if drawing breath. He drew one himself and released it with an arrow, burning with a dark light as it tore through the miasma. He did not miss. He never missed. From out of the mist materialized an elf, or rather, an elf long fallen to decay. Its flesh was rotten, tattered on the bone, its eyes sunken in darkness. *Wight.*

Aëros drew Löekeh's string to his eye as a hideous, seething laughter echoed from beyond the curtain of fog. It was familiar. Another wight lurched from the grey. It joined the first in death, another arrow drawn before the corpse hit dirt. But swift as Aëros was, it was not enough to forestall the horde that erupted from the mists. The onslaught overwhelmed him—immediately.

Aëros' reflexes slowed as the horde grew, more overflowing the remains of those he'd already slaughtered. They wore the faces of strangers. They wore the faces of friends. His arrows knew not one from the other.

His breathing became erratic, heavy, desperate. He slid in the mud churned up in the rotting heath, struggled to keep his footing

274

as the walls of rioting flesh closed in. Vain. The wretched laugh echoed again, arrogant, crooked with amusement. It echoed even as his fingers slipped on Löekeh's string, coated in sweat, grime, blood—his, strangers', friends'. Even as death crept out from his shadow, his rope running out. Even as his defense failed, as the undead overtook him, as the laughter boomed in the night.

Another death loomed over him, held him down, forced him into the gore of friend and fool that stained the soil, drew his rope ever shorter. It was calm in comparison to the roar within, quiet in contrast with the asylum, with the laughter chattering into the air. The silhouette beyond the mists loomed, watching. The Shadow watched too, urging him forward.

Move on.

He struggled against the horde, found the effort impossible. It was only then, as his breathing staggered and he choked on the mire churned up at his feet, that he realized the laughter had been his own. It was the sound of a fragmenting mind, overburdened, the sound of rattling in the asylum, shaking the foundation of his sanity apart.

As his laughter broke and his vitality dwindled, the wights wrenched his head upwards from the refuse. They held him in place, forcing him to fix his eyes on the silhouette that was still but a shadow in the haze. The mists thinned, the form darkened, the asylum shrieked—louder; *louder*; *LOUDER*. Dread swelled up from within. The wights standing before the Wayfarer parted, and from the gloom stepped another.

Aëros' eyes widened, wild, his breath rapid and rolling. *I don't understand.* He met the wight's eyes, finding them familiar, finding one missing, one a silver and sunken crescent moon, the sickly green glow of unlife liming it. He knelt there, restrained by the undead, staring into the eyes of himself, risen, rotting; seeing himself, undead. *I don't understand.*

275

Time ticked to a halt in Aëros' mind as he tried to make sense of what he was seeing. He could not reconcile what he knew with what stood before him. His confusion faltered and fell away in the face of his forgetting, knowing what he knew was that he knew nothing at all, the proof standing before him.

"Aëros." He spoke his own name like an echo of the nightmare past, reverberating with all the weight of its implications. The wight tilted its head, as if as confused as he was. It knelt before him, its decomposing eyes struggling, straining, trying to discern what he was as much as he was trying to discern it. It was no more able than he. It was a mindless thing, its interest in him a lingering instinct of curiosity so inherent to the nature of him it persisted even in a rotting corpse; he, a thing verging on mindlessness himself, tipping further and further over the rim with each moment.

The wight was him. It was what he looked like in the Waypoint, when he'd set to making Thrace uneasy. What he had looked like when the Lësh'unn had mostly killed him. What he looked like always, beneath the veil of his illusion. *Is this just another? Another hallucination?*

No.

Aëros' eyes flicked to the side, unable to turn his head for the wights which were wrenching it back, trying desperately to wrench it off. He found the Shadow sitting on a gravestone, staring at the undead doppelganger, its shadowy, sunken eyes betraying its bewilderment, its awe.

Smirking over the great irony, Aëros looked past the Shadow, the wight, and his doppelgangers, to the silhouette of Dún, to his journey's end. To the bones of a madman, the madness in them reaching out even now, tainting the world with the remnant of its will. The horde holding him, the him that was before him, one of a number, one of the undead. It was no different from any of the other wights. A witless, wandering husk. No will but that which was placed in it by the one who raised it: to seek, to slaughter, to devour.

The wights holding him gripped harder and began to tear him apart. To rend him, joint from joint, bone from bone, sinew from sinew. He felt his armor pulling, scale-mail stretched tight, leather tearing, hems ripping. Felt his joints creaking, his muscles screaming, his life flickering as his head was pulled slowly back, neck spasming against the strength of the dead, knowing another death, a shorter rope, frayed to its final threads. He found his undead doppelganger still knelt before him, frozen in its confusion, indifferent to his inevitable doom, having seemingly met it itself. He sought the Shadow as his neck went taut, finding it above him, standing upside down in the sky, its eyes holding his, his its, twined in twain.

And this, Wraith? Is this my death? So near my journey's end? At the hands of what seems to be myself? All for the bitter irony of it? Like Arök swallowing his own tail?

The Shadow did not speak. The asylum shrieked. Aëros was sure it would soon grow hoarse. He heard the echoes of his past lives in those screams, his past deaths, saw them in the rotting corpse knelt before him. The echoes of memory, nightmare; the agony of forgotten and festering things down in the asylum, buried in the sepulcher at the base of his mind. The mists retreated further, Dún darkened, the agony raged, rasped, and began to suffocate, to fade, his mind quieting, distracted.

The muscles in his neck creaked, tearing. He screamed and laughed with the pain. He stole his mind from death; bringing it far away, far within, to the rim of insanity. He stood there, staring at the Shadow, standing there beside him.

Is this my end?

Silence.

WRAITH!

His thoughts blurred, a haze layering them, a mist muffling his mind. Everything he still remembered, everything he'd forgotten, vanishing behind the same shimmering, dreamlike veil.

WRAITH!

Dark, empty, silent. Death. The Shadow was fading, the world was fading, dark around the edges. The wraith looked to the asylum, to the last of everything left to remember, the final memory, the seed of madness, of truth, the only salvation left.

There is no choice now, Aëros.

No one to save you but yourself.

You must remember.

You must take the truth,

Shoulder it to Dún.

Or you will wander in madness.

As this husk before you.

Knowing nothing.

Knowing no one.

Witless.

Ruined.

Hollow.

Aëros stared over the rim, feeling his death, listening to the shrieking of his madness echoing up from below, knowing there was only one way to salvation. He looked at his ring, at its promise, knew the weight of it, of what he would lose if he did not heed it, of whom.

Always forward. Always on.

He leapt over the rim of insanity and delved down into his unconscious and unknowable mind, ripping open the last thing bound by the asylum, the sepulcher of memory, which held the truth he was even now not yet fully ready to accept. He took it and willed himself to hold on, even as the horror of it tried to devour him, returning to him everything he'd forgotten. Mastery, misery, the riddle of himself no longer a mystery.

His mind rushed back from within to the world without, to the Barrows, the silver crescents of his eyes seething, rolling over black as coal, pooling with darkness, like Rifts into the abyss. His mask fell, and with it the illusion veiling his past deaths, his visage mirroring the undead effigy knelt before him. The wight's trance of confusion shattered into anger as it found itself now staring into the face that was its own: a massacre of scars, of deaths almost, mostly...and for it, fully.

Aëros evanesced into shadow, primordial, ancient, that which was when all else was not, his form melting into those cast by his doppelganger, the dying trees, Dún. He remembered everything, and what was more, he understood it. He willed the threads of his being to unravel, to become as the threads of Aūr that underlay them all, existing both everywhere and Nowhere, as an aurora, as a wraith. The horror wound up in that understanding would have overwhelmed him, but in this form his sense of reality was as distant as in the Wayshrine. It would not last. He could not maintain this state forever, could not linger in it long, not without fading into the Tapestry completely. When it went, the horror of his remembered past would fill its place. But not before he met his journey's end. Not until he stood before the bones of a madman, both the beginning of his journey and its end. Then he would submit, then he would choose—to keep what he had forgotten, or bury it back inside himself. Remedy or ruin. Memory or madness. Freedom or the asylum.

The Shadow watched as Aëros became a shadow himself, a wraith. It watched the slaughter as it had with the Fēl. Watched as the wights lurched forward at the Wayfarer's sudden disappearance. Watched as the Aëros that was undead staggered back. The wraith materialized from the shadows, rushing through the seams of reality, Löekeh glinting, shifting from blade to bow and back, sharpened Argynt, black luminescent arrows, and the needle of a promise dripping with the ichor of the undead, culling the horde before the Barrows could even begin to drink from the spoiled lifeblood spilled. It was not a cruelty, but a mercy, the severance from undeath a release into the slumber that was their due.

The Shadow's smile softened as the wraith, wreathed in darkness, materialized from the shadow of the wight that should not be, the wight that both was Aëros, inexplicably, and was not. It grasped the wight around its chest, dragged it back, set the tip of Löekeh above its heart, and drove the blade through to the hilt. The wight that was and wasn't Aëros gasped, the dull light of unlife flickering, fading, gone. The corpse slumped in the wraith's arms, the rooks and ravens circling,

The wraith—the Wayfarer—stood in silence. He looked around the field before him, piles of corpses mounded atop one another, the defiled threads of Anima holding them together now frayed, finished. Their bodies decayed as the unnatural time that had held them together at last left them, their flesh and skin and bone ashing away on the wind, fading into the haunting gloam of the Barrows where they would never again be disturbed from the quiet of death.

Beneath him lay the corpse of Aëros. The corpse of himself. The answer now revealed to him, his understanding resolved. The Shadow drifted up alongside him, staring down with him.

It's time to move on, Aëros.

They stood, Wayfarer and wraith, watching as the husk before them flaked away too, watching it vanish into the winds, back into the world as nothing more than dust, than ash. "I know."

Aëros turned away from his death, turned back towards the silhouette in the distance. Dún beckoned to him, beckoned in full now that he remembered what he'd imprisoned, buried, forgotten. He abided the summons, lingering in his phantasmal form as he went, not yet willing to confront what he'd freed. Not yet willing to choose. *Memory. Or madness.*

Passage V: Journey's End

"There is only one story. It takes many shapes. It is told many ways. It is the story of everything. The story of us."

– Unknown and unknowable

Chapter XXIX: Dún

• Stirring of Winter •

Aëros' stride lengthened as he felt his time lessen, his phantasmal form fleeting. As a shadow it passed over him, and as a shadow he passed over the Barrows, moving in those cast by tombstones and trees and great spires of stone, swiftening to the source of the shadow cast over it all, to Dún. He watched the memory play out with indifference, severed from it and its pain, a spectator viewing a story he'd written, lived, and forgotten. The Shadow was its narrator, as ever and always. His own form, his own voice, an enigma no longer.

"You will find no sanctuary in this world or any other, Athair." *You spoke to yourself, but he heard you. He knew you were coming. He was waiting.*

Aëros met a curtain of heavy rain, forcing the mists to fall away at last and revealing the threshold of Dún, its silhouette sharpening into the ruin itself, the mausoleum of memory. It sat perched atop a mound on the opposite ridge of a terrible chasm. The gash in the world collapsed into a pit of pitch, darker even than the home of the Shaēd, swallowing the little light offered by the lightning flickering through the sky. A stone bridge forded it, the only way to cross. He came upon it now even as he saw himself come upon it in the memory he'd forgotten, the memory that would devour him if he let it. He listened to his voice echo from that memory, grim and horrible.

You found the bridge, and pressed on. Dún was a ruin, decaying and unraveling with the Ages. You passed through the crumbling walls as a shadow under night, to meet a friend in betrayal.

Aëros found Dún other than his memory showed. Not as a ruin, but whole, healed, as if wrought and hewn not a season past. Its gate was thrown up, walls smooth and insurmountable. He knew he could pass through it, physical barriers being of no consequence to a wraith, knew too that it was unnecessary. He set his will on the illusion and tore it apart, unraveling the threads of Dräu that composed it. It was a phantasm intended to dishearten the curious, to ward off those who might reveal the secret buried there.

Rain beat hard through the collapsed roof as he stepped over Dún's threshold. He passed a wall fallen not from age, but foolhardiness, beside it a small cairn hidden in the rubble, the beginning of everything, once concealing brittle and broken bones, now just a memory.

There was no time to stray into regret. He found what he was searching for, a doorway set within the floor, sealed up by a solid slab of grey stone. He did not know how to open it, but he didn't need to. He moved through as a shadow, stepping onto a stairwell leading down into the crypt, into the darkness of death, into the depths of forgotten things now remembered, waiting in a sepulcher with the bones of a madman.

You found him in the crypt, sitting atop the nameless sepulcher at its heart, waiting. He did not appear as one responsible for omnicide might. No, he was rather too youthful, too familiar for that. Familiar? What a dissonant sensation. Beneath his darkling mane, his serpentine eyes, his ashen skin, he wore a smirk you knew all too well, all too proudly displayed. Such bitter currents of self-loathing and disgust arose in you at the empathy you felt. His youth and his familiarity were false, not an illusion like yours, but a suit of skin he wore while time stood still around him.

The dissonance between Aëros' mind and his memory was ending, the two weaving back together. He continued down the stairwell, knowing what waited for him, unsure if he could accept it when it was before him. The Shadow turned, knowing his thoughts, his trepidation.

Move on, Aëros.

Move forward.

For yourself.

For your promise.

For them.

Aëros looked to his false finger, his ring, and then to Dún, this doorway, his journey's end.

"Aūriel!" She was stooped, beaten and bloody, broken beneath his feet, a chain wrapped round her neck and held in his hand like a beast. You strode forward, bearing all the wrath of a beast yourself, a predator with eyes perceiving its prey.

"Now, now, Aëros," said Athair, producing a blade from Nowhere. A familiar blade. Yours. Löekeh, now pressed to Aūriel's neck. You understood what it meant. For you. For Tärin. You stopped, finding you'd already drawn an arrow, already set it to your eye, trained on your prey.

"Aëros, I—" Athair pressed the blade harder into her neck as she spoke, silencing her. There was no fear in her eyes, only a fury to match your own.

"Athair," you drew the bowstring back further, muscles flexing, wrath rising, "where is my son."

Aūriel caught your eyes, a wild sorrow overwhelming her as she flicked her gaze into the shadows of the crypt. You shifted your focus, slowly, to a figure hunched over in the darkness.

"That arrow looks so familiar, Aëros," said Athair, looking into the darkness himself. "Like those you used to fletch when we were young. The fruit does not fall far."

He beckoned into the shadows, hearkening the figure. It stood, turned, and out from the dark shambled your son. Or what was once your son, a dull green glow in eyes revealing what he'd become. A dead glow, like the vesta all those years past, like the little raven that began it all. Your breath staggered, halting as your mind caught up with what your eyes were seeing. "No..."

You threw your gaze to her, to your Aūriel, mother of your son, disbelieving. In her eyes you found a plea for forgiveness, a desperate apology for not doing more, for not being able to protect the boy that was yours and hers both. Your eyes told her she bore no blame, and never would. Your eyes gave her the forgiveness she could not give herself.

Laughter. Athair. He dropped off of the sepulcher, standing now, your wife on a chain held in his hand; your son, dead, revived. He tilted his head and smiled.

"What have you done, Athair..." Your words rumbled out, a deep, primal growl echoing out behind them. "This is my family..."

Athair's laughter died a disturbing death, his features running rigid with anger, framed by fury. "So was I!"

Darkness surrounded Aëros as he descended, wreathed in darkness himself. He had no need for light in this state. He saw the Shadow striding ahead, darker than the darkness, as indifferent to it as himself. The stairwell was silent, his footsteps featherlight, breath arrhythmic but stifled. He watched the horror of the nightmare unravel, knowing he should be sick, but feeling nothing as he displaced himself from himself, sensing only that his separation was swiftly ending—but not as swiftly as the stairwell. The final step fell away, the crypt running out before him. It was not vast, but it was deep; a well of memory, of regret, of sorrow. There, at its heart, rested a single, lonely sepulcher.

As his eyes marked the grave, his phantasmal form faded fully, mind and memory knitting back together, the sense of dissonance lost like shadow over a dark sea. He recoiled as he snapped back into awareness, as his emotions washed over, trying to drown him. He staggered forward, chest heaving with discordant breaths, sweat-streaked hair swaying before him as he staggered to the sepulcher with nothing but the weight of a promise and the will to see it done.

The grave seemed to approach him instead, drawing up to him, beckoning for him to return, to remember. He collapsed forward, catching himself on the lid and bowing over it, breath ragged, mind racing, knowing what rested inside. He understood it, understood what his journey had been: a distraction, an attempt to ease his mind into remembering what lay buried within it.

The sepulcher was identical to the one hidden in the depths of his inner asylum—of carven crystal, unyielding to the weathering of Ages. It was the last effigy of his past, the final tether to everything he'd repressed, everything he could not face, everything he'd forgotten on purpose, left to fester, to rot behind a pale illusion. A thin ray of moonlight pierced a split in the foundation above, indifferent to the clouds and the rain, falling upon the sepulcher's lid and revealing a name there engraved. Not the name of the one responsible for devouring a world. No, it was the name of the one who'd hidden such memories away, forsaken them. The name of a madman. His.

Behind the sorrow and the suffering in Aūriel's eyes lingered a sliver of hope, silver swirling in the aurora hue. A flash of metal, the slithering sound of slit flesh, the gasp of death. Löekeh was in Tärin's hands, in the hands of your son. He dragged it across his mother's throat, opening it, and watched—unseeing, unknowing, undead—as her hope poured away.

It could not be real. It was a phantom. An illusion. The last of your innocence died. Athair's laughter returned, basking in the horror of his design.

You roared, shaking the bones of the world beneath you, and loosed your son's arrow from your bow. It took Tärin between the eyes, snuffing out their undead glow. Athair staggered back a step, surprised, not thinking for a moment that you would have been so swift to do what you had just done. But you knew better than that. What you killed was not your son, not any longer. You would let your grief run through you, but not yet.

Your bow became a blur, your arrows a hailstorm, each one loosed with your wrath, tipped with the poison of your pain. They punched into Athair, shredding him. You spoke no more, gave him no more time to speak himself. Your arrows spoke for you, each one finding its mark, each one rending his flesh to ragged strands. He fell back, toppled away from your family, collapsing into a heap of himself. You dove, catching your wife and your son as they fell. You held them both to you, the dead and the dying.

"Aëros..." She was weak, life bleeding away, Dún drinking her. She would die, and there was nothing you could do to save her. She turned her head, looking to you, to her son. His body was ashing away, the twisted threads that had kept him animated unraveling the essence of him. "Tä... Tärin..."

You took her face in your hand and tilted her eyes to meet yours, taking her away from her pain. "Aūriel... We'll go home to the Fells. I'll bring you both stories. We'll be hap—"

Her smile interrupted you. The smile of her death, the smile she had worn with the whisper of a promise given in life. A promise of unyielding love. Of how she would feel on this very day, so long as she was in your arms when it came. "I am happy..."

Your tears fell like a winter rain, cold and unwanted. You looked at each other, saying nothing more, the time for words past. You watched the aurora scintillate and fade from her eyes, the radiance of a last falling star winking out, felt the weight of your son lessen, felt the loss of him as his body became ash, your family taken by the darkness beyond the horizon, forever.

Aūriel. Tārin. I love you. The thought came as Aëros watched himself, the echo of his memory, the reality he'd cast away, forgotten, buried alive. He watched himself stand there, a reflection misshapen by woe—vacant, lost, unsure what to do. He loathed what he saw. *You could have done something!* His thoughts railed at the echo of his past, as if it were not his own actions that shaped it. He could do nothing, could have done nothing. His doom was sealed with the rest of his world. He made his choices, and from one thread to another they wove the fabric of his sorrows.

You did not scream as she faded. That was a reaction for frustration, for anger. You felt something else entirely. Your sorrow bled into the world around you; the silence that came was wreathed in it. So much left unsaid. So many thoughts and partings and hopes taken by the indifference of death. All you ever wished to say raced through your mind, and all fell on the deafness and darkness of the grave.

Then, through the darkness, you heard something. Him. His laughter returning. You heard the insanity in it. It felt so familiar, so within reach. What would happen if you grasped it? If you succumbed as he had? You saw what it had done to him. Would it do the same to you? You looked up, slowly, as if in a dream, as if the world had taken on new weight, reality a new understanding. "Aëros, Aëros... So swift to kill your answers!"

"Why..." Your voice was brittle, hollow, void. "Why..."

"Why?" His laughter felt like a hail of his own arrows, rending your mind as you had his flesh. It cut off abruptly, sharpened into anger, into wrath, his words furious and fierce, foaming with hatred. "Why? Why?! Your betrayal! Here! In the ruins above! The way you looked at me that day, the way you saw me, judged me! This is where it began. It followed our friendship our whole lives, wore the guise of help when you

sent me to that asylum, when it was nothing more than an attempt to control what you held in disdain! You did not help me. You sent me away. You forgot about me! Forsook me! In Arkym you left me to rot! You brought me to this! You brought me to the rim of this insanity and kicked me over!" He gestured to your family with an arm shot through with arrows. "Her death, your son's, your friend's, everyone's: your burden, your fault. You'll never forget me again."

Head hung, you heard his words as if through the murk of deep waters, heard the ouroboros of your choices circling like a murder of rooks and ravens, feasting on themselves. You held her, your Aūriel, her body cooling in the damp cold of the crypt, still smelling of lemongrass, lavender, mint leaves. You thought of your son, of Tärin, of how much better a man he would have been than you. You thought of your friends, dead because of you. You thought of Arythos; all the innocents, the world itself. Your fault. All your fault.

But no. It wasn't, even if you believed it. It was Athair who had devoured your world, and would have regardless of betrayal. You'd seen it in his eyes the day the raven died, had seen it ever since. Your only failure was your hesitance to kill a friend, even if it meant saving the world from him. You hadn't forgotten him, not once. Not ever. You'd stood on those cliffs, overlooking the sea, your heart weighed down with regret, with uncertainty in your decision.

But your hesitance was gone now, dead with everything else, with everyone else, with every bit of your innocence. You placed her gently on the cold stone of the crypt's floor, resting in the pool of her hope, her love. You took Löekeh from where it had fallen, a gift never meant to be given back. A tear fell, finding the blade and running down its length as you stood. You didn't speak, could not, overwhelmed with your wrath. It wasn't in your posture, but it was in your eyes, for they hid nothing.

You drew a single breath and tore forward in your fury, Löekeh brandished, its edge honed with your hatred. You would feel the life drain from him as you had felt it drain from her. You would bathe in it, revel in it, your only vindication, your only reprisal. A life for a thousand, a world, a family. It would heal nothing.

His laughter rolled on and on. You overcame him, tore Löekeh through his mouth, removing the muscle of cheek from jaw, hoping to stop the laughter. He didn't flinch. His mirth did not cease. You raged, cleaving apart what remained, rending tendon from bone, pulling all the blood from his body. There was insanity in that blood, soaking you, seeping into your flesh, your bones, your mind.

He sunk to a pile of refuse, of viscera, of death. But death did not claim him, and he laughed still—that malignant, arrogant, joyful laugh. You rent and you rove and you reaped and still it pierced you, the laughter of what was once your oldest, dearest friend. Now a shapeless heap, a soulless wretch.

You slowed as you wearied, as your efforts failed. He was indifferent to his tattered shell, indifferent to death, indifferent to you. He could not die save for the shattering of the vessel that held his soul— a catharsis he would never allow you. You watched as the heap reformed, watched as the corpse knit itself back together, immortal threads disobeying and disinterested with death. He stood before you again, unwounded, unmarred, devoid of his soul. You understood what that felt like now, hollow as you were. He spoke to you through this shared familiarity, through the empathy of a fragmentary and pointless existence; the makings of insanity.

"Ah, Aëros." His mouth stitched itself back into a smile. "You and I are bound by our kinship, even in betrayal."

He spoke the truth, and it cut deep, deeper still because even though you knew it, you buried it. You'd kill the truth before you accepted it. Your blade arced towards him, but you froze, unable to bury it in his flesh. Something waylaid you. An unnatural cold, seeping out of him, the boreal nature of death. You leapt back as it crept over you, bewilderment in your eyes. The shivering air drew over your Aūriel and began to devour her. It aged her skin, weathered it black and frostbitten, unrecognizable. Your horror met your desperation, and you shifted blade to bow once more.

Your arrows ripped through the air, each aimed with the eye of a marksman too far gone into mastery to miss. Not a single one met its mark. As weak to the unnatural cold as you, each shattered as they met the will of the monster masquerading in the skin of a man. A red crescent appeared on Athair's face, a crooked smirk soaked with arrogance, with delight in the sorrow wreathing your own.

You stopped as the ninth arrow failed you, lowered your bow and stood there, staring, watching as her body was devoured, as darkness slithered into your soul and sunk into the asylum, weaving the rot of repression into the sepulcher of your madness. You stood unknowing and broken as the cold crept over your flesh and a haze drifted into your mind.

The moment became a lifetime, an Age. The tension betwixt you and Athair distorted the very threads of existence caught in the intervening space, and nothing save the death of one of you could sever it.

"Come now, Aëros." His voice echoed long in your thoughts, reaching you even now, from this distant vantage and displaced reality. "You cannot kill me. You know that."

You snarled, teeth bared. "Stop hiding behind your cowardice, and you will see what I can bring myself to do."

"There it is!" he laughed, overjoyed. "The binding thread between us! The feather of friendship! You wear a mask of civility, but beneath it you know you are a predator, a horror, no better than me in the end. No better than anyone." He stood to his full height, posturing, swaggering, teeth bared like your own, as hateful of you as beloved. "That is what makes your betrayal all the worse. An arrogant condemnation of the reflection of yourself you see in my—"

"ENOUGH!" you screamed into the echoing hollow of the crypt, the sound shaking dust from the death of Ages. You looked to your Aūriel, ashen grey, quiet and cold, then looked to him, your eyes gripping his, hunting. "I am a predator, I am prey; a lord of the hangman and the hanged; and your rope has run out, Athair. I have no more of my own to give you. If vengeance is all I have left to take, then I will take it and be done."

Athair listened to your words, accepting the truth in them. He reached beneath his cloak and took from it a lantern; beautiful, familiar. A work of your own artifice, a gift you regretted giving, a symbol of love, betrayed. You knew it for what it was now—the vessel of his soul, holding the essence of his immortality.

Your eyes widened. He held the source of his endlessness, apparent and bare before you. You drew your bow; the arrow shattered. Again and again you failed, ceaselessly, your want overwhelming your reason. You would never have your vindication. You would never have your revenge.

"If vengeance is all you have left, then I will take that from you too. My life is not yours to end, Aëros." He spoke even as your arrows flew and shattered, dusting the trinket of your desire. "Not by your will. Not by the will of anyone..." He stared long at the vessel, his soul, his immortality. He spoke the words that would take the last of everything from you. "Anyone but me."

"*Aëros Elwaē Arōaē.*" Aëros read the name upon the sepulcher in the depths of Dún, and as he did the sepulcher in the base of his mind slid open, revealing all. This grave was his, but it did not belong to him. The Shadow stood beside him, and he looked to it for what seemed the first time, seeing it for what it was. Not hallucination, nor symptom of delusion, nor phantasm of his psychosis. It was the Aëros of this world. The Aëros whose reality he'd stolen. The Aëros he stood in place of as an imposter, a doppelgänger, a phantom, the name upon the sepulcher his and his alone. He thought back to the mines, to the memory of him and Tärin, to the explanation he'd given his son of the nature of reality. *We share a thread of ourselves across all realities that share a version of ourselves, and sometimes those threads overlap.*

The Shadow was tied to him by the thread of mind that composed the asylum—that which knew him in full, even the secrets he hid from the shallow waters of his innocence. The secrets of his memories, those he'd willfully imprisoned, forgotten.

His world shimmered as memory returned, his delusion fraying away, truth revealed in its place as the Shadow spoke.

My world, bound up with your delusion.

Different enough only to leave you unsettled.

Uneasy.

You inscribed your name upon this nameless sepulcher.

Told yourself it was Athair's.

An impetus to embark.

A reminder at the end of a journey you framed for yourself.

So long ago.

You have done this many times.

In many worlds.

Never in a world where your family lives.

For fear of your delusion becoming too great a temptress.

For fear of breaking your promise.

I did not say it then,

To preserve your delusion,

But thank you.

Aëros listened to the Shadow, to himself, his heart heavy, tears pattering on the lid of the sepulcher. "…thank you?"

For freeing my family.

For freeing me.

Aëros looked at the shadow of himself, seeing everything he'd missed before, all there in its eyes as it had always been, if only he'd known how to look. The An'kou in the forest, a little boy and his mother. The undead him in the Barrows. He'd helped free this Aëros and his family, and envied the him that was not him his freedom. He looked back to the sepulcher, hoping to find his own.

Athair grasped the lantern, held your eyes, and with his will shattered the soul in each, shards of crystal exploding from the lantern, shards of silver in those moon-hued eyes of yours dimming, dying, dead. The cold of a thousand winters erupted from the trinket, and Athair fell, collapsed again in a pool of his own ichor, black in the dimness of the crypt. His laughter engraved itself in the air as his will fled into the world, into you.

"Our debts are settled, Aëros." He lifted his skeletal hand, gesturing to you with all the confidence of one on the doorway of death. "Depart, Walker Betwixt and Between Worlds. Ease your pain as only you can." His eyes fell over her, your Aûriel. "Forget me as is your way. Forget it all. Always forward, Aëros; always on."

You did not speak. You simply looked on, wrathful, despairing, apathetic. You could do nothing but watch. Watch as his life flickered, as the final threads of his consciousness unraveled, as the gleam of arrogance and sanctimony at last faded to the empty eyes of the dead.

His body blackened from the cold he'd conjured, still emanating from him even in death. The threads he'd twisted about his own soul tore at his flesh, tarnishing the guise of humanity he'd worn. His skin

297

rotted from his bones, falling like bark from an ailing tree, flakes turning to ash, dusting away as his soul dissipated, his eldritch immortality eating away at his very essence. He perished, your oldest friend, and with him any hope of reprisal.

You were alone then, the Slayer of Death and yourself slain by it, left with nothing, with no one. You stood there, over the blackened corpse of your wife, the ashes of your son, on the rim of insanity, wondering where it might lead you. To Athair's fate? To another, more horrible still? Perhaps. Or perhaps it would lead to ignorance, and bliss therein. It was worth considering. Death stood beside madness, but it was not a consideration. You knew then as you do now that it would offer you no peace. Insanity then, or the other unthinkable path. The only path that would offer you freedom from your suffering: acceptance. To move forward. To move on. To walk that path was to walk with suffering and pain your only companions, in hopes that with time they would fade.

Athair's words called out to you from beyond the grave. "Depart, Walker Betwixt and Between Worlds. Ease your pain as only you can."

You buried your dead in a world of ash and darkness, even those whose bones you did not have to bury. You took your memories—your nightmares—and pushed them down, imprisoning them in the asylum of your mind, in a sepulcher that was the reflection of the one that held the truth. You fled, imagination your only limit as you walked in dreaming delusion, to worlds every bit as real to the Aëros that named them home as yours was to you. Those Aëros were always dead, the world theirs no longer. But neither were they yours. They were false, and in such falseness your lie festered within you, devouring you. You banished your ability to go back, your world-walking ways, for the threads of Aūr were the sinew that bound the bones of your delusion together. You forgot everything that made you the Wayfarer. That was better than the truth. That was better than the pain. You knew it made you weak. You knew what she would have thought.

You made a promise, half-hearted and distant, but a promise nonetheless. Bowed before one central sepulcher of carven crystal, ringed *by five others like it, thousands of hewn stone in turn ringing them, all set in a world of ash, cooled in the many Ages of your gravetending. The thousands were for the nameless, the unknown. The five were for your closest friends, your family: Aūriel, Tärin, Thrace, Shaē, Jä. You looked to them all, binding yourself to them with your word. "I will return to you, Aūriel, Tärin. Everyone. I promise." The one was for you. You set yourself inside and sealed your world away behind its lid, arriving in worlds that were not your own. You've since walked in countless realities, repeating the same desperate journey time and again, unable to do what you must to end it, your rope shortening, sanity fraying, threads of self—forgotten.*

The memory faded, the last the asylum held, the seed of Aëros' madness buried in the sepulcher. It was beautiful, radiant crystal in the midst of the grey stone that entombed it. He placed his hand upon its face and felt the tremors of his memory within, hearkening him to return to what he had forsaken, as it had since he chose the way of forgetting, so long ago. The Shadow stood beside him, looking over the sepulcher, looking over him.

So few threads remain, Aëros.

You cannot do this again.

Athair's will brought you to this rim.

But it is your own that binds you here.

Here your soul will wither.

Ashen.

Hollow.

Here your mind will fade.

Witless.

Forgotten.

Move on.

Move forward.

As you promised you would.

Aëros heard the Shadow, and saw the truth in its words, for they were his own. It was the part of himself that had never forgotten. The part that knew he would need to return to this effigy of the past, that it was the only way to remember. Now he had, and it revealed a path he was not sure he could take. Images of a world of ash and darkness flashed in his mind, fear building within him, paralyzing him. Then he heard their words, and all fear washed away.

Always forward, my love. Always on.

The words came from... *Memory? No.* From somewhere beyond memory, beyond death, beyond time, beyond place, from everywhere, from Nowhere. *Aūriel.*

His tears fell like spring rain, soft and welcome, sinking into the roots of his ring, into the promise that threaded it. To return. The warmth of her voice enveloped him, an ember in the dark hollows of his madness. Not an ember to burn away his sorrow, but to warm it with the memory of love, threads as bitter as they were sweet.

Another voice, familiar; once innocent, now wise, the wisdom your father's, your own. *Tärin.*

Death ends no more than life begins.

Aëros heard him, saw him—could see them both, each in the other's embrace, longing for him to move on, to return. His tears swelled, falling harder. The echo of their voices faded, the Shadow's—his own—taking their place.

Move on from this world, Aëros.

Let it grieve, as it ever should have.

Its Wayfarer was lost, long, long ago.

But your world has not yet lost its.

Its Wayfarer still walks and wanders.

Return to it.

The last of it yet to move on.

See what the Ages have wrought.

Of ash

Of sorrow.

Aëros thought on the Shadow's wisdom, his own. He was so very tired, his weariness ancient. There was but one way to know rest.

Always forward. Always on.

The sepulcher was sealed in the same way his chest of memories had been, by what looked to be an ordinary lock. He set his will on his ring, the symbol of his love, the key to his promise, and it became the key to the tomb as well. He turned it, called it back, and slid the lid of the grave away, revealing nothing. No Athair. No Shaēd. No bones but the bones of his memory.

The way back was dark. Dark and so very deep. He climbed into the sepulcher and lay within, looking up, following the ray of light gleaming through the split in the foundation to the clear night above, the rain passed. Valrävn clutched the shattered moon, cradling it as it died. A streak ran across the dark, the thread of an aurora breathing itself into existence, flowing through the night in currents of scintillating iridescence. He dragged the covering of the tomb back into place, sealing himself away. He drew breath. Forgotten. Familiar. His own.

He waited in darkness—consuming, enshrouding, silent. He did not sleep, but he dreamt—dreamt away the night and its nightmares. The darkness settled and passed; a light shimmered and faded, and with its fading came the whisper of gentle wind. He slid back the lid, and awoke, finding that it was night no longer.

Chapter XXX: A Wood

• Stirring of Spring •

I t was like stepping over a threshold, simple and unremarkable. Aëros slid the lid above him away, and light poured in, blinding him. He sat up, the world without shimmering as his eyes adjusted, and it felt as if he were waking from a dream.

He found himself in a sepulcher like that he'd entered, around him the eternal fixtures of an ancient graveyard, all carved from crystal. It was a small, quaint, forgotten place of reverence. A familiar place, though the faraway familiarity of an old life half-remembered, from an Age older still. He read the scripture on each tombstone, knew every name in turn. *How I've missed you...* He saw them, faces and all; remembered them as they were, as they would ever be. Death had claimed them, but from their death came life.

The graveyard was not ringed by ash and darkness, but by the grove of a great forest. Ara in the likeness of nascent wōadglōam—somewhat different, the product of Ages passing, changing—grew with the dead, the underwood entwined with the crystalline cenotaphs as if to enshrine them and the memory of their Age now so far faded.

Midday sunlight drifted down on misty rays of summer warmth, wrapping Aëros in a shroud of welcome and return. The wind waxed soft, carrying the sweet and soothing scents of fallen rain and the forest's breath, his own breath calm, tranquil, rhythmic with the world's.

The denizens of the woodland noticed him as he stepped from the sepulcher, a familiar stranger, and were curious at his arrival. Hummingbirds flitted overhead, vesta peered through bush and umbel, Kodama chattered as they faded in and out of life and death. He heard laughter through the spaces in the trees; the laughter of children. He saw the silhouette of Ayl, of Ken, of

303

others. *Others?* He swallowed the thought in his throat, amazed. *I have been gone so very long.*

He was home, and his world had healed, moved on. The Age of ash had ended, long, long ago. His tears streamed; tears of sorrow, tears of joy.

Even ash of Ages gone, may grow a wood, a world, a home. Her words echoed to him out from memory, bringing with them the threads of her wisdom, and the song woven from it:

> *…Fair few still walk the ways of old,*
> *Those trails tread by foolhardy souls,*
> *Who wandered where none had before,*
> *Through grove, and moor, and silver shore.*
>
> *For in those elder days they say,*
> *To wander was the only way,*
> *In lands untouched, in lands unknown,*
> *In wood, and vale, and hall of stone.*
>
> *Their journey roved and wrought a word,*
> *For leaf, for moon, for bone, for wyrm,*
> *Each name a thread in stories told,*
> *Each tale, each myth, worn ancient old.*
>
> *Of dragons dark and brooding lone,*
> *Of forest eaves 'neath dusken gloam,*
> *Of havens hewn from argent white,*
> *Of realms beyond the seams of light.*
>
> *All memory scrawled upon a page,*
> *All fable passed from Age to Age,*
> *From ash to ash and shade to shade,*
> *A shade of dreamer's distant days,*

For even ash of Ages gone,
May grow a wood, a world, a home.
Where tale and myth may find yet still,
A youthful and foolhardy will.

To follow those wayfaring ways,
To know now and forever say;
Far into dusk their trail does go,
Far into dusk their trail does go…

Aëros heard the song as if sung aloud by his Aūriel, then realized it was. He stood in a graveyard filled with those he had built a life with, those he'd loved, those he'd lost. The Shadow wandered between the tombstones, and the souls of his loved ones appeared beside each, five souls for six graves—the sixth his own—each pair of eyes familiar. His own eyes welled, hot, terrified, distraught. He felt fury rise up within him; rage, wrath, hatred. Not for Athair, but for himself.

Their forms were ethereal, grey, hidden beneath the phantasmal haze that draped them. He knew them all the same. How could he ever forget? He saw them each in their eyes, for they hid nothing, even in death. Thrace, Shaē, Jä…

…Aūriel, Tärin.

Their eyes were wells of deep, longing sadness. Not for themselves, but for him.

They do not suffer.

They linger only for you.

The last of this world yet to move on.

The last of this world yet to know peace.

They wish only for you to rejoin it.

To return.

His friends. His family. Waiting for him, hoping. They did not speak, everything that needed saying in their eyes. He faltered with his own words, knowing them for what they were—worthless. He feathered a hand over his ring, Aūriel over hers, each a band of binding; of ardent memory, of soft, sorrowful serenity. A promise to return. She looked at his, his false finger, knowing him and his foolhardiness, his humanity. Loving him in spite of it, loving him because of it.

In memory they shall ever be, Aëros.

Until death comes to you as an old friend.

A familiar hand to guide you on.

To walk with them all as memory together.

Aëros looked to the Shadow, his tears sinking into his smile, grateful. It nodded, smirked, smiled, and was gone, returning to its own home, its own memories.

The summer's sun sat unfettered in the clear firmament, and it was kind to his bones. The wind blew fair through the trees, and the forest's underwood was soft on the soles of his weatherworn feet, bare as they always and ever were. It was a perfect day. It had been long since he knew one.

He stood then on the rim of reality and fantasy, memories drifting up from his mind. He saw in them his friends, his family. They stood before him and around him, embracing him with their sorrow and their hope. He embraced them in return, and with bittersweet wisdom willed them to depart—to their rest, to memory, where they would always and ever be.

They turned from him, knowing their hope was fulfilled. One by one they faded: Thrace, Shaē, Jä. The last, his Aūriel, his Tärin, he stood with 'neath wood and sun.

Aëros knelt to his boy and embraced him, holding him gently, knowing he could not hold on forever. He parted from him, gestured to Nowhere, and drew Löekeh from its shroud, shifting blade to bow and holding it out. "I think I no longer have need of this. Take it. Practice, so you can show me how you've improved when next I see you, Little Raven."

Tärin smiled, ear to ear, as a boy who knows the pride of his father must. He took the bow, an artifact of his father, a symbol of his pride, and drew the string back, an arrow appearing along its riser. He held it aloft, released, and the arrow sailed up, through the eaves of the forest, beyond the sky, a star in the day, falling beyond the horizon, falling for innocence. Aëros looked back to Tärin and found only his grave, his son at last fallen beyond the horizon himself.

A tear slipped down his cheek and Aūriel caressed it away, his sentinel, knowing more would come in its place; for their boy, for her, for all the sorrow he'd held hidden until now. Tears healed, and grief mended, the remedy of sorrow. They sat together, saying nothing, simply staying there in one another's presence. She saw his Shräud, torn, a work of her own skill, and set the needle of her will on the threads that composed it, mending its wound whole. His eyes, full moons once again, thanked her for the gift, for her love, for everything.

Her eyes held an aurora, flickering and iridescent, threaded with the same gratitude, the same love. They were strong, hiding nothing, as a tear fell. Aëros caressed it away, her sentinel. She gathered him in her arms, drawing his eyes to hers, their tears as one, each falling for the other, each silhouetted in sadness and in joy.

Her mouth crooked, wistful, smirking, smiling. *"Do you remember how we met?"*

"My Aūriel. My love," he brought her eyes to his and held them there, reassuring, raised over his own smirk, "I remember everything."

"I am happy," she whispered.

The words were familiar, easy. "As am I."

They held each other a moment longer, a moment all they needed. They parted wordlessly, all those unspoken held in their eyes, in their memories.

Always forward, my Aēros.

Always on, my Aūriel.

Aēros' tears fell alone, but not in loneliness. They fell in the heartwood of a forest, a grove ringing the graves of Ages gone, of memories forgotten, returned to. They fell upon a world shaded in familiarity, upon a home—his. It was not a new world after all, just one grown older, wiser, from the ashes of its innocence. He felt this in the threads of the world's existence, in the threads of Aūr that composed it. He did not set his will upon them, though he now remembered how. This was not a time for Rifts; it was a time for walking. He was a wayfarer after all. He had been gone so very long, and there was so very much to see.

An illusion shimmered over his face, veiling his past deaths, his humanity. Not for pride nor fear of the truth, but to reflect how he felt within—whole. He set his stride toward the sun, toward the spaces between the trees, to where the laughter of children echoed, to a home that had moved on. And he—Slayer of Death and by death slain nevermore, Wanderer Betwixt and Between Worlds, the foolish, the wizened, the Wayfarer—moved on with it.

Made in the USA
Middletown, DE
21 September 2021